But Not for Long

Unity Hall says she has been writing for a long as she can remember. A totally undistinguished school career in Wembley was just saved by pages and pages of ill-spelt, untidy essays.

Still unable to spell, she has worked in Fleet Street as a journalist since leaving school, apart from three years of living in the United States where her jobs were more varied, including waitressing, selling and making doughnuts.

Unity Hall is woman's editor of the *News of the World*. She travels widely for her newspaper, lives in London, and spends as much time as possible at her home in the South of France.

Unity Hall

But Not for Long

Pan Original
Pan Books London and Sydney

First published 1982 by Pan Books Ltd,
Cavaye Place, London SW10 9PG
© Unity Hall 1982
ISBN 0 330 26739 6
Printed in Great Britain by
Collins, Glasgow

For Olivia and Derek Shephard –
for always being there.

And, of course for You.

Chapter One

'Who's a pretty boy then?' Ingrid Pallia's husky voice was flattened by the lack of resonance in the heavily furnished bedroom.

'For Christ's sake,' Monique Berault said, 'you make him sound like a parrot.'

'But he is pretty, aren't you, darling?' Ingrid said, stroking the boy's bare arm. 'Just like me.'

The two women and the boy were reflected in the long mirror which ran the length of the back wall of the bedroom. Behind them was a huge four-poster bed, covered with a heavy silk hand-sewn patchwork quilt of many colours. The carpet beneath their feet was of shaggy white wool, and the windows to their right were hung with white velvet drapes, now drawn against the street noise of Park Avenue outside.

'He looks ridiculous.' Monique said. 'Bloody ridiculous.'

Ingrid regarded the boy who stood between them awkward and silent, his face made up in parody of her own – black mascara and blue eyeshadow and eye pencil bringing out the ice-blue eye colour they both shared. His pointed face was covered with a flesh-coloured foundation that hid the light blond hairs on his chin and cheeks, and his cupid mouth was outlined in red pencil and filled in with a dark lip-gloss.

'Why does he look ridiculous?' Ingrid pouted. 'He doesn't need blusher. He's like me. He has his own colour.'

'Look here —' the boy began to say. He could have been no more than seventeen, perhaps younger. Ingrid had not bothered to ask when she picked him up in the village. His shaggy blond hair had been combed into a passable imitation of her own short and artfully ruffled style, and for an instant he squared his narrow shoulders and looked around for escape.

'Don't annoy her, chérie,' Monique said, her voice silky, but with an underlying note that stopped the boy short. 'She hates her fun spoilt.'

From the other side of the bedroom door came the sounds of a party in progress. A muffled buzz of voices, and the underlying beat, beat, beat of a heavy rock disc on the stereo gently vibrated in the closed room.

'Yes,' Ingrid said absently, still raking him with her eyes. 'If you want your snort you'll have to be a good boy.' She turned to her secretary. 'Why does he look ridiculous?'

'Those jeans and no tits,' Monique said flatly.

'Give me time. I'm not finished with him yet.'

The boy was shirtless and his bare chest was painfully thin. His trunk and legs were covered in old patched jeans and he wore running shoes.

Ingrid was searching her wardrobe.

'A beautiful white silk shirt for a pretty boy,' she crooned, 'and white silk trousers to match.'

She had the mass of silk over her arm and her face, intent, was moving back towards the boy. She put out her hand and neatly undid the stud of the jeans and downed the zip.

'Off with them,' she said, 'and the shoes.'

The jeans slid over thin legs into a crumpled heap at his feet, and as if he realised that he now looked even more ridiculous so nearly nude, the boy hastily stepped out of them, and bent to pull off his shoes.

Naked, he stood up and stared at the two women defiantly from behind the make-up. Ingrid's eyes were fixed well below his waist.

'What's your name, darling?' she asked.

'Christopher,' he said.

'How appropriate,' she said. 'Christopher from Christopher Street.'

He flushed.

'I don't come from Christopher Street. I'm not gay.'

'Just a bit indeterminate?' suggested Monique.

'Well, maybe later,' said Ingrid, her eyes still on his genitals. 'After you've had your snort. Now put these on, darling.'

Embarrassed, the boy took the trousers and shirt from her

8

and pulled them on. Ingrid attended to button and zips, found a bright red leather belt from a drawer and put it round his waist. The clothing fitted. The shirt was loose enough and cut so as to give the illusion of the curve of breasts and the flared trousers clung over the boy's lean hips with a suggestive bulge at the crotch, obscene against the made-up face above. Though the boy was an inch or two taller, they were the right length. Ingrid normally wore them with high-heeled shoes, but his bony feet stuck out from below the folds of white silk, long, raw and pathetic.

'There now,' Ingrid said triumphantly. 'Couldn't he be my twin brother?'

She patted him affectionately on the cheek, beaming at her handiwork, a woman who appeared to be perhaps in her late thirties, small, slim, flat-chested with a perfect kitten face, ice-blue eyes, a full, greedy mouth and very white even teeth. Her husky voice had some faint trace of indecipherable accent, and she moved like a ballet dancer, each part of her body in perfect coordination.

'You want the pictures?' Monique said.

'Of course.'

Monique was younger. In her mid twenties, and taller, with a fine Latin bosom pushing up from the deep neckline of her skin-fitting black satin dress. She had elongated, Nefertiti eyes, a wild frizz of long black hair, and though her English was perfect, somewhere in her voice lurked the rolling r's and the lost th's of France.

A Polaroid camera in her hands she began arranging Ingrid and the boy against the white velvet curtains, standing back to look with narrowed eyes until she was satisfied with the posing.

'Stand still,' she said, and the dim hidden lighting of the room was raised by a flash. All three stood in silence as the picture slowly wormed its way from inside the camera.

'Let's see! Let's see!' said Ingrid, excited as a schoolgirl.

Wordless, Monique passed it over. Her expression faintly contemptuous.

'Oh, it's beautiful!' Ingrid said. She passed it to the boy. 'Couldn't you just be my twin?'

He looked at it with a sort of horror. The two of them, her

in a white sheath dress, revealing tanned, freckled shoulders, her head on his shoulder, and the two faces so alike, made up in the same colours and the same style – but his young and soft, hers diamond pretty, the harsh lighting revealing lines and shadows.

'Now,' Ingrid said briskly, 'you shall have your snort while Monique frames our picture. Then we'll all go to the party.'

She moved, narrow hips swaying, to a small white cabinet in ivory beside the bed, while Monique busied herself with a silver frame in which she set the picture. Then it was placed, beside others, all of Ingrid with young boys in make-up and bisexual clothing, on a white lacquer marble-topped dressing table.

'You're getting quite a collection,' Monique said laconically. Ingrid giggled.

'Want some?' she asked her secretary. She was holding a silver box, so intricately shaped that it required some thought or knowledge to remove the lid.

'Not now,' Monique said.

Ingrid turned to the boy who stood disconsolate on the white carpet, his eyes on the silver box.

'How do you want it – spoon or a hundred dollar bill?'

'Any way,' he said huskily.

'I expect you're more used to using a bill,' she said.

'Not a hundred dollar one,' Monique said, not looking at him.

Ingrid was carefully spilling the white powder in a thin line along the length of a banknote. Then she poured more into a small gold coke spoon for herself.

The boy's hand was shaking as he took the folded paper from her, and tipping his head back he snorted the coke.

'It's good stuff,' Ingrid confided. 'You can see, I'm taking it myself.'

More delicately, she sniffed up her own ration with a red-tipped forefinger, fastidiously holding one nostril at a time.

'Feeling better, chérie?' Monique said to the boy. 'No? Well you will in a minute. It is time for your public appearance.'

'I'm not going out there,' the boy said backing towards the bed.

'If you want another snort later you will,' Monique told him. 'I told you, she does not like her fun spoilt.'

'Oh, don't be silly,' Ingrid said, taking his arm, her full mouth pouting. 'You look beautiful. I can hardly wait, but I must show you off. I think he's the best yet, don't you, Monique?'

'A remarkable likeness,' her secretary said, expressionless.

As Ingrid opened the heavy wood door the noise of the party swelled into the room. She stepped into the enormous living room beyond, pulling Christopher with her, then let him go to stop, stand, fling her arms wide, her head back and call: 'Darlings – look! My latest twin!'

The lull was only temporary. Those nearest cheered and clapped, and Christopher was instantly whirled away by a tall, thin man with a heavy moustache and dark glasses.

'Come to poppa,' he said, as Ingrid stood laughing.

'Remember he's mine,' she shouted. 'He's called Christopher and he's not gay.'

'Wanna bet?' the man shouted back.

It looked like a good party, Ingrid thought as she gazed around her rented living room. The decibels were high, the forty or so guests all appeared to be drunk. Several couples were boogying on the white carpet and others were doing other things on the white carpet that might have been better done in the bedroom.

As if they had picked up her thoughts, one couple staggered to their feet and a braless, red-headed girl whose dress was unbuttoned to the waist said: 'You finished in there, honey?' as she pushed past into the bedroom.

'Do what you like,' Ingrid said, 'but watch that quilt.'

The quilt was just one of the things that went everywhere with her. Ingrid did not believe in travelling light. Her clothes, some of her furnishings, her collection of photographs and all her jewellery jetted around the world with her. She liked to feel at home wherever she was.

She hesitated. She enjoyed giving parties, mainly because she was famous for her parties, but she never quite knew what to do at them. What *did* one do at parties really? Dance, fuck, drink, eat. Never talk. It was too noisy. The coke was beginning to work and she felt like dancing, fucking and drinking. Absently she picked up a half-full bottle of Dom Perignon and poured herself a glass. Dom Perignon was pearls before swine, she thought, seeing the half-filled glasses littered around the room on the expensive white furniture, and more abandoned half-filled bottles on the floor. But then she always served Dom Perignon, people expected it. And the image had to be maintained. Particularly now things were not so easy.

The coke had worked on Christopher, too. He was boogying happily with the man with the moustache, whose name escaped her. She couldn't even remember who had brought him along, and she thought Monique shouldn't have let him in. Too plain. Ingrid only liked pretty people about her. Ugliness made her uneasy.

Christopher looked good enough to eat, shimmying in his white silk. And so he should, she thought. Hadn't she made him in her own image? He was too good for the moustachioed phoney macho and she decided to get her property back pronto.

A little unsteadily she pushed her way through the dancers. Someone had turned the lighting even lower, and the boy seemed to gleam in his white clothing as he moved his hips slowly and sugestively to the hard beat of the music. His mouth was faintly open, still bright red and glistening, and small beads of sweat gleamed on his upper lip. Black Moustache looked as if he were having an orgasm right there, Ingrid thought. She didn't mind sharing, just as long as she came first.

'Piss off, sweetheart,' she said without malice to the man. 'I found him.' She put her hand on the boy's arm to turn him to her, and like an automaton he swung to face her, never stopped dancing. She could feel herself getting excited, and she wrapped her arms around his neck, rubbing herself against him.

'Let's do it the old fashioned way,' she said.

'Sure,' he said. 'Why not?' And she detected a trace of the South in his voice.

'Do you like it here?' she whispered in his ear, running her tongue around its curves and curls. 'I bet you never thought you'd find yourself at an Ingrid Pallai party.'

12

'No, I never did,' he said.

He had put his arms around her, his eyes glazed, his hips rotating, and they danced until she said: 'Let's go somewhere quieter, huh?'

'Ok,' he said. 'Why not?'

'Jesus,' she said. 'You're dumb, but never mind – you're pretty.'

'Ok,' he said again, as she led him gently from the other dancers.

In the bedroom the redhead was on her quilt, naked, her partner on top of her, his white buttocks flailing. Neither of them reacted to the door opening until Ingrid, who had no objections to them screwing but considerable objections to what might have happened to her quilt, screamed – 'Get out of here! I told you to watch that quilt! Get off my bed!'

Reluctantly, the man raised himself on his elbows and said plaintively: 'Gee, Ingrid. Have a heart. I was just coming.'

'Well, go and come somewhere else,' she said crisply. 'What do you think this is – a whorehouse?'

'You could have fooled me,' the man said, leaning to pick up his trousers. 'Come on, sweetheart.'

The redhead staggered to her feet and without any attempt to dress, followed her partner out into the living room, where her nudity released a whoop of appreciation from those guests still sober enough to recognize a good thing.

Ingrid, ignoring the boy who stood smiling vacantly behind her, peered at her quilt, and picked up the redhead's small black panties from where they had been dropped, marched across the room, opened the door, flung them out into the living room, and then slammed the door and locked it.

'Now, twin,' she said. 'Our turn.'

Very carefully she folded the quilt and put it on the chaise-longue that stood across the foot of the bed. A heavy white blanket was underneath, and slightly squinting at the boy, who stood hesitant a full three paces from the bed, she said: 'Sheets or blankets?'

He made a do-as-you-please gesture of the shoulders and hands, and she contemplated the bed, the pink tip of her tongue outlining her lips and then said decisively: 'Blanket.'

13

She twisted one arm up behind her back and with a fluid movement unzipped her dress and let it slip to the floor. She wore no underclothes, and her body was boyish, small breasted, with flat stomach and a faint puff of blonde pubic hair. There was not an ounce of spare flesh anywhere. Before settling herself on to the bed, she stood in front of the long mirror and ran her hands over her breasts, stomach and hips, gently stroking herself, then lifting her breasts with the palm of her hand, she stepped back, and lay down – her pose studied, one hand holding a breast, one just covering the blonde triangle of hair, legs not quite apart, head turned sideways on the pillows to look at the boy, mouth wet and provocative.

'Come here, twin,' she said. 'I bet you never thought you'd find yourself in bed with Ingrid Pallia, now did you.'

'I sure never did,' he said. He stood looking at her as if he didn't quite know what to do. Languidly, she lifted the hand from her breast and beckoned to him. A higher flush of colour had come up on his fair skin, and his blue eyes glistened as he moved towards her. He was wiping the make-up from his face with his hand, and uncaring of the silk, pulling off the shirt and letting the trousers fall as if to assert the remnants of his masculinity.

'I'm going to fuck you, you bitch,' he said.

'That's the idea, darling,' she said gaily, deliberately rolling on to her back and very slowly opening her legs wide. 'You've caught on at last.'

He had just lunged towards her when the telephone rang.

'Shit!' Ingrid said. She rolled over to answer it as the boy stretched beside her, rubbing himself against the length of her back.

'Yeah —?' she said into the white telephone, her voice impatient.

'Ingrid? Good morning. And how are you?'

It was the slow, cultured English tone of her agent.

'For God's sake, Paul,' she said. 'It's four o'clock in the morning.'

'And when else would I actually find you in?' he said. 'Nor do I believe I've woken you up.'

'Not exactly,' she said impatiently. 'But it wasn't the best moment. What do you want?'

She could feel the boy's excitement as he pushed himself against her. His mouth was biting at the nape of her neck, and she thrust her behind into him, her mind barely on the phone call.

'I've sold your life story,' Paul was saying.

'How much?' she said automatically.

'If you tell all – and they do mean all – quarter of a million pounds for the book and newspaper rights. We hold the film rights.'

'Half a million dollars,' she said, her voice awed, pushing the boy away from her with an impatient wiggle.

'That's right,' he said cheerfully. 'Dependent on agreement of the copy. But Ingrid – for that money you're really going to have to talk.'

'Then it's not enough,' she said slowly; her mind was racing as she took in the implications of what he was saying.

'It's an incredible deal,' he said, and the steel that was always lurking under his English elegance and charm came through as he said: 'You are not Elizabeth Taylor, and they are spending that much money to hear – in detail – about your lovers."

'You mean they don't want to actually read about me?'

'You, but more about the men you've slept with. Your track record is pretty good.'

Suddenly she was frightened. The dangers of what else they might find out were so great. The boy's hands pulling at her breasts became intolerable. She turned to shove her elbow into his ribs.

'Oh – piss off!' she said.

'I beg your pardon?'

'Not you, Paul. Listen – I can't do it. There are things I can't say. You know that.'

'Kate Anderson's writing it. That's in the deal.'

'Kate's your little friend. Not mine. I don't even know her. And,' she added acidly, 'you've always said how professional she is. I've never met a journalist yet who didn't sell me up the river.'

'She doesn't sell people up the river. And there's more. I've been busy on your behalf.'

'So who's paying for this phone call?' Ingrid said. The idea

15

of Kate Anderson writing her life story had annoyed her.

'My fifteen per cent of a million,' Paul said. 'Plus my fifteen per cent of your new film.'

Ingrid felt her heart lift. She was dimly aware that the boy had turned his back on her and was lying in a foetal position. A new film, like a new important lover, had not come along in eighteen months now. She was all too aware that her fame rested on pictures of Ingrid Pallia arriving at London Airport, Ingrid Pallia arriving at Los Angeles. Ingrid Pallia arriving at Rome. And with the current lover in tow – when there was a lover these days.

'What is it?' she said and she couldn't keep the eagerness out of her voice.

'The new Pedro Bellino,' Paul's voice was laconic. 'He's making a film based on Colette's Claudine series.'

'But Claudine was a schoolgirl in the beginning of the series,' Ingrid said suspiciously. 'And a lesbian. I know I look young—'

'He doesn't want you to play Claudine, Ingrid.' Paul's voice seemed even more modulated and patient than usual. 'He wants you to play Claudine's headmistress. And he wants Jenny to play Claudine.'

She heard herself shriek.

'Jenny! No way! Not in a Bellino film. For Christ's sake, Paul, you know and I know what he does to little girls.'

'Jenny is no longer a little girl. She is sixteen years old. Nearly seventeen. Too old for him.'

'Listen —' Ingrid knew she was hissing between her teeth. 'As far as I'm concerned, and as far as the rest of the world is concerned, she is fourteen years old. Don't presume, Paul. I'm not ready to have a sixteen-going-on-seventeen-year-old daughter. I'm not going to be ready for a long time. I'm keeping Jenny in the background for just as long as I possibly can. And I'm not putting her in any Bellino film.'

'It's the publicity value he wants, Ingrid. Her father's won how many Academy awards? You're famous. It would be her first film. You supporting her, just as you always have.' Paul was rarely sarcastic, but Ingrid thought she detected a trace then. She screamed down the receiver. 'I'm not discussing it! I won't discuss it!'

'It's a lot of money, Ingrid.'

'How much?' she heard herself say, remembering the pile of bills in the elegant desk drawer of the elegant and unpaid-for flat that she had rented. And the price of coke, the price of Dom Perignon, the price of airline tickets and the price of popularity.

'Not settled, but it will be the best ever,' Paul said. 'With that and the book, you could land up rich.'

'Michael will never agree to her doing it,' she said.

'Michael Bolt has to be the meanest man in Great Britain,' Paul said. 'If it lets him off the hook for her support . . .'

She looked at the telephone receiver helplessly. If Paul himself had been there she would have scratched and clawed at him. She had done so in the past. He was the only person in the world who knew nearly everything about her. There were other things about her that nobody knew and never would if she were lucky. Paul she trusted implicitly, yet she had never laid him. He'd never even tried. She knew he didn't fancy her and never had, but he had always been on her side and kept her career ticking over.

She heard herself shouting again. All the euphoria of the snort had gone. She was facing reality.

'Listen,' she said. 'If you're going to earn all that much out of me, you can bloody well get off your arse and come on over here. Why should I discuss it on the phone at four in the morning when I've got the most interesting fuck I've had in ages just waiting?'

'I'll come with pleasure – but it'll be at your expense,' he said.

'If I'm going to be that rich, I can afford it,' she said. 'I'll expect to see you sometime tomorrow.'

'As soon as I can,' he said evenly.

She slammed down the receiver and sat glaring at the white piece of plastic.

Christopher from Christopher Street was groping again.

'I thought I told you to piss off,' she hissed at him, turning so swiftly that her knee met him somewhere near the groin. 'So piss off. Now.'

Her expression was so ferocious that instantly his thin white shanks were scrambling off the bed, and he was wildly looking around for his jeans and T-shirt, whimpering quietly to himself.

He found his clothes, pulled them on, fought with the lock of the bedroom door and stumbled out. Ingrid hurled the picture of him and her in its silver frame after him as he went. He was just ahead of it. The frame hit the door and broke into a shower of fragmented glass, and she rolled over on to her stomach, thrusting her face into the deep down pillow and wept. But not for long. Eventually she stopped and thought. She sat up – stared at herself in the mirror – pushed her hair back in order and shrieked for Monique, who came, slender, dark haired, sardonic and submissive but with an alertness that showed in the dark intelligent eyes.

'Get all those freeloading creeps out of here,' Ingrid demanded, 'and then come back.'

Monique stood silently looking at her sprawled and naked employer for a moment. 'Couldn't he make it?' she asked.

'Christ knows,' Ingrid said. 'I didn't stop to find out. I've got a lot to tell you. Get rid of them and come back.'

Monique's long eyes flickered over the nude body on the bed.

'I won't be long,' she said.

Chapter Two

Kate Anderson lay on the made-up bed in the Beverly Wilshire Hotel staring at the flowered wallpaper and willing the telephone to ring. She wanted to go home. She had had Los Angeles, Hollywood, Beverly Hills and California in a big way. Back home she would be missing the magnolia blooming in her garden and if they kept her here much longer the chestnut candles would be white on the tree outside her bedroom window. All the roses of California would not compensate – and besides, she was missing, aching for Paul Wingard.

The job had not been an easy one. An in-depth series on one of Hollywood's flamboyant male stars. His girl-friends had declined to talk. His wives had declined to talk. He, on the other hand, had talked at great length and not entirely truthfully. His enemies had talked with considerable candour, and the court records of his divorces and brushes with the law had been revealing and fascinating. She had dug as deep as was possible in a town she found hostile and hard, and she wanted to go home.

Her notebook with pages of scribbled messages to herself was lying on her stomach as she half-dozed. She had been awake since six that morning, two weeks on the other side of the world still not having resolved jet-lag. Now, at midnight, she was not ready for sleep, and if she could stay awake for another hour she might be able to catch the editor of the magazine who had commissioned her and tell him she had done the best she could. Then she could go home.

She had been writing to please herself as she waited for the time to pass and had scrawled on a clean page of the notebook:

Why do I think of you on trains,
Planes,
Leafy, berry bordered lanes
And in tall cities when it rains?
Why do I think of you in trains?
I think of you
Here and there,
Anywhere
In places that
We'll never share.
I think of you
For I'm aware
In this affair
There's too much that
We'll never share.

She read it through again, changed the last line to 'We dare not share', then, rejecting it as second rate, said: 'Oh, sod it!', tore the page from the notebook, crumpled it and flung it across the room where it narrowly missed the wastepaper basket.

She debated whether or not to ring room service for a late night snack and decided against it. There had been too many late night snacks killing time. Paul didn't like it if she got too plump.

Kate had verged on being plump since she passed thirty. A medium-sized woman, she had thick black hair, which she pulled straight back from patrician features into a pony tail, and glass-green eyes that seemed to have their own lighting system. She had a zestful appetite for food, drink and living and had been brought up in different parts of the world, her father having been a famous foreign correspondent for *The Times* until his retirement. Her mother, the daughter of an Earl, had followed him in a surprised and yet resigned fashion, turning each corner of a foreign field into her own little England.

There had been spells at expensive girls' schools in England, France and Switzerland, but Marius Anderson had believed that the simple fact of living abroad was the best possible education, and therefore hers had been sketchy in the formal sense.

She had grown up to be totally at ease with people in any walk of life. She patronized no one – child, servant, waiter or chance acquaintance. Paul Wingard said she was the perfect thoroughbred, adding that on occasions thoroughbreds could be difficult to deal with, and needed to be given their head. He was aware that she could roar like an express train into tantrums which only made him laugh. Yet she was an exceedingly good journalist of the type her father did not entirely appreciate. Her skill was delving into others' lives. The first impression she gave was nervous-making but very few people did not find themselves saying things they had meant not to say when confronted with her listening face and sympathetic eyes.

The phone rang and she snatched it from the cradle before its second peal.

'Hello,' she said breathlessly.

'Good morning.'

'Good morning, my darling,' she said, her voice lifting. 'What a lovely way to end the day.

'And to start the day,' Paul said. 'Are you all right?'

'No,' she said. 'I am not. I want to come home.'

'From sunny California? It's raining here.'

'I long for rain. I long for tall buildings. I long for proper streets. I want to get out of this nowhere, smog-ridden scrap heap.'

'What's wrong with glamorous Beverly Hills, home of the stars?' he asked, his voice teasing.

'Hampstead Garden Suburb with jacarandas,' she said, decisively. 'And it doesn't have you. I miss you.'

'In that case I have good news. What chance of your getting to New York tomorrow?'

'Why?'

'Because I am going to be there.'

For a moment she did not believe him, but Paul never lied.

'Paul! Honestly? Alone? Just you?'

'Just me.'

She let out her breath in a long whistle.

'I can't believe it. New York. Of course I'll get there. The hell with the story.'

'Don't mess anything up.'

'I won't. But Paul – first time ever. I've just been writing a poem about us in tall cities. I never thought it would happen. Darling, can we stay the night together?'

'I don't see why not. If we're very discreet.'

'Paul – aren't you excited? Aren't you pleased? We never thought it would happen!' •

He laughed.

'You are a schoolgirl,' he said. 'Yes, I'm excited, and I'm pleased. You'll know how much when I see you. And don't you want to know why I'm coming to New York?'

She sighed down the telephone. The reason seemed incidental as she pictured his grey eyes and angular face, and the way his brows made a shelf above the eyes. She was enjoying the warm hot feeling she always felt when she thought of his large, square-fingered hands touching her and the way the fair hair glinted on his wrists in sunlight.

'Why are you coming to New York?' she asked dutifully.

'Because I've a job for you.'

'Me?'

'You. I've sold Ingrid Pallia's life story and the deal with the publishers is that you write it. First for newspaper serialization and then as a book. We have to meet her in New York to discuss details.'

Kate was silent, and then she said slowly: 'Darling – is it a good idea, my writing it? You know I don't like dealing with your clients and I don't like Ingrid Pallia at all. Couldn't we just meet in New York? If I'm with you I won't want to work. I just want to be with you – with no guilts and no interruptions. It's the chance of our lives. Honestly, don't let's spoil it with kinky, cocaine-sniffing, much-laid Ingrid Pallia. I've had two weeks of the prototypes here. I've had enough.'

'The publisher insists on you,' he said. 'Nor have you asked what they are paying.'

She looked around the luxury of the Beverly Wilshire room, sighed and said: 'Ok, how much? The first time ever we're meeting away from home and all you're talking about is how much I get paid.'

He chuckled. 'You always did have a very proper disregard for money. How does £25,000 grab you?'

'Sounds like a lot of champagne,' she said, and let a little whistle escape through her teeth.

'It's a package deal. She's been paid £250,000 for the whole thing. You get ten per cent. 'I get fifteen per cent.'

'And I do all the work?' she said, mock indignant.

'Ah, but I arranged it. Listen – are you really through there—'

'Positively,' she said. 'If one more person is rude to me on the telephone I'll commit mayhem. In this town the PROs have PROs and their secretaries have secretaries, and even they won't speak to anyone. I'm just waiting to ring home to get all clear. I can write the series. It won't be quite what they expected, but it'll stand up.'

'That's my girl. What plane will you get?'

'The first I can in the morning. But I'll be a lot later than you. Darling—'

'Yes—'

'I'm excited. And I love you.'

'I know. It's a bonus. Now make your phone calls and ring me back. I've got to get myself to London Airport. I'll book us into the Royalton.'

'Your name or mine?'

'Two rooms. We won't use one.'

She clucked, exasperated, then said: 'OK. See you tomorrow.'

'Today!' he said

'Your today, my tomorrow.'

She noted with her writer's detachment that her heart was actually beating faster when she put down the phone. A thumping that she could hear in her ears and feel in her wrists. Knees up, she wrapped her arms around herself, hugging her body, still not quite able to believe what he had said. In five years they had never spent the night together. The opportunity had never arisen, and he had refused to create one, saying that would be disloyal in the extreme. Disloyal to whom? she sometimes wondered, after five years of love and total faithfulness on her part. But his problems were greater than her own. In fact, she had no problems at all – apart from loving him. She was free, well friended and well funded, successful enough to be rich in a way that still surprised her.

The price of the 'bonus', as he called it, would be dealing with Ingrid Pallia. Kate had interviewed her before, and found her cold, venal and conceited. But £25,000 was a lot of money, and there was even more for Paul whose commitments were hard to keep pace with.

She mentally began to rearrange her schedule of work – what could be put off and what could not. Ingrid Pallia would take at least two months, if not three, of solid work. If she could do the newspaper series before the book and then pad it out it would help. The newspaper would certainly be in more of a hurry for the words than the publishers. But however she arranged things, Pallia was going to take too long. And knowing the lady's globetrotting, jetsetting habits, it dawned on Kate that she would probably be trotting behind, and half the profits would be eaten up by air fares.

Still, every cloud had a silver lining. Paul and New York together. She let out a small and muffled whoop of delight and then grinned at the idea of how Paul would accuse her of being a schoolgirl. She felt like a schoolgirl.

On reflection, she decided she would not ring London for clearance. She would clear herself. If they told her to stay on it would ruin everything. She'd ring from New York, then if they wanted more done, she'd go back – after Paul had returned to England. And at her own expense if necessary.

But she wouldn't tell Paul that.

She decided to book her flight before sleeping, realizing she hadn't asked him for how long he would be staying. Not just the one night, surely, though it was difficult for him to be away from home for long!

She rang back his office, missed him but left a message on the answering machine for his secretary, the tart and faithful Bunny, who was the three wise monkeys in one when it came to her boss. Kate was pretty sure Bunny, a plain lady in her late fifties, knew perfectly well that Paul was having an affair, but she was even more certain that Bunny would never betray him.

She didn't sleep well. Genuine excitement kept her awake, just as it always had as a child the night before a party or a holiday. It definitely felt like Christmas.

She was up at seven packing, settling her bill and returning the too large hire car. She had breakfast in the Café of the Pink Turtle, choosing eggs as she did every morning, hoping that maybe this time they'd get them right. They didn't.

She decided to treat herself to a limo out to the airport as a little calm before the storm. She loathed Los Angeles airport rather more than she loathed Los Angeles itself. She was even more impatient than usual with the delays and confusions of travelling. Time seemed to be dragging. She wanted the day to pass quickly. It had been two weeks since she had seen him.

She scribbled again for herself on the plane. Another poem for him. He liked her to write poetry especially for him. Sometimes she thought that the only two romantics in their respective tough worlds had found each other. But her intuition told her there were many more gentle hearts beating under leather exteriors.

Today she was obsessed with the clock and she had written:

Time's metre's altered
His poetry's erratic
And nothing is certain
And nothing is static.

24

Our routines are shattered,
Plans change like the weather
Till time shuts his eye —
And at last we're together.

Together in four hours' time.

The man sitting next to her said something, and she turned
to look at him blankly. 'I'm sorry?' she said.

He was young, and she took in brown eyes and brown hair.

'I said what are you scribbling?' He had the leaning-forward,
eager look of a man trying to start a conversation or a pick-up
but she didn't want to be picked up or start a conversation with
anybody. She wanted to daydream and fantasize.

'Nothing in particular,' she said, and very deliberately turned to look out of the window.

He fidgeted uneasily beside her for a moment and finally
ostentatiously opened his newspaper. Only then did she judge it
was safe to go back to her notebook, until sleep took over and
she dozed for most of the flight.

New York was crisp as celery, with a bright blue sky and
rogue clouds scudding behind the comic crowns on the older
buildings. As her taxi came off the freeway, and the skyline
snapped on to the horizon, she felt her spirits lift. New York
always exhilarated, and knowing Paul was there, waiting, she
felt a high that no drug the Hollywood addicts used could
match.

Once through the Midtown Tunnel the scruffiness of the
town was apparent as the taxi jerked through pot-holes, and
skidded past black plastic bags of rubbish left on the sideways.
Nothing could detract from her happiness. The town had a
special magic all its own.

The Royalton was on 44th Street, with the Empire State
looming ahead on Fifth Avenue. The fountain played in the
cool marble foyer, and the desk clerk, indifferent as ever,
greeted her casually as if she'd left the day before.

'A message for you, Miss Anderson,' he said, after taking
her American Express card and stamping her bill.

In the lift, while the black porter carried her bags, she

25

opened the folded sheet of paper eagerly. His handwriting –
strong, but elegant, was there.

Darling, sorry not to be there to greet you. I'm at Flat 1920, 3781
Park Avenue, with madam. Can you come over as soon as you
arrive? We'll settle with her, and then we're on our own. Come
quickly – I want to see you. Paul.

'Oh, sod it!' she said out loud, and the porter grinned at her.
'Bad news?' he asked.
'Not really,' she said.
'That's good,' he said philosophically, and she laughed.
'As a matter of fact, it is,' she told him.
Paul had obviously taken the double room. Hers was small.
It made sense. He had to have the telephone to hand in case
Madeleine called. There was no one likely to call her, but she
would have preferred him to come to her room. Not that it
mattered. Once above the landing the Royalton was quiet,
comfortable and entirely discreet. No one would be interested
in where she spent the night.

Very quickly she changed into one of the simple uncrush-
able silk jersey dresses she travelled with. She chose a deep
emerald green plainly cut in shirt-waister style, but left the
buttons a little deeper open than the dress demanded. Paul
liked her to look sexy. She also changed into matching silk and
lace trimmed underwear. The minute bra had no support, but
she needed none. The panties were brief, showing a frilly
emerald green and black suspender belt and wispy stockings
with a fine seam at the back. He was old-fashioned when it
came to underclothes. Normally she wore practical tights and
snug pants with smooth-line bras, but Paul thought they were
dull. For him she brought naughty underwear. For herself it
had to be comfortable.

She made up her face carefully, three layers of mascara for
the thick lashes that fringed green eyes like a snippet of dark
silk, and then hesitated over which scent to use. She settled on
the heavy sweetness of Fracas because he liked it, though she
normally only wore it at night and with evening dress.

She was ready. She took her small tape recorder, just in case,
and put a notebook into her shoulder bag. Maybe he'd want

her to start work. It was best to be prepared she decided as she left the room and went downstairs.

A taxi was dropping to the Algonquin opposite. She called it and gave directions, enjoying the streets, watching the gusty wind lifting skirts and swirling paper in the gutters.

Ingrid Pallia's apartment block on Park Avenue was large, old and elegant. Also, Kate thought as she went up in the lift to the nineteenth floor, expensive. But if Pallia was about to earn herself not far short of a quarter of a million pounds, she could no doubt afford it.

Monique Berault, the secretary, was waiting for her at the doorway to number 1920. She was almost too good-looking in her slant-eyed, Egyptian way, Kate decided. Pallia wasn't keen on competition. Certainly not younger competition. It was said she couldn't even bear her daughter, who was turning into a beauty, near enough to dim her own star.

'She is waiting for you with Paul in the drawing room. Through there,' Monique said, her accent attractively and huskily French. 'I'll be in in a minute.'

'Right. See you,' Kate said.

She walked towards the door, telling herself to play it cool. Don't let her face show how pleased she was to see him. Play it cool. Play it cool.

But it was almost as if New York had released something in him. He was standing waiting for her and as she came through the door, he made two strides, and wrapped his arms around her, so that her face was pressed momentarily on his chest and she could hear his heart.

Then he pushed her away from him and grinned down, his grey eyes alight, the wrinkles around them enhancing and framing the smile.

'You made it,' he said. 'Good trip?'

'Usual,' she said. 'How was yours?'

'Usual,' he said, then releasing her arms, turned her by the waist to face Ingrid Pallia. 'You know Ingrid, don't you?'

'Yes, we've met a few times. How are you?'

'OK.' The actress's blue eyes were unfriendly.

Hell – hostile, Kate thought, and the professional in her coming to the fore said: 'You're looking terrific. And before

I forget – I really enjoyed your last film . . . It was a great performance.' It hadn't been; she couldn't even remember the title, but no matter.

The eyes had softened fractionally. Flattery would get you anywhere, Kate thought; particularly with actresses. But the woman still had made no move to ask her to sit down.

'Come and relax,' Paul said. He had settled himself on the sofa, a heavy tumbler of gin and tonic in his hand, his long legs stretched out in front of him. Casually dressed in a lightweight tweed suit, he looked as if he should have had a gun dog at his feet. 'Really, Ingrid,' he added, 'your manners. Get Kate a drink. She must be croaking for one.'

'What do you want?' Ingrid asked grudgingly.

'Gin and tonic would do fine,' Kate said.

Ingrid nodded and then shouted, the husky voice suddenly harsh: 'Monique – bring a gin and tonic.' She then settled herself back in a deep white velvet-covered armchair. 'So you're writing my life story.'

The hell with her, Kate thought.

'I don't know,' she said. 'I'm really not sure if I have the time. I thought we were going to discuss it . . .' She paused and turned a dazzling smile on both Pallia and Paul in turn. He was stroking his upper lip with long, square fingers, and she could see the hairs on his wrist and the sight was turning her on in small hot waves. She knew he was hiding a smile, and she knew he realized exactly what she was doing.

'For £25,000 I'd have thought you'd have found time,' Ingrid said petulantly. 'I gather the publisher insists on you.'

'Well, I don't know . . .' Kate said, making her voice doubtful.

Ingrid was looking at her with hard eyes, then suddenly she smiled: 'But I'd love to work with you,' she cried. 'You're so clever. Everyone says you're the best! I'm sure we'd get on.' The voice changed to the hard shriek again. 'Monique – where's that gin and tonic?'

'Here.' The secretary was in the doorway, a glass chinking ice in her hand. 'Sorry to keep you waiting.'

Kate took it and sipped slowly. The room was very silent. Monique was standing still and watchful, Ingrid tense in the armchair. Paul remained relaxed, his cigarette spiralling blue smoke towards the fireplace where an artificial log-fire burned blue flames.

'Well, what do you think?' Ingrid said. 'I think it might be fun.'

I could touch her for fifteen per cent Kate thought, but said: 'Well, in principle, let's say I'll do it. But you'll have to be very open with me. It's easier if you tell me everything, and then we decide what we can and can't put in.'

'Then you'll know everything about me, won't you?' Ingrid said.

'You also have to trust me,' Kate said. 'If you're anxious, Paul can give you a list of names of people I've worked with before. I've kept all their secrets. Ask them. There's no reason why I shouldn't keep yours.'

Ingrid got up from the armchair in one fluid movement. She went to the window, and stood with her back to the room, pulling at the blonde tendrils of hair around her ears.

'It's not an easy thing to do,' she muttered.

'You're right,' Kate said. 'It's a very hard and painful thing to do. Tiring as well. Reliving one's life can be very traumatic. You just have to keep saying to yourself: "Half a million dollars. Half a million dollars. Half a million dollars." '

'Yes,' Paul said, 'because for that much money you're going to have to be pretty frank, Ingrid. And it's got to be truthful. No lies they can catch you out with.'

She turned abruptly.

'I don't give a damn what I say about my lovers. It's what I say about myself I'm worried about. You know the problems, Paul.' She made a helpless little gesture with her ballet dancer's hands.

'Your age,' he said.

'I'm not having that printed. And I don't want to talk about Jenny.'

'Your age is difficult for anyone to check,' Paul said. 'And unless you've had an affair with your daughter, no one's going to be interested.'

Kate looked at him in surprise. The comment was out of character, but his eyes were pressed steel as he stared challengingly at his client.

'Listen.' Kate decided she should break in. 'Don't worry. You have complete control over the words. You're quite safe. If you don't want to do it in the end, well, *tant pis.*'

'I don't want to do it now.' Ingrid said, petulant again. 'But I need the money.'

'Don't we all,' Paul said grimly.

'Just do it,' Monique said suddenly. 'A few more years and no one will be interested. And look what telling it all did for Joan Collins.'

Ingrid was biting her lip. Then suddenly she sighed, shrugged her shoulders and said: 'OK, then. When do we start?'

'How long are you here?' Kate asked.

'Not long. We have to go and see Bellino about my new film in London the day after tomorrow.'

'We can work in London then?'

'Well, I was going straight on to Rome. He's filming there, and I've taken a villa in Parioli for the summer.'

'Summer in Rome – you must be mad, Ingrid,' Paul said placidly. 'You'll fry.'

'It has a huge garden and pool. And I like it hot. We can work there.'

Kate felt her heart sink. Rome meant more separations, unless he could get there too. Maybe New York would have broken the pattern. Maybe he'd leave Madeleine alone if he found she could survive without him. Suddenly she was impatient to be away from Ingrid. She wanted to be alone with Paul. She could smell the English tobacco of his cigarette, just see his angular profile with the positive nose that saved his face from being feminine, and in front of her his long legs and the good leather shoes on his long feet. He had good feet for a man. Well shaped. She liked to hold them.

'Why don't we get together briefly in London to make some arrangements?' she suggested. 'Presumably until you've seen Bellino you won't know exactly what's happening. But we ought to get started pretty quickly.'

'That's right,' Paul said. 'There's no publisher's advance until they've seen a couple of chapters and a synopsis.'

'I think that's a bloody cheek,' Ingrid said. 'I mean – I'm famous enough.'

'It's publishers' practice.' Paul had made his voice patient. He put down his gin and tonic on the glass table beside him. 'Jet-lag is catching up with me. And I'm hungry. Do you want dinner?' The question was for Ingrid.

'You know I never eat dinner,' she said. 'But we'll have lunch in London. Friday. Is that OK?'

'That's fine,' Kate said, thinking if Paul could stay on, they needn't leave until Thursday morning. And that would be two whole days together.

'Right then. We'll be off. That's settled. Contracts signed in London, OK?'

'OK.' Ingrid waved languidly, and stayed curled in her chair. It was Monique who took them to the door of the apartment.

'Listen,' Paul said to her. 'Make sure she's there for God's sake. Pedro Bellino's the best break she's had in ages.'

Monique nodded. 'Don't worry. She'll be there,' she said, 'definitely,' as she closed the door behind them.

The long corridor down to the elevator was empty and Paul stopped and pulled her into his arms. Her head went up to meet his, and she clasped her hands around his back, rubbing herself against him. His tongue was flickering in her mouth, and she let hers join his, clinging to him, knowing she was making small sobs of pleasure.

He pulled back, and as she did so, they both said simultaneously: 'I've missed you—' then they laughed, and Kate, running her hand lightly over the tweed of his trousers said demurely: 'So I see.'

'And so *I* see,' he said, his fingernail scratching gently at her left nipple, which stood rampant along with its twin under the soft silk of her dress.

They heard the whine of the elevator, and Kate pulled a mock-cross face, wriggled her dress back into place and began to walk again.

'You'll have to hide behind me if nothing subsides,' she whispered just before the elevator doors slid open. 'You shouldn't be so well endowed.'

'Just shut up,' he said cheerfully.

Even dropping the nineteen floors to the ground she was aware of him as they stood, playing at being two casual people, six inches apart, not speaking. But she noticed even the four bored New Yorkers who shared the journey were sneaking sideward looks at them, and the black operator grinned as he let them out.

Did desire show that much, she wondered, or did frustrated lovers carry a musk – like wild animals?

In the street the wind flattened her dress against her body, and he took her arm.

'Shall we eat?' he said.

She turned to look up at him, surprised.

'Not go back to the hotel?'

He shook his head, and on his face was the half-rueful, half-defiant expression which meant he had come to a decision she would not like, and from which it would be difficult to budge him.

'Why not?' she asked.

He hesitated.

'Let's spin it out. Let's behave like a normal couple who can enjoy a meal together and go home to bed as a natural progression of events. We don't have to snatch at anything today.'

She thought about it. She was still excited and wanting him, but she understood what he meant.

'OK,' she said. 'Where shall we eat?'

'You don't mind?'

'Yes and no. It's all right as long as I'm with you.'

He squeezed her arm.

'We'll eat at the Algonquin. Then we can just fall across the road and into bed.'

'Sounds good,' she said. 'The Rose Room?'

'Yes. I did book. But we're a bit early. Want to walk?'

'Umm,' she said. 'Walking with you in New York! Can't believe it.'

'Well, here we are.' He squeezed her arm lightly. 'And Park Avenue, too.'

'Very posh,' she said. 'As was that flat. How does she pay for it all?'

'God knows.' He shook his head. 'I expect she's in debt up to her eyeballs. What a bitch she is.'

'I thought you were a bit off her,' Kate said. 'What happened?'

'Well, Bellino's making a film based on Colette's *Claudine at School*. Gives him a chance to get his paws on little girls, I suppose, and he wants Jenny Bolt for Claudine.'

'And Pallia's jealous?'

'Not so much that as terrified about the age thing. You may as well know, the fourteen-year-old Jenny is really nearer seventeen. A bit too old for our Pedro. No, Pedro wants Ingrid to play Claudine's headmistress for the publicity value. It appears that Ingrid has had a cultural day, whipping through the Claudine series, and has decided that she'd rather play Rezi – the Lesbian who seduces Claudine. As she so succinctly put it – 'If anyone's going to mess about with my daughter, it might as well be me.'' '

'Yuk!' said Kate.

'Yuk, indeed. There's no script as yet, so whether the story will get as far as Rezi remains to be seen. Claudine is grown-up and married when she discovers her. I would think that Pedro will stay with the schooldays so he can indulge his tastes.'

'What nasty people you know,' Kate said.

'What nasty people we both know.' He was slightly defensive. 'Anyway, forget it. Look at this town. It's too much, isn't it?'

'It's too much! Much too much with you thrown in. Paul—'

'Umm?' He was striding at his usual brisk pace making her take two steps to his one in her high heels.

'How long for?' she asked.

He looked down at her, his face serious.

'I ought to go back tomorrow.'

'Oh no—' her voice was such a wail of despair that he almost smiled. 'Paul – that's not fair. Stay on. Please. I've never asked you before. This time *please*.'

'She was very shaky when I left.'

'She's always shaky.'

'I know. But she doesn't complain. And I feel a shit. She does too much. She will do too much, and the kids need so much attention.'

'They shouldn't. They're old enough to cope for themselves.'

'She spoils them, Kate. You know why. Don't be hard with me. It doesn't suit you.'

His voice was gentle and suddenly she felt ashamed.

'I'm sorry. But Paul now you're away . . . This time, for me . . . Something for me . . .'

'All right,' he said slowly. 'I'll stay tomorrow. I'll go Wednesday morning.'

'Can I fly back with you?'

'I don't see why not,' he said. 'We are on business.'

The small victory won, she giggled and rubbed her hip against him.

'We could become members of the mile high club. Want to?'

'I think I'm too large to perform in an aircraft loo,' he said, 'but we'll try if you like.'

'It's a deal,' she said happily.

In the end even he had been eager to finish with dinner and neither of them wanted coffee. They walked a little too fast through the dark oak and dim lights of the Algonquin foyer and into West 44th Street, across the road and into the Royalton. Once inside he seemed to slow down.

'I'll come and carry your things,' he said.

'You needn't,' she told him. 'I've put everything I'll need in one small suitcase in the room. And I ruffled the bed before I went out. You go on. I won't be long.

'All right,' he said. 'It's room 1414.'

He got out of the lift before her, and she felt a twinge of uneasiness. The chance to kiss her again had been there but he hadn't taken it. And he seemed a little remote. Guilt again. Guilt over his goddamn wife and her wretched, pitiful illness. That was the killer between them every time: her sickness, her courage. All that created the conviction that both she and Paul felt – a reluctant conviction on Kate's part, perhaps also reluctant on his – that it would be unspeakable to leave a woman who after twenty years of marriage and two children tragically had found herself stricken with a long lingering illness. Kate and Paul had been lovers for five months when he came to her, shaken and white, to say that his wife's failing health had been diagnosed as multiple sclerosis.

Kate had rationalized the situation. She loved Paul Wingard; she could not imagine her life without him. She wanted to be married to him, but knew it was not possible. Yet. For the time being she would take what was possible, and give him

34

what was possible. She felt no guilt. She even felt she was behaving rather well under the circumstances for she was totally secure in Paul's love for her.

The issue was not so clear cut for him, and she knew it. There were times when his conscience tormented him and he agonized over what he considered unforgivable disloyalty to his sick wife. He had never ceased to care for Madeleine, but the affair between him and Kate had been a thunderclap of attraction; a meeting of two people who were totally harmonious together – sexually, socially and when they were alone.

He couldn't give Kate up. But while she felt frustration at their snatched meetings he felt guilt.

Maybe she wouldn't love him as much if he didn't feel guilt, she thought as she cleaned her teeth in her own bedroom, slipping the brush and toothpaste back in her sponge bag before leaving. On the handle of her door she hung the 'Do Not Disturb' notice to keep the maids out in the morning. And then she went to his room.

The door was on the jar and she went in quietly, locking it behind her.

'Paul,' she called softly. The lights were very dim.

'Here—'

He was in bed, leaning up against the pillows, a script in his hand. She stood still, smiling at him.

'Not working?' she said.

'Not really. Waiting for you.'

'You undressed.'

'Umm – nothing erotic about a man undressing.'

She sat on the edge of the bed and leaned to kiss his cheek.

'Everything about you is erotic to me.'

He was half smiling at her, his arms brown on the white of the sheets, his chest thick with faintly greying hair. He put the script on the floor. 'Just come to bed,' he said.

'Yes, sir,' she said meekly. She stood in front of him, teasing. Slowly she undid the buttons of her silk dress and it fell in a glistening puddle at her feet. Then smooth-skinned and rounded in the scraps of underwear and high-heeled shoes, she lifted long bare brown arms and released the knot of hair at the nape of her neck. It tumbled into waves on her shoulder and down her back.

35

'No more,' he said softly. 'Not another stitch. Come here.'

He had flung back the covers, and he was splendidly erect. She approached the bed from the foot, and kneeling, took him in her mouth before stretching herself along the length of him, pressing her breasts into him, until her mouth found his.

He rolled her over on to her side, and they lay pressed together. He had pushed himself between her legs and she rubbed her nylon clad thighs on him. His hand was pulling at her breasts; the other clasped her firmly to him, as they kissed, tongues entwined, breath coming slow, a red glow between her legs.

'I love you,' she whispered throatily. 'I've missed you. I want you to fuck me.'

'I will.' He was whispering too. 'I will, but not too quickly. I love you and I've missed you too.'

His hand was roaming over her midriff and her curved belly, fingers lifting the silky edge of her briefs, stroking the dark hair below and parting it to caress her in the hidden spot that would make her arch her back, moan and beg him not to stop.

'Go in me quickly,' she begged. 'I can't wait. I don't want to be too wet. I want you to push in. Hurt me a little. It's been so long.'

Her hands were stroking her briefs down her legs. He took them and laid them under his face on the pillow, and she lay spread for him, one breast fallen from its cup, the other covered, the suspender belt and the stockings still on her body, as she took him in her hands, gently pinching the delicate string at the tip. 'Is that nice – is that nice?' she kept saying. Then she rubbed her fingers along the length and unable to wait swung her legs over his body and guided him into her.

He pushed hard and savagely, and she gasped; a small exclamation of pain. He drew back and pushed again. It was easier now. He was sliding in and out, probing her depth.

'Lovely,' she said, opening her eyes. His face, intent and serious seemed to swim before her. He was very quiet, the lines in his face erased, his eyes darker. 'Oh, lovely, darling one. Don't stop.'

But he had. Abruptly he pulled away from her, and her searching hand found that suddenly he was flaccid; limp on her palm. She continued to hold him lightly, and pressed her mouth back to his, rubbing herself against him in small circular movements, then nibbling at his eyelashes, his ears, his cheeks. She took his lower lip in hers and sucked it gently, then kissing him, thrusting her tongue deep in his mouth.

They lay quietly kissing while her hand still stroked, but he remained acquiescent in her hand. She twisted to lean down and take him in her mouth, her tongue licking, her breath warm on him. Some instinct stopped her turning so his tongue could explore her, but his fingers were searching so deeply she imagined he was touching her womb and his other hand was stroking, scratching and pulling at her nipples, almost to the point of pain.

The pent-up longing for him was too much. The dam had to break. She let go of him, and lay her head on his thighs, her loins raising and falling as his fingers found her rhythm and rode with it.

Gasping, sobbing she came in a great flood of feeling that lifted her body from the bed. His fingers never stopped.

'Come again!' He was commanding. 'Come again!'

Panting, she did. And again – her body bowed – her breath fast, as she clutched him convulsively. Then he pulled her from his thighs, turning her again until she was laying beside him.

'There's my good girl,' he said, stroking her cheek. 'Now go to sleep.'

She tried to sit up, but he held her down.

'What about you?'

'Just go to sleep,' he said.

Tentatively her hand reached down. Still quiet. Still limp. It had been like that at the beginning when they first knew how ill Madaleine was. His guilt had made him impotent. But that had not happened for a long, long time now.

She put her head on his shoulder, and tickled his chest gently without saying anything. The new situation was the problem. Spending the night together had thrown him. The atmosphere needed lightening.

'Do you have to take your teeth out or anything?' she asked, deliberately making her voice sleepy.

'What?' That had stirred him.

'Do you have to take your teeth out or anything?' she asked again.

'No, I do not.' His voice was indignant. 'What a question.'

'Well, how would I know?' she said. 'We've never slept together before. And while we're at it – what do you like for breakfast?'

'With luck – you,' he said.

She giggled, and nuzzled her nose into his neck.

'Good,' she said. 'I love it when you eat me.'

'But failing that,' he said, 'two scrambled eggs, bacon, toast and coffee.'

'Me too,' she said. 'But they can't scramble eggs in America. They sort of fry them all gunged up.'

'I'd better settle for you,' he said. 'If you're still speaking to me.'

She held him as tightly as she could.

'I am content,' she said, adding dreamily, *Je suis content. How do you say it in Spanish? In any language, I am content. And glad you don't have to take your teeth out. Not that it would have altered a thing, of course. Still, at fifty you're doing well to still have them all.'

'Bitch,' he said, one hand stroking her breast with love.

Somehow in the night while they slept she had turned away from him. Her behind was pressed into his stomach, his arm flung over her. She woke to feel him pressing into her, thick and hard while his hands were urgently rearranging her body so he could enter her. He took her from behind, in a sudden thrust before sleep had receded. She wasn't ready for him, and cried out, and then her muscles relaxed and she felt herself open like a grateful flower as he rode her, pressed against her, his hands over her breasts.

There was no way she could caress him. She lay accepting the length and hardness of him, moving with him, until she knew by his breathing in the dark, and the familiar soft gasps, that he was going to come.

Then came his long groan and she was coming too.

'Oh, I love you,' she said when he had fallen back away from her.

'And I you,' he said. 'Come back here.'

She turned to lay her head on his shoulder again, marvelling at the feel of his warm body in the darkness. And then they slept.

Chapter Three

'I don't understand why you want Jenny,' Ingrid Pallia said pettishly. 'You don't know her. You've never seen her – you don't even know what she looks like. And you've no idea whether or not she can act.'

'Oh, but I do know what she looks like, dearest,' Pedro Bellino said, regarding the very clean fingernails on his very long, thin clean hands. Everything about Pedro was long and thin. He looked remarkably like Don Quixote, even to the little pointed Van Dyke beard. Don Quixote or an extremely handsome menacing stork, Ingrid thought as she watched him warily from her armchair as he paced about the hotel suite.

'How do you know what she looks like?' Ingrid said. 'I've forbidden any photographs.'

'We met last year,' he told her with a smirk of triumph. 'At a *very* smart house party on Mustique.' His voice was all innuendo. 'It was when she was away with Michael. I must say he keeps very grand company, dearest, but I suppose since the divorce you wouldn't be persona grata any more. Not fair, that, is it? The man always gets away with more.'

'Jenny never told me she'd met you.'

'No, I don't suppose she would.'

There was a long silence while Ingrid struggled to control her anger. The inference was clear. And last year Jenny had been fifteen. A little old for him, but her innocence made her seem younger. And he *thought* she was younger. Everyone thought she was younger.

'So you know what she looks like.'

'Very beautiful, if I may say so.'

'And what makes you think she can act?'

'There were lots of charades. Well, you know – there are always lots of charades on Mustique. *She* likes them. Jenny was very good too. I told her so and she confided in me that she wanted more than anything to be an actress. And with you for a mother and Michael as her father, it ought to be there, oughtn't it?'

'And what was Michael doing while all this was going on?' Ingrid asked, her voice icy.

'Keeping a very close eye on her, unfortunately,' he said, regretful.

It had a ring of truth, and Ingrid breathed a little easier.

'Well, I don't know. Michael will never agree anyway, and we have joint custody.'

'Dearest, you know and I know that she's sixteen, she's domiciled in England and she can do what she likes.' His face was malicious as she was unable to hide her discomforture. 'Still, we won't tell anyone else will we? It's much better for the picture to have her only fourteen. I do congratulate you for getting away with it so long.'

'Pedro – may I ask you a question?'

He answered with a gracious wave of his long arm while she looked at him steadily.

'Why do you want *me* in your film? You quite obviously hate my guts and you always have.'

Answer that, you tormenting bastard, she thought, but he merely looked genuinely surprised.

'Good heavens, dearest,' he said. 'What does my opinion of your personality matter? We're both very good professionals when we're working. You are right for my film. You'll make a marvellous Mademoiselle Sergent – jealous, fiery, a schemer, tough as old boots and bisexual with it. The only flaw is that Mlle Sergent was a redhead. You wouldn't consider going red, would you?'

'I might,' she said cautiously. 'I'd have to wear a wig for the period anyway.'

Suddenly she felt easier. This open bitchery of the conversation was more her style. She too preferred to say what she thought and damn the consequences.

'So you would,' he was saying gaily. 'So what do you think?'

She got up from her chair and walked to the window, staring out at the grey Thames below. Pedro always stayed in the Savoy. He like to watch the river, he said, and he hated new-fangled American-style hotels.

'All right,' she said, not turning to face him. 'On one condition. You swear you won't touch Jenny.'

'Dearest, she's much too old for me.'

She turned to look at him. His assumed foppishness and his elegance could label him as a roaring poof. But he was a paedophile.

'Pedro,' she said, 'You're disgusting.'

He looked crestfallen.

'Ah, Ingrid – you disappoint me. And you such a naughty girl yourself. I would have thought you'd understand. I tell you, dearest, by 1985 no one will give a toss about my tastes.' He stopped and thought. 'Maybe 1990. I mean, just look how the climate of permissiveness is galloping. Lovely Sodom and Gomorrah! No, fifteen years from now in 1990 the age of consent will be twelve. And all those discerning gentlemen with the same tastes as mine will come out of the closet and be happily screwing schoolgirls who'll love it. And what a trade there'll be in ten-year-olds.' He sighed deeply.

'You are disgusting,' she said flatly.

'You only think so because you're a mother,' he said cheerfully. 'And I've heard you like them young yourself.'

She glared at him.

'Dearest, it is the *on dit*.'

He was smiling at her, the ends of his mouth curled up under the moustache that went with the beard, his dark brown eyes narrowed and twinkling. To end the moment, she picked up the glass of champagne she had been drinking and said: 'When do we start shooting?'

'In about three weeks' time. In Rome. But I'd like you there before for costume fittings and script consultations. Paul has your script, and a contract. One for Jenny too. Will he act for her?'

'As he acts for Michael as well as for me, I can see no reason why not.'

'Well, you toddle off and discuss money with him. I hate discussing money. But I think you'll be pleased.' He stroked his beard with all five fingers. 'By the way, you have read the book?'

'*Claudine at School*? Yes.'

'There's a lot of making love to ladies.'

'I'd noticed,' she said, her voice sarcastic. 'Who is playing the charming Aimée whom I seduce so skilfully?'

'Not yet cast, dearest. Anyone you fancy? Blonde, nubile and nineteen. And small enough to sit on your lap. Those are the requirements.

'I'll think,' she said. 'Sounds like a young Ursula Andress.'

'Don't be bitchy!' he said, then added slyly: 'The other *on dit* is that you don't mind ladies, either.'

She did not reply. She drained the champagne, picked up her small purse and her mink jacket and said: 'See you in Rome, then.'

'Can't wait, dearest,' he said.

She worried all the way to the foyer where a porter scuttled to find her a taxi. The script couldn't be *too* raunchy. It was a feature film and it was based on a classic. It was also big budget. It couldn't go too far. But it was a break she desperately needed; her bank manager was beginning to make threatening noises. It might be an idea to ring him and give him all the good news.

For a moment as the lift went down she felt a sinking feeling that came from something more than the sudden descent to the ground floor. It seemed as if all the covers, all the wraps, she had so carefully shielded herself with were coming off. Being peeled away one by one.

Telling her life story with all the dangers involved . . . making a near-porn film . . . Pedro knowing Jenny's real age . . . did he know hers? And the rumours about her sexual preferences. For a moment she felt exposed and naked.

But the feeling passed. And once in the taxi, she began to plot the spending of all that money that was coming her way.

Ingrid stopped worrying. But then, She never worried for long.

*

Pedro Bellino lit a long, thin cigar with great attention to detail and regarded himself in the large mirror over the drinks cabinet of the suite with some satisfaction.

He looked exactly what he would have been had fate not decreed otherwise: a Spanish grandee. His father – an ageing none-too-rich aristocrat – still ran the stud on an enormous burned brown ranch outside Cordova breeding brave bulls; a ranch that was not as profitable as it had been before the Spanish discovered football to the detriment of the ring.

His personal history had changed when his father had been made Ambassador first to London and then later to Washington. It meant that Pedro's entire childhood had been spent in English-speaking countries, his youth in Madrid, then Paris and Rome, where his grasp of all languages had given him entrée to the film world. He had begun as a translator in the days after the war when the European film industry began to flourish, became fascinated, then committed, until gradually he became a director.

As a young man, he had enjoyed older women. By nature he was both a pupil and a teacher and in his salad days the mature had appealed to him for what he could learn and he had been an avid and willing pupil. Even today he regretted the loss of that sexual experience which those women of certain age brought to a bedroom. But then the teaching of some dear young innocent was compensation – the gradually sweet deflowering; the enjoyment of the unmarked flesh, the unused face, the bud breasts and sweet breath of youth. And the act itself. Ah, the little cries, the small sobs – it was an initiation to all joys, a ceremony he performed with great art and one he liked best when there was blood to show for it.

He had been more riled than he would permit himself to show at Ingrid's flat assertion that he was disgusting. He saw himself as one who directed the young on the path of life. And she, the bitch, with her own penchant for the beautiful, should understand. There was no beauty in age, though he, considering he was nearing fifty, had managed to retain his looks. His stomach was flat, the grey in his hair tinted into oblivion, and he made sure he was always tanned. His little nymphets liked the older men – but only if the older man was pleasing to their candid, all-seeing eyes.

His secretary, Olga, a poker-faced and uncommunicative small woman in her late thirties had come into the room.

'Your auditions start in half-an-hour,' she said. 'But there's a girl outside, no appointment, insists on seeing you. How she got up—'

'What does she want?'

'An audition. Says she read about it in the *Mail* Diary.'

There had been a not too pleasing reference to the fact that he was auditioning for schoolgirls in the papers that morning, with veiled hints about his sexual preferences. Too veiled – a fraction more and he'd have sued.

He made a little tut of annoyance.

'What does she look like?'

'Small, blonde, aged about fourteen. Sounds American. Looks like an angel with naughty eyes.'

There were times when Pedro believed Olga shared his tastes. From the look on her face, this was one of them. It seemed it might be worth seeing the girl.

'Send her in,' he said.

An angel certainly, but a very confident one. She came through the door in long strides, stopped, stared around her, and said: 'Great! What an amazing view.' Her voice was American accented – high, clear and childish.

'I'm glad you like it,' he said, making no attempt to hide the sarcasm.

She moved closer to him, close enough for him to see the flawless skin with the faintest trace of freckling across the nose. Her mouth was full, the lower lip dangerously greedy. She had round blue china-doll eyes with long lashes; they gazed at him with candid innocence. Her hair hung thick and blonde down her back and over her narrow shoulders, curling at the ends. Her nose was perfect. It was a face from a strip cartoon, petite, yet larger than life, without an imperfection.

'I'm sorry. That was not polite,' she said, suddenly a schoolgirl in her flat-pleated skirt and neat white blouse, both held together with a red belt. 'I'm Bobbie Jean Dennison. I don't have an appointment because I don't have an agent. It was very kind of you to see me.'

She held out her hand like a well-brought-up little girl. It was a very small, soft hand and he took it, pulling her fractionally nearer to him. Her breasts, he noted, were barely formed, her narrow hips and pretty little legs in flat shoes heart-stopping.

'And why do you want to see me?'

'Because I want to be Claudine. I'm just like her. Truly. I'm naughty too.' It was said with a sudden lowering of the eyes that tried to bely the statement. 'I'm good at lessons, grown-up for my age . . .'

'Which is?'

'Thirteen.'

She could have been, but he didn't believe it, and his quizzical look said so. She grimaced.

'You're too clever. I'll be fifteen in two months.'

'And in what other ways are you like Claudine, Bobbie Jean?' He found himself amused by her.

'Well, I live with my father who's always preoccupied, except that he's interested in shits instead of slugs.'

The word came unpleasant from her child's perfect mouth. He winced.

'Well, they are,' she said defensively, a little girl needing her mouth washed out with soap. 'Politicians and people like that. He's with the American Embassy here. Your father was Embassy, wasn't he? I reckon Claudine's father was better off studying slugs.'

She had chattered her last remarks and now she stopped again and looked demurely at her small feet.

'And can you act?'

'Yes. I always get the lead in the school plays.' The limpid eyes were on him again.

'School plays? Come now! Which school?'

'The Lycée. My French is perfect. That's good for Claudine, isn't it? And you could screen-test me, couldn't you? I photograph awfully well.'

He could believe it. The aching in his loins was there, but he moved away from her, puffing at the cigar.

'Your father's a diplomat.'

'Aha, I hardly see him. We've lived all over.'

He knew the condition.

'Does your father know you're here?'

'As a matter of fact—' the eyes lifted to him supplicating, then yellow lashes, like streaks of gold, dropped to hide them. White teeth bit the tantalizing lower lip. 'He doesn't. I couldn't tell him, you see. He's in Brussels, and he won't be back until late tonight. To tell you the truth—' the newly raised eyes were anything but truthful '—it's as well. You see if you think I'm right for the part, we could perhaps arrange something . . .'

'Bobbie Jean, the part of Claudine is cast.'

He enjoyed the spurt of genuine tears of vexation; there and gone as quick as an April shower. She was emotional under all that bounce and bravado. Good.

'Oh, sh— dear,' she said. 'I couldn't play Anaïs – she's all tall, thin, dark and sour looking. I'd love to be Aimée—'

'Too young,' he said decisively, wondering why he was playing these games and knowing exactly why he was.

'Could I be Marie, the stupid one?' She sounded as if she didn't want to play the stupid one.

Suddenly he felt an excess of largess.

'Who knows? Maybe I will give you a screen test – if your father agrees, of course.'

'Oh, he'll agree to anything. I can do anything with him.' Her lips curved in a sudden secret flash of amusement and Pedro felt a pang for the father of this delectable girl who was forbidden to him. Or was she? Was that what the satisfied, pussycat smile meant?

'Well, I'll think about it,' he said.

'Oooh. You're fantastic. Fabulous.' Suddenly she had launched herself upon him. Her arms, soft and slight, were around his neck, she was on tiptoe so that her flat stomach was pressed against his uncontrollable erection, and her soft mouth and breath were on his face. Breath that smelt faintly of peppermint, and lips that tasted to him of honey. She had kissed him full on the mouth, and then pulled back, girlish, blushing, eyes downcast again.

'You need your bottom smacked, young woman,' he said severely trying to regain control.

'It's no good,' she said, laughing. 'I like that, too.'

He almost groaned, but she was chattering on.

'Would it be a good idea if I came back here tonight after

you've seen all the others? Then you can tell me what you've decided. Suppose I came about eight? Poppa won't be back until gone midnight, so it wouldn't matter if you had to keep me waiting. I wouldn't mind a bit. But I'd like to know my fate, as it were. It's awful hanging in the balance. You see, I want to be an actress, but there aren't many parts for girls of my age. When I read the papers this morning, I thought I had to try. Nothing ventured, nothing gained, don't you think?'

She was pink as a rose, her little feet almost tap-dancing with excitement. He had to keep his hands off her. For the moment, anyway.

'Are you a virgin—?' he heard himself ask abruptly. He hadn't meant to.

Now she was bacardi rose, deep red. A red that spread down to the opening of her white shirt. The tap-dance stopped, and the head hung genuinely, a rose too heavy for its stem.

'Yes.' Her voice was low.

'That's all right then,' he said briskly. 'You run along now. You can come back at eight. I'll tell you my decision.'

'Thank you. Thank you,' she said, hesitated and ran for the door.

After she had gone he called to Olga: 'Bring me in a large whisky.'

A line of coke wouldn't have helped, and he had to get himself together before the auditions began. But he knew that somewhere there would be a part for Bobbie Jean Dennison. Even playing the stupid one.

He had just about finished the whisky when Olga's unobtrusive figure came back into the living room.

'Frances Elliot is downstairs,' she said. 'Are you ready to see her?'

'Which one is she?' he asked, his mind still on the Dennison girl.

'The one whose agent sent the videos. She's done several children's TVs, small parts in a couple of B pictures, and one West End stage performance. You wanted to see her because you thought she looked the perfect Anaïs.'

'Oh yeah, I remember,' he said. 'The ugly one.'

'But, as you remarked at the time, a very good little actress.'

'I remember,' he said irritably. 'Just get her up here. I've got fourteen girls to see and four parts to cast by today. The casting director can fill the classroom.'

She took no notice of his bad humour. She never took any notice, but she did her job with remarkable efficiency. For a brief moment he wondered what her private life was like. It was a passing thought that occured often. Who the hell would ever want to lay her, he wondered? Still, attractive she might not be, good secretary she was. A professional. And he respected her for that.

This child Frances Elliot had appeared to him to be professional also. She had a gruff little voice, like a dog with a frog in its throat, a sallow little pointed face with eyes far too narrow for beauty. Her mouth was tight and mean, and there was a sort of odd decadent sexuality about her. Not the kind that appealed to him, but it was there for others with different tastes. More important, she could act. She reminded him of a young Glenda Jackson.

The door was opening again, and Olga was ushering in not one but two people. One was a young woman amazingly wearing hat and gloves, white gloves. The other unmistakably young Frances Elliot.

The young woman in the hat moved purposefully across the room towards him, her hand outstretched. Close up he could see she was not perhaps so young – nearing forty, but her very fair skin and blue eyes and tendrils of blonde hair escaping from beneath the garden party hat had misled him.

'Good afternoon, Mr Bellino,' she said in the plummy, mouth-contorting tones of the posher London outskirts. 'I'm Eileen Elliot – Frances' mother.'

That particular English accent always brought out the foreigner in him.

'Enchantée, madame,' he said, bowing over the hand with fulsome care.

'I came along with Frances because my husband suggested it might be helpful to you.'

He looked at her sardonically.

'Helpful, madame, or safer?'

She flushed bright scarlet under the fine English skin that was already cracking into faint lines.

'Not at all,' she said stiffly.

'I assure you, Mrs Elliot, I am very impressed by your daughter's acting talents. Nothing more is necessary.'

'My daughter is a fine actress,' the woman said, trying to be mollified, but not absolutely sure whether she should be.

She was a bore. Abruptly he turned to the girl who was standing regarding him boldly, but without any coquetry. Her look was interested, her head slightly to the side. With her beaky face and her punk hair, she looked like a canary. She also had a genuine confidence and self-possession. This one was no virgin.

'Do you know anything about Anaïs?' he asked her.

She nodded. 'Yes. I thought you'd want me for her—'

'Little girl,' he interrupted, 'this is an audition. I don't know that I want you for anything.'

She nodded, gravely, unabashed.

'Well, in mind for Anaïs,' she said. 'She is the plain one of Claudine's friends and the most experienced. Always falling in love. Sharp and clever.' She paused. 'I always get those sort of parts.'

She was perfect for the role. It seemed unnecessary to prevaricate. The professional section of his brain was rerunning the film-clips he had seen of her. They were good. No point in not saying that she would do very well for the role.

'I think you have another of them,' he said. 'Are you free?'

'Yes.'

'You'll have to get rid of that terrible hair.'

'I told you so, Frances—' the mother's refined tones intervened. He ignored her.

'And you'll have to spend at least four months in Rome. Are you still at school?'

'Yes.'

'There'll be a tutor.'

Mrs Elliot appeared to feel she was losing control.

'That won't be necessary,' she said. 'I am an ex-schoolmistress and I will tutor my daughter myself.'

'At your own expense, madame,' he said, smiling at her with spurious charm.

She stared at him, her blue eyes suddenly steely.

'My husband would not permit Frances to leave England

without me as a chaperon,' she said icily. 'She is not yet six-teen.'

'My dear madame, you will be very welcome,' he told her, 'but our budget does not cater for individual chaperons. There will, of course, be professionals. But if you should wish to come of your own accord, you will be very welcome indeed. You may well enjoy the experiences. But that is a matter for you and your husband to discuss.' He turned again to the daughter, whose eyes were making no attempt to hide her amusement. He warmed to her. What fate to be landed with such a mother!

'I'll be in touch with your agent, Frances,' he said, 'but you can assume, subject to agreement, that you will be Anaïs in my new film. That's all for now.'

Sometimes he thought Olga listened behind doors, her tim-ing was so impeccable. At that precise moment she knocked and came in.

'Your next appointment is here, Mr Bellino,' she said, and turning to Mrs Elliot: 'Shall I show you the way out?'

'Thank you.' Mrs Elliot said, with a twitch of her gloves.

He watched them go with interest, thinking it would almost be worth paying Mrs Elliot's expenses to see what the hot sun of Rome and its Romeos would do to her in four months.

One thing he knew. She wouldn't come home again in white gloves and a garden party hat.

Chapter Four

Frances Elliot was standing in a cupboard, her ear pressed to its back wall. The cupboard was in her bedroom on the first floor of the neo-Georgian house which her family occupied in Weybridge and she had discovered long ago that the walk-in where she hung her clothes made a perfect sound box into the living room on the other side of the hall and stairway. The knowledge had been useful for years – there was little that that went on between her parents she didn't know.

When her mother had said she would have to speak to her father about the part in Bellino's film when he came home, Frances had announced that she thought she would go to her room and read the Claudine book again.

'Why not, dear?' her mother said, fussing with ice and Martini glasses and anxiously checking the gin bottle. On the occasions when Alex Elliot did come straight home from his architect's office, he was much more amenable after two large, very cold Martinis, which he liked made with just the merest suspicion of Noilly Prat and a scrape of the zest of a lemon.

Frances thought that his recipe was no more than an excuse for drinking neat gin. But then she didn't like her father very much; nor her mother, come to that.

Her mother's awful voice was plumbing its way into the cupboard now, echoed by the deeper, grumbling tones of her father. Frances tiptoed across the room and took the little stool from her dressing table so that she could sit in comfort while she listened. She had an idea that this conversation was going to be a long one.

'How did your day go, dear?' her mother said.

'Usual. That damn fool Johnson is going to cost us the finishing clause money if he doesn't get the builders off their arses. I told him he'd set too early a date.'

'Oh, dear, 'Eileen Elliot said. 'Does it mean much trouble for you, darling?'

'Not for me, but plenty for Johnson,' her father said savagely. 'Don't worry. You won't have to curb your extravagance.'

Frances heard her mother's footsteps cross the room to the drinks cabinet, walk back, and then the soft sound of pouring. The second Martini was on its way.

Then there was silence. He'd be flipping through the *Standard,* Frances thought, and waited patiently to see how her mother would get around to the subject. So far she was showing remarkable restraint.

'Frances and I had a really fascinating day,' she said at length.

Her father grunted. He was probably deep in the city page.

''She's been offered the most wonderful film part, Alex – it's an incredible opportunity for her.'

There was a slap, as if her father had hit the arm of his chair.

'You know how I feel about it,' he said.

'Yes, but really this time—'

'Taking out all your thwarted ambition on the child—'

'But she is good—'

'It's nothing but bloody vanity on your part—'

'But this time, Alex—'

'And if she ever does make a go of it, you'll finish up being jealous as a bloody she cat at her success.'

'Alex, that's not fair—'

'Why the hell can't you spend more time interesting yourself in the business that pays for all this nonsense? Why can't you use all those marvellous talents you were meant to have to at least act as if you liked some of them and show an interest in what goes on?'

Her father was attacking to change the subject. There had been open warfare the previous week when her mother had refused to go to the firm's twentieth anniversary dinner. Her father had been furious, her mother adamant.

'When everybody knows you're having an affair with your secretary!' Elaine Elliot's voice had turned shrill. 'Why should I go there when I know everyone is laughing at me? You ask too much, Alex.'

There was another slap. Probably the newspaper this time.

'For the last time. I am not having an affair with Linda. But it's a great excuse for you to get out of doing anything, isn't it? Great excuse! Then you can act the sad little left-at-home for all your bloody coffee-morning friends.'

'When Linda leaves, I'll show an interest in the business.'

'Linda's not going anywhere. She's my right hand.'

'And the rest,' Elaine said, the round vowels slipping.

Alex Elliot merely grunted, and the newspaper was rustled loudly. Frances heard her mother cross the room again. This time it would be a Martini for herself.

More silence, and then a tentative 'Alex . . .'

'What?'

"We must talk about Frances' film. Hal Matthews says that Bellino needs your permission before the contracts can be signed. You know that. She's still under age.'

'Bellino?' There was a deep note of suspicion in Alex's voice. 'Bellino – isn't that the chap . . .' Frances heard more rustling of newspaper. 'Yes, listen to this —' and her father reading out from the paper said:

'Film director/producer, Pedro Bellino was a happy man today when a series of pretty little girls arrived at his Savoy Hotel suite to audition for roles in his new big budget movie *Claudine At School*.

Bellino, a Spaniard, is well known for his affection for the young and has been quoted on many occasions on his interest in guiding their careers and helping in their development.

Today he told our reporter that he believed he had already discovered some remarkable new talent as a result of the auditions. It was, Senor Bellino stated, all girl talent.

"There are no roles for small boys in *Claudine At School*,' he said. 'The film takes place before the days of coeducation." '

There was a silence broken by Elaine's defensive voice.

'Well, what about it?'

'For Christ's sake, woman, you're obviously as big a fool as you look. The man likes little girls, and you're suggesting that I sign something to let our daughter work for him!'

'It's a lot of money: five thousand pounds. Hal says it's very good. As her agent he recommends she does it. I mean, how many other films is she going to be offered? And she's no beauty.'

'Not like her sainted mother, who was fairer than them all, never had the opportunity, and now all you think about is money.'

'Sometimes, Alex, you go too far.' Her mother's voice was low. Frances had hardly picked up the words. 'I have already insisted that she be chaperoned.'

'By whom?'

'By me.'

It was a long silence this time, and Frances was certain she could guess what was racing through her father's mind.

'How long's this film going to take?'

'Four months,' her mother said evenly.

More silence. He was thinking of the opportunity. The opportunity to be alone with Linda with his wife out of the way.

'I don't want her to do it,' he then said flatly.

He was torn between the chance to be alone with his mistress and the moral welfare of his little darling – for Frances knew she was his little darling, in spite of her plain face and remote manner. Her father was afraid of her being assaulted by the naughty film director who liked little girls.

'Why not?' her mother asked.

'Because she is only a child and I don't want her subjected to that kind of situation.'

'You've let her do it before.'

'Little things. Nothing serious. Just to keep the pair of you quiet.'

'Well, she really wants to do this one. It's in Rome. It'll be an education. A marvellous opportunity.'

'In Rome!' Her father was shouting, and he himself crossed the room with heavy tread towards the drinks cabinet. 'In Rome! Making a film with a load of God knows what, with a man in charge who'll be trying it on, and her not even sixteen yet. Don't you care about your daughter at all?'

'I think it's a little late to worry about that,' Eláine said.

'And what do you mean by that?'

'Well,' Elaine paused, and then said spitefully: 'Would you say she's still a virgin?'

'Oops!' Frances whispered to herself.

'And if she's not, whose fault is it? Sending her to theatrical schools, putting her with a load of poofs and pansies—'

'They won't have deflowered her—'

'Making her grow up before her time. All because you thought you ought to have been Grace Kelly and never made it. Pretensions. Nothing but pretensions . . .'

Things were going pretty much normally, Frances thought. For years they had fought over her. As a child she felt like a bone between two dogs, but she knew how to manipulate the pair of them. It wasn't quite time yet. The moment would come.

'Why do you hate me so?' her mother was saying, tearful now. 'I've done the best I can. I know you only married me because of Frances. But I want her to have a better life than I did—'

'Is letting her go off with a degenerate bastard going to do that?'

'But I'll be with her.'

Again the silence.

'And who's paying for you?'

'We are. I am. Frances is. What does it matter? Just as long as she's protected. It's an important film, and Hal has negotiated an option for a part in whichever movie Bellino makes next. And he makes big movies.'

More silence.

'How long would you be in Rome?'

'I told you – about four months.'

A note of self-righteousness had crept into her father's voice.

'And I'm supposed to look after myself for all that time?'

'I don't doubt you'll manage,' her mother said, her voice totally expressionless.

It was the moment.

Carefully she crept out of the cupboard, putting the stool back by her dressing table. Then she opened her bedroom door, crossed the hallway in front of the stairs and went through the heavy glass doors into the sitting room.

'Daddy –' her voice was a schoolgirl squeal of delight. 'Daddy, how lovely – you're home. Have you heard the wonderful news? Has Mummy told you? I've got a part in a new film. An important part. Oh – isn't it exciting?'

She hadn't flung herself into his lap – that wasn't her style. She was uncomfortable at any physical contact with her parents. She let her face, her hands, her shining eyes do the work. She used what they had taught her in drama school, and the natural talent that was in her and her father responded exactly as she had expected.

'Well, I don't know,' he said, his voice gruff and uncertain.

She let the light go out of her eyes, her shoulders drooped and her hands fell, limp, to her side.

'Daddy! What do you *mean* you don't know!'

He was a big man, florid faced with greying hair combed straight back from his forehead. A coarse man who wore very good suits and was a first-class administrator in his own firm of architects. But he was putty in his daughter's hands.

'Well, only on condition that your mother goes with you,' he said.

'Daddy!' Eyes shining again, she walked to where he sat and very delicately imprinted a light kiss on his cheek. It was a rare gesture from her, and he touched his face briefly before saying: 'I don't approve mind.'

'You'll sign the papers, then?' her mother asked tentatively.

'If I must.' He picked up his newspaper. 'But keep away from this Bellino fellow.' he said to Frances.

She couldn't resist it.

'Don't worry, Daddy,' she said. 'I'm really far too old for him.'

Pedro Bellino shut the door on his bedroom firmly. The scene was set. All was prepared. He looked at his watch. Ten to eight. He was pretty sure that Bobbie Jean would be prompt, and he had sent Olga on her way. The suite was empty.

He himself was wearing a long pure silk, deep maroon, paisley dressing gown. Underneath he wore nothing; the sybarite in him enjoying the feel of the silk on his skin. He was unaccountably nervous, and not certain why. Involving himself with the daughters of diplomats was not truly a good idea, and yet danger had always added spice to his liaisons. He lit one of his long, thin cigars and sat back in an armchair, staring pensively at the Thames. It would be a bonus if the child could act, but obviously he would have to find something for her to do in the film. If things worked out the way he was hoping this evening, he would be open to blackmail and he knew the Bobbie Jeans of this world well enough. They knew their value.

The telephone rang sharply, making him start. It was the hall porter announcing there was a Miss Dennison to see him.

He said to send her up and then half smiled to himself, the moustache emphasizing the twist of the lips. This time she wanted it known that she was in his suite. She wanted witnesses. No creeping up the back-stairs, or whatever it was she had done earlier in the day.

It seemed to him that she took rather a long time to arrive. The faint knock on the door of the suite heightened the anticipation, but when he opened the door, he hardly recognized the girl standing there.

The blonde hair was piled up on her head in a elaborate coiffure some strands of which had begun to tumble leaving curling tendrils hanging behind her ears. She wore a very deep red lipstick, a purple eyeshadow which made the clear blue eyes look shadowed and older. She was wearing high-heeled tart's shoes with a tight black sweater tucked into a narrow black skirt with slits at the side and black stockings.

'Hello,' she said uncertainly. 'Am I too early?'

'Dearest, you are commendably on time,' he said, attempting to hide his disappointment. 'Come in.'

She tippy-toed into the room on the high heels and then swung round to look at him as he shut the door behind her. Reading his questioning look, she said: 'I wanted to show you I could look old enough to play Aimée. Don't you think so now?'

'You look like a little girl dressed up in her mother's clothes,' he said.

'The maid's, actually,' she said and giggled. 'Momma doesn't wear things like these.'

'And what does your mother wear?' he asked.

'Suits and things. Mink coats. She's a career woman back home. I live with my father. He's got custody.'

'Why?'

'I don't know. No one will ever tell me. I think it's because she drinks.'

He had settled himself down back in the chair, leaving her standing, and she pirouetted in front of him, unselfconscious now and as relaxed as if she had known him for years.

'Look, don't you think I could be Aimée?'

'No.'

'Why not?' she pouted.

'Because, dearest, I think you are going to have to play the stupid one, but we don't know until the screen test, do we?'

'But I'm not stupid.'

'A little,' he said, raking her with his eyes from heels to hair, and allowing a smile to escape. Stupid enough not to realize her charm was in her youth. But aware enough to know exactly what was in his mind. It never failed to fascinate him: the sexual sophistication of these little innocents who put out all the right signals, if only dimly understanding exactly what they were about. They made the running every time for men of his tastes and preferences. As young as nine – sometimes younger – they knew exactly what they were doing.

The only danger was the scream of rape, the cry of seduction and the reversion to the sobbing schoolgirl calling for mummy when the deed was done.

So far he had avoided that, but Nemesis always hovered.

Her round blue eyes were shining now, and more tendrils of hair had collapsed from the piled mass on top of her head.

'Am I going to get a screen test?'

'Yes.'

'When?'

'When my secretary has arranged it with your father. But you must ask him first.'

She grimaced. 'That'll be the tricky bit.'

'I thought you could do anything with him?'

Again the secret smile.

'I can. Most of the time. But he won't care for me being in Rome.'

'You will be very properly chaperoned . . . once the filming begins.'

The perfect little nose wrinkled into broadness, and the soft mouth became a clown's.

'Oh, shit!'

He tutted, then said:

'So, shall we enjoy ourselves now?'

He could see it was too abrupt for her, but he had intended it to be. She took half a pace backwards, her body movements suddenly defensive as she curled her arms over her small breasts.

'Come into the bedroom,' he said. 'I've something for you.'

She seemed to gulp, but very slowly followed him. He paused theatrically before the closed door, turned, smiled at her, and flinging it back said: 'Look.'

The eyes went rounder if it were possible, and the lipsticked mouth pursed into a perfect, kissable 'O'.

'How super!' she said.

Laid out on the floor of the bedroom, in the area in front of the bed, was a very expensive train set with stations, goods yards – all the gadgetry that Hamley's, London's best toyshop, could provide

'How did you know?' she said.

'Know what?'

'That I'm mad about train sets.' She was advancing into the bedroom and surveying the complex mass of track, stations, engines and carriages that he had arranged. 'Do you know, when my parents split, Mom got custody of my older brother, and the thing that really made my pop mad was that she got custody of the train set too. We had an amazing one. Up in the attic.'

'I take this with me wherever I go,' he said.

'You do. Why'

He stroked his moustache to hide the smile.

'I find it is a relaxant,' he said.

'Oh, sure – can we play with it now?'

'Why not. But in those clothes . . .' he paused delicately. 'Perhaps I could loan you one of my pyjama jackets.'

Her mind was on the train.

'Ok,' she said.

He picked one of red silk, banded with white silk cord. He was sure it was the shortest he owned, and then tactfully leaving her to change, went back into the living room.

He returned when he heard the stifled noise of an engine running around the track. She had settled herself with one of the control panels and was busy manipulating a long set of Wagon Lits with a car ferry trailing behind, dropping off mail bags with one of the more intricate gadgets.

'It really is great!' she said.

He stood looking at her, desire moving in him. She was kneeling, the soles of her feet pink and soft, the red silk of the pyjama jacket ending just at the bend of the back of her knee. She had let her hair fall in disarray down her back and the red lipstick was smudged.

As she leaned forward to correct the positioning of one of the toy stations the jacket rode up revealing the soft crease and curves of her buttocks where they met her firm legs. He felt himself tighten and stand under the silk of his own dressing gown and experimentally rubbed his hand over himself through the cloth, making the excitement grow. She did not see, she was too intent on the trains whizzing around the tracks, busy changing signals, and making small murmurs of pleasure to herself.

He had brought in two of the large cushions from the sofas in the living room, and he flung these on the floor, then taking the pillows from the bed to add to the pile. With this makeshift seating arrangement he settled himself on the floor beside her, close by the controls of the second electric panel, and casually put his arm around her so that her hair fell on his arm where his sleeve had slipped back. It felt as if she had stung him.

'Tell you what, dearest,' he said, 'I'll take all the goods train – you take the passenger trains, and I'll try to crash your stock, you try to avoid me. Do you know how to operate the points?' She nodded. 'That's it then,' he said. 'Everytime there's a crash you must give me a kiss.'

The look she turned on him was totally calculating.

'Right,' she said.

He was so excited that he found it hard to keep his mind on the movement of the trains and the switching of the points, therefore she was keeping her line of engines and carriages out of his way without too much trouble. He was silent, trying to concentrate on the controls, but aware of the talcum-powder scent of her, and of how the red pyjama jacket was falling away from her shoulder so that one delicate little shoulder-blade was visible under the white skin. But he could not catch a glimpse of her breast. She was giggling and bumping herself up and down on the cushions as her trains sped through the toy stations, and the buzz and rattle of the engines going faster round the floor added to his excitement, and he forced himself to focus only on the electric controls. It took a while but eventually he managed to topple the line of Wagon Lit from the track. His own line of goods trains fell too, and both set lay topsy-turvy, wheels still spinning with all the pathos of real wreckage.

'Oh,' she pouted, 'now look what you've done.'

She swung herself up so that she was kneeling in front of him, and then leaned forward to kiss him where he sat, legs crossed on the floor. As she came towards him, the lipstick mouth gleamed, and the red jacket slid forwards to show two small, immature bee-sting breasts. As they kissed, he could not resist any longer. His long fingered hands cupped her breasts, thumbs gently stroking the rose nipples.

She made no move to stop him, and her mouth, tight closed stayed on his. Very carefully he unfolded his legs so that they were each side of her and leaned back on the cushions, pulling her down on to him. He felt her tense a little, and murmured: 'It's all right. Relax.'

She had the bony softness that pleased him as she lay very still and rigid along the length of his body. He wondered if she could feel how excited he was, and wondered, too, just how experienced she really was. For the moment he decided to continue kissing her. He nuzzled at her lips, doing his best to remove the lipstick, and hoping that traces of it were not all over his face. Gradually her lips began to part and she was breathing a little faster, and very delicately he slipped the tip of his tongue just inside her mouth.

Then he pulled back.

'Do you like that'

'I think so,' she said. The strip-cartoon face was mirroring anxiety, but he felt the uncertainty was faked.

'Has anyone done that to you before?'

'One boy I liked.'

'Did he do it like this?' He kissed her again, more firmly, and this time let his tongue flicker in and out of her mouth until he felt her responding.

He had turned her on her back, making sure she was on the cushions. Behind them the neglected trains whirred and protested. Groping without breaking their mouth contact, he

61

turned off the electricity. It was suddenly very silent.

He was sitting now, looking down at her, and he took the cord of the pyjama jacket and gently pulled it.

'May I look at how pretty you are?' he asked.

She nodded, eyes round. Her mouth was slightly open. She had one arm behind her head in a Marilyn Monroe pose.

Slowly he opened the jacket, so that the red silk became a sheet behind her very white body. He ran his hand over the two minute breasts, over the curving, faintly bony ribcage, and down the small fluff of hair on the barely formed mount of Venus. Then she stiffened.

'What's the matter?' he asked.

'I don't let anyone touch me there.'

'Never have?'

She hesitated.

'Well, that one boy I liked.'

'What did he do? This?'

He ran his fingers through the fine hair, then parted the soft seam into the plumpness of the outer lips, gently stroking and exploring, restraining himself from what he would really like to do, and yet pleased with his own patience.

She lay very still, and now he was feeling between the inner lips, and searching for the little bump that should tell him whether or not he was arousing her. It was hard to find, not raised, and had he been able to look, he was sure not darkened.

Was she one of the cold ones, he wondered? All sex on the surface; all promise but with no fire or passion? Sometimes they were like that, these nymphets: aware that their bodies were marketable commodities. As young as twelve, already with a tart's mentality.

'Are you really a virgin?' he asked her, bringing his hand back over her stomach, making her jump a little, and then caressing her breasts again, with gentle tugs at the nipples, and circular rubbings with the palm of his hand. They at least had risen he thought, and it seemed her body was arched, more eager.

'Yes,' she said.

'Tell me what you enjoy. What pleased you with that one boy you liked?'

The violet eyes looked up at him warily.

'I didn't let him go below the waist. Not often anyway.'

'You let him touch your breasts, like I'm doing?'

She nodded.

'But no more?'

'Not often.' She seemed to consider and then said: 'I did let him rub himself against me, down there, you know, just once. But I wouldn't let him go in.'

'Why not?'

'My mother said I shouldn't waste it on schoolboys. It would be better with a man who could help me.'

Exactly what sort of help did she mean? he wondered, all the time working on the stiff little nipples, and feeling his own stiffness throbbing, hurting.

'And what happened when he rubbed himself on you?'

She grimaced. 'It made an awful mess. I was frightened I might get pregnant, but he said I couldn't that way. But I went home quickly and had a bath, just in case. You can get pregnant that way, can't you? I suppose he just didn't want to be responsible if anything went wrong.

Her voice was virtuous.

'So you don't take the pill?'

She giggled.

'Our doctor would have a fit. Anyway, I don't need to un- til—' she stopped.

'Until?' he prompted.

'Well, I decide. You know,' she said uneasily, her eyes flickering towards the place where his dressing gown was definitely lifting.

He laughed, and bent to kiss her again, then running his lips over her throat, worked on her breasts with tongue and teeth, trying pain, a little sharp bite, to see if perhaps that excited her. But she only made small protesting noises.

His fingers were in among the other lips, and perhaps she was a little damp, but no rich juices ran, and his disappoint- ment grew. He wanted her to cry out for him, he wanted her to cling to him and plead for relief. He wanted to arouse her, but in spite of her indifference, his own desire had not gone. She *looked* so perfect – the child woman, with her down of

63

pubic hair, her unused face, budding breasts and gentle jutting bones. He wanted her to moan for him. This one would not moan.

He was groping in his pocket with one hand for the French letter he had put there, just in case. It was a shame to have to use it, but she most certainly could get pregnant from what he was about to do. He would need the jelly as well, he thought, irritated that it was going to be necessary to make preparations that could only be clumsy.

He decided to put the tube itself at the opening to her, and quickly squeezed. She jumped at the coldness, and kissing her, he rubbed the sticky stuff in until his fingers could easily slide inside without hurting her.

Then he rolled on the French letter, and let his dressing gown fall open as he knelt above her opening her legs wide. She made no protest. He wanted her to take his erection in her hands and stroke him, but she did nothing. She lay there with a provocative tart's smile not looking at the body he was still proud of.

'I'm going into you now, Bobbie Jean,' he said lowering himself as slowly as he could on to her. He didn't want to hurt her, though his instinct was to plunge deep and sudden and make the cold little bitch scream out.

He had to manoeuvre himself to find the way; there was no help from her and he eased in, over the bony hump inside. It was smoother than he had thought it would be. His own care and the lubrication had helped so that she only gasped a little and made one little sobbing noise. As he rode with more confidence, he began to get angry. It should not have been like this.

Then he was riding her savagely, and she was twisting under him – almost responding – and panting, he came, crying out at the moment. Then he flopped on to her flat body and lay very still, drained and disappointed.

'I can't breathe,' she said plaintively, after a while.

'I'm sorry,' he said, and rolled off her. 'Are you all right?'

'I think so,' she said cautiously, and sat up, looking between her legs.

'Look,' she said triumphantly. And on the red of his

64

pyjama jacket was a darker red. 'I told you,' she said. Then her voice became wheedling. 'You will give me a part in the film now, won't you?'

'I will give you a part in the film,' he said wearily.

'Oh, goodie,' she said. They both lay tumbled on the floor in silence, the toy train ludicrous beside them. Then she said thoughtfully: 'Is that all it is?'

'That's all it is,' he said.

And he knew exactly what she meant.

The White Elephant Club was less crowded than usual, which was something of a blessing. Ingrid was certain that this drink with her ex-husband was going to end in a flaming row.

He was being his usual pompous self. Charming the waiters into a frenzy of activity with his studied courtesy, patronizing the lesser actors at the bar, smiling, smiling, smiling.

Publicly, she had never heard him say a cross word. He never swore, he never complained. The only criticism that was made of him was that he was as mean as mud. Paul, who was his agent as well as hers, had once said to her wryly: 'If a fool and his money are soon parted, Michael must be the wisest man in Christendom.'

Mean or not, there didn't seem much doubt that one of these days he'd achieve his ambition and get himself knighted. And, by God, he'd have earned it, she thought, wondering what the public who believed him to be the most charming man of his generation would say if they could see and hear him in private. Then the mask fell away and the real man emerged from the lifetime role he had cast himself; vain, mean, pernickety and narrow-minded.

Yet he was a fine actor. Probably the greatest after Sir Larry and Sir John. It rankled that he could never quite achieve their eminence.

He had played every boring classic, graced every cultural flop – sometimes actually saving them. He only appeared on TV in the most important series. It was said he had never re-married because he was dedicated to his craft. He occasionally escorted distinguished actresses to distinguished first nights. There had never been a breath of scandal about him. She knew people said how he had ruined his life marrying that bitch Pallia.

He was a prick.

Hating him, she sneaked a sideways look at the classic boyish profile, the smooth fair hair and the long tapering hands playing gently with the glass in front of him. He caught her glance and made a sudden movement that nearly sent his drink flying.

Michael Bolt normally never made a clumsy movement. He had to be nervous. But then it was possible he'd heard on the grapevine what she had to say.

'What's all this about Jenny? he asked abruptly.

'Oh, you've heard.'

'Vague rumours.'

'About Bellino?'

'Exactly.'

She took a sip of her champagne and said: 'Then you've heard right. He wants her to play Mademoiselle Sergent in a film he's making based on the Claudine books. Though you probably haven't read them, have you?' she said spitefully. She knew in spite of the impressive shelves of leather-bound classics kept in the study of his house in the Boltons, his true taste was for cowboy sagas.

'I don't read trash,' he said.

'Colette is hardly trash,' she said. 'Actually considered a classic in France.'

'Then how would you know?' he asked nastily.

Deuce, she thought, and ignoring the remark said: 'Anyway, I've told her she can do it.'

'Well, she can't.'

'Why not?'

The coin head was held in a posture of disdain.

'What do you think letting your fourteen-year-old daughter play in a Bellino film about Lesbians and little girls interfering with each other is going to do to my image?'

'Oh! You have read the books—'

He looked as if he would have liked to pound the table.

'There is no way. I won't have it.'

'I'm afraid you're going to have to lump it, Michael,' Ingrid

66

said, her voice a purr. 'You and I know that little as it suits either of us, Jenny is quite old enough to do what she likes legally, and you and I know she wants to be an actress. And Bellino knows it too.'

She paused, eyes big over the rim of the champagne glass.

'What I ask myself is how he knows it? Could it be something to do with your jaunt to Mustique with her when you were all playing lovely charades and sucking up to the gentry. And why the hell should you care anyway? God knows your affections for Jenny are zero.'

'That's not true.' The actor's voice was perfect indignation; the nostrils quivered. 'And if it were, you know perfectly well why—'

'Michael, she is your daughter. Whether it suits you or not, I assure you you are her father.'

'So you say,' he said, 'but even if I were not, I would still be very fond of her.'

'Well, it's a good opportunity for her. And just think – you won't have to pay all that child maintenance once she starts earning.' She was openly mocking him. 'And there's another thing . . .' She looked down at the table and then straight at him. 'Someone wants to publish my life story.'

He stiffened, and looked anxiously around the red and plush of the bar as if afraid someone was eavesdropping.

'What do you mean?'

Surprisingly, she found herself uneasy. She lit a cigarette, taking swift puffs, wishing she had taken a snort of coke before all this.

'Oh, kiss and tell, of course,' she said, keeping her voice light.

'Oh, Christ! You're not doing it?'

She stubbed out the cigarette and said defiantly: 'As a matter of fact, I am. It's a great deal of money. Too much to turn down.'

'How much?' he said. She could see he was very anxious and realized he was wondering whether to match the sum to shut her up.

'Too much for you to buy me off.'

'What are you going to say?' His whole manner was defen-

67

sive. He had drawn back from the table and was regarding her warily.

She hesitated, and then signalled the waiter to freshen her drink. Both were silent watching the bubbles float golden in the fluted glass. Michael caught the waiter's arm.

'I'll have a large whisky,' he said.

It was only when the whisky was served Ingrid spoke again. Then she too looked around to make sure she couldn't be overheard. The bar was filing up, the crescendo of noise growing. No one took any notice of them. The White Elephant catered for celebrities, and a visiting American film star seated by the window outranked them both in the fame stakes.

'About the early days I'm not exactly telling the truth,' she said. 'I can't tell the truth . . .'

His attitude had immediately become jauntier.

'So you won't be saying too much about me?'

She said significantly: 'I'll keep your secrets if you keep mine.'

She could almost feel his suppressed sigh of relief. Feeling safe, he ventured to criticize.

'But really, Ingrid, why are you doing it?' he asked. 'It's so common. Truly vulgar.'

'So is money,' she said, thinking of her unpaid bills. 'But necessary.'

'How much money?' he persisted.

She shrugged her narrow shoulders. Why not tell him?

'Quarter of a million.'

'What!' He had spilt his whisky as he started to put the glass to his mouth.

'You heard,' she said. It wasn't a bad idea to let him know the price that could be put on *her* fame. He was always so superior with her. 'I have slept with some rather spectacular people,' she said smugly.

'Not for a long time,' his voice was waspish as he wiped whisky from his chin with a very white handkerchief.

'How do you know?' she said sharply. 'And how would you know?' she added pointedly.

'Dear God!' he said. 'The wages of sin are a lot of money. And how do you think you'll ever work again when you've exposed all those spectacular people?'

'As someone pointed out – look what it did for Joan Collins.'

'It's sick,' he said.

'Wouldn't you do it for that much?'

'I haven't anything to tell—'

She burst out laughing.

'Oh, come *on*,' she said. 'Really, Michael – it's me, Ingrid, you're talking to. Come off it.'

'Anyway,' he said, and smoothed back his sleek fair hair. 'I would not. Not for a million.'

She laughed again.

'Maybe wise in your case,' she said. 'It's not so glamorous, is it?'

He glared at her with the blue eyes so like Jenny's. It was a pity, she thought, that he really was Jenny's father. Her other lovers had been so much more rewarding. At times Jenny could be as sober-sided as he was.

'What are you going to say about the early days?' he asked abruptly, obviously changing the subject. 'You'd better tell me in case anyone checks with me. I don't intend reading your opus, I can tell you. And what the effect will be on Jenny—'

That had been the thought that troubled her too, the imponderable she didn't want to think about. She ignored his comment and answered his question.

'Half truths,' she said, ticking off points on her fingers. 'I shall be half Italian, half German. I was born in Rome of an Italian mother while the war was at its height. I never knew my father. He was a German soldier who raped my mother. And she rejected me. She couldn't stand the sight of me for the awful memories. So, I was cared for by the nuns until I was fifteen when relatives in Boston, USA, agreed to have me.' She paused. 'Be patient, we've nearly got to you.'

He sighed theatrically.

'I stayed in Boston until I was eighteen when I went to Hollywood with this dream of being an actress. And there we met, darling, both aspiring young actors waiting in the same agent's office.'

'Oh, God,' he said, but she continued, relentless.

'We were so in love that we had our adorable little baby out of wedlock and we found a wonderful foster mother to look after her while we tried to make our way. We married when I was twenty-two, by which time you'd become quite successful and I wasn't doing so badly.

'Of course, I was a virgin until we met. It was only after our marriage break-up that I discovered the true joy of sex . . . That bit's true, anyway,' she said viciously.

'I don't like it –' Michael's voice was raised. He looked guiltily round the room, and repeated: 'I don't like it,' in a quieter, emphatic tone.

'Why not?'

'Admitting we weren't married.'

'I'll have to give them a bit of spice about you. And anyway, we *weren't* married. That part's pretty accurate, except for the timing.' She pouted at him. 'We are going to sound the most idyllic, loving young couple you can imagine when I've finished with us. Don't worry. You'll come out pure as the driven snow, I promise you. And I shall definitely be the one to seduce you.'

'Well, you did,' he said sourly.

'But I'll make it a lot more exciting than it actually was.'

'Oh, God,' he said again and gave a haunted look around the bar. 'Can't I persuade you not to do this? You'll regret it, you know.'

'Maybe. But I'll be ashamed of myself all the way to the bank.'

'Nobody's going to believe all that nonsense, anyway,' he said and he sounded desperate. 'Rape, nuns. Honestly, Ingrid!'

'Kate Anderson's writing it. She'll make it believable.'

'Graham Greene couldn't make it believable.'

'It's not a Graham Greene type of plot,' she said. 'How about Harold Robbins?'

'Well, I think it's appalling,' he said, his voice self-righteous. Self-righteousness had always been one of his least attractive qualities, along with the other things. 'And I warn you, I shall sue if you libel me in any way. You'll be worth sueing, at least,' he added bitterly.

'I thought you weren't going to read it?'

'My lawyers will read it.' He finished his drink and started to get to his feet. 'I have to get to the theatre. It's getting late. But I think we'd better discuss all this again sometime.'

He gave her a perfunctory kiss on the cheek for appearances sake, and she noted almost with pleasure that he hadn't paid the bill. Nothing changes, she told herself. What a prick he is!

The prick was tipping the waiter a coin in a highly ostentatious way, then the doorman. The prick gave her an actor's smile as he left, holding his prickish black, velvet-collared overcoat and gold-topped cane.

'Piss off!' she said, mentally, relaxing in her seat once he'd gone and enjoying the thought she'd upset his performance for the night.

She still had half a glass of champagne, most of the evening before her, and she didn't feel like going home. She called the waiter over, smiled and said: 'Mr Bolt said would you give me another glass of Krug, please, and put it on his bill.'

The waiter's Italian face was impassive, he knew as well as she the trouble the club would have getting the bill paid, but he brought her the drink.

As he turned away a mid-Atlantic voice said: 'May I pay for that?' She looked up to see a man, no more than twenty-two, standing at the table. He was dark, curly-haired with bright brown eyes, and lean in a dark suit and tie which seemed out of place on him. He belonged in jeans and a bomber jacket. He looked both familiar and very Californian. She knew him from somewhere. Then it dawned. He had a small part in a long-running TV Western serial. She sought her memory for his name.

'How kind,' she said. 'But I don't like to drink alone,' and indicated the chair that Michael had just vacated.

'Nor me,' he said sitting down. The brown eyes twinkled. Naughty eyes. Bedroom eyes. Let's-not-mess-about eyes.

It wasn't going to be a bad evening after all, she thought.

Bobbie Jean sat on her father's lap in the big leather armchair by the study fireplace. She had her arms around his neck, she was blowing into his ear and gently nibbling at the lobe. Her breasts were pushed into him, and she could feel the hard ridge of him pressing into her buttocks, and she wriggled very deliberately as she puffed and bit and hugged.

'Oh, please, Daddy, darling,' she said, 'please, please let me do it. I'll be safe. Mr Bellino's secretary says I'll be chaperoned all the time. Oh, Daddy, I want it more than anything in the whole world. I want to be a star. You say I'm your star. It's my chance. I'm so lucky. Please, Daddy, please, please, please don't say No.'

She pressed her behind into his lap more firmly, and shifted from side to side as she planted a soft, moist kiss on his cheek. A lingering one.

He groaned. A long, low desperate sound.

'Yes,' he said. 'Yes. Perhaps it's a good idea.'

Chapter Five

'I didn't believe a bloody word she said!' Kate slammed the frying pan down on to the built-in gas ring as if she were slamming it on Ingrid Pallia's head. 'She's a lying bitch, and I won't have my intelligence insulted like that.'

Paul was sitting on a high stool still in his business suit, the newspapers in front of him, his heavy black reading spectacles slipping down his nose. He pushed them further down and peered at her over the top.

'Why do you think she's lying?'

Kate was breaking eggs into a basin, slinging the empty shells in the sink.

'Because I have been interviewing people for far too long to to be taken in by a pack of lies. Now,' she said, beating the eggs with a fork and ferocity, 'I don't mind people lying if it all works and adds to the story, and if they tell me that they're bending the truth. What I do mind is the sort of idiotic lies where ninety-four people are going to come out of the wood-work screaming and shouting that it wasn't like that at all. And I end up looking an idiot.'

'What did she tell you?'

'You don't know?'

'I don't know. I can recite you chapter and verse about her lovers. I know nothing about what happened to her before Michael Bolt. Nor does anyone else. Maybe Michael. Maybe not even him. Maybe Monique, but she's only been with her for about five months so unless they're very close she won't know either. So I'm curious.'

She had been putting butter into the omelette pan, but she turned the gas off and perched on a stool leaning her elbows on the work service, pushing his newspapers out of the way. She wore a blue and white track-suit and her feet were bare. Her hair was screwed into a comic knot on the top of her head, and she was without make-up. He looked at her with affection. 'You do realize you look about twelve,' he said.

'But I'm not twelve, Paul.' She was very serious, the anger still simmering. 'You must tell her that lies won't do. If I'm going to do this job – and I didn't want to do it in the first place—'

'What did she tell you?' he asked, insistent.

'Huh! To cut a very long and very highly coloured story short – Italian mum gets raped by German soldier in the war, she is the unfortunate – and I do mean unfortunate – result. Mum rejects her and gives her to the good kind nuns, who look after her until she is a teenager. Then some obliging relatives in Boston, Massachusetts, of all places, take her to their bosoms. She stays with them until she is eighteen and then goes to seek fame and fortune in Hollywood. There Michael comes into her life.'

'It could be true.'

'But it isn't. I just know it isn't. I can smell it isn't. For a start, she's got to be older than that. It maddens me. Two hours of tape wasted. I'm not even going to transcribe it. No—' She got up from the stool and went back to the stove. 'I will transcribe it and pick out all the discrepancies. Then when I've done the rest of the interviewing, we'll go back to the beginning with a few tough questions.'

Paul had wandered across the open-plan kitchen/dining room to the drinks tray where he poured himself a gin and tonic.

'It might not be in her interests to tell the truth,' he said. 'And that's a pretty riveting story, true or not.'

Kate had just been about to pour the eggs into the hot pan. She put down the basin and stared at him. He had made no move to come back close to her.

'What do you mean?'

'She is my client,' he said, with the stubborn look that turned his eyes grey and set his full mouth in a narrow line. 'I have to protect her. Why don't you just write what she tells you?'

'What she tells me.' Kate was spluttering with anger again. 'What *she* tells *me!*'

'Kate.' His voice was very calm. 'I didn't mean it like that. I meant write the story that she tells you. A lot of your reaction is because you don't like her, isn't it? You're a good hater, my dear.'

There was truth in it and suddenly she laughed. 'And a good lover?'

'Very good.' His eyes were blue again.

'After lunch?'

'After lunch. Therefore I wish you'd get on with that omelette.'

With a dramatic gesture she picked up the basin and from a height emptied the eggs into the pan, then turned them with a fork as they sizzled.

'Two minutes,' she said. 'Get the salads out of the fridge will you, darling, and pour the wine.'

They had come back to her home in the mews for lunch; he from his office in Berkeley Square, she from the Dorchester where she had spent the morning interviewing Pallia.

They often lunched together at the mews house. She would cook something simple, quick and uncomplicated, which they ate at the table in the dining area, trying not to touch each other, but she never bothered to provide pudding or cheese. It was always wasted. They ate, watching each other's mouths, then he would lead her up the spiral iron staircase to the second big open space which was her bedroom, living room and study in one. They would make love on her big bed, then shower, dress and circumspectly return to their work never later than three o'clock.

Today they ate more slowly, the near quarrel still hovering.

'I see your point about protecting her,' Kate said. She always saw his points. There was no sense in not for he could be totally inflexible about things he believed and with him she never wanted to argue. It wasted their time together. 'But where does that leave me? Honestly, Paul, if she's not going to trust me, it's better if I don't do it.'

She had let him see he had almost won and he grinned at her across the table.

'Even if it means missing us being together in Rome?'

'What do you mean?' She put down her fork and stared at him.

'What I say. There are developments. Bellino has sent me a new client – some American child he's cast. That means I have three actresses on the film. Four clients counting you. And Bellino wants me to take them and the other starring child out there. Be a man about the plane, as it were.'

'But what about Madeleine?'

His face clouded.

'Actually, there's a development there. She's heard about a clinic in Bavaria where there's some special kind of treatment that she wants to try. I don't know. It may be some quack place, but I feel we've got to give it a go. She's finding out all the details today, and if it sounds at all helpful, I'll take her over almost immediately and then fly back to go to Rome.'

Her mind was taking in the possibilities while the journalist in her was already wondering if perhaps this might be a story. 'What do they do there?'

He shook his head.

'I don't know. I tell you – it may all be a con. But she wants to go.'

'How much does it cost?' she asked.

'I don't know.' He sounded slightly exasperated. 'I don't know anything about it. But if she goes I'm free to go to Rome without any complications. Her mother says she'll look after the children.'

She took a mouthful of her omelette thoughtfully.

'How long will she stay there?'

'About a fortnight.'

'Umm.' She wanted to feel elated, but she sensed a return of his guilt. Being in Rome with her while his wife was taking some kind of possibly unpleasant treatment was not going to make for perfect accord between them. The question was how to lessen his guilt? She decided to try reverse tactics. 'I don't think you ought to let her go,' she said slowly.

'Why not?'

'Well, the kids will be miserable with both of you away. You're probably right, it won't do the slightest bit of good and it'll cost you a fortune. Also, you'll worry yourself sick the whole time she's there. Better really if you brought her to Rome. It wouldn't be much fun for us, but at least you wouldn't be wasting money and worrying about her. Or alternatively you could wait until you can go with her.'

'But she wants to go now,' he said, still irritated. 'She's talked of nothing else.'

'Why don't you ask her if she'd like to come to Rome instead?'

He gave her an uneasy look.

'As a matter of fact, I did.'

She felt her stomach plummet. It wasn't the answer she'd expected.

'And—'

'She refused. Said it would be too hot for her. She wasn't keen at all.'

'Well,' she said. 'If you've offered, there's not much more you can do.'

'No, I suppose not.'

They ate in silence for a minute, and then, unable to help herself she said: 'Why did you ask her to come to Rome, Paul?'

He put down his fork and sighed.

'Usual reason. Guilt. I very much want to be there with you, and I thought if she refused I wouldn't feel so bad about it. Then she brought up this Bavaria thing and I instantly saw the possibilities and started plotting for us to be together. Then back came the guilt.'

She was still measuring her words.

'It seems to me,' she said, wiping her plate with a piece of bread, 'that you haven't any reason to feel guilty. You asked

76

your wife to come to Rome with you, and she refused. She wants to go to Bavaria and you're paying. You have to go to Rome for your job. You haven't any choice. The fact I'm there is really incidental. You'd still have had to have gone even if I wasn't involved with Pallia.'

'That's all very true,' he said doubtfully. 'Oh, but – you know me.'

It was time to change the mood.

'Yes,' she said cheerfully. 'I know you very well, my lovely.' She paused. 'You aren't half taking a time over that omelette. Do you want cheese? Or can I offer you something else?' The last sentence was in the most suggestive tone she could manage, and she licked her lips so they gleamed wetly, twisted her arm behind her head and pushing out her breasts pouted at him in a parody of a pin-up pose.

'You can offer me something else,' he said, pushing his plate away and grinning at her.

'Shall I go up first?'

'Yes – why not?' he said. 'Then I can pinch your bottom.'

'We're not in Rome yet,' she told him.

Not wearing shoes she was able to run up on the open-runged iron steps quickly, vanishing into the bathroom. There she washed and then put scent on her thighs, her breasts and behind her ears. Under the track-suit she was naked. She knew this excited him almost as much as the erotic underwear she generally wore for him.

Completely at home in her bedroom, he had already stripped to his trousers when she came into the room. His suit jacket jacket was over the back of the chair, shirt and tie neat on it so as not to be creased for the afternoon at the office. His socks were on her long-haired white carpet, and the shoes, splayed beside them. He was behaving like a husband she thought, amused.

'You're too quick,' she said, moving towards him and unfastening the belt that held up his trousers. 'I wanted to do all that.' She pulled at the zip, and then pushed her hand inside, fingers searching for the gap in his underpants. 'Ah!' she said. 'That seems very satisfactory.'

His trousers had slid down.

'Now look what you've done,' he said, laughing at her.

'What?' She was all innocence. 'This?' giving him a gentle tweak, 'or that – ?' pointing to his trousers crumpled around his ankles.

'Both,' he said. 'Now you can fold the trousers.'

'Yes, sir,' she said meekly as he lifted his long feet one at a time from the tweed. She picked the pants up, folded them, and laid them neatly over the chair, and turned to find him rampant and naked on her bed, his arms behind his head, smiling at her.

'Come here.'

'Wait,' she said. 'I'm overdressed.'

'Come here.'

'No.'

She stood at the foot of the bed and very slowly unzipped the long zip that fastened her velour jacket, then she pulled it back to reveal her full breasts, the nipples already rouging.

Very slowly she walked towards him as he watched her, and then she knelt on the bed and bent forward so that one pink tip fell near his mouth. He lifted his head to take it between his teeth, his tongue teasing. She just knelt, her eyes closed, making soft sighs of pleasure.

Then she pulled back and kissed him lightly on the nose. She slid off the soft velour pants leaving them crumpled on the floor, then jumped on the bed, stretching out alongside him, her head on the cushion of his shoulder. He wrapped his arms around her and they lay very still, until she sighed contentedly and twisted her head so his lips could come down on hers.

They kissed for a very long time, and then she softly nibbled him, exploring him with her tongue and all the while they gently stroked each other, their breathing deep and slow, their eyes closed.

Sometimes their lovemaking was gentle and calm like this. Practically without passion and yet almost more exciting than when their bodies generated a deep heat and they twisted and turned while she was impaled on him, hands, mouths and tongues frantic.

Today was a gentle day. They were not so much lovers as deeply in love. No pillow talk, no whispered hurried instructions from her as to what she wanted from him. He knew what she wanted. He stroked and petted her, pulling her tight to him until their faster breathing said it was time and he rolled her on to her side. She slid her leg under him, their bodies closed again, as he took her very slowly. In. Out. In. Out.

They clung to each other in the silent room and somewhere outside someone was parking a car, a blackbird chattered danger and the traffic of the main road beyond the mews was a dull roar.

'Oh, darling,' she sighed. 'Oh darling.'

They still did not speak at the very end, he only groaned softly in time with the last convulsive movements and her breath came quickly, panting.

'Yes?' she asked him a second or two after he was still.

'Yes. You?'

'Oh, yes. Yes—'

She lay relaxed, her leg still under him, her arms clutching him as she felt him fall way from her, small now, cool and velvety soft to her stroking fingers. After a while he said: 'Am I hurting you?'

'No, no,' she said dreamily. 'That's what your waist is for. To put my leg under.'

'Nevertheless,' he said, lifting his body from her so she could stretch beside him again. 'There. That's better.'

The room was quiet again, the curtains blowing gently at the partly open window. He was very still and she realized he was sleeping, his face totally relaxed and peaceful. She could see how he must have looked when he was much younger; the years always faded from his face when they made love. She felt a pang of keen regret for all the time they had not known each other.

She thought briefly then of his children, his wife and the clinic in Bavaria and then tried to push the thoughts away. Her greatest problem in coming to terms with the situation and the unknown, unseen Madeleine was that it was so difficult not to fantasize Madeleine's death. If she were dead she could be with Paul all the time.

These thoughts frightened her sometimes by their strength. Though Kate had no strong religious convictions she had her own positive code of what she felt was right and wrong and good and bad.

It was certainly wrong and wicked to wish anyone dead, particularly when the possibility of Madeleine's death was no idle fantasy. There was every chance that she would die in the not too distant future. The insistent wish that it would not take too long made Kate ashamed and deeply guilty, yet she could not exorcise the idea from her mind. The picture of her changed future if Madeleine had gone for good would return unbidden at night-time when sleep would not come and at moments like this when she and Paul were so close it seemed unnatural that anything could keep them apart.

But it was the forbidden subject – the one thing she could not discuss with him. The thoughts remained secret, unspoken. She wondered if he thought them too and felt more guilts to add to all his other guilts.

She shifted restlessly, and Paul instantly woke.

'What time is it?' he asked.

'Late,' she said. 'We wasted this time arguing about boring Ingrid. We'd better get moving.

He yawned and stretched.

'But let's share the shower,' he said.

'You great baby!' She gave his slack penis a gentle tweek, and laughing, jumped out of the bed to turn on the shower. He loved her to wash, scrub and dry him. And he enjoyed soaping her breasts and body, very slowly, so that the shower itself became an extension of their lovemaking. Sometimes when they were not too late he would want to make love to her again. She was not tall enough for him to take her standing in the hot rain of stinging water, so dripping wet they would lie on the fluffy white bathroom mat while he took her with urgency. Then they would shower again.

After, he liked to dry her with an enormous rough white bathtowel, finally wrapping her in it before they went back to the bedroom to dress.

'What are you doing this afternoon?' he asked, knotting his tie in front of the mirrored wall of the room.

'Nothing much,' she said.

'In that case you'd better come to the office and sign the contract for the Pallia book,' he said. 'Before you change your mind again.'

She screwed up her face.

'Oh, God!' she said.

'Remember Rome . . .'

She grinned. 'OK. It's true. Every cloud does have a silver lining.'

'A twenty-five-thousand-pound-lined cloud,' he grumbled. 'Ungrateful bitch!'

'I've decided it's not enough,' she said flippantly.

She had dressed in a grey flannel suit with a pleated skirt and white shirt and she went to the shoe cupboard to look for grey shoes.

While she searched he asked: 'When are you seeing Ingrid again?'

'Tomorrow morning,' she said. 'I think I'll get her talking about her lovers and deal with the history later.'

'Whatever you think.' He looked at her appreciatively. 'You don't look like a lady who's been ravished. Are you ready?'

'Just about,' she said. 'Some lipstick will do it.'

The quiet mood hadn't quite left them, and in the taxi back to his office, they held hands in companionable silence, her thumb tracing circles on his palm.

'I do love you,' she said, just once, and his hand tightened on hers. It was the only reply she needed.

They were laughing and arguing about the contract as they walked up the stairs to his first floor office.

'I've changed my mind,' she told him. 'I want fifteen per cent.'

'Too late!' he said. 'We had a verbal agreement.'

'Your word against mine.'

'You've forgotten. Ingrid was there.'

'Who'd believe her!' Kate scoffed.

'Try to – just try to,' he said, his expression imploring.

It was fortunate that as they went through into his outer office they instinctively let their hands fall apart. Bunny was sitting at her desk, grey hair combed flat and neat, her face expressionless. Standing by the desk, legs planted just a little too wide apart, one hand clutching the desk surface for balance was a doll-pretty woman, blonde, soft featured, with whistle lines around the mouth and deeper lines around the eyes.

'Madeleine!' Paul said.

Kate froze, the automatic smile rigid on her face. The woman took an uncertain step forward. If Kate had not known better she would have sworn she was drunk. Suddenly she felt sick, her stomach lurching, she wanted to get out of there.

'There you are, darling,' the woman had grabbed at the desk again. 'Did you have a good lunch?'

He had pulled himself together after that first involuntary exclamation.

'Only a working snack,' he said. 'Madeleine – this is Kate Anderson. You haven't met, have you? Kate – Madeleine, my wife.'

The blue, blue eyes seemed to be looking at her without hostility. In fact, Madeleine smiled, and her hand was extended, a little shakily, but in what appeared to be friendship.

'I've heard so much about you,' she said. 'It's stupid we haven't met before—'

Her voice was high and light, the accent faintly North Eastern.

Without waiting for an answer she turned to Paul: 'Darling,' she said 'I'm not interrupting anything am I?'

What did she mean! Kate thought frantically.

'No, no.' He had moved towards his wife and taken her arm. 'Why aren't you sitting down?'

She looked around vaguely.

'Well, I was. But when I heard you coming—'

'Sit down,' he said firmly, leading her towards a chair. 'You must learn to take it easy.'

Kate noticed the slightest trace of strain in his voice and thought that surely Madeleine must have noticed it too. They'd been maried so long. But his wife showed no sign of anything being amiss.

'You must be wondering why I'm here,' she said brightly, once he had settled her into a chair. Kate's trained ear instantly detected the false note.

'Why are you here?' he said dutifully, his own voice betraying an equal falseness. 'Not that I'm not pleased to see you, darling.'

They were behaving like strangers. Why? Were they always so formal?

'Oh, good,' Madeleine said, her small perfect mouth turning down at the corner, her blue painted lids dropping over the blue eyes. She was playing the little girl. A sick little girl in this case, Kate thought, noting the tremor of the well-manicured hands, a genuinely sick little girl.

'I wanted to talk to you about Bavaria. It's so interesting, darling. It might just help, too.'

Kate knew now she had to escape.

'Listen,' she said abruptly. 'I'll pop in tomorrow and sign that contract, Paul. There's no hurry.'

'Nonsense,' Paul said, his voice jovial. He turned to Madeleine. 'She's just trying to get out of signing a contract for the Pallia book,' he said. 'If I let her go now, I may never get her back.'

To Kate the message was clear. Was it to Madeleine? But the other woman reacted conventionally.

'You get your business over, darling,' she said. 'There's no hurry. We can talk all night.'

Again Kate felt her guts contract. 'No, really,' she said. 'I'll wait. You two carry on. Bunny will keep me amused, won't you, Bunny?'

'I'll make you a cup of tea,' Bunny said.

'Me too, please,' said Madeleine.

'Yes, all of us,' Paul said. 'Kate – will you give me five minutes with Madeleine. You're not in a hurry, are you?'

Hating herself, him and Madeleine, Kate agreed that she was not, the smile on her face seemed plastered there. There didn't seem to be anything else to do but wait. Solicitously, Paul helped his wife from the chair, and with his hand under her elbow led her towards the door of his private office. Madeleine clung to his arm, walking with a curious type of sailor's gait, and together they disappeared.

'She ought to use a walking stick but she won't,' Bunny muttered. 'Vanity.'

'It's part of her illness,' Kate heard herself say. When she

83

had learned about Madeleine's illness she had read everything she could about multiple sclerosis. 'They will try to do too much.'

'Umm,' said Bunny, noncommittal, busying herself with the electric kettle.

Kate looked at the closed door of Paul's office. Once she and he had made love on the sofa there, late at night, just for the hell of it. It wasn't necessary with her big bed waiting at home, but he'd said he wanted to remember her every time he went into his office. Was he remembering now, she wondered?

Was Madeleine sitting on that very same seat where they had fucked so energetically; her imploring him not to let her fall on the floor, and complaining that the sofa was too narrow for action.

The sudden unexpected sight of Madeleine had been a decided shock. She was prettier than Kate had imagined, and her first instinct had been to feel pity. That was now followed by a certain wariness. The pity could easily take over, she thought, but somehow she hadn't liked Madeleine. The question was, had she not liked her merely because she was Paul's wife? People didn't automatically become likeable just because they were suffering from incurable diseases.

'Tea,' Bunny said, breaking into her train of thought. The secretary's face was still expressionless, but Kate thought she could read sympathy in the woman's grey eyes.

'Thanks,' she said, and summoned up a grin. 'Think they'll be long?'

'Not too long,' Bunny said. 'Her wish is his command. She was telling me she wants to go to Bavaria next week to a clinic where they apparently don't do anything but make the patients feel fitter and therefore stronger to cope with the illness. It costs £1000 a week,' she added, 'and apparently it has to be a two week treatment at the least.'

'But if it works,' Kate said, damning herself for hypocrisy.

'Yes, if it works.'

They were both silent.

'I'll just take their tea in,' Bunny said abruptly. She rattled cups on a tray, knocked and disappeared. Kate stared at the closed door.

'Oh shit!' she said out loud. 'Shit!'

And picking up her handbag, she hurried out and away.

Paul looked around the table at the Savoy, stared at the pink smoked salmon on the plate in front of him and wished himself approximately six miles away. Outside, the Thames ran cold and grey, and the fresh green buds were pushing through on the trees in the gardens below. In front of him, his back to the window at the large round table, sat Bellino, elegant, expansive and expensive, caviare in a silver dish placed on the white cloth in front of him. Bellino, Paul was certain was either a little drunk or high on coke. He wasn't sure which.

Next to Bellino was Paul's new client, Bobbie Jean. She wore a white blouse with a broad black satin bow under the collar, a pleated black skirt and small flat red Gucci shoes. Her blonde hair was tied in a pony tail, and she sat, hands folded in lap, a prawn cocktail on the table in front of her, looking as if butter wouldn't melt in her mouth. Paul figured a great deal more than butter had melted in her mouth. She was gaol bait if he had ever seen it. Her father, a tall, thin, anxious, buttoned-down American, had come to his office to sign the contract for her to play Marie. Paul had promised the man to keep a strict eye on the child, but he hadn't much hopes of being able to do so. The current between Bellino and her was so obvious it seemed to make small sparks.

On Bellino's left and next to Paul was Jenny Bolt, whom Paul regarded with a great deal of affection. She was such a tiny little thing; it had been easy for Ingrid to pretend she was younger. Even now she looked no more than about thirteen. She had large brown expressive eyes and a small pointed face with full naturally red lips. Her dark hair fell long and straight over her shoulders, and though she was so small in height she had a perfectly formed little body, covered now with a sort of crêpe dress that looked vaguely twenties-ish. She was a very nice child, he thought. Intelligent, quiet – an oasis of calm in any gathering. He had known her since she was seven years old when Ingrid had first brought her to England. In those days she had been happier speaking Italian, her English heavily accented, but the years at expensive and necessarily out-of-the-way boarding schools plus summers in the south of France, Italy or southern Spain had made her a natural linguist.

On Paul's left was Bellino's third casting: Frances Elliot. She looked quite dreadful, with punk spiky hair which had been yellow and was growing out over a birdlike face with sallow skin. She seemed to be wearing some kind of second-hand blue uniform and when she spoke her voice had the faint Cockney trace and abruptness that the middle-class young cultivated these days. Terence Stamp and Michael Caine had a lot to answer for, he thought.

He could see why Bellino had chosen her for Anaïs, though. It was perfect casting, and she might well not be a bad kid under the defence mechanisms. The too narrow brown eyes were bright and intelligent and, in spite of the unattractive voice, her manners were good.

The sixth and last person at the table was Frances Elliot's agent, Hal Matthews, an amiable enough elderly man who normally specialized in representing young glamour girls. The fact that the plain Frances was on his books was another sign of the times, Paul thought. The starlet era was dead. Girls were still trying to look natural, like Julie Christie, and everyone was searching for a young Glenda Jackson.

Maybe Hal, who'd made his name and fortune in the fifties with the pin-up queens who had decorated every British film and newspaper front page (decorously covered with one-piece bathing suits), had found her, Paul thought, taking a quick sideways look at the child. He discovered he was feeling a pang of professional resentment that he had the gaol bait and Hal had the promise.

The three girls had not met before and had barely spoken since they gathered at the table. Paul had brought in his two clients, who appeared within seconds of each other, and Hal had arrived a little later with his. Bellino had been there, ready and waiting.

The girls had barely looked at each other, except for little furtive summing-up glances, and now they all sat like good children as they waited for their meal to be served.

The waiter was bringing the last of the first courses – Jenny had ordered an omelette – and everyone picked up their forks with relief once it was in front of her. Eating was something to do. Bellino beamed on his guests, one hand missing from the table – undoubtedly on Bobbie Jean's thigh, Paul thought contemptuously, wondering whether or not Bellino had made the kid.

He disliked Bellino intensely; he was sorry that Ingrid had agreed to Jenny working with him, even though it would have been professional madness to dissuade her. Jenny was being paid very well and there was the commission. Still, things did now look a little brighter with Bobbie Jean taking up the attention and it was possible that Jenny was getting a little old for the Spaniard's tastes. Then the uneasy thought struck him that he was responsible for Bobbie Jean as well. Two teenage clients on a Bellino film was two too many.

Bellino had announced when they sat down that work would begin in Rome in a fortnight's time, immediately after Easter. The Rome studios were cheaper and less troubled with union problems than the Paris ones, he explained. The British studios he dismissed with a gesture. They would be moving to the Dordogne for location scenes about the middle of June when the weather improved.

With this in mind Paul ate his crab cocktail thoughtfully, mentally working out his schedule but mostly worrying about Kate. When he and Madeleine had come back into Bunny's office three days before, Kate had disappeared. He could understand why. It had taken Madeleine an unconscionably long time to tell him about Bavaria and he could hardly cut her short.

Bunny had said, her face expressionless, that Miss Anderson had had to leave for another appointment and would ring him later. Paul knew there was no other appointment, but he also knew why she had gone. The first sight of Madeleine, so unexpectedly, combined with the way she appeared to be behaving, would have been a considerable shock. The minute he had put his wife in a taxi for home, he rang Kate's mews house. There was no reply – only the uninterested answering service. He left a message.

It was the same for the rest of the afternoon though he rang repeatedly. She was not at home; or just did not reply. In a panic that he had lost her for ever he stayed at the office until seven when he had to drive home to Hampstead. Once home there was no way he could call Kate to straighten things out. He was preoccupied and snappy, but Madeleine seemed to notice nothing. Her mind was totally on the Bavarian clinic.

Madeleine was going to Munich the following week. She had arranged it all including that he would fly with her and take her to the clinic. She would stay for two weeks at a cost of £2000, the object of the exercise being to make her fit and strong enough to combat the illness. They promised no cures. He had agreed that anything was worth a try, but the conversation and the decision had brought about a kind of despair. Did he want Madeleine to get well? His mind shied away from the converse. He only knew for certain that he had not loved his once beautiful and spoilt, now demanding and stupid, wife for many a long year and that had she been a fit woman and had there been no children he would have left her long ago.

Left her for Kate: he loved Kate. And anxiety gnawed in him that now Kate had met his wife, pathetic in her illness, she would want to end the affair. He had always told himself it could not last for long, but that was a kind of fire insurance. If he told himself it would end at any minute – it wouldn't. He didn't want to tempt the furies.

He hadn't been able to get in touch with Kate the next day either, and then yesterday she had phoned him.

'Sorry, darling,' she said. 'I had to think.'

'And what did you think?' He had tried to keep his voice light.

'That I love you.' It was a flat statement of fact.

'So?'

'Tomorrow?'

'Yes – tomorrow.'

It meant food and bed at the mews, and then Bellino had commanded this lunch. Kate was a professional herself. She had understood, but as he carefully put down his fork and the waiter refilled his wine glass he thought with a pang that by now they would have been in bed and he felt a wave of desire and great longing for her.

Damn Bellino, he thought, suddenly aware that the man was asking him something.

'Sorry, Pedro, I was miles away.'

'I was wondering how long you will be able to stay in Rome?'

'Only a week. I can't leave the business for much longer, and I have to bring my wife, Madeleine, home from a clinic in Bavaria.'

'How is Madeleine?' Bellino's voice was solicitous, as the muscles of his right shoulder moved slightly. He was touching up the child under the table. Her doll face was set rigid in an embarrassed smirk.

'Not good, not bad. It's one of those periods where the disease seems to get arrested for a while. We hope this clinic will help.'

'Umm—' Bellino must have seen how Paul's eyes watched his shoulder. Ostentatiously he put his long, thin hand on the table. 'And I believe Kate Anderson is coming to Rome.'

Was it a twist of the knife or as casual a remark as it sounded?

'She's writing Ingrid's life story,' Paul said curtly.

Jenny had turned to him, her round brown eyes wide.

'Mother's writing her life story?'

'Didn't you know?' The thought she hadn't been told troubled him.

'No.'

'She's not saying anything about you,' he said quickly.

'Well, she wouldn't would she?' Jenny said.

'Your mother is too fond of you to involve you,' Paul said mechanically.

'And she's led a very interesting life of her own, my dearest,' Bellino put in. The man was on form for bitchiness, Paul thought, looking at his secret smile as he smoothed the little pointed beard.

'I expect I'll learn a lot,' Jenny said laconically.

There was an awkward silence, which Hal broke saying heartily: 'Is it a good deal, Paul?'

'Pretty good.' It wouldn't do to say how good, he decided.

'Let's hope you can tie the publication in with the film,' Bellino said. 'One could help the other.'

'It's possible,' Paul said guardedly.

Bellino seemed to be getting drunker. He had already downed two glasses of wine.

'You girls will meet Jenny's mother in Rome,' he said. 'Where is she staying, Jenny? And are you to be with her?'

'That's the idea,' Jenny said without enthusiasm. 'She's taken a big villa in Parioli.'

'Very grand,' Bellino said. 'Did I mention that we have rooms in a charming pension in the Piazza Navona for you and your mother, Frances?'

'Where am I staying?' Paul saw how his new client, still too young to hide her feelings was suddenly apprehensive.

'I thought in at the Hassler – my hotel,' Bellino said.

Paul had promised Bobbie Jean's father that this would not happen.

'She must be chaperoned,' he said firmly, his eyes challenging Bellino's across the table. 'She's far too young to stay in a hotel alone. Sorry, Pedro. Her father insists. As a diplomat he can't afford any criticism.' He thought Bobbie Jean looked relieved and hoped the implied warning had got through.

'She could stay with us,' Frances said suddenly. 'If my mother is chaperoning me, she might as well chaperone both of us. You could pay her expenses, then Mr Bellino.'

The girl's voice was schoolgirl innocent, her face girlishly bright and eager, but Paul could have sworn there was a glint of mischief in her eyes. He warmed to her. He had been right. She wasn't a fool.

Bellino's face remained expressionless as Paul said quickly: 'That's a very good idea. Would you like that, Bobbie Jean? The Piazza Navona is charming. Old Rome.'

'I know it,' she said. 'Daddy was once at the Embassy there. For three years.'

'Do you speak Italian?' Paul asked.

'Yeah, and French. I liked Rome,' she added thoughtfully as if something interesting had happened to her there.

'The Eternal City,' Bellino said. 'Do you know it, Frances?' She shook her head.

'Then, of course, you don't speak Italian?' His voice was malicious, getting his own back, a spiteful schoolboy.

'I only speak English,' she said, 'and even that not very well.' She grinned at him, eating the last mouthful of her melon.

He wasn't going to be able to put this one down, Paul

decided, wishing again she was on his books and not on Hal's.

'We shall show you the Vatican,' Bellino promised. 'If there is a God he dwells in St Peter's.' His voice was sonorous. 'It is magnificent. A thing of incredible beauty. A towering reminder of the Creator.'

Bloody hell! thought Paul. He is pissed.

'I can't imagine him there,' Jenny said suddenly. 'It's too like a museum. Cold. I imagine him in fields, in country churches and on mountains.'

'You believe in God?' Bellino asked her.

'I was brought up Catholic,' Jenny said.

'That is not an answer.'

'I suppose I do.'

'And I believe in the Devil,' Paul put in jokingly, thinking that Bellino didn't look too unlike the popular conception of him either.

'But of course,' Bellino said positively. 'If there is good there must be evil. And, of course, the Devil is in charge. Look at these girls—' He waved a hand around the table. 'Fresh, young, beautiful and innocent. Created by God. It is not God's fault,' he added acidly, 'that Frances has chosen to desecrate her hair in that appalling fashion.' He shook his head and returned to his theme. 'But their innocence will pass. And every line that creeps on to their faces, the coarsening of the skin, the growing slackness of their bodies will be the work of the Devil.' His voice was now that of a preacher, saddened by sins. 'The Devil takes all that is young and beautiful, then ages and corrupts. All is ageing and corruption. The flower fades, the tree falls, the skin wrinkles, the hair greys. Corruption of beauty and youth are the Devil's doing.'

There was a long silence at the table. Frances looked as if she wanted to giggle and Hal Matthews was distinctly embarrassed. Bellino suddenly looked his age, his face lined and heavy as he drank again from his glass. He must be a lapsed Catholic himself, Paul thought, secretly haunted by thoughts of purgatory to come. And for now it was easier to blame his own corruption on some evil power; unloading the responsibility. But he couldn't help but feel a twinge of sympathy for the man, locked as he was into his own revolting perversion.

Perhaps Bellino was right. Perhaps God or the Devil had made him that way and he wasn't to blame. And who was he, Paul, to judge with his confused feelings about his wife, his need for Kate, and worse the self-knowledge that told him it wasn't so much sympathy, decency or caring that kept him with his sick wife and his two rather dull children, but the judgement of the outside world? How would it look if he left? What would people say? He hadn't the courage for their disapprobation.

If Jenny was right, he'd be judged in hereafter anyway if no secrets were hidden from God. If Bellino was right, it wouldn't matter much either way.

It was Frances who broke the silence.

'Well,' she said cheekily. 'Before we all go to rack and ruin, I'm going to enjoy my fish and chips.'

Bellino looked pained. 'Grilled sole and pomme frites, if you please,' he told her.

'If you've ever fancied a harem, you've got one now,' Kate said *sotto voce* to Paul. They were waiting in the departure lounge of London Airport, Terminal One, for the morning flight to Rome. There was Paul, there was Kate and there were Jenny and Frances, Bobbie Jean and Eileen Elliot, all in varying states of anxiety and disorganization, the girls trying to appear grown up, which they were not, and Eileen Elliot trying to appear well travelled, which she was not.

Paul had smoothly dealt with tickets and baggage, herding them kindly like prize cattle. Now he and Kate had moved to the bar and were drinking a coffee cognac.

'What a mixture,' Kate said. 'That awful mother!'

'Bit pathetic, I'd have said,' Paul suggested.

Kate regarded the woman. Eileen Elliot wore white gloves, a pale blue suit of which the skirt was two inches short for the correct fashion, a blouse with a frilled bib, high-heeled white sandals and a floppy white hat.

'Birmingham?' she asked.

'No, much posher. Weybridge.'

'Good heavens! No wonder the daughter dresses so bizarrely. And is that voice for real?'

'Both voices are not quite for real,' Paul said. 'But what do you think of Jenny Bolt?'

'Gentle?'

'And good. A nice child. And my new client, the bonny Bobbie Jean Dennison?'

'Cocky and frightened with it.'

'Could be. She's Bellino's choice.'

'He's had her?'

'Almost certainly.'

'And she doesn't want him any more if she can avoid it?'

'You're very perceptive.'

'If I'm not by now I never will be. Anyway they seem to be getting on. No signs of tensions.'

'It's odd, isn't it,' Paul said. 'They couldn't be a more different bunch, but since the photographic sessions last week they seemed to have palled up. Separately they're very grown up. In a group, they're a bunch of kids. Frances has been appointed ringleader, or voted herself in, I'm not sure which, but they seem to have formed their own gang.'

'United against Bellino, no doubt,' Kate murmured. 'I wonder why their fathers let them come.'

'That's what puzzled me. I wouldn't let my Mary within miles of him.'

The BA Rome flight was being called, and Paul went back to his shepherding while Kate bought all the daily papers, before ambling gently down the hard-on-the-feet passages of the terminal to Gate 21. In the big waiting lounge the girls had formed a little group of three and Paul was sitting with Eileen Elliot. He had saved a seat for Kate and she sank into it, handing over the papers to him.

'Want to have a look?'

He took the *Telegraph*, and Eileen Elliot asked in her plummy voice: 'Could I have the *Express*?'

Kate handed it over and took the *Mail* for herself. The three of them were quiet for a moment and then there was an exclamation from Eileen Elliot.

'Oh look!' she said. 'There's a picture of Frances.'

It wasn't only a picture of Frances, the shot was of the three girls together in a formal group wearing turn-of-thecentury dresses and classroom aprons; exceedingly sexy little French schoolgirls.

'How exciting!' the Elliot woman said. 'Isn't it exciting!'

There was a faint flush of pink on her cheeks and her blue eyes were pleased, sparkling. 'Shall I show it to the girls?' she asked Kate.

'Why not?' Kate said. 'But just let's read the caption first.'

The caption named the three girls and said that they had been chosen to play the schoolchildren in Pedro Bellino's new film, *Claudine at School*.

It added that Ingrid Pallia, who had just sold her life story for a quarter of a million pounds, was to play the school head-mistress while her daughter, Jenny Bolt, had the role of Claudine.

Wordlessly she passed the paper to Paul, who read it and whistled.

'Who's been talking?'

'Ingrid, of course,' Kate's voice was contemptuous. 'Who else?'

'Well, I suppose she's entitled if she wants to,' Paul said, and handed the paper to Eileen Elliot with a smile. 'Show it to the girls. I expect they'll be thrilled.'

They were thrilled.

'Fame at last,' Frances said perkily. She was looking much better. Her hair had been tinted to its natural colour, the spikes were growing out and it had been tightly curled so she had the head of a rather sinister looking little Botticelli angel. Bobbie Jean stared at the paper with china doll blue eyes circled and let out a squeal. Jenny was smiling, but when she read the caption she said: 'Is mother really getting that much, Uncle Paul?'

He hesitated. 'Better ask mother, eh?'

She understood instantly. 'But she'll have to tell an awful lot, won't she.' The candid dark eyes looked into his, and he said slowly: 'I'm afraid so.'

Kate put her hand on the girl's arm.

'Don't worry, Jenny. I won't make it nasty.'

'Thank you,' Jenny said.

They had been booked first-class seats and Eileen Elliot enjoyed a little too much champagne, the flush of excitement on her cheeks growing. Paul, sitting away from the others with Kate at his side, was still concerned with arrangements.

'Ingrid's sending a chauffeur and the Rolls for Jenny,' he said to Kate, wishing the first-class seats were as cosily together as the economy. 'I've got to take the other three on to the Piazza Navona and settle them in. Do you want to come or go on to the Eden?'

'I'll get a cab to the Eden,' she said, and gave him a sideways look. 'I'll freshen up and wait for you. By the way, who's got the big room this time?'

'This time we have a suite with adjoining bedrooms.'

'You are getting brave.'

'I am getting foolish.'

She looked at him quickly to see if he were serious. It was hard to tell.

'You know the thing I've always liked about the Eden,' she said, her voice conversational.

'The upstairs bar? Do you want to meet there?'

'Nope.' She paused, then said: 'When they modernized the place they left those enormous old-fashioned baths.' She gave him a great grin and a flirty wink.

'See you in the bath, eh?'

Chapter Six

The bedroom was enormous with a ceiling that soared high above the big bed. The ceiling itself was divided into squares rimmed with gold, and on every square was painted a small picture, of a nude, of lush bold angels, and small fat cherubs. Here and there a man and woman coupled. Here and there two women coupled. If the sleeper could not sleep there was plenty to regard, both sacred and profane.

No one in the dim room, the shutters drawn over long windows shrouding light from the heavy carved furniture, was looking at the ceiling. They were a tangled heap of bodies on a bed, intent only on each other.

Even a practised voyeur would have found it difficult to count the bodies and the limbs. In fact there were four and sixteen. Two feminine, two masculine, all naked.

And in the centre of the pile, centre of the attention, was Ingrid. She lay on her back on the white heavy linen sheets, her head in thick down pillows, receiving like a goddess.

Her secretary Monique knelt across her, leaning with her head between her employer's legs, her long dark hair falling in a black curtain to mingle with the crisp blonde body curls below. Her spine formed a perfect curve down to her tight rounded buttocks and her full breasts were swinging free. One was grasped and tugged by a hairy brown hand with a signet ring holding a diamond stone on the little finger. The other dark nipple was twisted between long whiter fingers on a hand above a wrist which wore a heavy gold identity bracelet. Her own hands were reaching slightly behind her to grasp and pump two columns, one nesting in sparse blond hair, the other rooted in thick curly black.

The goddess touched no one. She lay with her arms outstretched, her head turned on the pillow so that the blond man could lean over and kiss her mouth.

Between darting explorations with his tongue, he licked her throat and bit at her ears. The dark head attended to her small left breast, sucking it up into his mouth, while the right breast was caressed so expertly by the long, more slender fingers that the red point seemed greater than the white curve.

Ingrid writhed under their hands and mouths, moaning, her flat and muscular body making convulsive little jumps. The bodies were young and firm, in a tumbled and yet somehow precise pattern of flesh that had a kind of beauty. A collector of Japanese pornography would have recognized and applauded the real thing.

However it was not something that Jenny Bolt had wanted to see. She had quietly opened the door to her mother's bedroom wondering if her mother was napping, stopped appalled at what she saw, and equally quietly closed the door again.

Her brief intrusion had not interrupted the revels on the bed. The four were lost in a sex-scented, voluptuous, timeless sensual experience. This was the third time they had quadrupled in various patterns and combinations, but always Ingrid was the goddess; always taking, never giving, sexually insatiable.

She and Monique had met the boys who served them so enthusiastically the night before on the Via Veneto. They had been to George's for dinner, and strolled back towards where they had parked the car.

Clicking in high heels, Monique in red fox, Ingrid in mink, they decided to stop to take a nightcap at the Café de Paris. It was still too early in the year for the pavement cafés to be fully open and busy at night, so they had gone into the long, brightly lit bar and ordered two Remy Martins. Sipping them Monique had looked boldly over the range of customers. There seemed to be little talent. Some American women tourists, rustling with crimplene. A group of boisterously drunken youths and some obvious lovers scattered through a few businessmen. Once, in the Dolce Vita days, the bar had attracted the beautiful people of Rome. Sometimes, even if increasing rarely, it still did. It was always worth looking in.

'Nothing much doing,' Monique had said just before the two boys came through the door. They were perhaps twenty, one dark and one fair. Both were tall for Italians and wore good jeans with denim jackets. The dark one had a strong Roman face with the bold nose of a Forum senator. His hair was thick and curly and his black eyes raked the bar for talent, just as Monique's had. And their eyes met.

The other boy was slimmer with smooth fair hair and the neater looks of Northern Italy. He had gone to the bar to order and when he returned with two Grappa his companion touched him lightly on the arm, nodding towards where Ingrid and Monique stood. There was a brief discussion and then they both moved towards the women, smiling as they came nearer.

'Queer?' Ingrid asked quietly, taking in the heavy jewellery nestling in the hairs of the dark one's chest.

'Bi,' Monique said positively.

B.N.F.L.—D

'Safe?'

'Yeah, I think so.'

'Well, you've scored again, Monique,' Ingrid murmured. 'Congratulations.'

They found both boys spoke quite reasonable English, which made a change. No doubt they always pounced on tourists and the ability was necessary, Ingrid thought.

But not a lot of time was wasted on small talk. Half an hour later all four were in bed. The boys' ancient jalopies were parked in the drive of the Parioli villa behind Ingrid's convertible Mercedes and Monique's Lancia. No one had bothered with introductions, though Ingrid was pretty sure that they had recognized her.

It was a dangerous game she and Monique played with their pick-ups, she thought as she let them into the big pink villa. One day something could go badly wrong, though Monique had never made a mistake yet. Her instinct when picking up was unerring. She managed to net sexual athletes who went quietly come the morning, and who had never yet given either of them a dose of the clap.

It couldn't last for ever, and hopefully nothing would go wrong tonight.

It was crisp and clear as they stood on the doorstep while Ingrid fumbled with the unfamiliar keys. The moon bleached out trees, gates and the house itself, throwing black sinister shadows across the dark boy's face, exaggerating the strength of his nose, so that Ingrid felt a frisson of fear. She sometimes wondered if what she really wanted was for one of them to beat her up, rape her, steal from her. Did she perhaps want to be punished?

Inside, in the dim yellow lighting of the huge open hallway, the dark one looked just like a randy, sexual boy again. She could see by the contours of his jeans that the thought of what was about to happen had aroused him, and she wondered which one she would get. Her choice would be for him, and though she knew instinctively that he would not wear her clothes, she hoped that maybe the men could be persuaded into a foursome. She preferred the foursome. There were things that Monique could do to her with more skill than any man.

She had decided it must be because only a woman could really know what a woman liked. And Monique knew exactly what she liked. They still both preferred it with a man. When it came to the actual fucking it had to be a man, preferably well endowed. But she believed the sensuality of all the preliminaries came better from a woman. She couldn't understand women who shuddered at the thought. She and Monique could please each other very well, thank you, on the rare nights when Monique failed to score. Ingrid could not sleep without having had sex. Sex and coke: both were essential.

Now, unaware that her daughter had briefly witnessed the scene on the rented bed, Ingrid knew she was ready to be fucked.

She pushed the boy's mouth away from hers and gave the order.

'Now! Now!' she said.

It was the dark one's turn to have her. The tangled knot untied itself. Monique lifted her legs from around her employer's body so that the dark man could stretch out on Ingrid's narrow body, between her open legs which scissored around his back to bring him closer to her as she bit frantically at his shoulder.

Monique stayed as she was on her haunches while the fair boy knelt behind her, thrusting into her, moving fast as she clung to the end of the bed, his hands grasping her big, full breasts holding them from swinging above the white linen.

The only sounds in the room were of heavy breathing; then one strangled excited gasp created three more strangled gasps, and the four again were heaped, acquiescent, and still.

The breathing slowed, deepened. In the brooding light of the room where the shutters barred the bright early afternoon sun, they slept where they had fallen.

The jalopies should have tipped her off, Jenny thought. Once she had seen those two old cars, so different from her mother's style and preoccupation with labels and the fashionable expensive things of life, she should have known that something was wrong. But her mother had known she was arriving. She'd even sent the chauffeur. She must have forgotten. She certainly was occupied, Jenny thought bitterly.

She felt sick, shocked, frightened and excited all at the same time as she stood irresolute in the hallway of the villa, her black chihuahua clutched in her arms. He was the cutest little thing she had ever seen when her father had given him to her for a birthday present two years ago, and she had christened him Samson.

Now she hugged him to her as he sat in her arms like a small black monkey. He had been so quick to greet her, so pleased to see her that in this big, empty strange house she felt he was her only contact with love and affection.

'Oh, Sammy,' she said into his small black ears. 'What shall I do? Is she going to put *that* in her book?'

He wriggled in her arms and she put him down, noticing that on the hall table by the telephone a day-old copy of the paper was open at a page showing the picture that had been in the *Daily Express*.

The caption beneath it was much the same, except that it said the three girls would be arriving in Rome today. The item had been ringed in red crayon. By Monique? Or by her mother? Whichever, someone should have remembered she was arriving.

She thought of the tangled mass of bodies on the bed and was ashamed because the memory made her feel a heat at the pit of her stomach. And she was ashamed of her mother. What had all that got to do with love? She wondered if she had been conceived in such a tumble of bodies. She couldn't imagine her father in an orgy. She couldn't even imagine him making love. Perhaps, once her mother hadn't been like that. She had no memories of her mother until she was five years old. As far as she could remember she had never seen her before then though Rosa had said this was not true. She wondered where Rosa was now.

She had no idea what to do with herself. She felt she could not stay in the house. What would she say or do when the owners of those two old cars appeared? Her face would give her away, and she knew it. Her mother would guess she had seen something.

She went out on to the big porchway of the house and stared around her. There was a narrow drive fronting the house and swinging round to the back. There appeared to be a big garden and her mother had said there was a swimming pool. She did not want to explore in case the windows of her mother's room looked out at the back. She couldn't yet work out the geography of the house.

Across the road from the house, set well back, was a block of white painted flats, carefully insulated by trees. The street was quiet – nearly all blocks of smart flats. Theirs was the only villa. No one seemed to be about, but then it was a cul-de-sac, she noted, ending on nothing more than a small patch of parkland. The villa's side walls backed on to the piece of green.

Parioli seemed unnaturally quiet and still after the noisy drive through the town from the airport with the yellow taxis weaving snappily through the traffic like marauding wasps. Here there was no traffic. Only one car parked in the street, lower down, and not a sound of engines or gears or the faintest peep of a horn.

Samson had trotted to the closed wrought-iron gates and had turned to look at her inquiringly.

'You want a walk?' she said to him. 'Why not?'

She opened the gate, and he ran slightly ahead of her as she walked towards the patch of green.

It was bigger than it looked from the house, tree-lined and falling away in a gentle incline. At one point there was a fine view of Rome, St Peter's dome towering, ringed with other lesser domes. As Samson snuffled in the long grass she stood and stared at it feeling a deep sadness, remembering Bellino's promise to show them the cathedral, and remembering too his behaviour at Mustique. Why, she wondered, were so many older people so unpleasant?

She walked around the edge of the field, Samson trotting not far away, and just as she was returning to the gap that led back into the street she saw the stranger. He was lounging against a tree, and Samson, growling, comically fierce for his size, advanced on the man. He was burly with reddish curly hair and a heavy-jawed handsome face with full, drooping moustache. As Samson reached the turn-ups of the trousers of his dark suit, he casually but swiftly leaned down and picked up the little dog. Then suddenly there was a knife in his hand which he placed under the dog's chin.

101

'If you come with me quietly,' he said in heavily accented English, 'nothing will happen to the dog.'

Jenny stared at him in shock. The knife was glinting at Samson's throat as the dog struggled to free itself from the grip of a huge hand.

'What do you want?' she whispered.

'You are to come with me,' he said. 'When we reach the street I shall put this knife away, but remember I don't need it. One scream, one sound from you and I can snap the dog's neck with my hands. And I will.'

He had light blue eyes that seemed to have ice behind them. Very clear, very cold and glittering.

She still could not move.

'Why?' she said.

'Never mind why,' he said and grabbed at her arm. 'Just come.'

'Don't touch me,' she said, her voice rising. 'I'll come. I'll come. Don't hurt Sammy.'

He just grunted, and she found her legs moving as she walked beside him out into the street. It was still deserted, some yellow blossoms blowing on the trees in the garden in front of the villa where her mother cavorted in bed with three other people. A blue BMW was parked across the road at the gap leading to the green patch. The engine was not running, and a boy sat in the back seat. It was a two-door car and without haste the man opened the one away from the driving side. He pulled the seat forward.

'Get in the back,' he said.

She did as she was told, and in the split second of releasing the seat, he let his grasp relax on Samson, the dog wriggled free and leapt across into the back of the car and on to her lap.

'Get that dog out,' he said to the boy in Italian.

'No!' She was clinging to the small warm body. 'If you take him, I'll scream. I don't care. I'll scream my head off.'

'Let her keep the dog,' the boy said in Italian, putting out a hand to touch Samson's head. She turned to look at him. He was perhaps seventeen, thin, his shirt open to show a scrawny chest. He had the same pale eyes as the man but without

102

the strange glitter and his face was thin with high cheekbones, topped with curly black hair. She wasn't afraid of him.

'What does he want?' she asked in Italian.

The boy looked uneasy.

'You must be quiet if you don't want to get hurt,' he told her, and she sensed he was doing his best to sound menacing.

'Get her head down,' the older man was saying as he got into the driver's seat, 'and quick about it.'

'Lie down,' the boy instructed her, but he didn't touch her. It seemed wiser to obey. She curled her small body into a circle on the seat of the car, Samson between her knees and her chin. He was still growling gently to himself, the hairs on his neck bristling. It was just ten past three.

'Get the blindfold on her,' the man said as he started the engine.

It happened easily. Something held with a lot of sticky tape was slapped across her eyes, and with claustrophobic terror rising in her, she began to sob as she felt the car set off and drive away from the house where her mother was still probably lying on her bed with all those bodies attending her.

But she recovered some spirit as she felt the boy's breath on her ear, and heard his voice whisper: 'Please don't cry.'

It had gone three when Ingrid stirred. A ray of sunlight had penetrated the shutters and was tickling her eyelids. Slowly she woke, stretching and looking down at her sleeping companions. She still liked the dark one better, she thought, eyeing his genitals, where even in sleep there were signs of a growth to come. She liked dark men. Hairy dark men with hairs on the backs of their hands and on their chests and shoulders. Any man would do, as long as he was physically attractive. Old men, pot-bellied men, skinny men, bald men. None of those would do. She would rather have Monique. But most men, as long as they were performers and were young, would do. Old men began at thirty-nine.

She was debating whether to get the party going again when she suddenly remembered: Jenny. Jenny was due home.

'Oh my God!' she said out loud, and Monique opened her long, Egyptian eyes.

'What is it?' she asked, instantly alert.

'Jenny! She must be home. Get them out of here. Down the back stairs. Quickly as you can. Pay them what they want.'

'Shall I ask them back?'

'Yeah, but it'll have to be daytime. When Jenny's out.'

They had been speaking softly so as not to wake the two men, but the dark one was sitting up.

'What's up?' he asked sleepily.

'Her daughter's coming home.'

'What's she like?' he asked. 'Any good?'

He put his arms behind his head and grinned lecherously.

Suddenly Ingrid was angry.

'Get out of here, the pair of you,' she shouted. 'And don't try anything funny.'

She had pulled on a long kaftan, and was tearing lira notes out of a purse. She threw a large bundle on the bed.

He scratched through the hair on his chest.

'What's this?' he asked.

'Isn't it enough?' she snapped.

He grinned again. 'I was just about to pay *you*.'

She stared at him in icy silence.

'I am not a whore,' she said slowly.

'*Signorina*, you surprise me.' He stood and bowed naked.

'For God's sake tell her we fuck for fun,' said the other man's voice from the bed.

'Bastards,' Ingrid snarled at them and hurried from the room.

She ran downstairs, remembering her feet were bare. She'd tell Jenny she'd been napping. That was true enough. Jenny's luggage was in the hall, but there was no sign of Jenny; nor of Samson. The house was silent, and Ingrid remembered Monique had given the servants the day off so she and Ingrid could have their fun in peace.

Where was Jenny? The absence of the dog explained it, she decided. They'd gone for a walk. That was it. And now there was time to get those two gigolos out of the place without any trouble. Turning, she ran back upstairs again.

*

'What's that?' Frances and Bobbie Jean were hanging out of the window of their room at the pension where Paul had left them ten minutes before. Below was a great round fountain that poured endless water, decorated by statues of four huge, muscular robed men.

'Fountain of the Four Rivers,' said Bobbie Jean, who had been acting as a guide all through the journey from the airport into the town. She had pointed out the ancient monuments, naming them, and given a brief potted history. 'If you knew how many times I've been dragged round this lot—' she explained. 'We were here three years.'

Frances regarded the statue and pronounced: 'It's smashing. But what's he doing?'

Bobbie Jean gazed indifferently at the vast statue where one of the figures held its arm as if to ward off a blow.

'Something to do with the sculptor Bernini, not getting on too well with the architect who built the church next door. St Agnes somebody. We can't see it from here. They were rivals. And the god on the statue has his arm ready for the day when the other guy's church falls down. Something like that. I can't remember exactly.'

'I like that,' Frances said. She moved from the window and said: 'I wish Jenny was with us. It must be terribly boring for her, stuck with her mother.'

'Well, we've got yours,' Bobbie Jean pointed out.

'Yes, but there are two of us. And my mother's easy to deal with. No trouble at all. Hers must be awful, don't you think?'

'Haven't thought,' Bobbie Jean said.

'Well, writing that book.'

'Doesn't sound bad to me. Not for all that money.'

'There are more things in life than money,' Frances said darkly.

'Oh, I don't know,' said Bobbie Jean. 'I want to be rich.'

'I expect you will be,' Frances said, but without malice.

They returned to looking out of the window, then Frances said thoughtfully: 'Look at that ice cream place opposite. I could go for an ice cream. They say Italian ice cream's fantastic.'

'Me too. It is. Why don't we go?'

'Why don't we? We'll be back before she wakes up.'

Eileen Elliot had retired to her bedroom, her head spinning from the flight, the champagne and the excitement. She had immediately dropped into a sound sleep.

They left the room quietly and ran down the stairs to where the entrance of the pension opened discreetly into the narrow street behind the Navona.

'*Buona sera, signora,*' Bobbie Jean said to the whiskery old concierge who let them out into the afternoon sunshine. An alleyway led into the *piazza* and once confronted by the dignified oval square with its three fountains and graceful buildings, Frances said: 'It's very splendid, isn't it? I'm longing to explore.'

'I'm longing for an ice cream,' said Bobbie Jean. 'Come on, let's go over.'

A man had materialized in front of them – a big man with reddish hair in a chauffeur's uniform, his cap held respectfully in two hands. His broad body was blocking them and he said: 'Signorina Elliot?' He was looking at Bobbie Jean.

'No, that's my friend,' Bobbie Jean said.

'You are Signorina Dennison?'

'That's right.'

'The Signor Bellino has asked me to fetch you both to the dressmakers for your measurings.' His English was good, but not quite perfect. 'It is not permitted to bring the car into the *piazza* but it is not far away.'

The girls looked at each other, Bobbie Jean resigned.

'We'll have to tell my mother,' Frances told him.

'No – we are late – the traffic. The studios will telephone her to say that you will be back in one hour.'

'Beastly Bellino! What do you think?' Bobbie Jean said doubtfully. 'Is it the costume? What does he want?'

Bobbie Jean had told the girls Bellino had made a pass at her. Nothing more.

'Must be,' Frances said. 'Or he'd just send for you. He doesn't like me. Anyway, he can't do anything with two of us there. We just have to stick together.' She turned to the man who was watching them with oddly intent blue eyes. 'OK. We'll just go and get an ice cream and be right with you.'

106

He hesitated for a second, then laughed showing large white teeth that crossed in the front.

'You may stop for your ice cream. We pass the *gelateria*.'

'Cheek!' Frances whispered. 'Who does he think he is? We may stop for our ice creams, indeed!'

He waited some paces from the shop. 'Doesn't want to be seen with kids buying ice creams, I suppose,' Frances said. She had taken a dislike to the man. 'Take your time choosing. He can wait.'

They settled for a strawberry flavour for Bobbie Jean, chocolate for Frances, and sauntered to join him, licking at the cornets.

'This way,' he said, and led them along the *piazza's* wide pavement towards the Vittorio Emanuele. Once out of the square he plunged into a tiny almost deserted side street where a white car was parked. A boy sat in the back seat.

'This is it,' he said, and opened the door. 'You in back,' he said to Bobbie Jean. His tone was a fraction too authorative for a chauffeur and Frances thought indignantly he was coming it a bit. But Bobbie Jean did as she was told.

'Hold that,' she said, handing her half eaten cornet to Frances.

As she negotiated the awkward climb into the back and sat down, momentarily off balance, the boy's left hand came across swiftly just as she started to say 'Hi' to him. He held a large pad which he thrust over her face, forcing her head down with his right hand so the pad and her nose were wedged on the back of the front seat. He looked skinny but he was stringily muscular.

She tried to struggle as the sickly sweet smell of chloroform hit her, but his hand had her trapped by the neck. She could not move in the narrow space between the seats.

For one second too long Frances was frozen. In that second the big man grabbed her from behind and very casually, as if he was helping her, pushed her into the passenger seat. But she could see the knife glinting in his hand. His arm lightly around her waist, the steel was pressed into her stomach.

'Don't shout,' he said. 'Don't struggle. Don't do a thing. Claudio—'

Bobbie Jean had collapsed half on the seat, half on the floor. The boy clambered over her and in a swift movement leaned to press the pad over Frances' face. Terrified, she tried to move her head from side to side to escape the cloying smell. The knife gently pricked her neck.

'It'll be easier if you don't struggle,' the man said, smiling his big-toothed smile. 'Just relax. Just relax.'

Only when she had flopped unconscious in her seat did he walk slowly round to the driver's seat, chinking his keys as he walked. Once in the car, he made a quick look round to see that no one was watching them, pushed Frances' inert body on to the floor, moving her, but gently, with his foot away from the gear shift.

Seconds later the white BMW drove away. From the street only two people could be seen in the car – the boy in the back, and the driver. It was ten to four.

In the gutter where the car had parked, two ice creams, one pink and one dark brown, melted in the sunshine.

The bathroom of one of the Hotel Eden's grander suites was awash with soapy water. Every bath towel was sopping wet on the floor and Kate and Paul jammed together in the large, white enamel tub were helpless with laughter. Her soaked hair was escaping in straggles down her back, her eyelashes were rimmed with bath-foam. The foam clung in the hairs of his chest, and the wet hair at the back of his neck was springing into small curls.

'I don't believe it's possible,' he grumbled.

'It's the foam. I used too much. It's made it all slippery.'

'Shall we give up and go to bed?'

'No way,' she said.

She had meant it to be glamorous. At Vincenti Airport, Jenny sent off safely in her mother's chauffeur-driven Rolls, Paul had asked Kate to give him about two hours – until four o'clock. Even allowing for Rome traffic and Mrs Elliot's fussing he should have settled them into their pensions and got himself to the Via Ludovisi where they were staying.

Her own taxi had been driven by one of Rome's rare and welcome sedate drivers and it had taken nearly an hour to get from the airport through the suburbs and the clogged old city up to the Ludovisi.

She had brought Paul's luggage with her, and installed in the elegant suite she unpacked for both of them. She spent so much of her life in hotels that it was important that the room was made as homelike as possible. She rang down to the desk to ask for flowers and a bottle of Krug to be sent up. She put out her little travelling clock, hung her clothes and decided which drawers would be for underwear, which for sweaters and which for his things. Then she put books on the bedside table and poured herself a long glass of mineral water from the small well-stocked refrigerator in the room.

At ten to four she began to run the bath in a small trickle, adding a long thick stream of greeny-yellow Badedas. Anything can happen in a Badedas bath, she reminded herself. She carefully wiped off her mascara so that it would not run into long trickles down her face, and screwed her hair tight into the Javanese knot that always made him laugh.

As she had no intentions of getting her hair wet, she splashed a great deal of Fracas behind her ears, and then putting on a long white towelling dressing gown settled down to wait. At the turn of the key in the door, she intended leaping into the bathroom and into the bath and reclining there, bubble-covered. The Krug was already in its ice bucket in the bidet, glasses frosting in the fridge.

When she heard the key, she hurried into the bathroom, slipped off her robe and climbed into the bath cautiously. The water was somewhat on the hot side and made her grit her teeth. It also seemed to be turning her a rather bright red very quickly.

'Where are you?' he called.

'Where I said,' she called back.

His face came around the door and he grinned at the sight of her, bubbles up to her chin, her hair twisted high.

'Hello, darling,' she said, one hand languidly plucking at the foam, 'your bathrobe's on the bed. Come and open the champagne, will you? There are two glasses getting nicely cold in the fridge.'

He bowed, still grinning and disappeared without speaking.

He was back quickly, almost as if he hadn't bothered to fold his trousers, she thought, wearing a heavy blue robe. He had two glasses in his hand, and still without speaking, he took the bottle from the ice bucket and opened it.

'Showers are all very well,' she said dreamily, 'but they lack the finer things. The leisure to brood in a cloud of steam, the possibility of drinking without getting drowned, the chance to make love in warm water, sitting down without being rained upon.'

The cork came out with a pop.

'You've forgotten the bit about turning your fingers and toes all wrinkly,' he said.

'No cynicism, please,' she warned and as he handed her a brimming glass, 'this is our first bath.'

He had slipped off his robe, and she looked at his broad-shouldered body with pleasure as he stood on the bathmat, smiling down at her.

'Who gets the taps?' he asked.

'Come, come,' she told him, 'the gentleman of course.'

'With what I've got in mind you ought to have the taps.'

'Sounds rude, but OK.' She twisted herself round from one end of the bath to the other, careful to keep under the cover of the foam. 'It's not very comfortable,' she complained.

'Keep your legs up,' he said. 'Make room for me.'

Obediently she drew up her knees, and with some speed he got into the water and started to sit down. Two things happened; a tidal wave splashed over the side of the bath, and he leapt straight up and out again, shouting: 'Jesus Christ! That's hot.'

'Oh, God – I forgot to tell you,' she said. 'I've got used to it.'

'You also forgot Archimedes' theory,' he said, regarding the lake on the tiled floor.

'Eureka!' she said mournfully, peering over the edge. 'Do you think it will go through downstairs?'

'Don't know – but since I'm out . . .' he took the bath towels from their shelf, and scattered every one on the floor. 'That should mop it up.'

'And so how do we dry ourselves?'

'On our bathrobes,' he said. 'Hang on, I'm coming back in.'

110

Gingerly he climbed back in, and sat down very slowly.

'I hope it cools down in a minute,' he said. 'You're all red.'

'I like it hot,' she lied, and scooping up some bath foam, leaned to put it on his nose, and leaned further to kiss it off again.

'What are we supposed to do with our legs?' he asked.

'Stretch out and I'll sit between them, then I'll put mine round you.'

A lot more water was displaced with the manoeuvre and she began to giggle.

'Now if I wriggle up a bit,' she said, 'we can do *something*.'

'What?'

'Well, this—' She groped in the water and found his penis and began to stroke. At the same time he found his way between her thighs and did the same.

'It's rather nice in water,' she said tentatively.

'It's very uncomfortable,' he said, mock cross. 'I'm too old for this lark.'

'You are a spoilsport. It's not that you're too old, you're just too large to fit. Anyway, what was it you said you had in mind?'

'Turn round,' he instructed. Carefully she did so. 'Lean back—' She leaned back. He put his arms around her and began to soap and stroke her breasts, throwing water over them in gentle little waves, pulling at her nipples.

'Nice?' he asked.

'Umm—' Something hard was pressing against the base of her spine and putting her hands behind her back she felt for him again. 'That's too good to waste,' she said and turned to kneel over him, lowering herself on to him, knowing there was little doubt she would be wet enough for him to enter.

'Oh darling!' she was saying, as she pressed down. 'Oh—' the second 'darling' turned into a long shriek as her knees slid from under her, and she sprawled, face down in hot water, her chin hitting on a splendid erection. His arms were instantly pulling her up to rest on his chest, and he was laughing so hard that her head was rocked by the laughter.

She drew back and looked at him indignantly. 'Not funny!' she said and then she, too, started to laugh.

'One thing's for sure—' she managed to say, 'a blow job is definitely out!'

'Definitely,' he said, turning her head to kiss her. 'But I still want you. Any suggestions?'

She moved the water with her hand thoughtfully. 'It's got to be possible. Everyone does it in porno films, not that I've ever seen a porno film . . .'

'You haven't?' he said.

'I've never believed in spectator sports,' she said primly, adding – 'and this is no time for conversation.'

Her hand was caressing him under the water again, and his fingers were in her, while they exchanged foamy kisses. She drew herself up, a little breathless, and said: 'Got it. But you have to have the taps. It's more upright that end. The bath I mean!'

He turned and she leaned over the side to pick a sopping towel from the floor which she placed over the taps to protect his back, and then when he was sitting upright, she knelt, took his shoulders firmly in her hands, told him to put his arms around her, and again lowered herself on to him.

She gave a little gasp of pleasure as he entered. 'For God's sake don't slip,' she said. 'Hold me tight. I'll do the work.'

She moved her body up and down on him faster and faster, her knees clamped tight around him. His eyes were shut and gradually he was thrusting upwards to join her. The water around them seemed to be boiling with movement, their mouths were clinging and wet, until he threw his head back and a long cry dragged from him.

She made one last frenzied push, and for her the deep, exciting contractions began. 'Stay with me, stay with me—' she gasped, and he thrust again into her. 'Come! Come!' he commanded until he felt the tensions go out of her body. Then they both stayed still, breathing slow and deep.

After a while she wriggled in his grasp.

'This water's getting cold,' she said. 'Let's get out.' Then rather shyly – 'Did you like it?'

He kissed the face that was just inches from his. 'Very much,' he told her. 'Now let's go and do it again. In bed.'

*

They didn't do it again. By the time they had dried themselves and the bathroom floor, finished the champagne and lain down, her head on his shoulder, his arms around her, they fell asleep.

At nearly six the phone rang. It was Eileen Elliot.

'I'm so sorry to disturb you.' Her voice was timid, anxious. 'But you haven't seen the two girls, have you?'

'No,' Paul said, stifling a yawn. 'Should I have?'

'Mr Wingard, I'm worried. I fell asleep after you left us, and when I woke up about an hour ago, there was no sign of either Frances or Bobbie Jean. The concierge says she saw them go out about four. I can't think where they can be.'

'Sightseeing I expect,' Paul said comfortingly. 'There's a lot to see in Rome.'

'I'm sure Frances wouldn't just go for so long without telling me.'

'She's got the naughty Bobbie Jean as a bad example,' he said.

'Maybe you're right, but I'm worried. What shall I do?'

He decided, convinced in his own mind that they'd found the shops and maybe a couple of Roman youths, and were just enjoying themselves, and he told her so.

'Give me a ring if they're not back by seven,' he said. 'But I'm sure they will be.'

'What's up?' Kate said sleepily, sitting up and running her hands through still damp hair.

'Frances and Bobbie Jean seem to have gone off on a spree. Mrs Elliot's worried.

'Found the local talent, I expect,' Kate said. 'God, I'm hungry. Can we go to the Piccolo Mondo?'

'If you like.'

'We'll have to be early to get a table.'

He shook his head. 'I'll have to wait until she rings back and says they're home. I told her to ring by seven if they're not.'

'Oh well, I guess I can survive that long. But with a drink,' she said. 'Let's raid this mini-fridge.'

It was about ten to seven when the phone rang and Paul picked it up expecting to hear Mrs Elliot saying that the girls were home. But it was Ingrid.

The conversation began in much the same way as the earlier one.

'Paul, you haven't seen Jenny, have you?'

'No,' he said, puzzled. 'Why?'

'She's not here. Her luggage is here. Verde says he dropped her home around three, but there's no sign of her since. Or the dog.'

'She's probably taken the dog for a walk.'

'For four hours!' Her voice was rising.

'When did you see her last?' he asked, a faint nudge of anxiety beginning to trouble him.

'I haven't seen her.' There was a pause. 'I was asleep when she came in.'

'Listen,' he said, 'Frances and Bobbie Jean have gone missing too. She couldn't have met up with them, could she?'

'She could,' she said doubtfully, 'I don't know. How long have they been out?'

He did a quick calculation. 'Not as long, I don't think. Look, stay there and I'll ring Mrs Elliot and see if they're back. She was ringing me at seven.'

'If they're out too, you're probably right. They're all together somewhere. But ring back quickly, won't you?'

Frances and Bobbie Jean were not back, and Mrs Elliot was in a state bordering on panic. 'It's terrible,' she said, 'I don't know what to do. I can't speak the language. Mr Wingard, I'm frightened.'

He put his hand over the phone and spoke to Kate who was sitting on the bed filing her fingernails.

'She's in a state and she is alone there. Do you mind if we go over?'

She grimaced but said: 'Not if you think it's necessary.'

He went back to the phone. 'Kate Anderson and I will be right over.'

'Do you think we ought to call the police? What does one do in Italy in this sort of situation?' Eileen was asking.

'Call the police,' he told her grimly.

'Bobbie Jean, are you all right?' Jenny had thought she heard the American girl say something and got up from the mattress where she had been lying for the past hour or so. Both girls had been unconscious when the big man carried them in and

114

Jenny had been terrified that they were dead. He left them on the other two mattresses in the room, limp and white. She rushed to hear if they still breathed after he'd gone and found they did: slow, shallow breaths, but definitely breathing. Then she lay down whimpering quietly to herself until, exhausted, she dozed off for a while – how long she couldn't tell. The room was dark but some light crept in at one or two points; through shutters, under a door and through what appeared to be a fanlight in the ceiling, high above. It was just enough light to see and she was sure the sun still shone outside.

'Is it Jenny?' Bobbie Jean's voice whispered.

'Yes. Are you all right?'

Bobbie Jean looked up bewildered.

'I feel nauseous,' she said. 'I remember. Oh, God – that man. Where's Frances? Where are we?'

She was trying to sit up, but grimaced as a wave of sickness hit her.

'I don't know,' Jenny said. 'They brought me here about twenty minutes before you.'

'Jenny? Bobbie Jean?' Frances' voice was drowsy but she was able to sit up and look around her.

'You're awake!' Jenny said. 'I was so frightened, Frances. I thought you were both dead when he brought you in. You were so white. You looked terrible.'

'I feel terrible,' Frances said. 'Where are we?'

'We don't know. It's a big room with three beds. There's a little bathroom and lavatory at the side but all the windows are barred and I haven't seen anyone since they brought us here.'

'What's it all about?' Frances said. 'Who was that man?'

'I think we've been kidnapped,' Jenny said apologetically, as if it were her fault. 'There's an awful lot of it in Rome.'

'Kidnapped!' Frances' voice wavered terror and excitement. 'I wish I didn't feel so sick.'

All three girls were now sitting up on the mattresses which were the only furnishings in the big bare room. On each mattress were the only furnishings in the big bare room. On each mattress were two blankets. There were no pillows.

'Did they do it to you?' Frances asked Jenny. 'Put you out? He got Bobbie Jean in the car first. Before I could do anything, he'd got me too.'

'Who?' Jenny said. 'Was it a big man with red hair and funny eyes and a boy? Quite a nice boy?'

'He wasn't a nice boy,' Frances said. 'It was him that did it. Put the stuff in our faces. I suppose it was chloroform.'

'They didn't do that to me,' Jenny said. 'The man just threatened to kill Sammy, my dog. I've got him here, under the blanket with me. I'd taken Sammy for a walk. My mother . . .' The awful scene in the bedroom flashed through her mind in the darkness. 'My mother wasn't in. And just as I was coming back this man grabbed Sammy and put a knife under his chin. He said he'd kill Sammy if I didn't come quietly. They put me in a car, and then the boy put something over my eyes so I couldn't see. A bit later the car stopped and I think the boy got out and someone else got in the front. Anyway, it was a different man who left me in here. They took the blindfold thing off once I was in this room.'

'They told us Bellino wanted us for costume fitting,' Frances said. She had crept off her mattress to sit with Jenny and Bobbie Jean had followed. 'Then when he'd got us in the car, he chloroformed us. He and the boy. Oh, God, my mother will be having a fit. We never even told her we were going out. We only wanted an ice cream.'

There was silence in the dimness for a moment.

'It's not so bad with all of us together,' Bobbie Jean ventured. 'Imagine being alone.'

'I thought I was at first,' Jenny said, her voice trembling with the memory of it. 'It was awful.'

'What happens now?' Frances asked.

'They kill people sometimes, don't they?' Bobbie Jean said.

'Not if they get the money,' Frances told her. 'I don't think my parents have got much money, though,' she said thoughtfully.

'Nor my father,' Bobbie Jean said. 'The alimony he pays my mother is horrendous.'

They were too polite to mention that Jenny would have the least problems.

'We'll just have to escape,' Frances said. 'When it's light, we'll make a plan. If we could work out where we are . . .'

'Well, we're not in the country,' Jenny said. 'Listen to that noise outside.'

They listened. There was a background buzz of traffic; the muted sounds of angry hooters.

We're in a town,' Frances said, 'but not on a main road. Probably an alley like the one he grabbed us in.'

A distant sound of a police car's siren could be heard and Bobbie Jean said: 'Think they're looking for us?'

'Too soon,' Frances said decisively. 'At the moment everyone will be furious with us, convinced we've just gone sightseeing without telling anyone.'

'They'll think I've picked up a boy.' Bobbie Jean said. 'I wish I had.'

'My mother probably hasn't even noticed,' Jenny said, burying her face in Samson.

'Well, mine will have, she'll be having kittens,' said Frances. 'Right. We're not in the country. Rome?'

'Oh, yes,' said Jenny. 'The journey wasn't long enough for anywhere else. And how could they have picked you up and brought you here so quickly if it wasn't near the centre?'

'Two cars?' suggested Frances. 'What colour was yours?'

'Ours was white,' Bobbie Jean said promptly. 'A new BMW.'

'Mine was blue,' Jenny said. 'I don't know what kind.'

'So that's it. We're not far away. If we can escape . . .'

She stopped speaking at the sound of a key turning in a lock. A door opened flooding in a long panel of yellow light, and then a light switch snapped and the room was boldly lit from one uncovered bulb hanging from the centre of the ceiling.

The boy was standing there with a tray. Someone behind him slammed the door shut and locked it again.

'Food—' he said.

No one spoke, and looking embarrassed he crossed the room and bent awkwardly to put the tray on the floor. 'It's a pasta,' he said.

'Please,' Jenny spoke to him in Italian. 'What are they going to do to us? Please tell us what it's all about.'

'You mustn't ask me questions,' he said woodenly. 'He'll tell you later.'

She had got to her feet, and he put out his hand to scratch gently between the dog's ears.

'Do not worry,' he said. 'No one will hurt you.'

Abruptly he turned and hurried back to the door. He knocked. It was opened, and he left without a backward look.

'What did he say?' Frances asked, kneeling on the mattress.

'That there was no need to be frightened, no one would hurt us,' Bobbie Jean said.

Jenny was stroking Samson's head thoughtfully. She did not speak.

'Well,' said Frances. 'Let's hope he's right. In the meantime we might as well eat.'

On the tray were three plastic plates and spoons and a large enamel dish. She lifted the lid off and sniffed. 'Just spaghetti,' she said. 'No sauce.' Then, still in the kneeling position, she looked up at the other two girls.

'It's a bit exciting, isn't it?' she said and giggled nervously.

'Your name's Claudio, isn't it?' Jenny said when the boy came back for the tray.

He looked frightened and backed towards the door.

'How did you know?'

'Frances remembered, from the car. That man called you Claudio.'

'It's my name.' he muttered.

'Claudio – I have a problem.'

He looked at her warily.

'Sammy – that's my dog – has to go out. I suppose you won't let me take him. Will you walk him?'

The boy looked at the dog and Jenny knew she had got it right. He liked Sammy.

'He's really called Samson,' she added. 'As a joke.'

'I'll take him out for you,' the boy said.

'On one condition—' the boy's face said that she was in no position to make conditions but Jenny hurried on '—that you bring him back. Will you swear on the Holy Virgin to bring him back to me?'

'If I say I will bring him back I do not need to swear,' the boy said. 'Give him to me.'

'Be careful in the street. He's not used to traffic.'

'I shall take him in the courtyard, not in the street,' the boy said, as Jenny put the wriggling little dog into his arms. She then picked up and handed him the tray. 'Is that what you came for?' she said. 'It's all gone. We had to give Sammy some as well.'

'In future I will feed him,' the boy said as he went out of the room. Someone locked the door behind him.

'I don't like the sound of that "in future" much,' Bobbie Jean said. 'Sounds as if we'll be here for ever. He seems to like you. Can't you find out what's going on?'

'I'll try,' Jenny said. 'I rather like him.'

'A kidnapper!' Frances snorted. 'I do wish I could understand what everyone's saying. You two are lucky being able to speak the language. It makes me feel lonely being left out.'

'We might try to teach you,' Jenny said. 'It would be something to do.'

The light had been left on, which lifted their spirits and sent them looking for possibilities for escape. There were none. And when Sammy was pushed through the door without it being fully opened, the bulb in the ceiling went dark again.

The light that filtered through the sealed shutters now was of a different quality. Outside it was dusk and the street noises seemed to be intensified.

'I think we're in Trastevere,' Bobbie Jean said. 'It sounds like Trastevere. It's the noisiest place in Rome. Particularly at night.'

'Where's Trastevere?' Frances asked. She had lain down on her mattress again, Jenny was sitting on hers, stroking Sammy, and Bobbie was at the window, listening.

'The other side of the Tiber. Sort of old Rome. There's lots of little alleys and things and it's not a good place to walk at night. Daddy used to bring me to a restaurant there a lot: Sabatini's it was called, but he always got a cab back to the other side.'

'So we're in Trastevere, so what?' Frances said.

'Well, if we do escape we at least know where we are,' Bobbie Jean said. 'Though how? These shutters are nailed.' She beat briefly and impotently on the mosquito netting covering the shutters then lay on her own mattress.

'We've nothing to sleep in. No clean clothes,' she grumbled. 'Is there any soap in that bathroom?'

'A bit,' Jenny said.

'You'll have to ask the boy for things we need,' Frances said. 'You'll have to flirt with him.'

'Aren't you frightened of him?' Bobbie Jean asked.

Jenny shook her head.

'Aren't you frightened at all?'

'A bit. It doesn't seem real, does it? Like an adventure, really.'

'It's better being together. It would be awful to be alone,' Frances said positively. 'I wonder how much they want for us if we are kidnapped.'

They were silent for a moment, each thinking her own thoughts. Then Frances added: 'I hope it's not too much.'

Chapter Seven

'Perhaps you would be kind enough to explain to us exactly who NAP are.' Charles Dennison was speaking perfect Italian. 'I think we would all prefer to be completely *au fait* with the situation, however unpleasant. I'm sure I can speak for all of us,' he added, looking around the silent and anxious group.

Kate, as the only other person in the room who could fully understand what was going on, found herself enormously impressed by Dennison. His terrors were no less than anyone elses, but he showed only a calm and courteous front. He was handling a difficult and emotional situation with diplomatic aplomb.

They were gathered before an examining magistrate and an inspector of the Pubblica Sicurezza, both of whom had been delegated to work on the kidnapping of Bobbie Jean Dennison, Frances Elliot and Jenny Bolt.

Two days had passed since the girls disappeared. After fruitless searching by the *carabinieri* – hampered by the fact that Ingrid could not pinpoint the time when Jenny had last been seen – the word kidnapping had begun to be mentioned. Paul said bluntly he believed this to be the answer and that the girls' fathers must be contacted immediately.

Charles Dennison and Alex Elliot had flown from London on the first available plane. Michael Bolt had come, reluctantly, that morning.

He had arrived at the Parioli villa to a scene of frenzied activity. Half an hour earlier Ingrid received, by ordinary post, a communication from a terrorist group who called themselves Nuclei Armati Proletari. They claimed responsibility for the kidnapping of the three girls. The villa was full of policemen, headed by Inspector Garoni of the political branch of the Pubblica Sicurezza.

It was he who had called all three families to meet with the Rome magistrate who would be empowered to issue warrants for the arrest of the kidnappers – if and when they were apprehended.

When the Elliots, the Bolts, Charles Dennison, plus Paul and Kate who had gone to give moral support, were settled in the big room, the magistrate outlined to them exactly what the police now knew, which was frighteningly little – in fact no more than they knew themselves. Charles and Kate took turns to translate what he was saying and it was all taking a long time.

NAP, as they knew, had kidnapped the three girls. They were demanding a ransom of half a million pounds for Jenny and a quarter of a million each for the other two girls. The money was to be paid in used Swiss, German or British banknotes. In seven days' time NAP would contact the parents with instructions as to where and how the money must be left. The complete sum of one million had to be paid at once so that all three girls could be released at the same time.

The letter had gone to the forensic department, where nothing had been learned. There were no fingerprints. The notepaper was cheap and ordinary; the postmark Rome, but that, the magistrate pointed out did not necessarily mean anything. The girls could be anywhere in Italy.

'In fact,' he said, 'we are of the opinion that they are not in Rome. That would explain the delay between the kidnapping and NAP's contacting you today, *signora*.' He inclined towards Ingrid.

The atmosphere in the big room was tense. Ingrid's hands

were shaking as she chain-smoked. Charles Dennison was managing to keep his diplomat's urbanity, but his foot tapped restlessly as the magistrate spoke. Only Michael Bolt seemed unconcerned, Kate noted. But for the rest, the strain of the past days was showing.

'Perhaps you would like to explain the details, Inspector,' the magistrate suggested. He was a small fat man with pebble glasses and balding dome. He was sweating in his light grey suit, but Kate thought he seemed kind – doing his best to relieve their fears.

'If you wish,' Inspector Garoni said, with a slight bow towards the magistrate. He was an elegant man. Tall and thin, with a sharp clever face, his brown eyes watchful, dark hair swept straight from his brow, he wore plain clothes; a suit that could have been tailored in London – a white shirt and quiet tie. The sergeant who accompanied him wore a comic-opera navy blue uniform with a purple stripe down the trousers. He sat stolid and quiet, his gun nestling at his plump hip.

'NAP, as we call this terrorist group, have been in operation since the beginning of 1974. Just for a year,' Garoni explained. 'They come originally from Naples and they were born out of a split in another left-wing movement called Lotta Continua. This kidnapping is very much in character. They are one of the few of our many Italian right- and left-wing terrorist groups who kidnap for money. They are a self-financing organization and it is by kidnapping that they have raised their funds in the past.'

Charles Dennison translated quickly then asked: 'They've kidnapped others?'

Inspector Garoni nodded. 'Last year they held a Neapolitan gynaecologist, Antonio Garguilo, for a ransom of seventy million lire. That would be about £40,000 in your money. Then in December last year they became more ambitious and kidnapped the cement king, Guiseppe Moccia. For him they exorted a ransom of one billion lire.'

'And they got away with it both times?' Charles asked.

'They did,' said Garoni. 'But they are not, on the whole, an efficient group. They have a propensity towards collective suicide. They use explosives and frequently manage to blow themselves up—' the trace of a smile crossed his face. 'Only about six weeks ago a bomb exploded in one of their hideouts. It killed Vitaliano Principe, one of the leading Nappista, and it seriously wounded his friend, Alfredo Papale, who will not be involving himself with any terrorist activities for a long time.

'Their leaders, Maria Pia Vianale, Franca Salerno and Silvio Nuscio recently distributed millions of counterfeit banknotes. They were easily traceable. It seems that someone may have persuaded them the notes were genuine or at least passable. We have already arrested many of their members. If it's any consolation we are confident that the end of 1975 will see the end of NAP.'

'And in the meantime?' Charles asked.

'In the meantime I would suggest that you try to raise the ransom money. I appreciate it is a great deal, but sometimes it is possible to bargain with these terrorists. Maybe we can, particularly with NAP, who are not as professional as the Red Brigades.'

'In other words you think everyone is going to have to pay?' Kate asked.

'It is rarely that people do not have to pay in kidnapping cases in Italy,' Inspector Garoni said. 'Kidnapping has become the Italian crime. And make no mistake – they will kill if they do not get what they demand.'

'Kill children!' Kate said. 'I thought Italians loved children.'

'These are hardly little children,' Garoni said defensively. 'Nor are you dealing with ordinary Italians. You are dealing with terrorists. Terrorists anywhere in the world are a race apart.'

It was the truth. Kate made a helpless little gesture.

'Is there nothing else that we can do?' Charles Dennison asked.

'Please keep me informed of everything that happens. I would suggest that if it is possible you all move into the villa at Parioli. It seems that is where NAP have decided to make contact with you. We will put a man permanently on duty in the house. We will also make sure there is another telephone installed so that the one on which the kidnappers may call you is free at all times. We will attach a tape-recording machine to the telephone. Other than that there is little we can do except wait until they make contact. We will do nothing that could endanger your children's lives, I can assure you of that.'

'Thank you,' Charles said. 'I speak for everyone in this room when I say that getting them back safely is all that matters.'

Ingrid shifted in her chair. She had been sitting stock still. 'Is he suggesting that you should all move into the villa?'

'Right,' Charles said.

'That would be no problem,' she said. 'It's quite big enough. And I'd be glad of the company.'

'I think that goes for all of us,' Eileen Elliot said. 'I couldn't stay in that *pension*. I'd go mad.'

'Will you and Paul come too?' Ingrid asked Kate. 'It'll be easier for working, and Paul will create his usual oasis of calm. We'll need that.'

'I'm not feeling very calm,' Paul said. 'But if you've room . . .'

The magistrate was speaking rapidly to Garoni, who nodded and turned back to Charles.

'I think we have done all that is possible for today,' he said. 'Please rest assured we will do our best to find your children, and that we shall keep in touch with you at all times.'

'And much good that looks like being,' Charles muttered in English. But he half bowed to both the magistrate and Garoni, proffered thanks on behalf of the group, and then led the way out of the room.

Disconsolate, they walked down the stairs, out into the street below, and stood disorientated, aimless on the pavement, uncertain of what to do next.

'Let's all go back to Parioli now,' Paul said in officer's tones, 'and work out some kind of campaign.'

Charles Dennison agreed. 'A good idea.' he said. 'We must decide how to deal with this.'

'Surely only the police can deal with it,' Alex Elliot said belligerently. It seemed to Kate that Frances' father had lost weight even in the short time since he arrived. His self-important puffed-up air which was the first thing she had noticed about him had vanished. His eyes were set deep in his head, and his hands twitched nervously at a newspaper which headlined the news of the kidnappings.

Of course,' Dennison said, his voice patient. 'But we have things to discuss. The ransoms . . .'

'Standing on the street corner is no place,' Paul said firmly. 'Mr Dennison, if you'll organize a taxi for yourself, Michael Bolt and Ingrid, Kate and I will take Mr and Mrs Elliot with us.'

The life of the city, noisy, hard and uncaring, went on around the group as the two men went to look for a taxi rank. It was getting warmer, and standing silent on the corner, Michael Bolt surreptitiously wiped his wide brow. He was bored and almost disinterested, Kate thought, and making no attempt to hide that he was twitching to get away from all this unpleasantness. He reinforced all her prejudices about the acting profession. Did he care a damn about Jenny, she wondered? He kept muttering that he must leave for tomorrow's performance. He couldn't stay away long. His public . . . his management . . . Kate longed to ask about his daughter.

Ingrid looked as if she was in a state of shock. Her age was showing, her eyes black-rimmed, her cheeks sunken. She seemed to have taken the kidnappings harder than the other parents. And it was a genuine distress, Kate decided. No acting involved. Monique was at her side, her face as expressionless as always and she had not spoken once. Now she was holding her employer's arm tightly.

The Elliots were reacting strangely too. Eileen, as they now called her, was upset, but not sufficiently so. The father was blazing with an anger barely hidden. He looked as if he wanted to hit someone, kill someone – preferably, Kate thought, his wife. He was distressed as well as angry, as his haggard face showed. He had cut himself shaving, and the bloodstained piece of tissue paper still clung to his fat cheek, incongruous above the silk shirt, silk tie and heavy silk suit. It was probably the first time in his life he had let himself be seen to such disadvantage.

There was no conversation on the noisy ride back to Parioli. Alex Elliot stared straight ahead, ignoring Rome. Eileen

125

Elliot, her face set, looked out at the Via Flaminia as if it were of enormous interest. Paul and Kate tried to make conversation, failed, and abandoned the project. It was a relief when the taxi stopped outside the large terracotta villa, set around with cyprus trees.

Inside, the formal sitting room was easily large enough to take everyone. Kate settled herself on a hard-backed chair near the window to detach herself from the main group, and Paul, with the same thought that this was not entirely his business, sat near her. Then they waited to see what would happen.

Quite naturally and without fuss, Charles Dennison took control. He was very Harvard and Ivy League in his grey suit with a conservative shirt and tie. The archetypal diplomat, his voice measured, almost ponderous, and with just a faint trace of the Southern States softening the Washington hardness. Tall and thin with greying fair hair and grey eyes, he was a similar physical type to Michael Bolt but with a steeliness and strength that Bolt came nowhere near to possessing. Charles Dennison was very much a bloke, Kate decided, in spite of his narrow shoulders, lean body and faintly anxious maner. It was as well he was here, if only for the fact he spoke such good Italian.

'It is the ransom we must discuss,' he said. He was standing while the others sat, his back to an ornately carved mantelpiece, his hands, without anything to hold, still easy. 'The half a million for your daughter, sir—' he looked at Michael Bolt. 'Is this a possibility?'

'Not from me,' Michael said, on a note of alarm. 'But her mother . . .'

The diplomat showed. Without a flicker, Charles turned to Ingrid.

You have this money?' he asked. 'Forgive me, but this is no time for the niceties.'

'Someone wants to buy my life story for half that money. It said so in the Rome papers,' Ingrid said, her voice not quite steady. 'Maybe that's what gave them the idea. Kate is writing it. But we haven't even begun. I have things I can sell. But not enough. And they want the money so quickly.'

'We all want to release our daughters quickly,' Alex Elliot said. 'But I don't have £250,000. If I sold the house and the

126

business . . . well, I could raise it . . . but it'll take time. There's a bank loan already on my firm . . .'

'Perhaps Inspector Garoni will get them back safely,' Eileen said from her seat in the room's most comfortable chair.

'I think we have to be prepared to pay,' Charles said quietly. 'We must act on the assumption that we are going to have to pay. If the police succeed, we shall be fortunate. We may be fortunate to get our daughters back at all.'

Alex Elliot sunk his head into his hands, hiding tears.

We should never have let her go,' he said, his voice muffled. 'Never.' He looked up, and the anger was suddenly released. 'It was you,' he said, shouting at his wife. 'You and your God-damn ambitions. I should never have let it happen. I knew it was wrong.'

She looked at him coolly, her hands folded in her lap.

'You only let us come so you could be alone with your mistress. You are as much to blame. It must have been a difficult decision, your mistress or your darling daughter.'

The room had taken on the atmosphere of an encounter group.

'Stop it,' Charles said firmly. 'It may be that we all let our children come here for the wrong reasons. I know I did. But it's done now. We must get them back safely. Let me explain *my* position. I have very little money. My ex-wife, Bobbie Jean's mother, is an alcoholic. I have paid her vast amounts in alimony for many years, and I have also paid for many expensive and useless treatments. She was Bobbie's mother,' he said, as if explaining the reasons to himself. 'The sum £250,000 is beyond me. My salary is high, but it has always been spent. I shall have to appeal to my government.'

'Do you have a house you can sell?' Alex asked.

'A modest one in Georgia. I could perhaps get a loan on it, but not sufficient.'

'It's the time limit,' Ingrid said. She brushed her hand through her short blonde hair distractedly. 'And do we really have to get all the money together before they'll release any of the girls?'

'One million pounds in used notes, the amount to be reckoned on the interest rates of the day,' Charles said. 'They are very businesslike kidnappers, in spite of the inspector's doubts.'

'I wonder why not lire?' Kate said suddenly. 'Are they anything to do with foreign terrorist groups?'

'Christ, I hope not,' Alex said. 'It must just be that they want a hard currency. From what I've seen here they'd need a lorry to take that much money in Italian lire.'

'True,' Paul said.

'Paul, do you think the publishers would give me the money for the book now?' Ingrid asked. 'And can we get any more?'

He hesitated.

'They might advance the lot. They'd look pretty unfeeling if they wouldn't. But on the other hand, I doubt if they'll do anything without something on paper. You see, Ingrid, from their point of view, once they've paid you, you could renege, and it could turn out to be the tamest book ever, worth the usual £5,000. The big money of course comes from the newspaper. That's different. With this new situation going on, they'll probably pay even more, and give you a lump sum down for exclusive rights on what's happening now. But they'll want something on paper too.'

Ingrid had lit a cigarette and was pulling on it nervously.

'I didn't really listen before to what it was all about. I just heard the figure. It sounded like such a lot, Paul. Now it doesn't sound enough. What is the situation?'

'The Sunday newspaper is paying you £150,000 for the exclusive newspaper rights. This means that for that sum they can use the material in their Australian and American papers. The publisher is putting up the other £100,000 for worldwide book rights. We only have magazine rights left. I can try to sell those quickly.'

'So you have little problems other than time, Miss Pallia,' Eileen Elliot said.

'She has the same problem as anyone of us,' Charles Dennison said. 'If one of us can't raise the money, all our children are in jeopardy.'

'I hate to say this, it sounds so ghoulish,' Kate said tentatively, 'but you could probably make a bit of cash by selling your stories exclusively to one newspaper or another. You should let Paul handle it for you. He won't want any commission, will you, Paul – and he'll get you as much as possible. It won't be anywhere near the amount you need, but it'll be something.'

'That might be difficult for me,' Charles Dennison said.

'I can see that, but you could perhaps sign for Bobbie Jean to sell her story on her release. You'll find the English press will be here in droves any minute now. It must be a big story at home. And they'll be bargaining.'

Charles Dennison looked as if he loathed the idea, but said: 'All right. Let's be practical, how much do you think they'll pay?'

'With luck you should all get about £15,000.' Kate said. 'More, if you refuse to speak to any press person from any country without being paid something.'

There was a long silence.

'It's a long way off target,' Alex said. He turned to Charles. 'You really think we're going to have to pay up?'

'It's Italy, not England. I think we shall have to.'

'I'll fly back tonight and start trying to raise money,' Alex said. 'There's nothing else to be done.'

'And in that case,' Kate said briskly, 'I think that you and I ought to start working full pelt, Ingrid.'

'Anything,' Ingrid said. She turned to Michael Bolt who had settled himself as far away from the main group as possible and who sat, smoking, staring at the smoke.

'Michael – couldn't you raise anything on the house in the Boltons? You know I've no property of my own. And you must have some cash.'

'Sell your jewellery and your furs, dear,' he said. 'I am not selling my home or depleting my bank balance.' He stared at her defiantly, his expression implacable. 'The Italian police will get them back. It'll all turn out to be a publicity stunt of Bellino's.'

The group looked at him in varying degrees of astonishment. 'You shit!' Paul said softly.

'Oh, don't all look like that,' he said pettishly. 'And don't call me a shit, Paul. After all, none of you would sell your home for someone who wasn't your daughter, now, would you?' He stubbed his cigarette out with a vicious wrist movement. 'I really must get myself back to London. I've got my living to earn,' he said. 'Let me know what happens, Ingrid.'

He rose to his feet, gave the room a casual wave and moved towards the door.

'Michael.' Paul's voice was dangerous, and the actor recoiled at the suppressed anger fizzing from Paul's big body. 'Michael – it's not going to read well in the papers.'

'Nor is the real truth about Ingrid.'

'And nor,' Ingrid said wearily, 'is the real truth about you.'

'I don't think any of us would dare, ducky,' he said. 'See you in London.'

After the door closed behind him Ingrid stared at Paul helplessly. 'The bitch of it is,' she said, 'he is her father.'

'I'm going to tell you the truth about Michael,' Ingrid said. She was unaware that the cigarette between her fingers had nearly burned down to the filter. Kate got up and took an ashtray to where she sat in the big chair by the ornate fireplace. She took the cigarette and stubbed it out. Ingrid didn't seem to notice.

They were alone in the drawing room. The others had gone back to their hotels and pensions to pack and return. Paul was making the move for himself and Kate.

The room was very quiet. The tape recorder was on, and Kate waited without speaking for Ingrid to begin to talk.

'Michael has to be the biggest shit since Caligula,' Ingrid said bitterly. 'You know he's mean. Everyone knows he's mean, but he's meaner than anyone could imagine. Christ, you can't get meaner than denying your own child. I don't care. I'm going to tell it all, whatever he does.'

She lit herself another cigarette with a gold Dunhill lighter, balanced it in her hand and asked ruefully: 'How much do you think I'd get for this?' She sighed and put the lighter back in her small handbag. 'Anyway, I met Michael when I was a kid. He was a kid too. It was in Los Angeles and we were both trying to get the same agent to represent us. We met in this waiting room somewhere on Wilshire Boulevard. Michael had the first appointment, and when I came out after mine he was waiting for me. I think at first he just wanted to know whether I'd had any more luck than he had. I hadn't. We'd both been turned down and we were both broke so we went and had a cup of coffee and shared a Danish and commiserated with each other.

'The only difference was I had a pad.' She hesitated. 'I used to earn the odd bit of money modelling and could just about keep a roof over my head. Michael had been chucked out of his room that morning for not paying the rent. It was a typical Hollywood story of those days. There weren't too many of us who got picked up in drug stores and catapulted into instant fame and fortune.'

'What year was this?' Kate asked.

Ingrid's blue eyes looked at the ceiling. 'Oh, I don't know. I'll work it out later. Anyway to cut a long story short, I took him in with me. I fancied him a lot. He was marvellously good looking as a young man. Well, you know. You must have seen pictures.'

'There was only the one bed – and it was quite big enough for the two of us, but he still suggested he slept on the floor. After a night of that, he decided he would share my bed. And he didn't do a goddamn thing. He'd just lay there, stretched out, away from me, carefully not touching me. That went on for a week. It was just about the most frustrating experience of my life. I really wanted him.

'Anyway, after seven days of this, with both of us still trying to get work and getting nowhere, and me not even able to get modelling, I decided we both needed a little comfort. I took that matter into my own hands, as one might say. I just put my arm over him and started fondling him. He responded. He liked it. He finally came, but he didn't want to touch me at all.

'The next night I did the same thing. He seemed to enjoy it, but I wasn't getting much back, and neither of us even mentioned what had happened the next day.

'The third night, I made it. He fucked me. It took a while and it was hard work, but he made it. He was capable of it – though not what you'd call terrific. I was inexperienced enough in those days to be satisfied. We went on making it for about five weeks, and then he stopped. He told me women weren't really his scene even though he loved me. By then I was pregnant. So it was all a bit of a shock, even though I'd suspected.' She paused. 'The odd thing was he didn't want me to get rid of the baby, and he offered to marry me. I was still crazy about him so I agreed. I really thought I could turn him on again eventually. Boy – I'll never make that mistake again!'

'He believed then that Jenny was his?' Kate asked.

'Yes.'

'What made him change his mind?'

'That was after.'

'After what?'

Ingrid's voice took on that too precise note that Kate had learned meant she was lying.

'After it suited him not to be responsible. After he began to get well known and other things happened.'

'When you say women weren't his scene do you mean he was – sorry, is – queer?'

'As a clockwork orange. Does that surprise you?'

'Not a lot,' Kate said. 'Particularly after the performance this morning. He lost control and it showed.'

'Yes,' Ingrid said bitterly, 'he doesn't often let it show. He didn't let it show with me, either. He said he wanted a normal life. I suppose it suited him. He was installed in my place. I went back to modelling when I could and still tried for film work. When I got too pregnant to work a small part in a film came his way, and he started to pay the rent. He didn't speak any more about marrying me, but as he'd made me keep the baby I decided he was going to have to. He absolutely refused to do it when I was so pregnant looking. In fact, Jenny was about two months old when he did finally marry me, by which time I'd decided motherhood wasn't for me. He wasn't too keen on fatherhood either, with the baby in one room, the landlady complaining about the crying, and one of us having to stay home with her all the time. We decided to foster her. The local priest found us an Italian family who were hard up and mad about bambini and we left her there.'

'And what were the other things that happened that made him believe she wasn't his?' Kate asked, convinced something was being omitted from the story.

Ingrid lit another cigarette from the stub of the last one. She took her time over it and then said: 'Well, he was getting quite steady work, and I was earning a bit. I kept us for a month or two after Jenny went to be fostered when his work petered out, but after that things seemed to take off for him.

'We moved to a better place, and he was very much the rising actor with the pretty young wife. That suited him fine. It kept him out of trouble with the studios. In those days, you remember, all the queers had to be dated up with some starlet or another to make them look macho and available.

'I went along with it, because his success started mine. I began to get the odd job because I was Mrs Bolt. What the public didn't know was that back at the ranch Mrs Bolt slept in one bedroom and Mr Bolt slept in another. He got so he couldn't bear to touch me. But he'd discovered that with me as a smoke screen he could get away with his own thing.'

'And what was that?' Kate asked.

'SM,' Ingrid said, laconically. 'I came home one day just a fraction too early. There were a couple of leather-clad louts in our living room, swaggering, laughing at me. They had their filthy-booted feet on my sofa, and they were drinking my booze. I told them to get out. Michael said if I didn't like it I could get out. They were his friends.

'I had a pretty good idea what was going on, but I wanted to make sure. I came home even earlier. They were in his bedroom – these two greasy yobos. Whatever they'd been doing, they'd finished doing it. Michael was lying on his bed, on his stomach, his bottom and his back covered in weals. They'd been beating him. I can still see those red weals on his skin. He's very fair, and they looked like streaks of bright scarlet lipstick scrawled there. He liked it. When I came into the room one boy was standing with a birch, and the other one was pulling on his leather trousers. Michael was furious I'd appeared. We had a screaming row after the louts had gone. I remember clawing his face, and his expression said "more! more!" Then I knew all this wasn't for me. Anyway, I'm a sexy lady,' she added defiantly. 'I wasn't getting anything for myself having to act the feminine role in the rising young Hollywood couple. I was having to play it straight – not that it occured to me to do anything clse those days.

'So, we made an agreement. We got a bigger apartment and he had his life and I had mine until we were both established enough to regretfully announce our mariage was over. It lasted about five years.'

'And Jenny?' Kate asked.

'I used to go and see her all the time. She was such a tiny child. I smoked a lot when I was pregnant – maybe that had something to do with it. Anyway, when she got to be five, Michael and I decided it would be better if she was three and a half – she did actually look that young. And then we brought her home. We could afford a nanny so it was all right. And then just after we split, and I had to start boarding her out again so I could work. Michael had to pay me alimony, of course, but it was always like getting blood out of a stone. Still is,' she added.

'Why did you make her younger?' Kate's voice was totally impersonal.

'Oh, come on! I'd have been a schoolgirl mother,' Ingrid said. 'Listen I'm older than I say but I don't want my age mentioned in the book anywhere. In fact. I didn't really mean to tell you about Jenny's age. I don't really want Jenny mentioned if we can avoid it.'

'Frankly,' Kate said, her voice cool, 'there's not too much of what you've just told me we can mention either. Michael Bolt's sex life would make fascinating reading, but it would fascinate his lawyers too.'

'You mean you can't print it?'

'I think that the writs would be falling like hailstones,' Kate said crisply. 'But I still don't understand why he decided to disown Jenny.'

'I told you.' Ingrid sounded impatient. 'It didn't suit him to acknowledge her.'

'At what stage was this?'

Ingrid thought. 'Pretty early on.'

'Before she was born? After?'

'I can't remember. Anyway, if we can't print it, what's the point?'

'Oh, we can print that,' Kate said cheerfully. 'It's only his funny little ways in bed that won't do. Did he pay child support for Jenny?'

'Yes.'

'He never publicly disputed she was his then?'

'No. It was a bit more smoke screen,' Ingrid looked as if she wished she had never started the conversation. 'It was only to me, privately – and maybe to his lovers for all I know – that he said he didn't believe she was his. But she is. Totally his.'

Kate wondered about the 'totally' and said so.

'Well, because there wasn't anyone else it could have been. No one at all,' Ingrid said. She got up abruptly, looking as if she might walk out of the room. 'It's maddening. He gets away with murder. Everything I do gets found out. I don't want to talk about it any more.' She sounded like a petulant schoolgirl.

'OK,' Kate said. It was time to drop the subject. 'Tell me what happened when you were living this open marriage. How did you manage that?'

'Well, my first lover—' Ingrid began eagerly, off on her ego trip. Kate let the tape do the listening while she wondered to herself exactly what it was that Ingrid had left out. There was a great gaping gap. What sort of modelling was it that Ingrid had earned her living by at that time? She made a small bet with herself that Ingrid had been on the game. It seemed the most likely solution. But would she ever admit to it? And if she did, would it add or subtract from the value of the story? That was the question.

The kidnapping was causing heartaches and headaches among more people than the immediate participants. Pedro Bellino in particular was busy having a nervous breakdown, torn between the problems of the money he had already spent and would have to go on spending on *Claudine At School* and the unbelievable publicity he was getting gratis for the venture. The newspapers world wide were running stories about his actresses and his film – actresses who at the moment were mising. He was torn as to whether or not to film around the three girls, as difficult as that might be. If he did begin shooting, would it look callous? Would the world boycott his film for lack of taste? His backers, all of whom had put up hard cash, were pressing him. Decisions, decisions! He decided to start work quietly, gloomily aware of how difficult it was to keep anything secret in Rome. He told himself that he could always plead that stopping production would be jeopardizing other actors' and technicians' livelihoods.

The others at the storm centre were equally disturbed but for better reasons. Alex Elliot had returned to England to attempt to raise the ransom for his daughter. The moves from the others' various hotels and pensions had been quickly made, stage-managed by Paul. The Parioli villa was quite large enough to hold everyone. Paul and Kate had taken two attic rooms for privacy, both with a spectacular view of the city below – the city where somewhere the three girls might be hidden. Eileen Elliot and Charles Dennison, both of whom had stayed in Rome, had guest suites. Eileen had remained in Rome because she could not think of anything else to do. Charles was needed for his ability to speak the language, and because he was the obvious one to deal with both the police and the kidnappers when the contact was made.

For two days there had been silence. It had been four days since the girls had been taken, five days since they arrived in Rome. To everyone involved, it felt like five years.

The police were trying their best but there was little they could do. They had attempted to round up a couple of the Nuclei Armati Proletari and had come to the conclusion that whoever had snatched the girls was not in Rome. 'Someone from outside,' Garoni had told Charles. 'It makes it more difficult. But they'll make a mistake. They're bound to.'

Charles said to Paul that he dreaded them making a mistake even more than having to find the ransoms.

'When terrorists make mistakes it can be lethal for everyone,' he said.

Paul had been appointed to cope with the hoards of journalists who had camped in rotas outside the villa. The world newspapers were snatching every crumb of the story, concentrating mostly on Jenny. He was beginning to be anxious about getting to Bavaria to collect Madeleine. He knew it had to be done, but he hated to leave the situation where he was also needed. He and Kate had seen little of each other. Their first night in the villa she had sat up until four in the morning transcribing tapes from the day's interviews with Ingrid. She had related the story of Michael's particular perversion to Paul

136

with gusto and told him that she did not want a percentage for her work unless by some miracle the ransoms did not have to be paid. He had come to the same decision.

'But don't kill yourself working,' he protested.

'Listen,' she said, 'if I'm not getting paid I want to finish it quickly, don't I?'

He looked at her, smiled, shook his head and leaned to kiss her.

'Liar,' he said fondly.

'It's for Jenny – not her!' she said.

It was one o'clock in the morning and Kate in her dressing gown had padded bare-footed into his bedroom, announcing she had to sleep. He was sitting up in bed, waiting for her.

'Come on in,' he said, throwing back the covers, 'you need a cuddle.'

'I do, I do,' she said. 'Her voice on those tapes is beginning to drive me mad.'

'You don't like her any better?'

She was sliding down in the bed to lie alongside him in their familiar comfortable position, her head on his shoulder.

'Darling, she has slept with everyone famous in the Western hemisphere as far as I can see. Plus quite a few no one's ever heard of. Chapter and verse, I've had. Size of their equipment, how they did it first time, second time, last time. Zips are being unzipped all over the place, dresses falling in soft heaps of silk around her dainty little feet. And she's always in love. Every blooming time she's in love.' She mimicked Ingrid's faint accent: ' "I looked at him and I was in love." For Christ's sake, she's old enough to stop confusing love with good old-fashioned lust.'

'You didn't answer the question – you don't like her any better?'

She sighed into his shoulder.

'Well, she's really trying to cooperate, and she is worried sick about Jenny. I wouldn't have thought she'd care, but she does.'

'She hasn't talked about Jenny yet? Or the early days?'

'No. I haven't pushed, I've got a feeling she'll come to it in her own good time.'

Her voice was drowsy, and his arm tightened around her.

'Go to sleep, sweetheart,' he said.

'I think I'm going to have to.' she said. 'What a waste of our time, my darling . . . maybe in the morning . . .'

And her voice trailed away into sleep.

They never saw the man with the glittering eyes and the red moustache. It was always Claudio who came in with their food, took Sammy away and presumably fed him, as Sammy seemed quite content. They all called the boy Claudio now. He was their only contact with the outside world and they welcomed his arrivals. But he would only speak in monosyllables. They could not persuade him to talk to them. The food they were given was adequate and they felt very little fear. Boredom was the basic ingredient of their emotions. After the first full day, which had seemed endless, they had the impression that they had been in the big room much longer. They walked around, their feet clacking on the bare tiles, as Frances insisted they must have some exercise, they washed out their underwear and hung it by the barred window to dry, they began to teach Frances Italian, and they talked. There was nothing else to do.

It was at night in darkness with the street noises keeping them from sleep that the confidences began.

'It's my own fault I'm here,' Bobbie Jean said abruptly on the third night. 'Do you think it's a punishment?'

'For what?' Frances asked.

Well,' Bobbie Jean hesitated. 'I did it. With Bellino.'

'You did!' Frances' voice sounded no disapproval, only interest. 'What was it like?'

'Nasty and sort of nothing.'

'You didn't like it?'

'No.'

Jenny had been listening, laying flat on her back staring at the glitter of night light through the small window high in the ceiling where fredom was.

'He tried it with me,' she said.

'How did he do it?' Bobbie Jean said.

'Well, he didn't. He just tried. It was on Mustique last year. I had a stomach ache – a curse pain – and I'd gone to my room to bed. He came in and sat on the bed and he called me a poor

138

baby, and he started to rub my stomach. He said it would help. I quite liked it really, and then he started to get lower and lower and he suddenly picked up my nightie and put his fingers there . . .' She paused remembering her confusion of feelings as he touched her.

'What did you do?' Frances asked.

'I told him my father was coming up to see me, and he'd better go. He did. And after that I kept my bedroom door locked.'

'It wasn't like that with me,' Bobbie Jean said. 'I knew exactly what he was going to do. I didn't particularly want him to do it, but I did get the part in the film. That was why I did it. He had a train-set in his room at the Savoy, and we were playing with it on the floor. If the trains came off the track I had to give him a kiss. And it kind of went on from there. On cushions, on the floor. He put some jelly stuff in me,' she added, her voice indignant. 'It was messy. Yuck!'

'I've never done it,' Jenny said suddenly. 'You really didn't like it?'

'Well, it wasn't anything,' Bobbie Jean said. 'I don't know what all the fuss is about. It's just yucky.'

'Not if it's with someone you like,' Frances said. 'Then it's fabulous.'

'You've done it too,' Jenny said. 'And you're both so much younger than me.'

'Well, you've been locked up in a girls' school,' Frances pointed out. 'Not much opportunity.'

'I think my mother's put me off,' said Jenny. In the veiling darkness she felt the urge to tell what she had seen just before the man had threatened Sammy and taken her away. 'My mother's had masses of lovers. "This is your Uncle whatever" ' she mimicked. 'It's put me off. And then something terrible happened that day we arived in Rome—' Her voice faltered, the picture of the tangle of bodies a clear picture behind her eyes.

'What?' Frances urged.

'I got home,' she said slowly. 'I put my luggage in the hall, and there was a newspaper with the bit about us arriving in Rome in it. She knew I was coming home. She sent Verde with the Rolls. She had the newspaper. I thought she might be asleep and the house was so quiet and empty except for Sammy that I went looking for her. It was awful—' Tears were forcing themselves from her eyes, running down her cheeks and on to the bare mattress. 'She was lying on the bed and there were other people, all naked, all doing things to her and she was sort of moaning. One of them was her secretary, Monique. And there were some men. I don't know how many. It was disgusting. People are disgusting.'

'Wow!' Frances said. 'An orgy! Poor Jenny. What did you do?'

'I just shut the door ever so quietly and went for a walk with Sammy. And then that man appeared.'

There was a silence until Bobbie Jean said: 'It's funny, isn't it? What men are like. I'd never done it before, but I let Bellino because I wanted to be in the film. I've always got things I wanted by being kind of cute and provocative and playing the little girl. I never had to go that far before, though. I can get anything out of my daddy if I kiss him and hug him and sit on his lap. You know, I sometimes think he'd like to do what Bellino did. In fact, I know he'd like to do what Bellino did. But why when it's such a nothing?'

'It isn't. I keep telling you, it's super. I've done it lots of times,' Frances said.

'Who with?' Bobbie Jean asked.

'Well, there were two boys at school . . . older boys . . . My mother knew but she didn't care.'

'But what's it *like*?' Jenny pressed. She needed to hear it was idyllic, marvellous, romantic. She wanted details that added up to love.

'You'll find out,' Frances said cryptically.

Jenny said crossly: 'It's all right for you. Your family's normal. Not like ours.'

'My family!' Frances said. 'If you call having a mother who hates your guts and a father who hates her guts and who's got a mistress for a secretary normal, I suppose we are. And they both drink too much,' she added for good measure.

'Not much fun growing up, is it?' Bobbie Jean said mournfully. 'No fun at all.'

*

It was the morning after their fifth day of incarceration when Claudio began to talk to the girls and a small parcel arrived mysteriously at the villa in Parioli. Later Paul decided that someone must have posed as a journalist and joined the early morning assault on the door. But however it had arrived, there was the parcel.

'Better not touch it until the police come,' Charles instructed. 'They'll want to fingerprint it.'

There were no fingerprints, and Garoni himself straight from headquarters opened it in the formal drawing room, in a deathly hush and with an audience of eight, including his sergeant and Monique.

Inside the parcel was a cassette; an ordinary, innocuous cassette.

'Can someone get the tape recorder from the telephone?' Garoni asked, after it, too, had been dusted for fingerprints and none found.

'Use this,' Kate said. Her own small Sony was in her handbag and she took it out and handed it to the inspector.

'That's a neat little job,' he said approvingly. 'Is it efficient?'

'Very,' said Kate.' Play the tape and see.'

She showed him how to use the machine and once he pressed the replay button the voice they heard was speaking in rapid Italian. The tape had been re-recorded at a faster speed in an attempt to make the voice unrecognizable. It sounded like Donald Duck.

Kate, Dennison and the inspector listened intently. It was difficult to catch the words.

'What does it say?' Ingrid asked Charles when the inspector stopped it, her voice anxious.

'Roughly that the girls are safe, confirming they're being held by the Nuclei Armati Proletari,' he said. 'It goes on about the decadent classes, and says that soon we will be told where to bring the money if we want to see our children again. It adds they know we have been to the police, but if any harm comes to any one of their people they cannot answer for the safety of our children.'

'Their first mistake,' the inspector was saying with some satisfaction. 'If they think speeding the tape like that will disguise the voice, they are wrong. We just slow it again, and pronto! the voice is normal.'

He pressed the button to set the tape moving on. For a second or two there was only the gentle whirr of the spool turning, and then Bobbie Jean's voice came through clearly. She was saying: 'I did it. With Bellino. I knew exactly what he was going to do. I didn't particularly want him to do it, but I did get the part in the film. That was why I did it. He had a train-set in his room and we were playing with it on the floor. If the trains came off the track I had to give him a kiss. And it kind of went on from there. On cushions, on the floor. He put some jelly stuff in me.'

Charles' face had turned greeny white, and he sunk his head in his hands. His daughter's voice went remorselessly on.

'It's funny, isn't it? What men are like. I'd never done it before but I let Bellino because I wanted to be in the film. I've always got things by being kind of cute and provocative and playing the little girl. I never had to go that far before though. I can get anything out of my daddy if I kiss him and hug him and sit on his lap. You know, I know he'd like to do what Bellino did!'

'Oh, my God!' Dennison's face had turned scarlet and he looked round the room as if desperate for escape. All his diplomatic *sang froid* had disappeared. He was a man hot with embarrassment and self-loathing. Everyone in the room sat rock still, not looking at him, as the inspector said politely: 'Someone will have to translate for me, Mr Dennison.'

Charles made a strangled noise, and the tape clicked and then it was Jenny's voice: 'My mother's had masses of lovers. "This is your Uncle whatever." And something happened that day we arrived in Rome. She knew I was coming home. She sent Verde with the Rolls. I thought she might be asleep and the house was so quiet that I went looking for her. She was lying on the bed and there were other people, all naked, all doing things to her and she was sort of moaning. One of them was her secretary, Monique. And there were some men. I don't know how many.'

Ingrid was staring at the tape recorder as if it had hypnotized her. She was white, her hands clenched in her lap. Beside her,

142

Monique sat with her head so bowed that only the clear white parting in her dark hair showed.

'What does it say, *signor*?' the inspector was saying impatiently.

'Nothing.' Charles moved to switch off the machine, but he was too late. It clicked again and as Eileen gave a little sharp exclamation, Frances was speaking. 'It's super. I've done it lots of times. There were two boys at school. Older boys. My mother knew, but didn't care. My family normal? If you call having a mother who hates your guts and a father who hates her guts and who's got a mistress for a secretary normal, I suppose we are. And they both drink too much.'

'Oh, God help us! God help us!' Eileen was whimpering.

There was complete silence in the room as the tape wound on. Everyone stared at it; willing nothing more to happen. The inspector was silent, looking from one to another, his expression alert.

'Those tapes have been edited,' Paul said when the final click came. 'They could have said something quite different. It could all be out of context.'

'But it was true—' Eileen whispered. 'True.'

Charles' and Ingrid's expression confirmed what she had said.

'*Signor*, I must be told what has been on those tapes,' the inspector said quietly. 'It is evidence and may be important.'

'Inspector,' Kate said quickly, 'the tapes are very private and personal mesages from the girls to their parents. They speak of things that only their parents should know, in order for the identification, you understand.' Her Italian was deserting her in her haste to stop him taking the cassette. 'It would be an invasion of privacy if these tapes were to be heard by anyone else at all.'

His expression one of deep distrust, Garoni said: 'Will someone please tell me what is on the tape.'

Charles wiped his forehead.

'He wants to know if we will tell him what is on the tapes,' he said mechanically.

'We can't let him have them,' Ingrid said. The first shock over, Kate noted, all Ingrid's instincts of self-preservation were taking over.

143

'*Inspectori*, they are private,' Charles said.

'They are evidence,' Garoni said. 'I shall take them back to headquarters for translation.'

They watched him helplessly as he fiddled with the various buttons on the machine until he found the one that made the cassette spring out into his hand.

'It is evidence,' he said, as he went out of the door.

'Claudio,' Jenny was wheedling, her dark eyes spaniel-pleading, 'Claudio, get us a nightgown each. Please, Claudio. If we had a nightgown, we could wash our clothes. It's horrid sleeping in these clothes. *Could* you, do you think, Claudio?'

He looked uncertain.

'I'll try,' he said finally.

'Thank you, Claudio.' Now she was grave, as if sorry she had been so girlish. 'We would appreciate it.'

He came back quarter of an hour later with three nightgowns, one voluminous in a plastic bag. The girls giggled; Jenny and Bobbie Jean got into the tent-like one, two heads emerging rumpled from one neckline. Claudio was trying not to laugh.

'Claudio!' said Bobbie Jean. 'These nighties are damp. Where did you get them?'

'From off a clothes line,' he said sheepishly. 'I couldn't buy them. I had no money. And besides, he wouldn't have let me. You mustn't tell you have them.'

Jenny and Bobbie Jean were doing a ridiculous sand-dance under the white cotton folds.

'We won't tell, we promise,' Frances said.

'No, we won't,' Jenny said breathlessly, slipping out from under the gown. She moved across to where the boy stood near the door and kissed him on the cheek. 'Thank you, Claudio,' she said. 'You are very kind and we would have been frightened without you.'

He had turned bright scarlet, and without speaking he scuttled to the door and knocked to be let out. As he disappeared and the key turned again, Jenny was looking after him as if she did not want him to go.

•

An hour later a large Trastevere housewife who had been following the case of the kidnapped teenage actresses avidly in every edition of the papers noticed that some of her washing was missing, one of her nightgowns and two of her daughters'; all three were gone from the washing line above her ground-floor window.

She stood with pursed mouth, angry at their disappearance. Nothing else had been touched. She checked, reeling in the line. There was still one nightgown left. Her husband's shirts, all her bits and pieces of underwear and her daughters' things were still flying in a light breeze. She looked across to the bare wall opposite in her courtyard where her washing line ended its journey. It was deserted.

Why nightgowns, she wondered? And why only three?

Thoughtfully she went back into her apartment and put her hand on the telephone to ring the local police.

Then she decided No – it couldn't be! Just someone with a kink, she thought. A kink about women's nightgowns, she reasoned as she went to her kitchen to start preparing the family's supper.

Chapter Eight

No one could look another in the face in the big drawing room after the inspector had gone. Ingrid, making an exit worthy of Sarah Bernhardt, had announced she was going to her bedroom – the interview would take place there today. Silently, Kate had picked up her tape recorder and followed.

Paul muttered something distractedly about warning Bellino what had happened. 'Over my dead body,' said Charles Dennison, but Paul left the room looking as if he would make his own decisions.

Monique had melted away; the sergeant returned to his

post in the hall. Eileen and Charles were left. They stood awkwardly, avoiding each other's eyes.

'I want to kill myself,' Eileen finally muttered, half to herself, half to him.

'I want to kill Bellino,' Charles said grimly. 'And I may.' He moved to take her arm. 'Here,' he said kindly. 'Sit down. Stop blaming yourself. You came out of that pretty lightly compared to the rest of us.'

'None of you dislike your own child. Hate her guts, as Frances put it.'

'I've never thought it obligatory to like any relative, including a child,' Charles said. 'You've never done anything to harm her. That's the important thing.'

She sat where he put her and stared hopelessly into space.

'Alex was right. I was just trying to make her live out my own ambitions. We'll all be ruined for it. I wanted to be an actress. I gave it up when I married. I had to get married,' she said bitterly. 'Alex still throws it up at me. It spoilt both our lives. We've never been happy. He's never loved me. I've always blamed her for everything, but her father adores her. I suppose I'm jealous.'

She was crying, looking distractedly around for her handbag.

'Here—' Charles handed her a very clean white handkerchief. 'Don't cry. It's not going to help.'

'It's helping me,' she sniffed. 'I haven't cried for years.'

He stood looking down at her gravely. 'All men lead lives of quiet desperation,' he said softly to himself.

'Women too,' she said, looking up. 'Can you imagine the humiliation of your husband having a public affair? An affair that even your child knows about?'

'Oh, yes,' he said. 'I can imagine that. My wife had quite a few. She was often drunken publicly as well. Blamed me for it all.'

'It's different for men,' she said. 'They can escape. They're harder.'

'It's not at all different for men,' he told her. 'Women never believe that men feel emotional pain. I assure you that men hurt just as much as women. You hurt right now. So do I. What my daughter said was true. I have had what you might

146

call carnal thoughts about her. She knew it. She played on it. My daughter is a beautiful little opportunist. Sexually aware and probably as cold as charity. But I love her to distraction, and I shall do anything to get her safely home again. Whatever she's done, and whatever is happening to her now, she is still only a child. She is fifteen years old. The child is still close to the surface under all her attempted sophistication. But I don't think she's ever been truly innocent,' he added, his voice trailing away.

'I don't even know Frances,' Eileen said. 'I have no idea at all what goes on in her head, what she really wants. I don't know who she is, and she's my daughter. I suppose that's because I've never cared for her enough.'

She looked up at him, her large blue eyes brimming with tears. Her mascara was trickling down her cheeks, her customary steel-helmet of hair in disarray. She was wearing a pair of plain black trousers and a black sweater. Even with her eyes swollen, her nose pink, she looked like a human, breathing crying woman – and not the marionette she had always appeared.

'Listen,' he said on impulse, 'nothing's going to happen until they tell us where to bring the money. I'm waiting to hear from the State Department; you're waiting to hear from your husband. This is the third day we've been in this house without a sight of the world outside. I think we should go out and have some lunch.'

She looked surprised, then she hesitated. 'I can't. Suppose anything happened?'

'I don't think anything is going to happen today. The deadline for the money isn't reached, and they're going to keep us on a string for a long while yet. That's terrorists' technique.'

'I'll have to change. I can't go out like this.' Her voice was doubtful.

'Don't change,' he said quickly. 'You look great. Really you do. Just touch up your mascara. Don't do a thing more.'

She looked at him oddly.

'Are you sure you want to go with me?' she said.

'Sure. I wouldn't have asked you if I didn't, now would I?' he said.

'I shan't be good company.'

'Nor I. We'll be bad company together.'

He wasn't really certain why he was urging this woman to join him. He had disliked her on sight; decided she was pretentious and probably had a common little mind under the prissy exterior. But now they were in the same boat, sharing the same problem. It had given them something in common. She was someone he could talk to who would understand and he found himself in need of company; some company, any company that would make it easier to squash down the fear that had settled somewhere in his guts.

'Where shall we go?' she asked.

'I don't know. We'll have to get a taxi wherever. There's nowhere round here. I know – if we have to get a taxi, I'll take you to an old favourite of mine. Sabatini's in Trastevere on the other side of the river.'

'Is it far?' she asked.

'Nowhere's far in Rome,' he told her. 'Go and fix your mascara.'

When she came back downstairs the little Fiat taxi was waiting and he gave thanks that she hadn't changed into one of her more awful outfits. She had stayed in the black pants and sweater but added a brightly coloured scarf. He suddenly realized he would have been embarrassed to have gone into Sabatini's with her in her usual style of dress. Even in this situation he could not lose his diplomat's sense of what was *comme il faut*.

'Will I do?' she asked.

'Very well,' he told her. 'Come on, the taxi's waiting.'

His welcome at the restaurant left him choked with emotions. Sabatini was delighted to see him, and genuinely concerned about Bobbie Jean.

'We read it in the papers and saw it on the television, of course, Signor Dennison. Our thoughts have been with you and your daughter. Let us hope she is soon restored to you,' he said courteously. 'And let us try to give you and the *signora* a small respite from your problems.'

He seated them in a quiet corner and, when they had ordered, Eileen said: 'I just wish I understood what it's really all

148

about. It's so frustrating not to speak the language when things are being explained. I couldn't grasp what the inspector was saying, and the translation didn't seem adequate. Could you bear to explain it to me again?'

'I'll try,' Charles said. 'But Italian politics are pretty complicated, and I can't tell you much about these NAP people. They didn't exist when I was in Rome. I left in 1970, though I did see the beginning of what the Italians call the strategy of tension. It started in 1969 with extreme right-wing groups practising intimidation and the odd act of terrorism. And the left wing had also got itself into full flood after the 1968 French student revolution. Do you remember about that?'

'Vaguely,' she said. 'Didn't they pull up paving stones and things?'

He half smiled, thinking explaining any political background to Eileen Elliot would not be easy, but at least both their minds were occupied and they had something positive to talk about. 'That's right,' he said, 'and that all led to the birth of student-backed movements to the left of the Communist party in Italy. One of those was Lotta Continua – it means "permanent struggle" – which the inspector said our NAP had broken away from.'

'So they are Communists who've got Frances?' she asked.

'Much further left than the average Italian Communist,' he said. 'You have to remember that the Communists have always been a very strong factor in politics here. They always take a hefty proportion of the vote. Sometimes they win. People say this country is ungovernable, but it's been my experience that the Italians are very good at looking after themselves and governing themselves even in situations of emergency. The national temperament thrives on muddle and confusion. At the moment, the Christian Democrats and the Communist party are working towards what they call a "historic compromise". This alliance has made the far left even more threatening, it's annoyed the far right and it seems that there has been a sort of polarization between the extreme right and the extreme left.'

She was listening intently, and he was pretty sure she didn't understand a word he was saying. But he ploughed on. 'Mind you, the government seems pretty stable at this time. Aldo Moro has been leading a coalition of Christian Democrats and Republicans since December of last year, and they seem to be holding their own – unusual for Italian governments. They're inclined to fall like confetti at a wedding.' She nodded. He'd struck on something she'd heard about. 'Anyway, while I was here the roots of this left-wing terrorism were being planted in student movements which developed at universities all over Italy. In the last two years I was in Rome there were continual riots and demonstrations and a new left which contested the Communist party on its own territory was born. Lotta Continua was one of the groups. Not the Red Brigades. They didn't get going until 1971 after I'd been posted to London.

'The Red Brigades do a lot of kidnapping too. Last year they kidnapped a judge. They didn't want money. They see themselves as ideological purists. They're in a state of disarray at present, but their leader has just escaped from prison, so they could be back in business any minute now. I'm afraid our girls came to Rome at a time of maximum uncertainty when political kidnapping is the "in" thing.'

She had been picking at the food on her plate while he talked but he was pleased to see that she had eaten a little. None of them had been eating very much for the last two days and he was having to force himself to swallow the Roman artichokes that he had chosen as his first course.

'What do you think their chances are?' she asked.

'Pretty good,' he said, making his voice cheerful. It seems that NAP haven't any record of killings – except themselves. And anyway, somehow we'll get the money together.'

'It's the end of Alex and me,' she said, as if talking to herself. 'He'll never forgive me. He'll have lost everything he's built up over the years and I put Frances into this terrible danger. Our lives will never be the same.'

'None of our lives will ever be the same again,' he said. 'But from the sound of it, when Frances is safe again, yours could even change for the better if you've been so unhappy.'

'And yours?'

'Mine?' He sighed and shook his head. 'God knows.'

The *padrone* refused to accept money when Charles asked

for the *conto*, saying he hoped that the meal had helped to take their minds off their troubles. Charles felt a curious reluctance to go back to the gloomy villa and as they came out into the sunlit *piazza* he said: 'Shall we walk back to the river?'

'If you like,' she said. They had both stopped to look at the serene square, a fountain in the centre. 'What's that?' she asked, pointing to the building opposite.

'It's a church – the Santa Maria di Trastevere. It's supposed to be the oldest in Rome.'

'I think I'd like to go to St Peter's and light a candle for the girls,' she said slowly.

'Are you a Catholic?' he asked.

'No, but lighting a candle couldn't do any harm.'

He laughed shortly.

'St Peter's isn't too well endowed for simple things like lighting candles,' he told her. 'You'd be better in a little church – like that one. They say that oil gushed from the ground where the Santa Maria stands to presage the birth of Christ. Go and light your candle in there.'

'You're not coming?'

'No. I'll wait for you here.'

She smiled at him and went, her wedge-heeled shoes clicking on the uneven pavements of the *piazza.*

As he stood waiting for her, standing by the fountain and watching the people drink at the square's open-air café, he wondered again what had made him take her out. And he wondered where in this noisy, shabby city of monuments and fast moving people were their daughters? He was certain they were in Rome for no reason he could have explained. Rome had always seemed a small town to him; now it seemed frighteningly big.

Eileen was coming back towards him, looking calmer than she had for days. She smiled again, and he noted that her mouth lifted from its usual half-sad, half-cynical downward droop and she looked much younger. He'd always assumed she was nearly forty. Now he saw that she was probably nowhere near that.

'All right?' he asked her.

'All right,' she said.

151

He began to lead her through the back alley that would take them on to the Ponte Sista, and on impulse where the roads were cobbled and difficult he took her arm.

She looked at him, surprised, and then leaned gently against him. And he thought he heard a soft sigh.

'How old are you, Claudio?' Jenny asked. They were sitting with their backs to the wall, near the door, the tiles cold under them. It was the furthest they could get from where Bobbie Jean and Frances sat on the mattresses near the barred window. Bobbie Jean was patiently telling the days of the week to Frances: '*Domenica, lunedì, martedì, mercoledì . . .*' and Frances was repeating them after her.

They had already done the numbers, the months, and all the pleases and thank yous and a lot of declining of verbs. Frances was a willing pupil. There was nothing else to do.

'Nearly eighteen,' he said. 'How old are you?'

'Nearly seventeen.'

He looked at her gravely. He hardly ever smiled, she decided. She might try to make him smile.

'I thought you were younger at first.'

'Everyone does,' she sighed. 'I don't expect I'll grow much any more. I'm not even five foot. You're lucky – you're tall.'

'It upset me that you were so small,' he said, his eyes still on her face. 'I thought you were just a little girl.'

'Why did it upset you?' she asked.

'Because I did not join the Cause to make war on little girls,' he said flatly. 'The others were different. They looked older. And besides – we were told . . .' he stopped.

'What were you told?' she asked. She had tried to get information out of him for the past two days, but though he was prepared to sit and talk to her, he had given nothing away. 'And what cause?' she added.

'We were told you in particular must not be hurt.'

'Why me?'

'I don't know.' And looking into his eyes she realized he genuinely did not know.

'But what cause, Claudio?'

'I mustn't tell you.' He sounded miserable.

'We are kidnapped?'

He nodded dumbly.

'How much are they asking for us?'

'I don't know.' His voice was stubborn but she decided he did know. 'More for you,' he added. 'It's not fair.'

'My parents are richer than the others,' she said. 'I suppose that's why.' She was quiet for a moment, analysing her feelings. She should have been upset but she wasn't. She realized that all her life she had been lonely. Locked in this room, with Frances and Bobbie Jean and the boy she liked more and more all the time, she was part of a group and not for one instant had she been lonely or felt alone. Frustrated sometimes. Sometimes a little scared. But never lonely.

'I think you're very brave,' he said in a rush.

She considered. 'No. I'm not brave. Sometimes here I have been scared. But it's funny, right now, I'm happy, sitting talking to you. I feel I'm with friends and I belong.' She stopped and thought, and then added as if she was astonished at a revelation. 'I've never belonged anywhere in my life before.'

'Your mother is a bad woman,' he said flatly.

'What do you mean?'

He looked down at the floor. 'I know about what you found when you came home the day we brought you here.'

She looked at him, her head on one side, eyes wide open. 'How do you know?'

'I know,' he said mysteriously. 'And I know that you are a good girl. Not like the others.'

She thought about this statement for a second and then she said indignantly: 'You've been listening to us! You could hear what we were saying!'

He did not reply and she said: 'I think that's awful. Really sneaky.' She felt a genuine anger, and for the first time truly threatened. 'Really, Claudio. I didn't think you'd do a thing like that.'

'It wasn't me,' he said. 'And it was necessary – for the Cause!'

'The Cause!' she said, and snorted. 'What cause?'

Again he was silent, and she too, had nothing to say.

'I'm sorry they listened,' he said after a while. 'They're not listening now.'

153

'If they do anymore, will you tell me?'

'I can't promise,' he said, and he sounded miserable again. 'But that man who' – he hesitated, embarrassed '– that man who touched you. He will be punished. He was very angry when he heard what that man had done.'

'Who was very angry?'

He looked doubtful again, the grey blue eyes avoiding hers, and then said: 'The man who was driving the car that day.'

'The red-headed man with the moustache? Who is he?'

'I can't say,' he said. 'I'm not really sure.'

'How is he going to punish him?' she asked.

'I don't know. But he said the man will never molest a child again.'

Jenny looked alarmed. 'They're not going to kill him, are they?'

'I don't know,' the boy admitted. 'Maybe.'

Suddenly Jenny started to cry. 'They mustn't kill him,' she said. 'They mustn't.'

Claudio looked distracted: 'Please don't cry,' he said. 'But what would it matter if they killed him. He's bad; decadent.'

She looked at him, her brown eyes wide with terror.

'Because if they can kill him, Claudio – they can kill us.'

'No. No,' he said. 'Not you. I swear not you.'

'Can you swear about Bobbie Jean and Frances?'

He was silent.

'Oh, God!' she said. 'Oh, God, Claudio. Now I'm frightened.'

'Is there any news about the money from the publishers?' Ingrid asked Kate once they were in her bedroom. Ingrid had stretched herself on the bed, staring at the painted ceiling, one hand on her forehead. Kate had put the tape recorder on the marble bedside table, and settled herself in a deep armchair.

Looking around the big gloomy room and at the huge bed where Ingrid's narrow body seemed almost lost, she had a sudden vision of what Jenny must have seen, and shivered. There could be nothing worse than the horror of finding one's mother in such a sordid grouping. With men it would have been bad enough, but the Lesbian aspect was piling horror on horror.

She looked at Ingrid and wondered what she saw in other women. She did not look butch. She did not behave butch. Just a slut for whom anything went, she decided, disliking her more by the minute.

'Hopefully, yes,' Kate said. 'When Paul flies back to London the day after tomorrow he's going to take what work I've done – a very detailed synopsis – and he's pretty confident that there won't be any problems. The newspaper has already agreed in principle, as long as they have an exclusive on all that's going on here. I've been filing any developments. Paul should be able to bring their cheque back with him but he has to collect his wife in Munich and take her back to England first.'

'What about the others?'

'I think they're still trying to raise money. It'll take time.'

'Will they have theirs ready by the seventh day?'

'I don't know,' Kate admitted. 'Will yours be ready?'

'I don't see how—' Ingrid rolled on to her side so that her back was to Kate. Her voice was muffled, and with amazement, Kate realized she was crying. 'Christ – what am I going to do! Monique is selling everything I have as quietly as possible to get the best price, but it's not amounting to much. When they sell you the jewellery,' she said bitterly, 'they tell you what an investment it is. And when you try to sell it back, they tell you nobody wants second-hand stuff and it's good only for the weight of the gold and the stones.'

'How much have you raised so far?' Kate asked, wondering whether to try to be comforting or to pretend nothing was wrong.

'With the Rolls and one of the Mercs, about £80,000. It's not worth selling the furs, they're offering so little.' Suddenly she rolled over again to face Kate. 'It's impossible. What can I do? I've got to get Jenny back safely. I know you think I'm a lousy mother and I am. I've always resented her when she got in the way of my life. I'm not very good at real love, I suppose, but in my own way I do love her. She is the only thing in the world that's truly mine. There's one thing about this – it's made me realize just how precious she is. But supposing I don't get her back—' She seemed to be speaking to herself. 'If

I could put the clock back. If I hadn't stayed in bed with those –' she couldn't find the word '– if I'd been home waiting for her, maybe it wouldn't have happened. And wherever she is, she's got the memory of her mother being fucked by three other people at once. It's not going to be an easy thing to live with. For either of us.'

She sat up and lit a cigarette.

'Don't think I'm guilty about the fucking,' she said defiantly. 'I'm not. It's my way of life. But I didn't want Jenny to know. That's another reason why I've always kept her out of the way. It wasn't entirely selfish. But how am I going to get my hands on half a million pounds? In three days?'

Her voice was despairing. Her left hand clutched and unclutched at the brightly patterned quilt that covered the bed. For the first time Kate felt sorry for her.

'Will Bellino advance you anything on the film?' she asked.

'He was only paying me £30,000 anyway, and at the moment it looks as if there won't be any film. His backers are backing out all over the place. He's got his own money problems. Not that I care about him.'

'The bank?'

'The bank! You've got to be joking! If you knew the size of the overdraft I already have. This money from the book was going to get me out of all my troubles. Now I'll just be deeper in.'

'There must be something,' Kate said.

'There is.' Ingrid stubbed out her half-smoked cigarette. 'It's something I didn't want to do, but I'll have to. Listen, if Monique and I go away for a day or two, can you cover for us? Say I'm here, having a nervous breakdown, say anything. I don't want anyone to know I've gone.'

'I can do that,' Kate said. 'But where are you going?'

'It's better you don't know,' Ingrid said flatly. 'You can tell Paul I've gone. He's been keeping my secrets for a long time. No one else.'

'OK,' Kate said. Curiosity was prickling, but she decided to ask no more question. 'It'll give me time to put something together for Paul to take back.' She paused, then said tentatively: 'Perhaps today we ought to talk about the early days. Fill in some of the details.'

'We've done that.'

'Have we?' It was a direct challenge.

For a moment the two women stared at each other. Kate's expression was implacable; Ingrid's defiant. Then she bit on the full lower lip and shrugged her shoulders. 'OK,' she said, 'what do you want to know?'

They concluded the interview at four in the afternoon. Ingrid was exhausted, her skin an unhealthy pallor, small freckles Kate had never noticed before showing like brown age-marks on her skin. Once she had begun to talk, she had continued in a flat monotone. There had been no need for Kate to ask questions, she merely sat very still and listened. Sometimes Ingrid had cried; sometimes old angers had burst through. Once or twice she had laughed.

Kate herself was exhausted, still shaken by the story she had heard; but she wanted to transcribe the tapes; get the words on paper. Then she could put together a long synopsis for Paul to take back, and Monique could make a fair copy of it.

She put the first of the tapes on the machine and started the play back. Ingrid's voice sounded higher and younger recorded, and she spoke slowly enough for Kate to be able to type along with her words, fingers flying over the keys.

'I'll start from the beginning,' Ingrid's voice said. 'I was born in Berlin in 1931, and was christened Ingrid Marie Pallia. My father was French; a hotelier. He was training to be an hotelier when he met my mother. I'm not sure where. When I was born he was working at the Aldon. I was the youngest of three. I had an elder brother Franz who, if he were alive, would be about forty-nine. He was six years older than me. Then there was my sister Joanna. She was three years older than me.

'When the war came in 1939, my father just disappeared. He'd have been in his mid-thirties by then, I suppose, but suddenly he wasn't there any more. My mother never said anything in explanation even though he'd taken my brother with him. I think perhaps they went back to France. I've never really known what happened, but as I grew up that seemed the most likely explanation. I used to ask for my papa a lot – I liked my papa best – but all my mother said was that we'd see him again when the war was over.

157

'We stayed in Berlin all through the war, and it was pretty terrible towards the end. All through the winter of 1943 into the following spring we were bombed every night. There were appalling food shortages, we were always hungry. And there was the never-ending bombing. Everything in Germany was collapsing, and young as I was, I knew it, and I was frightened. My mother was frightened too. Maybe I caught the fear from her. My sister was the bravest. She was sixteen and seemed to think it was all an adventure. It was some time in the spring of 1944 when all the things my mother had been frightened of happened. Our apartment block was bombed and my mother and sister were buried alive. They never got them out in time. God knows why I was the lucky one. I was in a cupboard under the stairs when the bomb fell, and only the stairs remained standing in the building. I don't know why they weren't with me. I can't remember. I was screaming and crying and they dug me out.' Kate had to strain to catch her voice on the tape. 'I've never been able to bear to be alone in the dark since.

'I was thirteen when it happened and all the family papers were in a box under the stairs with me. That was all I had left in the world. I supose war makes children grow faster. I knew I was going to have to survive on my own. I looked older than my age. I had good breasts, and I was pretty – very blonde. Everyone thought I was older; I was definitely sexually precocious – bit like that Bobbie Jean kid. So I took my sister's papers, which made me sixteen, and I found myself a place to stay in a near derelict building where at least I had a roof and the old boy who owned the place used to give me money and share the extra food I got by using my mother's and sister's papers.

'Some weeks later the Russians arived. Four of them raped me. Well, I suppose you could say they raped me. I knew what they were going to do. There wasn't much doubt about it when they started to pull down their breeches and wrench open their buttons. I decided I wasn't going to fight. They were great hulking peasants and I couldn't win. So I smiled and fawned and they all had me one by one on the floor of my hideyhole, and by the fourth I didn't care any more. I didn't care at all when when they gave me some bread and some garlic sausage. That could be just about the best meal I ever had in my life.

'The Americans came through after that, and they had a great deal more *politesse* but the end result was the same. I got laid and I got a candy bar or a tin of spam or something that kept body and soul together. And that's the way it went on until I met Lucky . . .' There was brief silence and then Ingrid's voice continued, less sombre. 'He was only nineteen. It's hard to think how young everyone was in those days. He'd come up through the Rhine with his regiment and he was a private first class. PFC Angelli, son of first generation Italian Americans in Boston, Mass. He fell in love with me. He didn't know how young I was. He didn't know I'd been whoring. We couldn't say much to each other; his German was minimal. He just saw an attractive young girl, living in a hole in the ground, half-starved and all alone in the world. He took me on. He was getting out of Berlin himself. He had a posting back to Paris, I suppose that was because he was so young and he'd had a pretty rough war. God, he was a beautiful boy. Tall and thin, black hair, grey eyes and a neat little nose and chin. Almost pretty. He was a driver, so it wasn't difficult to put me in the jeep and take me along. I certainly hadn't any baggage to take with me. Just the family papers. I had to hide a few times, but we made it. We got to Paris.

'I suppose I was as near to being in love with him as I have been with anyone. We were both babies, but even at that age I had too much sense to tell him the truth about anything. I wanted to get to the USA. I wanted it so bad I could taste it. And Lucky was going to be my passport there. I had this vision of Boston – a big city, untouched by war. Food. Ice creams. Nylons. Lipsticks. Fruit. Luxury. All the things I hadn't seen for years. Things I hardly remembered. The USA had got them and I wanted them too.

'Lucky found me a little room in Paris on the Boulevard Montparnasse. He used to say it was there that the gods – and one goddess – lived. Me. I didn't have to whore any more and Lucky asked for permission from his commanding officer to marry me. I don't know if they were stalling, but the papers didn't come through in time and Lucky got repatriated State-side.

'But I was lucky too. He didn't forget me for the girl next door. While I went back to whoring with the US Army, he raised heaven and earth to get me to the States, and he did it. I arrived on some ancient prop plane with about forty other would-be GI brides in New York in the winter of 1947. He was waiting at La Guardia airport and we just fell into each other's arms. Very touching it must have been.

'The only problem was, Boston, Massachusetts, wasn't quite what I'd expected. The Angellis had a small delicatessen in a place called Neponset on the Neponset River, south of Boston. It sounded glamorous. It wasn't. The river was a dried-up stinking stream, the Angelli third-floor walk-up cold-water apartment overlooked the railway lines. Their deli, on a parade of scruffy shops, hardly supported them and their three other kids. All the neighbours were poor white Irish Catholics. Papa Angelli was a slob, Mama Angelli didn't care for me. I wasn't Italian, I wasn't Catholic and I wasn't one of them. Mama Angelli had her suspicions about me, and she wasn't far off the mark.

'Nor could Lucky get a job. There wasn't much work for the brave boys who won the war and my handsome young lover wasn't bright enough to take up the GI Bill of Rights education offers. I couldn't get a job either. My English wasn't bad, but it certainly wasn't good. My Italian was getting better – that's all the family really spoke. I was more miserable than I'd ever been in my life. If this was the US of A they could keep it!

'I stuck it for nearly a year, doing terrible jobs in plastic factories – anything I could get. Nobody mentioned the wedding. Even Lucky. Neither of us thought it was such a great idea any more. Our only problem was where to fuck.

'I shared a room with his two sisters. Lucky shared with his brother. And there wasn't any way in Mama's Catholic household we were going to be able to have it off. Lucky would borrow cars, and it was all back-seat stuff – uncomfortable, but better than nothing. One night we were at it and the police suddenly wrenched open the door, shining a great torch into the

160

car. I was angry more than anything – caught with my pants down. Lucky – he cringed. He begged them not to do anything. He was like a whining schoolboy. He made me sick. I fell out of love with him then and there.

'I was desperate to get away. And the only thing I could do was go back to whoring. I quite liked whoring. It was better than making plastic for twenty dollars a week. Whoring was easy money as long as you could pick and choose a bit. I had this idea that I'd become one of the high-class variety. But I knew I was going to have to start low.

'In 1948 Boston was full of sailors. Even Brits sometimes. I'd heard people talk about Scully Square and what went on there, so I got myself on the street car, and then the Met and I went to Scully Square. It was really rough in those days. Burlesque, whores, cheap joints. I just walked up to the first tart I saw and asked her how I got started on the game. I didn't want to find myself being carved up for trespassing on someone else's pitch.

"How old are you, honey?" she asked. She was a mulatto girl, I remember, big and probably in her twenties. I told her I was eighteen. She sort of sighed and she gave me an address in Appleton Street, off Berkeley Street. It was a brothel.

'The madam there was very happy to take me on. So I packed up my bag and my baggage – all one small attaché case of it – and moved to Appleton Street, which was the start of a pretty successful career in up-market whoring. I stayed there four years, the first two always dressed as a schoolgirl. I was doing very well, but I decided the madam was doing better than I was, and it wasn't on. I wanted to branch out on my own. I'd got a fair bit saved, so I had a long think about what I was going to do. It had to be California, I decided – the sunshine land of opportunity. And maybe, with my looks, I could get into films as well. But I sure knew I wouldn't starve.

'Nor did I. I built up slowly until I met Michael when I was twenty-six. I had a rather better pad than I led you to believe the other day. In fact, it was pretty luxurious. I was making a lot of money as a call girl. The work had grown by recommendations. I suppose I had some interesting tricks to offer. European tricks. I'd been doing it a long time. And I like my work.

161

I've never minded being fucked. Ever since the fourth Russian.

'The mistake I made was falling in love with Michael. That really did screw things up in one way, because I couldn't go on with the game while he was around. But it did make me try harder for film work. He was costing me my savings and, just as I was getting worried, he got a job, as I told you, and started to contribute. Being pregnant was a disaster, except that I thought it might keep us together – he was so keen to have a baby. And at that time, I wanted him around.

'Well, after Jenny was born and we were married he stopped screwing me, so apart from being broke, I was getting pretty damn frustrated. For God's sake I was only twenty-eight, officially twenty-two. When one of my old clients called one day and Michael was out, I agreed to have him come round. I needed both the money and the fuck.

'He brought a friend, and we all finished up as a happy threesome and – you've guessed it – Michael walked in. What you might not guess was that Michael also joined in. He wasn't doing much for me, but he was doing a lot for them, and they didn't mind a bit. I think Michael would have been quite happy about the whole scene, if he hadn't seen my clients pay me. Rather well. That changed the whole complexion of the thing for him. It was all right to fuck fellas for fun, but being paid for it wouldn't do. His British sensibilities were outraged. We had a screaming row, which finished with him saying: "I can't be married to a whore. Not in my position!" It didn't seem to occur to him that he'd been poncing off me for years. But at least after that he really tried to get me film work. He wanted to keep me off the game. Every now and then I'd take a special client just to keep my hand in, and to spite him. For the rest of the time I had lovers. Discreet lovers like heavily married film producers who could put a bit of work my way. At that time any lover I had had to be married. It was safer. But from the moment Michael realized how I'd been earning my bread, he wouldn't accept Jenny. He insisted she could be anyone's. I suppose it suited him to think that.

'And so it went on. He and I split, and my career took off. I did all those second leads in those musicals and comedies of the period, and I didn't have to whore any more. I almost missed the work! For the last few years I've been the one that's doing the paying when I pick up some gigolo. It gives me a sort of funny satisfaction. Like getting my own back on men.' There was a long sigh and then a small giggle.

'I do wonder now, when all this is over, if I'm going to have go back to the game. I'm going to be finished financially. But I don't think they'll pay as much as they used to. Except maybe for the privilege of fucking someone famous. What do you think?'

It was a question Kate didn't answer because she didn't know what the answer was.

The unlikely collection of occupants of the villa had fallen into a kind of gloomy routine. Each night they dined early in the big, sombre dining room: Ingrid and Monique, Paul, Kate, Charles Dennison and Eileen Elliot; six people forced into a reluctant intimacy.

After dinner they returned to the drawing room, where each one had created their own little territory. Ingrid and Monique always sat on the long sofa at the side of the fireplace. Eileen Elliot had the big comfortable chair on the other side. Paul and Kate sat together on a smaller sofa that was placed in the centre of the room, and Charles Dennison sat at the far end of the big sofa which was quite big enough to leave a fair gap between him and Monique.

After one coffee, Kate generally went to her room and her typewriter. Paul and Charles would talk until Inspector Garoni made his nightly call to report progress. There never was any progress. Nor had he mentioned the contents of the tapes. He would ask what their situation regarding the ransom money was. There was no great deal of progress there either. Alex Elliot generally telephoned about eight. He and his wife would have brief whispered conversations. The money was coming together slowly, she said when she had put the phone down. He had borrowed £90,000 on their house. After brief congratulations, everyone fell silent. It was a long way off target. They had all made their arrangements with the press, and for the time being the media seemed to have lost some interest. The crowds outside the villa were dwindling.

At around ten o'clock, Ingrid and Monique generally said goodnight. Eileen would follow them a few minutes later, leaving the two men to drink a last brandy and discuss endlessly the possibilities of where the girls might be; if the police could find them, and where the ransom money would come from eventually. Every conversation would end with Charles saying: 'I don't give a damn about anything as long as they are safe and we get them back in one piece.'

'I'll drink to that,' Paul would say fervently.

Paul and he would make their way to their respective bedrooms at about eleven but Charles found it impossible to sleep. He had not, in fact, slept since Bobbie Jean had gone. His cheeks were hollow, his eyes deep set. Once in bed, with sleep refusing to come, he tried to force himself to read, but the words on the page danced in front of his eyes and nothing made sense; not even the simplest of detective novels.

He was in bed, the book on his chest, resting half upright against the pillows blaming himself again for agreeing to let his daughter come to Rome, when there was a faint knock. He got out of bed, put his dressing gown over his dark blue silk pyjamas and opened his bedroom door.

Eileen Elliot was standing there in a pale blue nylon negligée covered with white-edged frills. Her eyes were wild, her hands like claws. 'Forgive me,' she said. 'I had to talk to someone. I haven't slept . . . I can't sleep . . . Charles, I'm so frightened . . .'

She put her hand over her face, and sobbed, the other hand reaching blindly for his. He took her arm, led her into the room and closed the door behind them. 'I'm sorry,' she was saying, 'but I'm so frightened. Lonely and frightened. Guilty. I don't know what to do. And I do love her. I realize how much I love her. What if they kill her? We'll never get the money. Only £90,000. It's so far off.'

He put his arm around her and held her tight to him. There didn't seem to be anything else to do, and besides, the human contact helped him too. He knew what she meant. Frightened, lonely and guilty: they were the three emotions plaguing him night and day.

She let herself be held, and leaned her head on his shoulder,

164

still crying. He could feel the dampness of her tears seeping through his dressing gown. He wished he could cry too. It might help.

After a while the storm lessened, and she was sobbing quietly.

'Now,' he said, 'come on. Sit down. We've all got to be brave. We mustn't break down. It's not going to help anything.'

He sat her on his bed, and she folded her hands in her lap and said: 'I know. I'm sorry. I seem to keep crying all over you. I don't usually do this.'

'I know. I know,' he said. 'Here – blow your nose.' He padded into his bathroom and came out with a handful of Kleenex. 'It's all better now,' he said and realized he was saying the things he used to say to Bobbie Jean when she had cried, thwarted from having something she wanted. And again the wave of sheer terror that he felt when he thought of her swept over him.

The woman sitting on his bed was blowing her nose, delicately.

'Come on,' he said encouraging, 'give it a good blow.'

She half laughed, half sobbed, and blew harder.

'That's better,' he told her as she sat watching him, the Kleenex crumpled in her hand.

'Charles,' she said quietly. 'I'm sorry to ask. But can I stay here? I don't think I can bear another night alone. It gets worse all the time. I don't think I can stay there by myself. Please, Charles, may I stay?'

He hesitated and he didn't know why, because he knew exactly what she meant. The nights were the worst. Long, dark, unending; full of fear and loneliness.

'Please,' she said quietly and with considerable dignity.

He nodded, not sure whether he could speak. He took her shoulders and stood her up again, slipping the peignoir from her arms. Underneath there was a double knit nylon matching nightgown, and he felt relief that it was not sheer. That would have been all wrong.

'Lie down,' he told her. 'And cover yourself up. I'll stay in the chair.'

'Don't sleep in the chair,' she said urgently. 'Please come

into the bed. Not for sex. For companionship. I need someone near. Don't you?'

'I think I do—' he told her.

She turned back the covers again for him, and faintly embarrassed he took off his dressing gown and lay down beside
her. On impulse he turned out the light. It felt more normal
in the dark. She was resting on her back, her breath still coming fast from the crying, punctuated by a small near hiccup
every now and then. He lay beside her, staring into the black-
ness of the ceiling until his eyes adjusted to the night light that
came in through the shutters.

'Are you all right now?' he asked her.

'Better,' she said, her hand groping until it found his. She
curled her fingers around his fingers tightly. 'That's much
better,' she said. 'Thank you.'

She was sleeping from sheer exhaustion in seconds, and he
found that the sound of her regular, slow breathing was sooth-
ing. He felt no sexual need for her at all, but it was good she
was there. Gradually his eyelids dropped until he too slept.

When he awoke a grey early morning light was flittering
into the room, and he found that in the night they had both
turned so that now she lay with her back to him, her buttocks
pressed into his stomach and his arm around her as he had
once slept with his wife. The position was achingly familiar.
She still slept, breathing deeply. Her blonde hair, disarrayed
on the pillow, was tickling his nose, and he found to his embarrassment that he was erect. He tried to tell himself it was
only an early morning stand, but it showed no signs at all of
going away. And he was beginning to feel an urgent need. The
most sensible thing to do seemed to be to get out of bed, but
as he moved away from her, lifting his arm carefully from
around her, she made a soft little grumbling noise and turned;
blue flickering between her half closed lids, and firmly put her
arm around him.

'Umm,' she said. 'Umm.'

He knew that if she were half awake she must feel the condition he was in. He tried cautiously to pull away again, but
this time the blue eyes were wide open, looking at him.

'Good morning,' he said. Perhaps she felt his excitement.

Perhaps not. But her eyes widened, and her mouth opened just slightly, and she was staring into his face, while he stared back at her, seeing the neat nose, the naturally red mouth, the faint lines in her delicate skin that now seemed endearing. Very slowly they both leaned towards each other, their heads barely leaving the pillow, until their mouths met and they were kissing. It was a very simple kiss. Her mouth felt soft and yielding, but she did not part her lips sufficiently for him to slip his tongue into her. He liked the chasteness of the kiss. It seemed right, and with a little exclamation he moved to pull her closer to him, not caring if she felt his erection; wondering what she would do.

He felt the nylon of her nightgown as he pushed between her legs, and she moved back from him her eyes wide again, but made no attempt to push him away. He liked the feel of the nylon against him and moved against it. He realized her hips were moving with him. He pulled the nightgown off her shoulder and his hand slid down to cup a full, rounded breast, damp with the light sweat of sleep. His fingers found that her nipple was as erect as he was. He left her mouth to sample her whiteness and rouge, as he gently bit her nipple, he felt her tongue exploring his ear, nibbling at the lobe.

Then he felt her warm breath and she was whispering in his ear.

'Charles – do it. I want it. It's been so long . . .'

'And for me,' he said.

She was lifting her nightgown with one hand, sliding off the other shoulder with the other. When the fabric was bunched around her waist, she pulled him, insistently on top of her. 'I like the weight of you,' she said breathlessly. 'Touch me there. Am I wet?'

She was joyously wet; open and waiting for him. He found the tender place and stroked until she moaned.

'Do it! Do it!' she said. 'Now. Right now.'

He could hardly wait himself. He lifted himself and plunged. He heard her gasps and sobs as an extension of his own. It didn't take long for either of them. He felt as if dams had burst, rivers flooded, clouds opened.

Like she had said, it had been a very long time, and still between her legs, he slept.

167

When they woke again he said, full of remorse, 'I shouldn't have done that.'

'Why not?' She was laughing at him. Confident.

'Your husband . . .'

'My husband hasn't touched me for four years. And anyway, he won't know.'

'I suppose it was natural,' he said. 'Fear does that to people.'

She looked serious and nodded. 'It made us forget. And I slept. Did you?'

'Yes, I did. For the first time since Bobbie vanished.'

'It's easier to face things after sleep,' she said thoughtfully. 'And easier when there are two of you. We made it through the night. Look, it's morning.'

Stray sun was striping the bed.

'I'd better get back to my room,' she said. 'I don't want to ruin your reputation.'

'No one in this house has any reputation after those tapes.'

'Kate and Paul?'

'You don't think they're lovers?'

'I hadn't thought about it,' she said. 'Too busy thinking of other things. Yes, I suppose they are. Discreet, though.'

'Well, perhaps we had better be too. Off you go,' he said and gently smacked her bottom.

She laughed, rearranged her nightgown, patted her hair and put on the peignoir before moving towards the door. Then she turned to look at him.

'Thank you, Charles,' she said. 'Thanks a lot.'

Chapter Nine

'It doesn't seem possible we've only been here six days,' Kate said. 'It feels like an eternity.' She was still in bed, her bare shoulders above the sheets, her breasts covered. Paul, in white jockey shorts, was standing at the sink, shaving. 'What time will you have to leave tomorrow morning?' she asked.

'Not too early, if I'm away from here about 8.30 I should be at the airport in plenty of time,' he said. 'It's going to be a long day by the time I get Madeleine home, though.'

'Wouldn't it be better to stay the night in Munich? It's not a long flight to London.'

'No. There's too much to do getting that money together. I've really got to push everyone. And they've all got to read your stuff. I can't get Jenny and Frances out of my mind. I'm even feeling for the naughty Bobbie Jean, though she may be better equipped to deal with whatever situation they're in.'

Kate leaned to take her dressing gown from the chair beside the bed and said: 'Ingrid mentioned something in that interview yesterday that made me wonder if it's perhaps not as bad as we think. She said her sixteen-year-old sister wasn't frightened of the bombing in the war; regarded it as an adventure. I don't remember being frightened of anything when I was fifteen. Maybe they're not either.'

'Let's hope so,' Paul said. He rinsed his face then patted it dry, and she thought how 'married' they had become in the last few days. It was going to be painful, dreadfully painful, when his family life was back to normal, and she went back to the mews with only lunchtimes to look forward to. She wondered for a second how Madeleine's health would be after the treatment and then made her mind skitter away from dangerous ground.

'What else did she say yesterday?' Paul wanted to know. He'd come back to the bed and settled down beside her, pulling the sheets and blankets over them both.

'It's all typed out. Horrible childhood in Berlin. Raped by Russians. Off to the US with a GI. You can read it. She was on the game for years. That's why Michael won't believe Jenny's his child. He's convinced she could be the child of anyone of the men that Ingrid was entertaining through the period. Ingrid, though, still insists that Jenny is his. Funnily, I believe her.'

Paul was difficult to surprise. All he said was:

'Well, Jenny does sometimes remind me of Michael, in her

169

stern moments; and Ingrid won't be the first nor will she be the last actress who's started off whoring. I can think of a few equally famous names whose backgrounds wouldn't bear too much inspection.'

He had slid her down the bed so that she could lay with her head on his shoulder. She pushed one leg under his and wrapped her arm over his chest.

'But where is she going on this mysterious trip with Monique?' Kate asked, pressing her nose into the hollow of his neck. 'Now what's that all about? Any ideas?'

'Not a one,' Paul said. 'Ex-lover she's going to blackmail? How's that?'

'Possible but improbable. Difficult to get people to cough up large sums of money these days for a sexual peccadillo. Maybe she's having another go at Michael. Maybe there's more she hasn't told me about him. You know,' she said thoughtfully, I've got a feeling there is something more. I can't think what, but there's a missing link. I feels it in me bones. And that's an instinct that doesn't often let me down on a story.'

'I can't imagine what it could be,' Paul said. 'It sounds as if she's run the gamut of everything dramatically possible. Raped by Russians, GI bride—'

'She wasn't—'

'Well, nearly. On the game. About the only thing she's missed is being a beautiful spy.'

'A spy?' Kate considered the thought. 'No, the dates wouldn't fit. Not for the war anyway. She really would have been too young. Mafia maybe, later on. Maybe that's why Jenny had an Italian foster mother.'

'What could she have done in the Mafia?'

'Pushed drugs? Or she could have been run by the Mafia while she was whoring. It's a five-year gap in California after she left Boston and before she met Michael. A lot could have happened.'

'I think she'd have been a lot richer if that had been the case. How about daddy being an SS man and she's off to Brazil to get money from him? Or long lost brother? More likely. Long lost dad is probably dead.'

'She can't do Brazil and back in two days, not unless she can fly like Peter Pan or the Angel Gabriel,' Kate said.

'Interesting you used masculine similes,' Paul said. 'A psychiatrist would make something of that.'

'It's that Lesbian bit with Monique. It gives me the creeps. And Monique is so uneasy-making too. Do you notice how little she says and how she watches and listens all the time. They both give me the willies and the idea of them in bed together . . . yuck!'

'Well, I suppose if they like it – whatever turns you on! Be more tolerant.'

'Well, I'm not,' Kate said shortly. 'I had moments when I warmed a little to her yesterday, but she's such a tough, cold charmless bitch. It's not that she's been a whore or anything that she's done. It's her horrible personality. Don't worry, though – I'll make her sound the most pathetic, misunderstood lady since Lucretia Borgia by the time I've finished the book.'

'I don't know how to take that,' he said as she giggled into his shoulder. 'Enough of Ingrid. Are we getting up or are we making love?'

'Love, please—' she said. 'For once I'm actually awake. Nice gentle loving love. That's what I want.'

'So that's what you shall have, my darling,' he told her.

After, languid with contentment, she was dreamily making up her face at the mirror. He'd bathed her as if she was a baby when they finally got out of bed, declining to join her in the tub.

'Once was enough!' he said.

She was stroking mascara on to her long black lashes while he sat and watched her when he said abruptly: 'I'm going to miss all this.'

She twisted on the dressing table stool to look at him.

'But you're coming back? We've got a little more?'

'Madeleine was talking about coming back here with me.'

She shut her eyes as she felt her stomach plummet as if she were in a plane in an air pocket.

'And you won't dissuade her?'

'Not if that's what she wants to do. On the phone yesterday she said the treatment had made very little difference. She felt fit, but if anything she was losing more coordination. I can't deny her anything, Kate my darling. You must see that.'

She remembered the woman in his waiting room, balanced on uncertain legs.

'No, of course you can't,' she said; then with a rush of resentment: 'But why can't you, Paul?'

'What do you mean?'

'I mean tell me your exact reasoning, your exact feelings.'

'You mustn't press me, Kate.'

She stared at him, green eyes angry.

'I am pressing you. Answer me.'

'All right.' He gave her a 'you-asked-for-it' look, his blue eyes turned grey. 'Because I once loved her. Because though today I don't like her very much and haven't done so for many years, there are times when I still love her. And she's going to die.'

It had been said. Kate rejected it, seizing on the earlier reason.

Crudely, deliberately so, she said: 'When you say you still love her – do you mean you still fuck her?'

He winced.

'Sorry,' she said, 'was that too vulgar a term to use about screwing your sainted wife? OK, do you fuck her, lay her, screw her, poke her, shaft her . . . ?'

'Yes, I do,' he interrupted and she burst into a storm of weeping.

'How could you?' she cried. 'How could you!'

'Shush—' He had his arms around her, but she fought him off, pummelling her fists against his chest. Finally he managed to hold her so tight that she could not move.

'You shouldn't have asked me,' he said. 'Kate, Kate, what do you expect? She is my wife. I have to be her husband. I can't deny her what she has so little time left to enjoy. I make love to her out of kindness; respect.'

'I don't understand how you can even do it,' she said fiercely.

'My darling, you'd understand perfectly well if it were anyone else. It's just because it's us you can't see straight.'

'Well, I thought we were different. I hate you for doing it.'

'With all your sophistication and all your experience you

172

can't see that it is different – you and me, and me and her. I lie in bed with her, darling. She touches me—'

'I don't want to hear.'

'Kate. I love you. I love you more than life. I can't do without you. But I can't deny my obligations. Please try to understand.'

'I understand you want your cake and eat it,' she said bitterly.

Then he was angry. 'That is not true and you know it. If you think that, we can say goodbye right now.'

'Then Goodbye—' she said, her eyes glaring green at him.

'Very well,' he said. 'Have it the way you want.'

He turned to leave the room but before he could turn the handle of the door, she was on him clinging to him, her face pressed into his back.

'I'm sorry,' she said. 'Forgive me, please forgive me. I was jealous.'

He turned to pull her back into his arms again. 'You don't have to be. You really don't.'

They stood silent for almost a full minute and then she said: 'Women will never understand men. At least not their own man.'

'And men will never understand women,' he said. He kissed her. '*Vive la différence.*'

It was 11.30 when the telephone in the hall rang for the first time. Charles Dennison ran to it, signalling the sergeant to put on the attached tape recorder.

A slow, calm voice speaking over a background of café noise said in accented English: 'Who is that?'

'Charles Dennison.'

'The father of *bella* little Bobbie Jean. *Cattiva* little Bobbie Jean.'

He did not answer.

'We know the police are in the house. We know they are looking for us. They will not find us. Do you have the money for your daughters' release?'

'We think we may have about half,' Charles said, his voice expressionless.

'Is that all? You will have to do better. You have two more days. Sometime in the next two days, one of you will be told what to do with the money. You will be very wise not to pass this information to the police. If you do, and we shall know if you do, you will never see your daughters again. You may tell the sergeant that he can switch off his tape recorder now. I have nothing else to say.'

The line went dead.

Everyone had come into the hall, and Paul signalled the sergeant to replay the tape. They listened in silence.

'What shall we do?' Eileen Elliot whispered.

'First we call Inspector Garoni. After that we make decisions,' Charles said. 'And for the meantime, we all pray that they are still safe.'

The red-headed man ambled back to the bar after he had finished the telephoning and leisurely finished his small cup of strong black coffee. The life of the café milled around him, Romans impatiently ordering, sipping their drinks in quick urgent sips; eating almost on the run.

He was thinking that next time he would have to use another telephone; one further away. They'd be sure to tap this one, though he hadn't given them much time. But it was as well not to hang about. The *carabinieri* could be astonishingly quick on occasions.

Leaving the cup on the table and wiping his moustache with the back of his hand, he left the café and plunged into the heat of the Via Vittorio Emanuele. His office, import/export, was just a few doors away. Not that much importing and exporting went on – just enough to allay suspicions and give him an excuse to be calling France and Germany so frequently.

Since leaving the girls at the house in Trastevere he had not been near the place. He'd left young Claudio and Mario to keep watch, and he was reasonably confident that nothing much could go wrong there. The rest he was handling himself. He wouldn't have trusted the NAP lot as far as he could throw them. A load of bungling amateurs, but useful for the moment.

This sprat of kidnapping to catch the mackerel of Scimitar was going very well. He wasn't entirely sure that they were on

174

the right track, but the lucky break had been when he approached the girl. She'd turned out to be a natural. She'd driven a hard bargain and it might even be worth keeping it. She could be useful again perhaps. And then there was discovering that she was such a sexy little bitch; a bonus, as the whole thing would have been twice as difficult had she not been around.

If all he remembered of Ingrid were still true, she would lead them to Scimitar. She had been a greedy, grasping, selfish child. If her character as an adult was the same there was no way she would part with that much of her own money. Not if there was the slightest chance of getting it from someone else's pocket.

The only danger was that she was not in touch with, and never had been in touch with, Scimitar. In that case, the exercise would not be as useful as he had planned. But at least they'd get a million out of it for the kidnappings.

It was now taken for granted that, when the girls were given their meal, instead of going away Claudio sat against the wall, talking to Jenny and stroking Sammy. Sammy now became a wriggling mass of joy when Claudio came into the room. Frances and Bobbie Jean teased her about her boyfriend, but neither showed resentment. His friendliness to Jenny gave them a sense of security too. In the darkness of the night when fear did attack, they consoled themselves that it must be hard to kill or hurt those with whom you had been friendly.

'What's it like in America?' Claudio had wanted to know.

Jenny thought. 'I don't really know,' she said. 'I was born there, but I was fostered out as a baby. I stayed with an Italian family in Echo Park in Los Angeles. It's a very poor area and we all spoke Italian and we all ate pasta, and we listened to a lot of opera, and Rosa, who looked after me, used to fly into screaming rages with us children and then she'd kiss us all and smother us with hugs. I suppose it was really more like being in Italy than in America.'

'How long did you stay with this family?' he asked.

'For years, on and off. When my mother could afford it and I was older, I went to boarding schools, but she picked

English ones. Well, British actually. I always seemed to be somewhere in Scotland.'

'She is not a good mother,' Claudio said positively.

'Not really. I suppose she isn't,' Jenny said. 'But I do love her. At least I think I do. She is the only mother I've got,' she said ruefully. 'My father's very funny with me. I don't think he likes me though he sometimes takes me places with him. My mother doesn't want me interfering in her life, but she does love me. I'm pretty sure she does.'

'Would you mind if you never saw her again?'

Jenny looked terrified. 'You're not thinking of punishing her?'

'No! No!' he said. 'It was just a question.'

She thought about that, her small chin in her hands. She had finished her supper of veal stew and pushed it away on the floor. 'No,' she said. 'I don't think it would matter too much if I never saw her again. As long as I had someone to love. Someone else I belonged to.'

There was a silence between them, and Claudio was looking fixedly at the floor. 'I'd like it if you belonged to me,' he said, his voice shaky.

'I'd like that too,' she said quietly.

They neither said any more, but Jenny was conscious of a soaring happiness. For the last two day she had thought constantly about Claudio. She could have described him in the minutest details to anyone, from the way his brows drew together, coming into little peaks when he was puzzling about something. The way one of his dog-teeth was just slightly crooked, and the sweetness of his rare smile. Jenny was not at all sure, but she had a strong suspicion that she had fallen in love. She fretted that they could not be entirely alone and she wondered what it would be like if he kissed her. Jenny had never been kissed. She'd heard about it in detail – and more – from girls at school and now Frances and Bobbie Jean who seemed to spend a lot of time talking about boys and what they had done with boys. She had no experience to offer these conversations. She felt, as he slid his hand into hers, that there could be no greater happiness than she was feeling at that moment. They sat silent in the dim room, listening while

Bobbie Jean and Frances chattered as they ate their meal. When they had finished, Claudio closed her hand, got to his feet and loaded the tray with the plastic dishes and spoons. Then he knocked for the door to be opened, with a quick backwards look he smiled at her as he disappeared into the corridor outside, and she knew what it meant in books when the heroine's heart turned over.

The taxi had been waiting very conveniently outside when Bellino left his host's apartment in Eur. He had dined with one of his backers, a rich industrialist whose more usual method of making money was manufacturing synthetic fibres. The meal had been good; the conversation stimulating and, most important, Bellino was pretty sure he had calmed the man's fears about his investment in *Claudine at School*. When the film was made the publicity value of the kidnappings and all that still had to happen would be uncountable. The only snag was the waiting to get the girls back. Bellino intended to hold them to their contracts when they were released.

He was even debating whether it would be a sensible move to advance all the salaries. They would then all be tied to him, and he had no doubts that they could use the cash to put towards the ransom.

He climbed into the waiting taxi, said briefly: 'Excelsior,' and settled back in the narrow seat of the little Fiat. Preoccupied with his thoughts, he wasn't taking much notice of the direction the driver was taking from the smart suburb and back into the City until he realized they were driving down the left bank of the Tiber, towards the Vatican.

'Excelsior Hotel, Via Veneto,' he said crossly. The driver did not reply, but continued driving steadily. 'Driver!' Bellino said. 'The Excelsior Hotel.' He spoke as to an idiot and the taxi skidded to a stop by the Ponte San Angelo.

'If you dislike the route I'm taking, you can get out of the taxi,' the driver said.

Bellino puffed with rage and for the first time looked at the man in the front seat. He was thick-set with reddish hair, and the face turned to look at him over the back of the seat had a heavy moustache and angry pale eyes that caught the light from the street lamps.

'I will do no such thing,' Bellino said. 'And you will drive me to the Via Veneto and charge me the correct fare.'

'*You*,' the driver said softly, 'will get out of this taxi.'

'Certainly not!'

'Are you sure?' There was a glint of steel in the man's hand. He leaned over the seat and with one quick movement, the point of a knife was at Bellino's throat.

'Very well,' said Bellino with dignity, acting as if he had not seen the knife. 'But don't expect me to pay you what is on the meter.'

'Just get out,' the driver said, each word separately enunciated.

It was only when he was out on the entrance to the pedestrian bridge where no cars passed that it occured to Bellino that the taxi had perhaps been a little too convenient in Eur. That he had not inquired if it was the one his host had telephoned for, and that it was odd the driver spoke such good English. All these thoughts flashed through his head as two men appeared from the flight of stairs that led down to the broad sandy bank of the Tiber and took up positions each side of him.

Again he felt steel, this time in his ribs, and without speaking both men held an arm and urged him back down the steps from where they had appeared. It was a long flight, he could see in the moonlight. Three separate gradients. What were they going to do? Drown him? Rob him? He began to feel a sheer terror. He needed to scream and he opened his mouth to do so, but a garlicky hand clapped across his face. 'I shouldn't if I were you—' a voice said in Italian.

They stopped moving where the third flight began and pressed him back against the stone wall. They both stank of garlic, he noted.

'What is it you want?' he said frantically. 'I'll give you my wallet. Anything.'

'Take off your trousers,' one of them, a thin faced dark man who might have been Sicilian said in Italian.

'What?' He could not believe what he had heard.

'Take off your trousers.' The man's voice was impatient, and the other smaller, plumper man with a drooping moustache pricked him urgently with a knife.

What the hell were they going to do? His mind flittered around all the possibilities as he desperately tore at the belt and zip of his trousers, scrambling out of them, dignity gone. He ought to shout, but who in the general clamour of Rome would hear him? If they wanted his trousers, they could have them, and his wallet – anything as long as they didn't hurt him. He could hear himself whimpering as his elegant dark trousers slid to the ground. The cold and the fear had made his bowels rattle. He was afraid of losing control of them.

'All right,' he said ingratiatingly, 'is that what you want? My wallet is in the back pocket.'

He was speaking Italian. These louts would not understand English.

'Now the underpants,' the taller one said.

'Underpants . . .' he said stupidly.

'The underpants . . .'

What was it. What did they want? He again did as he was told, and along with the terror was the frantic thought of how he was going to get back to his hotel without either trousers or underpants. What *did* they want?

The underpants joined his trousers on the cold stone steps and both men were looking at his genitals. They couldn't be queers. Surely they couldn't be queers.

The knife flashed as one of them held up Bellino's shirt tail. Suddenly he knew what they wanted. His shriek of terror as he understood startled the birds nesting under the bridge. And his second scream, louder and longer, was one of the terrible physical pain.

The reddish-haired man was waiting on the bridge, leaning below a sorrowing statue of an angel who held the hammer that had nailed Christ to the cross. He was looking at the vast circular bulk of the Castel San Angelo on the other side of the road.

'Is it done?' he asked.

The Sicilian who had performed the surgery grinned, showing yellow and rotting teeth.

'Didn't you hear?'

'I heard. What did you do with the remains?'

'Food for the fish. He'll never molest a child again.'

179

There was a rustle of notes.

'*Grazia*,' the smaller man said. 'Was it your daughter?'

The red-headed man hesitated. 'My niece,' he said. 'My sister has no man.'

'So you did the job for her, eh?' the Sicilian said.

'No. You did the job. Ah, here he comes . . .' Bellino had appeared, dragging himself and moaning, at the top of the steps, blood pouring down his bare legs. 'We'd better be off.'

The three of them melted into the night, the Sicilians running lightly across the bridge while the red-headed man left the taxi, the keys inside, and strode briskly down towards the Via Conciliazione, where there was a café with a telephone. He dialled 5100, explaining to the ambulance service that there was a grievously hurt man on the Ponte San Angelo. He then hung up, making his way to mingle with the promenading tourists and pilgrims who walked the length of the Via Conciliazione to marvel at St Peter's Square by night.

Thoughtfully he lit a long thin cigar of the type that he had known Bellino smoked. And he congratulated himself on having well stage-managed an unpleasant but very necessary task.

Dusk was falling and the worst of Rome's interminable rush hour was over when Ingrid and Monique slipped out of the villa and into the Lancia which Monique had parked in the street outside. The journalists were beginning to lose interest in the story and no one was about.

Parioli itself was as quiet as ever, but Ingrid had said she was anxious about the main roads to the Via Del Foro Italico and on to the autostrada. 'We've got a long way to go and very little time to do it in,' she said.

'Now will you tell me where we're going?' Monique asked once they were settled in the car.

'Marseilles,' Ingrid said briefly. 'Sleep when you can. You're going to have to share the driving.'

It was a long way, Monique thought, trying to work out what the mileage could be.

'And why Marseilles?' she asked, trying to sound disinterested.

'Why not Marseilles?' Ingrid said, forestalling any more questions.

She drove competently and very fast, pushing the Lancia to its limits once she had reached the autostrada to Florence. The journey was long, but totally motorway, then almost entirely autoroute to France. Monique after some mental arithmetic reckoned it would take ten hours.

She lit a cigarette and puffed at it, regarding the red dot of light in the darkness of the car. Night had come and she sat totally relaxed as the speedometer moved up until Ingrid was driving at 110 miles per hour, the long beams of the headlights striping the road in front so that it seemed they were speeding through a tunnel.

She was more than curious about what her employer was up to but decided that no doubt all would be revealed in the fullness of time. Why Marseilles, though? She had bet with herself it would be Switzerland. Marseilles was unexpected.

'Do you think Jenny will be frightened?' Ingrid asked abruptly.

Monique turned to look at the set profile beside her.

'Probably not too frightened,' she said. 'Not if the three of them are all together.'

'But we don't know that, do we?' Ingrid said sombrely. 'They might have split them up. It's easier to hide one person than three.'

'I'd have said the other way round,' Monique said. 'You'd have to find three safe hiding places instead of one.'

'I hope it's somewhere clean and comfortable,' Ingrid said. 'Whatever else I haven't done, I've always made sure she was somewhere decent.' Monique felt surprise at her employer's concern for Jenny. She should have been concerned earlier, she thought, yet threw out a crumb of comfort.

'She's young,' she said. 'The young adjust very easily.'

'I suppose so. I know I did.'

There was silence in the car as it swept on and up the wide curves and banks of the autostrada. Ingrid was intent on the road.

'Want a cigarette?' Monique asked her.

'No thanks. I'll have one when you take over.'

She was obviously nervous. Normally a relaxed driver, now all her attention was on what lay ahead, both hands firmly on the wheel, eyes unblinking so that all Monique could see was the pretty profile with its small flared nostrils and bowed mouth.

'Do you want me to take over now?' she asked.

'No, when we get to Florence.'

'That's a long way.'

'Not far enough on this journey. About 170 miles.'

'I'd call that far enough.'

Another silence, and then Ingrid suddenly asked: 'Where do you come from, Monique?'

The younger woman chuckled and said softly: 'I thought you'd never ask.'

'Well,' Ingrid's voice was defensive, 'you're not exactly forthcoming about yourself, are you?'

'And you're not exactly interested in other people, are you?'

An electric silence until Ingrid sighed and said: 'Don't give me a hard time, Monique. Not now. If you don't want to tell me where you come from, forget it.'

'I was born in Algeria.'

'You're not Algerian.'

'Sort of. My father was in the French army there. My mother was born there. A *pied noir*. She was his mistress. So I'm what you'd call a little bastard.'

'Were you brought up there?'

'No. My father set us up in the South of France.'

'How come you speak such good English?'

'Simple. My mother and I didn't exactly hit it off. When I was sixteen I went to England as an au pair. I was lucky. I ended up with a couple who both wrote, who were interested in language and made sure that I left their home speaking like a native. Actually, I stayed with them for three and a half years. I was happy there. I learnt a lot.'

A lot more than she was prepared to tell Ingrid.

'And then what?'

'All sorts of jobs with travel agencies and things until I drifted into the film business and met you.'

Ingrid just nodded and Monique remembered her father and how he had said: 'Always tell as near to the truth as possible. It saves complications.' Fortunately Ingrid's interest threshhold in other people's lives was pretty low. She wouldn't have welcomed too much more detail.

'Do you like working for me?' Ingrid asked.

It was a surprisingly easy question to answer.

'Yes I do,' Monique said. 'It's about the best job I've ever had.'

'Better than the au pair?'

'That wasn't a job – they spoilt me. They had no kids of their own. I had it made.'

'Why do you like working for me?'

Monique considered. Her work hadn't always been with very interesting or lively people. Frequently it was monotonous and boring. 'Because I've seen a lot working with you. Travelled. Learnt how the other half live,' she said flippantly.

'Do you like me?'

'What a question!'

'Well, do you?' Ingrid was persisting.

'I couldn't work for you if I didn't.' And when she analysed the statement to herself, it was true. She didn't dislike Ingrid. At the moment she was an object, and objective and her *raison d'être*, but she liked the woman's fighting spirit, her determination to live exactly how she wanted. And then there was the piquancy of the situation with the man. In an odd way, she liked them both.

The signs for Perugia were in front of them. Ingrid was making good time. If she kept up the speed that she was driving at they could be in Florence in less than an hour. She was more relaxed now. The tenseness had gone from her shoulders, and she clicked her fingers at Monique. 'Maybe I will have a cigarette now,' she said.

Monique lit one and leaned to put it in the pretty greedy mouth, thinking how odd it was that since Jenny's disappearance there had been no sign of the coke and the white powder. That had been a relief. At times she had been obliged to take some of the stuff herself for appearances' sake, and that had been a problem. Monique liked to be in control of herself always, and it was hard to stay together after sniffing.

Instead of sniffing, Ingrid had chain-smoked. Maybe her cocaine supply had run out. Maybe with so many police about she had been afraid to chance it. But the coke habit seemed to have been abandoned. Probably only temporarily.

'What are we doing in Marseilles?' she tried out, casually.

'You're not doing anything,' Ingrid told her, almost rudely.

'Sorry I asked,' Monique said, mock humble, but her employer only grunted. Marseilles? Why Marseilles? It shouldn't have been in France. Maybe a boat from Corsica? But Corsica wasn't right either. Anyway, it would take too long. Why the *hell* Marseilles? She needed some help and advice.

At Florence she took over the driving. They had to stop for petrol and the change was made without wasting time, Ingrid hustling on the attendant. The autostrada to Pisa was quiet and it was easy driving; she kept the car at a steady 110 miles per hour without difficulty. The car clock showed it was creeping on to nine o'clock and Monique was getting hungry. After over 170 miles to Genoa she was going to be even more hungry, she decided. Then as if anticipating her thought, Ingrid opened the glove compartment and took out some chocolate.

'Energy,' she said briefly.

'My!' Monique accepted a piece gratefully. 'You eating chocolate.'

'I told you – it's energy,' Ingrid said. 'I'm going to sleep for a bit. Just take the Genoa autostrada from Pisa. I'll take over when we get there.'

It was a fair division of the driving. By Genoa they had both been at the wheel for nearly 175 miles and it was gone eleven of a crisp, clear night. A crescent new moon floated in the dark sky and Monique was ready to sleep when she woke Ingrid, who had been slumbering uneasily beside her. They were just outside Genoa. An opportunity was needed.

'Your turn,' she said, 'there's a petrol station ahead. We might as well fill up, and I want a pee.'

'OK,' Ingrid said, rubbing her eyes with the palm of her hand. 'I could do with a pee too.'

'Then you go ahead,' Monique said, 'and I'll deal with the car.'

Wherever they went it was always her job to handle the money. Ingrid, like royalty, never carried any. All the business transactions were left to Monique, and she had to put in detailed expenses of every cent she had spent. Ingrid would spend wildly on herself and on parties, but when it came to the day-to-day expenses, she had the mentality of a bank teller.

Monique noted with relief that Ingrid had taken her make-up bag with her as she got out of the car and looked around for the toilets. She could be a while. Monique had been looking around too, for the telephone. As soon as her employer had disappeared and the gasoline was ordered, she hurried to the booth, fishing *gettoni* from the bottom of her handbag. The number she dialled rang out and was answered quickly.

'It's Marseilles,' she said. Then: 'I know. I am, too. Listen, we're in the Lancia. Pick us up at the autoroute turn-off for Marseilles, just before Aix . . . I don't know . . . You work it out . . . We're at Genoa and we're keeping a steady 110 at least . . . Christ . . . she's coming back. I'm off.'

Ingrid was coming across the forecourt as she hung up.

'That was quick,' Monique said.

Ingrid's eyes were hard. 'What were you doing on the phone?'

'Trying to ring the house. I hadn't a *gettone* so I asked the operator to get the number. She couldn't get through. I thought I'd find out if there was any news.'

'I don't want anyone to know I'm away, I told you,' Ingrid said impatiently. 'For Christ's sake – why don't you listen? Don't make any contact. Remember.'

'I just thought—'

'Don't think. Do what you're told.'

Without replying, Monique headed for the toilet herself. The bitch could be as bad tempered as she liked. It didn't matter. She had made contact.

Ingrid drove the Lancia as far as the frontier while Monique slept deeply. Her head jerking on her shoulders woke her a few times, but she opened her eyes refreshed, knowing that sleep would have come harder had she not been able to make the phone call. The responsibility was no longer hers.

'You can do the rest of the driving,' Ingrid said after they had shown their passports to a sleepy frontier guard and edged slowly into France where they went through the same procedure. 'Wake me when we get to Fréjus.'

As it happened there was no need to wake Ingrid. The autoroute petered out after Monte Carlo. The changing engine note disturbed her and she was alert to the drive over the last stretch of the Corniche and then through the Promenade des Anglais when they picked up the autoroute again at St Laurent du Var. 'Are you still OK to drive?' she asked Monique.

It was nearly two o'clock in the morning. Monique knew that if she relinquished the wheel she would sleep instantly but she wanted to finish the drive for reasons of her own.

'I'm all right,' she said. 'You go back to sleep.'

Ingrid did not go back to sleep. She sat alert in her seat as they sped through the Provence Alps on a road that was as familiar to Monique as her own face in the mirror.

'Where around here were you brought up?' Ingrid asked idly.

'Oddly enough, Marseilles,' Monique told her.

Ingrid did not seem pleased. She was silent until they reached the turn-off for Fréjus when she said: 'Right. Stop here, fill up and I'll drive.'

It wasn't really important who was driving, Monique thought as she got out of the car to pay the attendant and ask for a bill. The car number was known. There could be no error and she was tired. Ingrid, who seemed to have recovered all her energy, was waiting at the wheel when she came back, drumming her fingers impatiently.

'Christ, they take their time, don't they?' she said. She was twitchy again, Monique realized. Her shoulders thrust forward over the wheel as she peered through the night, accelerating just a trifle too much. Two more hours to Marseilles. Perhaps less. An hour and a half to the pick-up. It was all going well. Too well. As they reached the Le Luc exit, Ingrid slowed and joined the slip road to come off the autoroute.

'Hey,' Monique almost shouted, 'you've come off too early.'

'No.'

Goddamn her! Monique thought, but said: 'Where are we going?'

'You'll see.'

So near and yet so far! Someone was going to have a long wait at the Marseilles turn-off and there was nothing she could do for at least an hour. With Ingrid speeding east along the old N7 and Brignoles ahead, events were out of her hands.

'Fed up with motorway driving?' Monique ventured.

'No.' And as Ingrid spoke she turned the car left on to a secondary road so abruptly that Monique missed the signpost.

'Now where are we going?' she asked, her voice resigned.

'Taking you to a beautiful hotel,' Ingrid said. 'You'll like it.'

I'd have liked it a damn sight more if it had been on the autoroute after the Marseilles turn-off, Monique thought.

'Guess where?' Ingrid said, all her attention on the road in the darkness. 'You should know if you're a local.'

'On the coast?' Monique decided to join in the game.

'Yes.'

'Near Marseilles?'

'Not far.'

'Your class of hotel?'

'Yes.'

'Got to be the Roches Blanches.' Ingrid just nodded. In fact it did have to be the Roches Blanches. Monique had suddenly realized on which road they were. It was the D15, it cut straight across country to Cassis and it was a stinker to drive, particularly at night. But Ingrid seemed relaxed again now she was on the last leg of the journey. She was driving the the curves and bends with easy confidence.

But why the Roches Blanches? Monique asked herself.

'Are they expecting us?' she asked. 'They don't usually receive their guests this late.'

'They're expecting us,' Ingrid said laconically.

And when had that been arranged? Ingrid wasn't one to make her own reservations, not when she had a dogsbody to do it for her. Who else had made the booking?

Conversation dried again and she even found herself dozing as the Lancia roared on over the mountains until they pulled in to Cassis. The hotel, just outside the town, was in darkness except for a light in the entrance hall. Ingrid stayed at the wheel, the engine running while Monique got the bags from the boot and rang the bell.

'Someone's coming,' she called to Ingrid as she saw through the glass the night porter plodding wearily towards them.

'Good,' Ingrid said through the open window of the car.

'See you later.' And she put her foot on the accelerator, revved the engine, turned in a circle and disappeared back down the drive to the road. There wasn't a thing that Monique could do about it except make another telephone call.

She was asleep when Ingrid came back. Early morning light was flooding into the room someone had booked for them and she could hear the sound of the sea under her window. Their room had two double beds, but Ingrid, naked, climbed in with her.

'Wake up,' she was saying.

Monique had come back from some deep fog where she had been driving through black tunnels that never seemed to finish. Tunnels that had no light at the end. She woke in a panic to find Ingrid wrapped around her, repeating: 'Wake up, wake up.'

'What is it?' Monique said.

'Wake up!' Ingrid said into her ear, and then firmly and painfully bit the lobe.

'Ouch!' Monique sat bolt upright. 'Ingrid, stop it,' she protested. 'What's happened?'

Ingrid's head tipped back on her slender neck so that two strong sinews became prominent. She licked her lips, lowered her lashes and said: 'I got it.'

'A good fuck and a skinful of coke, by the look of it,' Monique grumbled.

'No. The money. The ransom. The whole fucking lot. Every sodding penny.'

But she had had coke. Maybe something even stronger, Monique realized. Ingrid only swore when high. Whoever had given her the money had given her coke. And where the hell had she gone to get it?

It was pretty much what Monique had expected. The journey had to be to get the ransom. No way in the end would Ingrid Pallia have totally bankrupted herself for her daughter. The old survivor had come through again. But *where* had she gone to get it? Had anyone followed her? Could anyone have had time to follow her? Monique knew there wasn't a chance. But had the provider of the cash come to Marseilles especially to meet her? Or was that now his homing ground? Unlikely.

The thought still nagged her that it ought to have been Portugal. And that she'd failed, but through no fault of her own.

'I got it! I got it! I got it!' Ingrid was saying, her voice slurring. The coke or whatever it was was taking over. 'I got it—' she said on a dying fall, and suddenly slept.

Disgruntled and disappointed, Monique decided she might just as well do the same.

They started the drive back at 10.30 the next morning. They had woken at 9.30 and Ingrid could have had no more than a couple of hours' sleep. Monique wasn't sure how long she had rested. She had no idea what time it had been when Monique returned to the hotel.

They took breakfast on the terrace, the Mediterranean blue below, pines scenting the air, but Monique's only thought was to get to a telephone without Ingrid knowing.

'I was high last night,' Ingrid said abruptly as they got into the car. Monique was driving. 'I don't want you to mention anything I told you about the money.'

'OK.' Monique looked in the mirror back at the charming hotel and wished they could have stayed longer. 'You didn't say much anyway. Only that you'd got every fucking, sodding penny of it. Where from?'

'I don't want to talk about it.' Ingrid was frowning; evading the question.

Monique shrugged. She could hardly announce that she did.

'And remember,' Ingrid added. 'I haven't been away. I've been in bed, sick.'

'And where have I been?' Monique asked, 'putting all that mileage on the Lancia?'

'To see your mother in Marseilles, if you need to say anything.'

Monique laughed. 'It's about the last place I'd think of going, since she's been dead and buried in the cold, cold ground for three years now, but if you say so, OK.'

They arrived at Parioli just after ten o'clock at night, and Monique, who had driven the last lap from Perugia, let the car

189

glide the last few hundred yards. Then very quietly Ingrid slid out of the Lancia, shut the door of the car and slipped along the driveway around to the back of the house. She had chosen to go in through the servants' entrance so that she could appear as if she had come from her room and down into the kitchen to get herself some food.

Monique watched her glide away and disappear before reversing a short way back down the road and then using someone's driveway, turned to drive back to the Via Flaminia and looked for a café with a telephone. She found one on the square where she made a brief call. As the phone was answered she said:

'She's back. She has the money.' A pause. 'No. She wouldn't tell me.' She listened, looking out into the café where the impatient Roman's customers stood, gulping their *cappuccino*. 'Tomorrow?' she said eventually. 'Where? OK. See you later, then.'

She put down the phone and then rumaged for another *gettone*. She was smiling, pleased with herself, as she picked up the receiver again to make a second brief call and she sighed with relief as she put the phone down. Very tired, she hurried from the café, hoping the *padrone* would not notice she had only used his phone.

There was a buzz of noise coming from the drawing room of the villa and she quietly let herself into the house. The hushed silence of the other waiting evenings was gone, and the group were up later than usual. It was not quite eleven and by now they had generally gone to their various rooms.

Though her intention had been to go straight to bed, curiosity made her decide to join them. She pushed open the door from the big dimly lit hallway and the scene in front of her was lit like a stage set. Every lamp was full on. The fire had been lit and Ingrid was standing with her back to the fireplace, wearing an uncharacteristic woollen dressing gown, her hair scraped back and no make-up. She was almost managing to look as if she had been in bed, sick for two days. Over-acting again, Monique thought.

Kate sat in her usual place but there was no Paul. Charles was standing against the arm of the sofa where Eileen Elliot was sitting. He had his hand lightly on her shoulder.

Ingrid was the first to spot the open door with Monique standing hesitantly.

'Oh, you're back,' she said. 'Quick, come in. There's so much news.'

She'd had a shot of coke, Monique thought dispassionately. It showed in the too bright eyes, the gleaming mouth and the fact that Ingrid had permitted herself to appear in public looking so unglamorous.

'What news?' Monique asked. 'Are the girls back?' Her expression was eager and anxious, and she wondered if she, too, were over-acting.

'No,' Kate said. 'But Paul's coming back tomorrow with £300,000 in banker's drafts. And with what we've got, that's enough for Jenny's ransom.'

Monique looked across at Kate. Her oval face was pale and she like Ingrid, wore no make-up. Her mouth, usually turned up at the corners in the beginnings of a smile was clown-drooped. She wore a blue and white track-suit.

'Paul's done it?' Monique said.

Kate just nodded.

'But what about Bobbie Jean and Frances?'

'Paul is bringing Mr Elliot back with him tomorrow,' Kate said, quietly. 'He can't quite make the figure. He's going to try to negotiate with the kidnappers.'

'And you?' Monique asked Charles Dennison. She was aware she was taking more part than she should in the proceedings; exposing herself a little too much – but even without coke she was feeling the same high as Ingrid.

'I too am going to have to negotiate,' Charles said sombrely. Both he and Eileen were watching Ingrid, their faces mirroring bitterness and envy. She did not seem aware.

'There's more,' she was saying. 'The most incredible thing has happened—'

Monique raised her eyebrows in query.

'Bellino. The kidnappers got him. They castrated him. He's in hospital in intensive care – but only for loss of blood. He'll be all right. But he won't be interfering with little girls again,' she said with satisfaction.

Monique felt a profound sense of shock, followed by a frisson of fear. Bellino had done nothing to the kidnappers. If they could be that ruthless . . .

'You mean NAP did it?' she asked.

'Yes. NAP,' Ingrid was saying with relish. 'They did it. They rang here and claimed responsibility this morning. Don't you think that's marvellous.'

'It's certainly poetic justice,' Monique said trying to show no expression.

'They rang,' Kate said wearily, 'and said that if the decadent society could not take care of it's children, they would. Then they claimed responsibility for Bellino. I'm surprised you didn't know. It's been all over the front pages.'

'I've been to see my mother in Marseilles,' Monique heard herself saying. 'But castration!'

'Castration,' Kate said. 'Not poetic justice. Rough justice. I'm not sure he deserved that.'

'He deserved that and more,' Charles Dennison said. He had moved a pace or two forward, almost threateningly. 'I hope the bastard dies! And painfully.'

Eileen Elliot had put out a restraining hand to him.

'You couldn't be expected to understand,' she said directly to the two younger women. 'Neither of you have children.'

Monique stifled a retort. It seemed only she and Kate had realized the danger to the girls from the evidence of NAP's violence.

'Of course not,' she said. 'I'm so pleased Paul has the money, Ingrid. If only the others can bargain, perhaps it will all come right.'

Ingrid's face was hard.

'There'll be ways,' she said.

'Of course,' Monique said. 'But if you'll forgive me . . . It's a long drive. *À demain.*'

She wanted to go up alone and think, but there was no chance.

'Wait for me,' Ingrid said. 'I'm coming too.'

192

Chapter Ten

Rome before dawn was as grey and dismal as any city, Kate thought as she looked out of the attic window and across the open space by the villa to the domes and campanili of Rome. From here she could almost count the seven hills, and the sky was sombre but with a thin yellow stripe of light that arranged itself as a backdrop to the distant dome of St Peter's.

She could not sleep and sat in her dark blue silk dressing gown staring out into the dawn. At just a little later than this, the day before, she had been dressed ready to go downstairs with Paul. He had been packing and he too was dressed; in a dark good suit with a plain dark-blue-and-white spotted tie. Full of misery, she had watched him, intent on securing the lid of the small leather suitcase.

She had asked: 'So, she'll be coming back with you?'

He had straightened.

'I don't know,' he said. 'She only suggested it.'

'Will you persuade her?'

'No.'

The flat firm little word had cheered her. She knew he would not lie.

'So it's fingers crossed?' she had said.

He had moved his shoulders uneasily. The questioning note in her voice was out of line. She was probing at his loyalties and that was something they normally tried to avoid. He resented it and there was no reassurance or joy in it for her.

It was as the streaks of light split the sky that she had suggested they go down. The taxi was due.

He had nodded, shut his eyes briefly and sighed, the rumpled bed behind him and the visible signal of his departure, the suitcase on the white linen sheets. He moved to take her in his arms and her head was on his shoulder. She had pressed herself against him as hard as she could and hugged him with all her strength.

'Do you want to pack it up?' he had asked into her hair.

'Do you?'

'Kate!' His voice had been strained, maybe because she was

holding him so tight. 'Please, darling. Not now. It's not the moment.'

'You started it. Do you?'

Again the explosive, truthful 'No!' She had let him go. And they had kissed once before going down to the hallway together.

Now watching the dawn stripes widen in the midnight blue sky she was remembering that 'No.' and praying that Madeleine would not come back to Rome with him. It would be a situation she felt she could not handle, for all her sophistication. If Madeleine came, she and Paul would be sleeping together in the next room, and he had said that they still made love. She tapped on the wall by the bed gently. Could you hear, she wondered? She would not be able to bear hearing the sounds of their lovemaking, but then she thought that Paul's sensitivity would not let that happen.

She wished she had asked him what was happening when he rang with the news of the £300,000 – but she did not want to seem pressing. And he had volunteered no information. She thought gloomily that if Madeleine had not been coming to Rome he might have been more likely to give her some news.

Now she had no wish to sleep so she returned to work on Ingrid's life story. The tapes of the conversations were transcribed and she was cutting up the sheets of typewritten words, sticking them into some rough order of continuity. Engrossed in the work, making notes where she needed more detail from Ingrid, she managed to forget her problems.

The anxiety returned when hunger and the sun streaming through the window sent her downstairs for a late breakfast. Charles and Eileen were already in the dining room, heads so close together that they were startled when she appeared. She wondered what Charles saw in Eileen Elliot, for it was patently obvious that some kind of affair had started. Eileen had blossomed in two days. Her eyes were brighter, her hair softer; she seemed more relaxed. Her voice was as awful as ever but maybe, being an American, Charles didn't realize how affected she was. As she said good morning, he went to the long table where coffee and bread and rolls were prepared. He poured Kate a cup, putting in the correct amount of milk and sugar. As a group, she thought, they had acquired a superficial intimacy regarding each other's likes and dislikes. He knew, for example, that she never ate breakfast and he brought her the cup and saucer making no attempt to offer her anything else.

'Paul's coming back today.' It was a statement, not a question.

She nodded and took her cup of coffee.

'At what time?'

'About four, I should think.'

'With £300,000 for Ingrid,' Eileen put in. She was wearing plain white linen pants and a deep blue button-through cotton cardigan. She looked years younger than the woman who had arrived in Rome just eight days ago, but her face, thinking of Ingrid, set in disagreeable lines.

'Yes,' Kate said.

'The wages of sin is a lot of money,' said Eileen bitterly.

'Yes,' Kate said again.

Charles put his hand on Eileen's arm.

'The fact that she has got her ransom may give us bargaining power,' he said. 'From the kidnappers' point of view half a loaf may be better than no bread and they can't keep the children for ever.'

'Maybe.' Eileen sounded sceptical, then she added: 'Alex is coming back today.'

'With Paul?' Kate asked.

'Yes and with Paul's wife,' Eileen said. 'Alex said that Paul suggested they might as well all travel together.'

Very carefully Kate put down her coffee cup. Another sip would have made her vomit on the spot.

'Well,' she said brightly, 'I'd better get upstairs and earn that £300,000 for Ingrid. See you later.' And with her back very straight she walked from the room.

'She didn't know Paul's wife was coming,' Charles said. 'Did you see her face for an instant there? Stricken.'

'I know how she feels,' Eileen said.

'Because Alex is coming back?'

She nodded.

'Guilty?'

'No.' She shook her head emphatically. 'It's just that I don't care if I ever see him again. It's going to be difficult.'

'Then I'm guilty,' he said quietly.

She half closed her eyes and sighed.

'Don't be. I've not been so happy for years. It was worth it.'

He went to pour himself another coffee, trying to unscramble his very confused thoughts.

Last night Eileen had come to his room and again they had slept without touching each other. This morning he had woken early with the same rise, and again she had turned to him and they had quickly and simply made love. Then as before, she had returned to her room.

Right at this moment he found himself wanting to make love to her again. Not simply. He wanted her naked, without the nightgown bunched around her waist. He wanted her hair in disarray on the pillow. He wanted to taste her, bite at her, lose himself in her. And he wasn't sure why. Melting the ice-maiden? Not that she had been all ice; just restrained. True affection? Or the fact that she was the first woman he had had in so long and that their joint anxieties had created a special need and bond?

Whatever the reasons, he found himself wondering how he could suggest that they went back to bed. The moment passed as the door opened again and Ingrid came into the room wearing a pale blue silk kimono printed with writhing dragons. Monique was close behind her.

'Good morning,' Ingrid said and sat down at the table. 'Coffee, please, Monique,' she ordered, 'and a croissant.' Monique busied herself at the serving table, and there was an uncomfortable silence as Eileen stared at her hostess with unfriendly eyes.

'Have you really raised the money?' she asked.

'Looks like it.' Ingrid took the coffee cup from Monique and took a sip, looking at Charles over the top with big innocent eyes.

'But it's not going to help if Charles and Alex can't get it,' Eileen said.

'Oh, I don't know. I shall try to bargain,' Ingrid said. 'They might let Jenny go. Silly to keep all three girls when they can get their hands on half a million for a start.'

'How could you be so selfish?' Eileen looked as if she was going to burst into tears.

'Now, Eileen,' Charles said. 'You'd do the same if it was for Frances. I know I would for Bobbie Jean.'

She was silent, her head bent, looking at the table and making a pattern with a few crumbs from the bread she had eaten.

'It's true, I suppose,' she said, and then looked at him. 'Will it hurt things for us if she gets her way—?' she jerked her head contemptuously in Ingrid's direction.

'God knows,' Charles said helplessly.

Monique had settled herself with coffee and bread. Her black hair was sleeked back with what looked like some kind of jelly and she wore a dark green track-suit.

'I can't see why it should do any harm,' she said. 'They can only agree to let Jenny go or they can refuse. What difference can it make to the other girls?'

'Then why did they ask for the money for all three at once?' Eileen asked belligerently.

Monique shrugged, and Charles realized he had never heard her voice an opinion before.

'Because of the dangers of two money-drops, I suppose. The girls must have noticed something about where they have been kept. They should be able to give the police some clues.'

'More likely they'll take the half million and still keep Jenny,' Charles said wearily.

There was an anxious little exclamation from Ingrid but Monique looked thoughtful. She chewed on her bread, eyes unfocused.

'No, I don't think they'll do that.'

'Why not?' Ingrid said sharply.

'I don't know. I just don't somehow,' she said vaguely.

Charles looked at her, considering, something like a suspicion forming in his mind. He had felt all along that it was possible that NAP could have someone planted in the house or at least close to their group. If his suspicions were right now he thought about it, it had to be Monique. Or Kate? Or Paul?

Neither seemed likely. Monique was the joker in the pack. And sitting there her face unmade-up, the very black hair sleek and shiny, flat to her head, the long eyes looking at nothing, she looked very foreign and far too exotic to be no more than a film star's runabout.

'How long have you worked for Ingrid, Monique?' he asked abruptly.

The long, black eyes were suddenly alert, watching him with quick intelligence.

'About five months,' she said.

'Not longer?'

'No. Why?' It was asked casually, but he sensed a challenge beneath.

'I was thinking how lucky Ingrid is to have you at this time.'

The girl shrugged. 'I haven't been so much help, I'm afraid.'

'Oh, yes you have,' Ingrid said suddenly. 'And would you believe, she costs me peanuts.'

Monique looked as if she wished that had not been said. She got to her feet and sighed: 'Well, I haven't that many proper qualifications. Rotten typist, can't do shorthand. I'm a very good gofer, though. And now,' she added, 'I'm going for a jog. I need some fresh air. *Ciao*. See you all later.'

With a light wave, she padded out of the room, her white sneakers slapping on the mosaic floor.

Charles watched her go, and then said to Ingrid: 'Where did you meet her?'

'In LA first,' she said. 'I think she'd been trying to break into films and then she was working as a kind of production assistant on that film I made in Paris. They'd taken her on because of her English. We kind of hit it off and it went on from there.'

Los Angeles and Paris, Charles thought. Would NAP go that far to set up this particular kidnapping? Five months ago Bellino's film had only been a vague thought in the man's mind. They couldn't have known Jenny would be cast, certainly not that Bobbie Jean would be cast. No, it didn't make sense. Monique couldn't have been planted that long ago. Not unless they'd roped her in much later and for money. But from what he knew of Italian terrorists, that wasn't their style. He must have got it wrong.

Ingrid and Eileen had been making polite conversation and now Ingrid was drifting out of the room, her kimono outlining her tight high behind. She was announcing that she thought she'd get dressed. It was suddenly very quiet and still. The room itself felt expectant and he saw that Eileen was sitting quietly, just looking at him.

'Shall we go back to bed?' he said abruptly.

For a moment she was statue-still then all she did was nod. To reassure her, he took her hand and led her out into the big hallway where the sergeant slumbered at his post, waiting for his early morning relief to arrive. He did not see them go by and mount the big open staircase up to Charles' room on the first floor. And Charles, again to lighten the moment, put a warning finger to his lips. She half smiled and when they got to the bedroom door, it was she who went in first.

The maids had already been in to clean and tidy. The bed with its white lace spread was neat, the shutters were drawn against the sun and the morning light filtered in dancing splashes over the walls and the heavy dark furniture.

The door closed behind them, she stood uncertainly in the centre of the room, looking at the bed as if she were not sure what to do about the bedspread.

He moved towards her and took her into his arms, her head dropped on to his shoulder and then lifted to look at him. He bent to kiss her and they stayed, clinging together, the kiss lingering while the soft sigh of their breathing was the only sound in the room.

Eventually he pulled back from her and, still without speaking, very gently and slowly began to undo the buttons on the front of her cotton cardigan. She moved uneasily and he realized she was nervous.

'Sshh,' he said, letting his hand slip under the cotton to cup the full breast underneath. She stood unresponsive but without complaining as he slid her cardigan over her shoulders and off her arms. Her hands loosely at her side, she watched him, her blue eyes anxious, until he turned her and unfastened the plain white brassiere she was wearing. Then he flung it and her cardigan over a chair and turned her to face him again. 'Beautiful,' he murmured, lifting the full heavy white breasts, one in each hand. 'Beautiful. Take your clothes off. Please.'

199

'All right.' She took off her trousers and panties swiftly, her back to him. Then she slid quickly into bed, hiding her face.

'What's the matter?' he asked her.

'I don't know.' Her voice was muffled by the pillows. 'I'm nervous, maybe.'

'You weren't this morning,' he reminded her.

'It wasn't so –' she hesitated '– open. We were in bed.'

'So you were hiding?'

She turned to look at him.

'Maybe, in a way.'

'Don't you want me to make love to you?'

'Yes, but—'

'But what?'

'This is different. I don't know what you expect from me. I don't know what to do.'

'Could you touch me and kiss me?'

'Where? Here?' She touched him lightly. 'I've never kissed . . .' her voice trailed away.

He found himself wondering fleetingly if this had been the problem with her marriage.

'Why not?'

'Because Alex said it was disgusting.'

'Well, it's not.' His voice was firm, correcting the misapprehensions of a child.

Quite suddenly she rolled over and sat up. She put out her hand and grasped him, moving him with considerable skill.

'That's what Alex liked,' she said, and her voice was angry. 'That's all Alex really liked.'

'I like it, too,' he said. 'But other things as well.'

He took her hand from him and laughed at her worried face. He knew that if he was to unlock this woman's sensuality – and suddenly it had become important to do so – he had to break her of old habits; teach her new ways and pleasures. And he found he had a willing pupil.

'You are a very sexy lady,' he said eventually.

She moved against him uneasily.

'Do you really think so?'

He chuckled. 'Yes, I do.'

She made a small self-satisfied noise. Then said: 'I've never done it in those ways before. Well, to be truthful, I've hardly done it at all.'

'What a waste,' he said. 'Well, there are lots more ways. We'll just work through the lot.'

'Can we really?' she said, burrowing her head in his shoulder.

They were still in bed at two o'clock in the afternoon. Between naps, small dozes and shared confidences, he had kept his promise and showed her how supple and responsive the body could be. She was sated, her hair damp and clinging to her forehead, her body coated in light sweat and smelling of sex, perspiration and love. Her lips were swollen and bruised. Small traces of mascara touched her cheeks like freckles, and she lay, greedy and happy, sucking at his shoulder until she had raised a black love bite. Then she sat up and peered at her handiwork.

'Frances came in with one of those on her neck,' she said. 'I was jealous. I've never had one nor given one.'

'Then I shall give you one,' he said. 'And then we must get up. The English contingent will be arriving soon.'

'Oh, my God!' she said. 'Alex! No, don't give me a love bite.'

His teeth and tongue were already tugging powerfully at the flesh at the base of her throat where her shoulder began. He let her go and said: 'Too late. You'll just have to wear a high-necked blouse.'

She giggled.

'I don't expect he'll notice.'

He looked down at her ripe body, her sleepy eyes and red mouth and said: 'I think maybe he will.'

'Not a chance,' she said. 'He hasn't looked at me for years.'

She believed it as she said it, but when they had showered and dressed and she looked at herself in the bathroom mirror, even she could see the change. Some kind of rigid control had gone from her. She looked softer. As if she were loved, she thought, and wondered if Charles did love her: hoped he might. Love was a word that hadn't been spoken.

She was sitting demurely in her chair in the living room with

Charles and Monique when they heard the taxi draw up outside. Someone rang the bell, and she could hear Ingrid running down the stairs. There was no sign of Kate.

She knew she ought to get up and greet Alex at the door, but somehow she could not. She was hugging the memory of the day to her, and yet was guilty that she had not thought once of Frances while it had been happening. All she had been aware of was her body and his and their responses to each other. She felt a wave of regret, both for herself and for Alex, when she thought of the lost years of her own sensuality.

He was coming into the room now, ahead of Paul, who was leading a pretty blonde woman who tottered on her feet. Alex was thinner and crumpled looking. He seemed aged and she stared at him, trying to equate this worried, beaten man with her bullying, insensitive husband. Impulsively, she got to her feet and moved to him, kissing him on the cheek.

'Alex—' she heard herself say. 'You look so tired.'

'I'm all right,' he said with only a touch of the old belligerence. 'What about you?'

He was searching her with his eyes, and his expression changed. He looked as if he were about to say something, and then turned abruptly away.

'Is there any news?' he asked Ingrid, who was standing in the doorway.

Before she could reply, the telephone rang. She turned and rushed into the hall where the sergeant, suddenly galvanized into life, was switching on the tape recorder. Ingrid grabbed the receiver, and stood, as if at bay, staring at the rest of the group who had gathered in the doorway.

'*Pronto*,' she said into the phone. Paul moved as if to take it from her, but she swung round to turn her back and clutch the receiver to her. 'Yes. Yes,' she was saying. 'I have it. I have my money . . . I have half a million pounds for you in Swiss francs. Let me have Jenny back. The others are still searching. You can have my money if I can have my daughter.' She was gabbling, babbling, while Paul and Alex stood watching her, both their faces stricken. 'How? How?' she said. 'No – tell me, don't go.' Her voice was frantic. Then she swung around again to look at the others. 'He hung up,' she said tragically. 'He just said he'd think about it. Oh, shit!'

'Ingrid – how could you?' Paul said. 'How could you!'

She tossed her head, the small nostrils flaring. 'Easy,' she said.

By the time Kate came downstairs an almighty row had begun. Alex screaming at Ingrid: 'You bitch. You fucking cow! You don't give a toss for anyone but yourself . . .'

Paul was trying to calm him as Ingrid shrieked back: 'I'll do what I like. If you can't raise the money, why should Jenny suffer?'

Madeleine was clinging to the jam of the door, standing with her feet planted wide apart, her face pale, she swayed gently on stiff legs. Monique was watching and silent.

It was Charles who managed to create quiet. He did it by taking Alex firmly by the arm and saying in a major-general's voice: 'That will do. And you be quiet too,' he said to Ingrid, raising his hand as if to slap her.

There was an uneasy silence and Kate asked, pausing at the last step: 'Whatever's going on?'

Charles turned to her. 'Ingrid has suggested to the kidnappers that they let Jenny go as she has raised her share of the money. Alex is angry.'

Kate thought about it. They all seemed to be looking at her as if she were expected to give judgement.

'Well, perhaps it's sensible, though they did say they wanted all the money at once. And,' she added, 'there's no guarantee they'll actually let Jenny go if we do give them the cash.'

'Exactly,' Charles said. 'It's not foolproof. But if NAP agree and Ingrid wants to take the chance we have no right to stop her.'

'I want to take the chance,' Ingrid said stubbornly. The high colour in her cheeks was subsiding, leaving unnaturally white patches. 'And so would you, if it were your daughter—' she flung at Alex.

'You never even gave us the chance to bargain,' he said bitterly. 'We ought to have been able to bargain.'

'That's the truth,' Charles said. 'No more of that, Ingrid. We're all in this together. In future, when they ring, Paul deals with it. Right?'

203

'It's my house, my phone and my daughter,' Ingrid said. I shall do what I like.'

Charles momentarily looked defeated.

'Oh, no you won't,' Kate said pleasantly. 'Or I won't write a word of your sodding book.'

'I've got the money.'

'No, you haven't, Ingrid. I've got the money,' Paul said. 'And I'll damn well keep it unless you behave yourself.'

'You can't do that.'

'Try me,' he said.

Her face reddened again. 'Oh, fuck off, the lot of you—' she said, brushing past Kate to go upstairs again.

They all watched her disappearance around the bend in the stairs and then Kate said tiredly: 'Why don't we all sit down?'

'Yes,' Monique murmured. 'I'll arrange for some tea.'

'I'd rather have a drink,' Alex said heavily, staring at his wife and then at Charles. He wasn't such a fool as he appeared, Kate thought.

She had tried to avoid looking directly at Paul, but her innards had contracted at the sight of him, grave faced and serious. He was helping Madeleine into the drawing room and settling her on the sofa in the place where she, Kate, had always sat since they arrived. She felt a wave of blinding resentment. Madeleine was smiling up at him, head cocked to one side like a canary. 'Thank you, darling,' she was trilling. Then she looked straight at Kate, saying: 'Am I in anyone's place?'

Paul looked momentarily stricken as he realized what he had done.

'Well, Kate usually sits there,' Eileen said. 'But I don't suppose she'll mind, do you Kate?'

It wasn't malice, Kate realized, just sheer insensitivity.

'Not at all,' she said. 'And anyway, I've got to get on with some work. It was only the din that brought me down. I'll see you all later.'

And for the second time that day she left the room feeling as if her stomach was in her throat.

Paul came to her about half an hour later. She was sitting, staring blindly at her typewriter as he knocked. She got up and pressed her back against the desk as he came into the room to see her facing him. He walked to wrap her in his arms; held her tight and buried his face in her hair.

'I'm sorry. I'm sorry. I'm sorry,' he said.

'What for?' Her voice was muffled.

'Everything. Be patient with me. I had no choice.'

'I know.' And she realized that she did know and felt a devastating wave of love and desire. She put her arms around him and hugged him. 'It's all right,' she told him. 'Truly.'

'It isn't really,' he said sadly. 'It's all wrong. I didn't want to do this to you.'

She wanted to reassure him.

'*It's all right,*' she said, emphasizing each word, then more casually: 'Where is she now?'

'Just finishing her tea. I'm meant to be checking on your progress.'

'My progress is fine. You'd better get back.'

'I suppose so,' he said doubtfully. 'You won't forget I love you?'

'No.'

'I'll try to be with you when I can.'

'No, it's better not.' She pulled away from him. 'Off you go. Don't worry. I'm all right. Just as long—' she stopped.

'Just as long . . .?' he prompted.

'. . . As you don't make love to her.'

'I couldn't. Not with you so near,' he told her as he went.

Alex Elliot was exhausted. His eyes felt as if someone had sandpapered them, he could hardly keep his hands from trembling. The strain of the past few days had taken its toll. The nightmare of trying to raise money on the house, on the business, on the few valuable pieces of furniture and jewellery that he had accumulated over the years, had made him realize just how little he had achieved in real terms now that the chips were down.

He had come back to Rome to try to bargain with the kidnappers, offering the amount of money that he had been able to raise, but that fucking bitch had got to the phone first. He felt a terrible despair and a gnawing fear that he would never see his daughter again. He knew with total certainty that the only thing that meant a damn to him in the world was Frances. For Frances he had sacrificed his life to the affected silly bitch he had had to marry. And now he had a strong suspicion that that affected silly bitch had been up to something while he had been away. She had the look of a woman who had been well laid. He knew the look intimately from the afternoons and early evening he had spent in the arms and the bed of Linda Bellamy. Before going back to Weybridge he would leave Linda with the same cream-filled look. That same near bruising of the mouth and the same languorous look in the eyes.

He did not care to screw his wife. The act of impregnating her reminded him too forcibly of the first time he had done so, and the consequences thereof. He loved the consequence, Frances, but he felt his life had been wasted on the woman who had by sheer chance borne his daughter.

But nevertheless, his wife was no one else's to screw, and as they drank their tea and ate pastries in the drawing room his bloodshot tired eyes darted from Eileen to Charles. It had to be Charles. There wasn't anyone else.

Suddenly he had to know. He put down his cup so that it rattled in the saucer and said abruptly to his wife: 'Come along.'

She looked up, surprised, and then flushed as she saw the look he was giving her. She half hesitated, half turned to Charles Dennison, decided against it and rose to her feet.

'Of course, dear,' she said dutifully.

She walked up the stairs three paces behind him, her head bent, as anger boiled in him. Once in their bedroom he looked around for signs of any sexual activity. There were none. She must have gone to his room, he thought. The slut.

'Would you like me to unpack for you?' she was saying.

'I'll do it myself.'

She shrugged and walked to the mirror, looking at herself, half smiling and curling a tendril of blonde hair around her finger. She was shameless.

'What have you been doing while I've been away?'

She turned from her reflection to look at him.

'Just waiting for you to come back,' she said.

'Just waiting?'

Her eyes widened. 'What do you mean?' she said, and the way she pronounced 'mean' enraged him.

'What I mean,' he said, sounding the word with its correct long double 'e', 'is have you been waiting alone?'

'Of course not,' she said. 'We have all been waiting. There is nothing to do but wait.'

Her face was bland; the eyes not quite looking at him.

'You haven't asked me how much money I've got together.'

'You told me on the phone. Not enough.' Her voice was vaguely contemptuous, and the rage boiled over.

He moved and grabbed her hair, jerking her head backwards.

'At least I'm trying. At least I care,' he said.

'I know.' Her eyes were slightly narrowed with the pain of him pulling her hair, but she watched him steadily. Now close up he could see her lips were bruised. He decided to bruise them some more, and bent to grind his mouth into hers, pushing his tongue between her unresponsive lips.

With sudden strength she pushed him away.

'Don't touch me.'

'Why not, you cold bitch?'

'I am not a cold bitch,' she said through gritted teeth.

'Oh yeah,' he said. 'Who says so. Charles Dennison?'

She froze, and then relaxed and a small smile turned up the corners of the swollen red mouth. 'That's right,' she said.

He stood speechless. Confession he had not expected.

'You filthy slut,' he said softly and unable to help himself, smashed his hand across her face so that she fell back on to the bed. He had the urge to rip at her clothing and to take her by force. He found he was erect as he had not been for her for years. But disgust for the whole situation filled him. His anger had gone. He stared at her.

'What sort of woman are you?' he asked her. 'Fucking around while your daughter is in danger of death. Christ. What sort of woman are you?' His voice was unbelieving. 'You've always been a lousy mother, but this—'

She was sitting up and her face crumpled. She dropped her head into her hands, hiding the angry red mark on her cheek where he had hit her and she was sobbing bitterly.

'It's too late to cry,' he said, and walked out of the room, picking up his unpacked suitcase. 'I'll be at the Eden if you want me. Tell Dennison you're all his – and he's welcome to you.'

Chapter Eleven

When Monique came back from her jog the next morning she wasn't altogether surprised to find Ingrid anxiously watching out of the front window of the villa for her return. Nor was she surprised to find Ingrid hurrying to open the front door, close it behind her, taking Monique's arm to walk her back down the gravel driveway and away from the house towards the swimming pool.

'I must talk to you,' she said.

'What's the matter?' Monique was sweating gently and she wiped her velour-clad forearm over her forehead.

'Look at this—'

They were out of sight of the windows, a bank of trees bordered the edge of the pool, giving them cover. Ingrid was handing her an envelope.

'Verde found it this morning. Stuck in the windscreen wipers of the Merc,' she said.

Monique sat down on the grass and turned the envelope over in her hands. It was addressed to Signora Pallia, and inside there was a single sheet of notepaper. The message was badly typed. It said:

Scimitar's daughter, send the dark girl who works for you with the money to the Piazza del Popolo to the café on the right at the end of the Corso at 4 p.m. today. She must order a cappuccino, come alone and wait for the signal to hand over the money. She will be told where the girl is to be found. Do not show this to any other nor to the police if you wish your daughter to be found alive.

'Somewhat overdramatic, isn't it?' Monique said. 'Scimitar's daughter? Who's she?'

'Never mind that; will you go? Will you do it?' Ingrid said impatiently. 'You will. I know you will.'

'Of course I will,' Monique said. 'But Kate's right. Supposing they just take the money?'

'Do you think they will?' She puffed on a cigarette, her hands shaking.

'How the hell would I know?' Monique said. She was not going to be drawn again. She was still angry with herself for dropping her guard the morning before.

'We have to chance it, don't we?' Ingrid said. There were small droplets of perspiration on her upper lip.

'I think we do.'

Ingrid was chewing on her full, pink lip. 'God!' she said. 'I'll have to get that banker's draft from Paul before she comes home. He'll keep the money for the others if I don't. He's got to think I've paid the ransom with the money for my book.'

'Yeah, you'd better do that,' Monique said, her face expressionless. Ingrid had a problem if Paul wouldn't part with the bank draft, but what was interesting her more was that now Ingrid was truly frightened – and frightened for her own skin.

Monique left far too early for the rendezvous. She told Ingrid it was better to go well in advance in case of traffic problems. She took the Lancia and parked it at a spot where there would be no problem finding a taxi, but before she picked up a cab for the ride to the Piazza del Popolo she went back to the café from which she had phoned the night before. Again, she made two brief phone calls.

This time she had time for a coffee before leaving, a dark blue suitcase on the floor beside her feet. There was no hurry. It was only three o'clock and she had only one more errand – a call to make in person on the Via Veneto.

Had the three girls known it, it was twenty-five to four when the door of the room opened and a strange man whom none of them had seen before came in. Claudio was lurking behind him, his face unhappy, lips turned down, shoulders bowed.

The girls stared at them resentfully. The bare room with its three mattresses had become their pad. Claudio had been let into their enclosed world. The stranger, an ordinary looking man in jeans, black bearded and with strong arms under a short-sleeved T-shirt, was an intruder.

'You—' he said, pointing at Jenny. 'On your feet.'

They were sitting crosslegged on their mattresses and Frances had been speaking Italian with them. She had learned a great deal and now she decided to try it out.

'What do you want her for?' she asked belligerently.

'None of your business.'

'It's all right,' Claudio burst out. 'They're letting Jenny go.'

The three girls, bedraggled and not too clean, stared at him.

'But why me?' Jenny said uncertainly.

'Never you mind,' the man said.

'What about the others?'

'They stay,' he said. 'Come on. Get moving.'

Jenny looked around her wildly. Frances' odd peaky little face was set, the mouth a thin straight line. Bobbie Jean's eyes were brimming with tears. They both looked very frightened. And Jenny remembered again when she had asked Claudio to swear that Frances and Bobbie Jean would not be harmed and he could not. The look on his face had haunted her from the time they had been incarcerated in this room.

'No!' she wailed. 'I'm not going. I won't go. Not without the others.'

'Please, Jenny.' Claudio's face was pinched. 'Please come with us.'

'No.' This time it was a scream. 'I won't. Claudio, you're wicked. You're wicked, and I loved you. You mustn't. You mustn't take me away.' She was sobbing hysterically, and she had somehow managed to wrap herself around her narrow mattress, arms and legs curled tight on it as the only thing in the room to cling to.

Bobbie Jean and Frances were clinging to each other.

'Don't cry, Jenny,' Frances was saying. 'Please, Jenny. Go and be safe. We'll be all right. There's two of us. It's not like being alone. You must go.'

'I'm not going. I'm not going. I'm not going,' Jenny screamed.

Claudio looked as if he was about to cry himself, and the man came across the room with a muttered oath and tried to shake Jenny from her stranglehold on the mattress. 'Get up,' he said impatiently. 'Let go. Come on. Let go.'

Samson was barking wildly, darting at the man's ankles. He gave an impatient kick, and the barking turned to a furious yelp as Samson vanished through the open door.

'Get that dog,' the man shouted at Claudio, still pulling at Jenny who clung tighter to her mattress. 'Quick, before it gets out.'

Claudio vanished with an anguished backward look, and as he went there was the sound of a telephone ringing.

'*Stronzo*!' the man said, and let her go. He hurried from the room, slamming the door behind him. They heard the key turn in the lock.

Very cautiously Jenny untied herself from the mattress.

'Jenny, you must go,' Frances was saying. 'It's silly to stay if you can go. Please, Jenny, be good and go. We will be all right, won't we, Bobbie Jean?'

'You don't know. You don't know,' Jenny sobbed. 'I won't go. I won't.'

'What don't we know, Jenny?' Frances asked quietly.

Jenny scrubbed her knuckles into her eyes.

'Listen, you mustn't let them take me away. Claudio promised – he swore – they would never kill me. I don't know why. But he couldn't swear about you two. Now you see. You must go in my place. They won't kill me. I know they won't.'

Frances and Bobbie Jean looked at each other.

'God!' Bobbie said. 'What do you think, Frances?'

'I don't know. I just don't know.'

'You've got to go. Not me,' Jenny insisted.

'But how?' Bobbie Jean said. 'How shall we manage it?'

It was quarter to four when Monique paid off her taxi in the crowded Piazza del Popolo. The tourists were in Rome in their thousands, and she wondered again why people came to swelter in the Holy City when they could have stayed at home. The square was impressive but dingy; needing a facelift, yet visitors gawped at the twin churches flanking the Corso, and

211

trudged in the heat up the hill so they could say they had seen the fountains in the Pincio Gardens. She watched them, the sun beating on the back of her neck, holding a large black suitcase firmly in her hand and thinking how surprisingly heavy paper-money could be.

, He was early too. The white BMW came from the direction of the Via Flaminia. He could not get close to the pavement where she waited– there were too many cars parked, and the old man in charge of the parking looked alert, ready to deal with another customer.

She threaded her way through the cars, got in beside him and with some difficulty slung the suitcase into the back seat.

'*Tu l'a?*' he asked.

'*Oui. Pas de problème.*'

'*Bon.*' He grunted and began to weave his way through the archway into the Corso. 'It went well?'

She continued to speak in French.

'I told you. No problem. I'm sorry about Marseilles.'

'It shouldn't have been Marseilles.'

'I know. It threw me too. She left me without transport at the damned hotel. There was nothing I could do.'

'How long was she away?'

'Abou three hours. She came back high. I thought she might have driven a lot further, but there was only about forty miles extra on the clock. She must have just stayed with him and he got her coked up.'

'She hadn't seen him for a long time. They probably had a lot to discuss.' His voice was sarcastic. 'And now she's parted with the money?'

Monique laughed softly.

'She's amazing. What a survivor. She got it twice, you know. Once from him and once from the newspapers. For her it's an ill wind.' She shook her head, then asked. 'Are you really going to let the girl go?'

He hooted at an old woman bent on suicide before he replied. 'I gave instructions to get her out by 4.30. She and the boy are getting too fond of each other. I don't want the responsibiliy of that, and in sight of the Vatican too!' He grinned wolfishly, the strange bright blue eyes alert below the reddish hair as the white mass of the Vittorio Emanuele loomed nearer. 'Still, I think we might just change things a little,' he said. 'Why don't we let the other two go, and keep the one? She was always a greedy bitch, my little Ingrid. I can send the boy away. It might just set the cat among the pigeons to send Ingrid back to Scimitar for more. And this time, don't lose her.'

'Good thinking,' said Monique approvingly. 'Very good thinking. The mention of Scimitar's daughter scared the shit out of her this morning. That'll throw her into total confusion.'

'Well, look for a telephone,' he told her.

It was just ten to four. And it was five to four when she got back into the car. Without speaking he started the engine and drove off.

'I ought to get back,' she said, but he only grunted.

She knew what he had in mind and how it was going to be. She felt that she probably should be resentful as acceptance was just part of the job. Or was it?

The truth was it was almost a bonus. Something in his casual, uncaring use of her and her body pleased her. Because what he didn't know was that she was using him too.

He had circled round and he was driving back towards the basement in the Porta Pinciana. He parked the car half across the pavement and got out, pulling keys from his pocket. He left her to get out herself and lock the car door before following.

She understood why he always chose the basement. There were no chairs – only the straight hard wooden kitchen kind. In his office on the Corso Vittorio Emanuele there was a big, deep comfortable leather armchair, and a thick pile carpet. The violence in him preferred the desk top in the bare dusty room.

In silence she followed him down the stairs, her heels clacking on the uncarpeted stairway. In the storeroom he snapped on the bare overhead light, strode to the desk and removed the green metal lamp which was all it held. Then he turned to her where she stood waiting, passive, a few paces away.

'Come here,' he said, his voice thick and the ice-blue eyes too shining, almost mad.

Still passive, but a heat of anticipation burning low in her, she walked towards him. He grabbed at her shoulders and swung her so that her back was to the end of the desk.

'Lift up your skirt.'

She raised the red cotton, pulling and bunching it around her waist. He just grunted.

His left hand was unzipping his fly, his right tugging at the small red briefs she was wearing. He got them as far as her thighs and she could already feel the warmth and wetness in her. Quickly she slid them the rest of the way down her legs, kicking them off into a scrap of crumpled nylon on the dusty floor. But she was no longer conscious of her surroundings, only of him: big, looming over her, his shoulders blotting out the bare light.

He had arranged her on the desk so that she was stretched out, her legs hanging to the floor. This was the moment at which he knelt before her, thrusting his face into her musky dampness. She liked him kneeling before her, and she liked what he did, but it never lasted quite long enough.

He got to his feet and pushed her further back on the slippery surface of the desk. Then he pushed her legs wider apart, raising them so she was bent at the knees, and then he flung himself on her, his hands gripping the sides of the desk. He was built like his shoulders, broad and strong. And the first thrust, in spite of her need for him, hurt. She groaned. At the beginning he moved fast, and then slowly in tantalizing probings. Then it was fast again, and she knew him well enough to know when it was nearly over. Sometimes the excitement of his cavalier treament of her made her come first. She did today. It was all part of the excitement of what she had just done – and wondering what he would do when he found out.

He was pounding into her frenziedly now, and then came the familiar long cry as he collapsed across her body. Only then was she conscious of the hardness of the desk; the stiffness of her back and his weight.

Thank God, he would not permit himself the weakness of resting. He was almost instantly on his feet, zipping his jeans, turning his back on her as she climbed from the desk, retrieving her panties.

'You'd better get back to work,' he said.

*

As the key turned again in the lock and the man came back in, the three girls stood huddled and scared in the centre of the room. Instinctively they had all held hands.

'All right,' he said, 'have it your way. The other two can come instead.'

All three girls seemed to be in a state of shock. Bobbie Jean looked at Jenny as if asking to be forgiven and half moved towards the door. Frances looked apprehensive. 'Did he say we're to go?' she asked Jenny, who nodded.

'Why has he changed his mind?' she asked.

'*Che?*' he said impatiently, and Jenny repeated the question in Italian.

'Orders,' he said. 'Now come on.'

'Do you think they're going to kill us now?' Frances asked Jenny, her face white.

'*Per favore,*' Jenny said humbly to the man. 'You're not going to kill them?'

Claudio was back.

'No. They're going home, Jenny. I swear it.'

She sighed. She believed him. 'It's safe. It's all right,' she said. 'You can go.'

They both stood irresolute and Jenny turned her back on them, looking towards the shuttered window. 'Go on. Go,' she said.

She did not see them leave, but it sounded to her as if their feet were dragging. 'See you soon, Jenny,' Bobbie Jean had said. 'Good luck.'

'I'll see they find you.' Frances' voice was trying not to wobble. 'Don't worry. And thanks.'

The door slammed and the key turned again. She looked around, tears blinding her. She wanted Sammy. But Sammy wasn't there. If he'd got away, he'd be run over, she knew it, and she burst into a storm of noisy weeping, her face buried in the mattress, telling herself she was weeping for Sammy and not for herself. She was crying so hard that she did not hear the door open until a light touch on her shoulder made her leap in terror. It was Claudio. He was kneeling beside her.

'Please don't cry,' he said.

'Where's Sammy?' she said accusingly. 'You've lost him.'

Claudio's head drooped.

'He got into the courtyard and ran under the door,' he said. 'I couldn't catch him, he's so little. And then they called for me. But Sammy will be safe. Someone will pick him up. It'll be all right. Look. I've bought you a present.'

She sat up, sniffing. He was carefully holding a white dress with a soft lacy collar and a ribbon sash. Like the nightgowns had been, it was damp.

'I'm afraid I stole it,' he said apologetically, 'but I thought you'd look so pretty wearing it.'

She looked at him and then his worried face. She half laughed and then she began to cry again as she flung her arms around him. He held her close and they clung to each other, silent, two children afraid of the dark.

'I want that banker's draft. It's mine. You've no right to keep it.' Ingrid's face could have been carved in ice, and her voice would have shattered glass, but Paul remained unimpressed.

'No,' he said. 'I'm not chancing it. If you've got the money, Ingrid dear, you'll behave badly. I want Jenny to be safe, but I want all three of those girls back equally safely, and next time there's a phone call, I'm doing the talking.'

'You've no right . . .'

'Maybe not,' he said placidly. 'But that's the way it's going to be.'

She was silenced, frustrated, her mind running over the possibilities of what would happen when Jenny was found. *If* Jenny was found. While Paul held the banker's draft, they'd guess she'd had money from somewhere else. He'd put pressure on her to use the money he held to release the others. She didn't give a damn about the others. She had the problem of Scimitar's daughter to deal with too. How did they know? What were they going to do?

She couldn't think of a way around any of the problems and, furious, she beat her fists on the side of the chair, debating whether or not to tell him about the note she had received. That wasn't a good idea either for too many reasons. Four o'clock had come and gone. Monique was back, and her errand done, she poured drinks for Paul and Madeleine, who sat quietly taking no part in the conversations. In a minute the others would be coming down. She was stymied.

The phone rang. She half leapt to her feet, but Paul gave her a warning glance. He left the living room quickly and went to the hall. Again the sergeant switched on the tape recorder.

She heard Paul say: 'No! That's incredible. That's fantastic—' She could also hear feet hurrying down the stairs as Eileen and Charles, alerted by the ringing of the phone, left their rooms. It had worked, she thought with a flash of triumph. Jenny was free. But how the hell was she going to explain? She could have killed Paul for hanging on to the money.

'Yes, we'll be right over,' he was saying. 'Only as long as it takes to get there.'

'What's happened?' It was Charles asking.

'Congratulations!' Paul said. 'Bobbie Jean's free. And Frances. The police found them wandering near the Colosseum.'

Bobbie Jean and Frances? Ingrid leapt to her feet and ran into the hallway.

'Jenny – what about Jenny?' she was shouting.

Paul hurried and took her hands tightly in his.

'They haven't got her. I don't know why. We'll find out. But it's all right – you have the money.'

She looked at him unbelievingly, and then she began to laugh, louder and louder, clutching at her side hysterically, until Charles stepped forward to slap her sharply around the face.

She was instantly silent. 'That's true,' she said. 'I've got the money. You have to give it to me now. You can't keep it any longer.'

And to her own consternation, she burst into tears.

The two girls were in the examining magistrate's office where Garoni, beaming, was waiting with them. Alex was already there. Paul had rung him instantly at the Eden, which was ten minutes nearer and as Charles and Eileen came into the room, followed by Kate, Paul and Ingrid, both girls flung themselves into their parents' arms.

Eileen was openly crying as she clung to her daughter: 'Oh

baby – I'm so sorry. It's my fault. I do love you. I do, I swear it. Oh, Frances, I'm so sorry. So sorry for everything.'

'It's all right, Mum.' Frances hugged her. 'I know. I do know.'

Charles' throat was moving as he held Bobbie Jean and stroked her hair. Her arms were tight around his waist and she was howling unashamedly.

'Don't cry. It's all over. You're safe,' he kept saying.

'But Jenny's not,' Bobbie Jean wailed. 'They've still got her.'

'That's why you must stop crying and remember every single thing you can about what has happened to tell the police,' Charles said. 'Now, sit down the both of you and tell us exactly what went on. Why have they kept Jenny, do you know?'

Very gently he led Bobbie Jean to an armchair, and then extracted Frances from her mother's grasp.

Frances was the more composed of the two, and she said: 'At first, they wanted Jenny. They were going to let her go. But she wouldn't. Claudio had told her that they would never kill her – he didn't know why, but that they might kill Bobbie and me. Or least, he wouldn't promise Jenny they wouldn't kill us. She was frightened they would. That's why she wouldn't go.'

Kate was swiftly and quietly translating and Garoni said: 'Ask her who Claudio is.'

'Just a boy,' Frances told Charles. 'About seventeen. He brought us our food all the time. And he fed Sammy. He was nice. Jenny really liked him.'

'I think we were in Trastevere, Daddy,' Bobbie Jean suddenly said. 'It kind of sounded like there. Noisy, you know. All night.'

'You were in Rome?'

'Definitely – they didn't take us far enough to be anywhere else. And it only took about a quarter of an hour before they shoved us out of the car today. We had to pull each other's blindfolds off before we could see.'

'Was Jenny all right?' Ingrid asked. She looked shell-shocked; all hysteria gone.

'She was crying when we left,' Frances said. 'It was awful, leaving her, but it seemed the right thing if they were going to

218

kill us and not her. Was it selfish?' She was asking Charles Dennison.

'It wasn't selfish at all,' he said. 'It was sensible.'

'I promised we'd get her out,' Frances said. 'We must.'

'It's all right, Frances,' Paul gently. 'She'll be OK. Her mother has her ransom.'

'But why did they let us go?' Frances said. 'Did you pay, Daddy?'

Alex Elliot, haggard, his thinning hair dishevelled, shook his head.

'No, we didn't pay,' Charles said. 'We couldn't raise the money.'

'I wonder why they let us go,' Frances said thoughtfully. 'You'd have thought they'd have wanted the money. Claudio kept talking about the Cause. What cause?'

'We'll explain later,' Charles said. 'For now you must answer the questions and not ask them. Then we can get you both bathed, cleaned and into bed. You look as if you need scrubbing. I've never seen such raggedy kids.'

Helped by Kate and Charles, Garoni took them through their description of the kidnappings, of the red-headed man, the cars and what they could remember about the place where they had been kept.

'First they blindfolded us and then we got into the car in what I'm sure was a courtyard,' Bobbie Jean said. 'Claudio had mentioned a courtyard. He used to take Sammy there for his walk. I heard them opening gates. They sounded like wooden gates, scraping on the ground as they opened. Then I think the car was the same BMW they picked us up in. It smelt the same. And it was two doors, like before. Then they drove off and suddenly they just pushed us out into the street. It was a long wide street and no one about, and when we'd pulled our blindfolds off, the car was gone. We could see the Colosseum in the distance so we walked towards it until we saw a policeman. Was he pleased to see us, and,' she added, 'were we pleased to see him.'

Garoni's phone was ringing. He answered it, listened, asked a few questions and then hung up and smiled at the girls.

'They were right,' he said to Charles. 'It was almost certainly Trastevere. A policeman has just rescued your daughter's little dog,' he said turning to Ingrid. 'It was roaming at the back of the Piazza Apolonia. The man recognized it from the pictures in the newspapers. That was ten minutes ago. The question is – how far did the dog roam?'

'I remember now,' Bobbie Jean said. 'Sammy ran out while Jenny was clinging to the mattress. But we forgot all about him after the phone call.'

'What phone call?' Charles asked.

'There was a phone call and then they came back and said it wasn't to be Jenny that was released. It was to be us.'

Her eyelids were beginning to droop and her voice was drowsy. Charles looked questioningly at Garoni.

'Too long ago now to be sure exactly where in Trastevere,' the inspector said. 'Even a small dog can cover a lot of ground in an hour or two. A pity. But we'll search the area. And for now, why don't you take your children home?'

The fat Trastevere housewife was not pleased when her daughter's confirmation dress – the one that had been worn by all the girls in her family – vanished from the washing line in her courtyard. But she was thoughtful when she read the papers the next morning. Blazoned headlines said that two of the kidnapped *bambini* had been found. The third was still missing. It was believed that she was hidden in the Trastevere area.

First, three nightgowns and now, just as the two girls returned, the dress had gone. Was the last little one now wearing her daughter's dress? Had all three worn the nightgowns? She looked out thoughtfully over her courtyard and the wall behind where the empty house was. The house that had just recently shown signs of life. The coincidence was too much.

The *signora* picked up the telephone and dialled the *carabinieri*.

Chapter Twelve

It was quiet in the big drawing room that evening. Alex had taken Eileen and Frances to the Eden with him. Bobbie Jean had been put to sleep in what had been their room.

Ingrid, complaining of a headache, had gone to her room. She did not look as if she had a headache. She looked like a Persian cat with a gold saucer of caviare. Paul had given her the bank drafts, and the sight of so much money had been an instant turn-on.

Madeleine, tired after the journey, went up to bed at nine, leaving only Kate, Charles, Paul and Monique to share the big drawing room.

Kate was in her usual seat again, Paul next to her, and she found she was beginning to come to terms with her own situation. The fact that she genuinely disliked Madeleine was helping. When dealing with his wife, Paul's face took on downward lines; as gentle and kind as he was with her, it seemed obvious that his attention and help were given from some sense of duty rather than as a labour of love. Madeleine herself did not seem to notice this. Maybe her illness gave her something genuine to be selfish about, but she was obviously a demanding woman, and probably always had been.

They were having a second brandy to celebrate the return of Bobbie Jean and Frances when the phone rang.

'Jenny!' Kate said. 'Please, God, it's about Jenny.' Paul hurried into the hall.

It was not about Jenny. It was a call for Monique and by the time she had had her brief conversation, Ingrid, again in the dragon kimono, was back downstairs wanting to know what had happened.

'Would you believe,' Monique said, 'a date for me!'

Her voice was light and gay, but something about her body showed tenseness as she stood by the fireplace, smoothing back her strong black hair.

'You're not going out?' Ingrid's voice was surly.

'Do you mind? I'd like to. It would be a break.'

'Who is it?' Ingrid demanded.

'No one you know. A guy I met in London. He's here for a few days.'

'Okay.' It was a grudging agreement. 'But before you go to bed, come in and make sure I don't need anything.'

'Right,' Monique said. 'I'd better go and change.'

Another demanding woman, Kate thought, watching Ingrid's bad-tempered face as her secretary left the room.

After mistress and employee had both gone upstairs, Charles asked, his face serious, 'What do you think of Monique?'

'Opportunist,' Kate said briefly. 'Swings whichever way does most for her.'

'You don't think she's kind of – well, mysterious. I can't fathom her.'

'In what way?' Paul asked.

'Well, do you think perhaps she knows more about this than we do?'

'You mean, is she involved?' Kate said. It was a thought that had not struck her before.

'Surely not,' Paul said. 'She's been with Ingrid for ages.'

'It's just that NAP seem to know what's going on in this house all the time. And how did they know where to find Bellino? He'd told Ingrid he was dining with his backers.'

'Bellino? What about Bellino?' Paul asked.

'Oh, my God! You don't know,' Kate said. 'Tell him, Charles.'

Charles told him, and as he listened, Paul's hand went involuntarily to cover the fork in his trousers. Charles nodded. 'It's psychologically interesting, but every man hearing that story does just what you just did. Serve Bellino bloody well right!' he added viciously.

And the discussion that followed about Bellino drove the subject of Monique out of their minds.

When Charles left them for his bed, Paul sat smoking, the grey plume of his cigarette drifting up to the high ceiling. It was so quiet in the big room Kate could hear the ticking of the ormolu clock on the mantlepiece and she watched a dazzled moth flutter dangerously around one of the small wall lights. She knew how the moth felt, she thought, amused at her own pretension. Then she slid along the length of the sofa so that

222

Paul could put his arms around her, and she lightly rested her head on his shoulder.

'Well?' he said, his hand stroking her bare arm.

'Well what?'

'Is everything all right?'

'Umm. I hate it, but in a way it's a good thing. Knowing her makes me understand things better. She is very shaky, isn't she?'

'Very.' He took a deep breath. 'I don't think it's going to be very long, Kate. Be—'

She knew he was going to say 'be patient' but he couldn't quite do it. It was the nearest they had ever got to the rocky, dangerous depths of the subject. It was best to say no more.

'I love you,' she said. 'It doesn't matter we're not going to bed together. I love you more than that.'

He bent to kiss her and it was a gentle, closed-mouth kiss. More a nuzzling of two mouths. Almost the kiss of friends.

At 11.30 Ingrid could not sleep. She loathed being on her own in the dark; all sorts of fears and self-questionings attacked her, and tonight there was too much to be afraid of: Jenny's safety, NAP knowing about Scimitar, the banker's draft burning a hole in her mind . . . How could she get to keep the money? It wasn't fair. None of it was fair. She'd always had rotten luck. If her father had taken her with him instead of Franz her life would have been very different. But it was too late to brood on that now.

She was also randy as hell. Ingrid didn't mind masturbation, but her sex life had started so early that she had never truly got the habit. She knew it pleased other women, but it did little or nothing for her. She'd always had the real thing handy to calm her nerves and her fears – a person, not an object to stimulate her – and she wanted the real thing right now. How long was Monique going to be?

Tonight, though, Monique wasn't the answer. She wanted a man, she decided. She wanted some good serious fucking. And some fun to take her mind off things. She considered Charles briefly but he wasn't what she wanted. She wanted someone in her own image again. So, she thought, she'd better go out and find someone.

She took the Mercedes which was parked outside the house. She hadn't bothered too much with clothing. She'd pulled on high sandals with transparent heels and a raspberry pink silk jersey dress, cut like a tube. With no bra, no pants underneath, no guy was going to need imagination. She had combed her short blonde hair, and used a little mascara – nothing more. It had taken her five minutes to dress and get out of the house.

She drove down to the Via Veneto and parked the car on the pavement in the Via Ludovisi, then heels clacking, she set off back to the Café de Paris – always a happy hunting ground.

The pavement seats were crowded, and she debated, deciding to go into the bar itself. She would be more conspicuous there. She smirked to herself thinking of how she let Monique do the work when they were together. She, from long experience, could pick up fellows faster than her secretary any day. But that was experience she'd rather her secretary didn't know about.

And that was another worry. All that stuff she'd told Kate Anderson. She'd done it in the emotion of the moment and in desperation, but she wasn't going to let it be printed. That was something she would have to wriggle out of. She felt a deep sense of self-pity. All her life she was having to worry about wheeler-dealing, wriggling out of situations and none of them were really ever her fault.

She ordered a Grappa which she had no intention of drinking. Alcohol was bad for the skin. Champagne was her drink. But Italian champagne was disgusting. She leaned against the bar and spotted her prey. A boy who was just her type. A blond, slim youth, almost certainly German, with very light blue eyes. He was dressed in white jeans and a black T-shirt with white moccasins. He had just the right look: her look. From her careful inspection of him, he had no underwear on either. He was almost certainly bi, if not queer, but she had found she was pretty good at dealing with near-queers. There was something strong and masculine in her, her tits were tiny, her stomach flat, and they could pretend she was a boy.

She looked at him boldly, and he left the group of twenty-year-olds he was with and came over to her.

224

'Waiting for someone?' he asked in English. He was German. She recognized the accent.

'I was, but as I was nearly an hour late, I think he must have gone,' she replied in German.

He looked pleased. 'You are German?' he said.

'I was born there – left when I was a kid.'

'Will you have a drink?'

'I'm fine,' she said, but gave him the sort of look that meant he could make other suggestions. 'And anyway, it's hot in here.'

He took her point and she said chattily: 'Are you visiting?'

'Yeah.'

'Have you seen much of the town?'

'Not a great deal.'

She gave him a bold look.

'I've got my car outside. Would you like a guided tour?'

His eyes flickered over her.

'OK.'

She could see he was considering how much it was going to cost him, and to put him out of his misery she said: 'You don't recognize me, do you?'

'Should I?' he said cautiously.

'I'm Ingrid Pallia.'

He looked at her more closely.

'I see now. But isn't your daughter—' he hesitated.

'Kidnapped. I've got the money together. I'm just waiting to know where to take it. I couldn't sleep. I needed to get out—' She looked him full in the eyes and licked her lips. 'I needed a change – diversion.'

She couldn't make out what he was thinking, but he said: 'That's good. So, you shall show me the town, eh?'

'Yeah, I'll do that,' she said.

She left the Grappa on the counter while he turned to wave at his friends and they walked out of the café together. He was silent, and there didn't seem to be much need to talk, so she merely led him round the corner and into the Via Ludovisi and pointed to the car.

'A German car,' he said.

'Of course,' she told him.

She had no intention of driving far. They both knew it was a formality. She showed him the Spanish Steps, drove down the Corso to the Victorio Emanuele and back to the Piazza Navona. As she drove, his hand was caressing her thigh, but she wasn't having him in the car. Too dangerous.

'You must see St Peter's in the daytime, not now,' she told him. She was driving the car to go through the Borghese Gardens and that way into the Piazza del Popolo. Once in the huge square, she said casually: 'We're right near my place. Like a drink and see a Roman home?'

'Why not?' he said.

He didn't say very much, she thought as she drove down the Via Flaminia, and his fingers digging into her thigh were hurting a little. But conversation wasn't necessary. She took her right hand from the wheel and stroked the front of his jeans. All was exactly as it should be. A long, hard ridge.

'That's nice,' she murmured, and he slid his hands between her legs.

'Wait – nearly there,' she said.

The villa was in darkness, except for the light in the hall where the sergeant slumbered. Ingrid just regarded him as a piece of furniture. Without even bothering to say goodnight, she led the boy up the stairs to her room.

'What's your name?' she said, as she opened the bedroom door.

'Hans.'

'Come in, Hans,' she said.

It was he who shut the door behind them, and strode over to the bed where she was standing. Without speaking he took her shoulders and ran his hands over her body, checking that there was no underwear.

He started to tear at the neck of the tube dress but she moved back and pouted at him. His eyes were very light in the dim room.

'Naughty,' she said. 'Mustn't be impatient. Just wait a minute. There are things to do.' He looked interested; the look of a man expecting something good and something different.

She laughed, and went to the wardrobe where she kept the special things. She took out the white silk trousers and shirt, the red belt.

'In a minute you can put these on for me,' she said. 'But first let me comb your hair.'

His expression had changed to one of deep suspicion. Was he affronted? She wasn't sure.

'Sit down,' she coaxed.

Reluctantly he did so.

She picked up the brush and comb from her dressing table and combed his blonde hair into an imitation of her own. Then she picked up a lipstick.

'Pout at me,' she said, holding it ready to apply.

He was beginning to realize.

'Oh, no—' he said, and his hand came out swiftly. As she gave a little protest, he grabbed the lipstick, stood up and very deliberately snatched at her hair with his left hand and pulled back her head. Then he scored the lipstick in thick greasy strokes over her face. And still he did not speak.

He let her go and as she looked at herself in the mirror seeing with horror the clown face staring back at her, he took the silk shirt and trousers from the bed where she had thrown them. He tried to tear them, but they would not, so he ground the lipstick into the white silk, and then he turned back to her.

'That's what you like, is it? Boys dressed up as girls. Not sure who you are, eh?'

She was suddenly frightened. His eyes were so light, strange. He moved towards her, cat-footed, menacing. 'Don't touch me,' she said backing away until she was pressed against the dressing table.

He still came on. His hand, broad and brown and with blond hair on the backs of the fingers, grasped at the neck of her dress and tore in a downward movement. It split completely at the back seam and fell to the ground in one piece. He looked at her naked and cowering and said: 'No tits,' eh?'

She could hear herself panting, knowing that she should scream, knowing that she should do something. But somehow she was excited. It was almost as if she had been waiting all her life for this moment when some man, some pick-up, would do her grievous harm – maybe kill her. It felt like the fulfilment of a prophecy. They way perhaps her life ought to end. The way she deserved to die. And so she didn't scream. She stood, staring at him, waiting to see what would happen next.

'Are you going to kill me?' she asked.

'Nothing so dramatic, Fraulein Pallia,' he said. 'I'm going to fuck you. But you may not like it.'

He was letting his jeans fall to the floor; his T-shirt ended just below his navel, and his erection rode over it, red against the black.

She was almost disappointed that it was only to be another screwing when he suddenly spun her around, grabbed her waist and pulled her back from the dressing table, and at the same time forcing her head down so that her small tight behind was presented to him. And then he lunged.

The pain was excruciating, and then she did scream.

Equally suddenly the pain was gone and it was he who screamed. She straightened up and turned to see Monique standing, holding the boy with his arm twisted around his back. His face was contorted as Monique pressed higher and harder.

'What the hell's going on?' Monique demanded.

'Oh, my God.' Ingrid limped to the bed and sat down. 'He hurt me.'

'You shouldn't pick up people without me.' With her knee she thrust the boy round to face Ingrid. 'Can't you see he's no good? You silly bitch. Go and wash your face while I get rid of him.'

Her knee hit the boy painfully at the base of his spine and she twisted his arm up higher. 'Move,' she said. 'Unless you want your arm broken.'

Ingrid didn't wait to see him go. She moved to her bathroom, walking carefully. She doubted she'd be able to sit down for a week. She felt a fool – ridiculous, and the sight of her lip-stick-slashed face in the mirror did nothing to change that. Age was catching up with her. She needed the bait of the younger girl for things to be right.

She was in bed when Monique came back. She knew she looked small and vulnerable on the huge mattress, with the sheets pulled up to her chin, her neat little head on the white pillow, and she said: 'Thank you, Monique. Stay with me, please. Until I sleep.'

The other girl just grunted and began to undress.

'How was your date?' She wanted to make Monique speak to her.

'Fine.'

'You were clever with that – that boy. Was it a sort of unarmed combat?'

'Sort of.'

'You're angry with me?'

Monique grunted again and said: 'You're a fool. You'll get yourself killed one of these days.'

Ingrid was silent, a frisson running through her. It sounded like the prophecy reiterated. She recalled her feeling when she had thought the boy was going to kill her. 'I know,' she said quietly.

To be violent with that vicious little German creep was just what she had needed, Monique thought, as Ingrid snuffled quietly.

Had she convinced him? She thought she had, but Franz had been deeply suspicious. She had spent one of the most difficult evenings of her life, and though Ingrid's life might have been in danger, hers had been truly so.

He wouldn't have hesitated to dispose of her, of that she was certain. It was amazing how alike they were, her two employers. Ingrid and Franz: both ruthless, both only concerned with their own lives and goals. Anyone in the way, or causing complications, was just swept aside. Not that Ingrid would resort to murder, she thought.

Her worry now was how they would react while they still held Jenny as a hostage to fortune – everyone's fortune.

She knew that convincing them could be the end of Ingrid; maybe Jenny too. But she felt Franz would not harm the girl. Jenny was innocent of everything. She could not help her birth.

The trouble with the job was that just sometimes conscience got in the way and had to be firmly put down. You had to get to know the principals in the game too well. And sometimes affection set in. She had even felt a stirring of desire for Franz as he interrogated her, with the others watching and silent. in that bare room. Ah well, she told herself, imminent death and sexual desire have always shared an unlikely alliance.

She sighed at the thought, and seeing that Monique slept, left for her own bed.

*

The first phone call to alert the household the next morning was from Inspector Garoni. Had the girls been brought night-gowns by anyone, he wanted to know, and what were the exact circumstances?

Bobbie Jean was woken and sleepily confirmed that indeed there had been nightgowns, damp ones, taken from someone's washing line. One had been huge. It had made them laugh. And yes, Claudio had stolen them. Did she have any idea where from? Garoni had wanted to know.

'Well, nearby,' Bobbie Jean said. 'Jenny asked him, he went out and he was back in about quarter of an hour.'

'*Bene*,' Garoni said. 'Now we know exactly which area to search.'

The phone's ringing had as usual brought everyone down to the hallway, including Ingrid. But as the last one to arrive, when it trilled yet again almost instantly she was the nearest to the instrument. She picked it up just as the tape recorder began to whirl again.

The others returned to the hall; saw her turn ashen, the deli-cate nostrils pinched and angry, saw her sway on her feet and clutch the telephone table for support. Then she cried: 'It's not true. You're lying. You're making it up to get the rest from me. I don't believe you. I don't!' She was shrieking into the receiver and then she slammed it down, and swung to face the startled group watching her. She shouted: 'It's a lie! It's got to be a lie! He wouldn't do that to me.'

Who wouldn't do what? Kate wondered. Paul without speaking had gone to run the tape recorder back and set it to replay. Ingrid had collapsed on the bottom stair, crumpling the hem of the dragon robe in her hands. The others stood, awkward and puzzled, waiting to see what was wrong.

The tape buzzed gently and then they heard the same half-whispering voice that had been on the other recording.

'Scimitar's daughter?' it said. 'Ingrid? That was a mistake. You should not have done that. You are a dirty, double-crossing little bitch. Where did you get it, all that funny money? Half a million pounds' worth. Has no one told you it is against the law to pass forged notes. Particularly Swiss notes, Ingrid. Those Deutcher Swiss in Zurich get very angry.' The voice

230

hardened. 'And so do we. I would not give much for Jenny's chances now if I were you. You'll have to go back to Scimitar, won't you? We've changed our minds. We want a million for Jenny now.'

'What the—' Charles said softly, but Paul was returning the tape to play it again. He had taken a note pad and pen from his pocket and was busily scribbling notes as they all stood and listened for the second time.

When the tape stopped, Paul, white with anger, his blue eyes turned grey, moved towards the stairs and dragged Ingrid to her feet by the arm.

'You've got a lot of explaining to do,' he said grimly. 'And you can start right now.'

'I don't have to explain anything,' Ingrid said, trying to pull herself free.

'Oh, yes you do,' Charles had moved to take her other arm, and he and Paul frogmarched her into the drawing room. They pushed her into an armchair and stood over her, threatening in their fury.

'Right,' Charles said. 'What money was this?'

'It's nothing to do with you.' Her ice-blue eyes were defiant. 'I'm not telling you a thing.'

'Would you rather tell the police where you got half a million pounds' worth of forged Swiss francs?' Paul asked. 'Because they're going to want to know. In fact, you might as well tell us, because they're going to *have* to know. So get your story together right now.'

Kate could see that Ingrid's mind was racing. What tall story would she come up with this time, she wondered, definitely intrigued?

'All right,' Ingrid said, her voice slow and deliberate, 'though I don't see why I have to tell you a thing. Anyway, you should be grateful to me,' she said, her voice full of moral indignation. 'I gave them the money for your daughters. Not mine. And it worked. You've got your daughters back, haven't you?'

Her pretty face was set in the precise and too-good-to-be true look Kate was so familiar with.

'She's lying,' she said resignedly.

'What happened, Ingrid?' Paul's voice was steel.

'Someone gave it to me.'

'Who? The one you're going to have to go back to?'

Ingrid was silent.

'Who is the one you're going to have to go back to? Who is Scimitar?'

Who was Scimitar? It rang a bell. A very distinct bell. Then Kate noticed that Monique was with them. She had been so quiet, her presence had gone unrecorded. It was the quick little flicks of her eyelids at the last question that caught Kate's attention. And Kate suddenly recalled the conversation begun and abandoned with Charles the night before.

'I didn't know they were forged,' Ingrid said, ignoring the question. 'I thought they were real. I've been tricked too.'

'Is that the truth?' Charles asked.

'For God's sake, do you think I'd deliberately risk Jenny's life with forged notes . . .'

Kate's quick journalist's mind had been racing and suddenly some of it fell into place.

'So the pay-off *was* for Jenny.' Kate looked at her with growing contempt. 'I suppose you wanted to keep that money Paul brought back from England. You weren't going to say a word about having got the ransom from elsewhere. But where from, Ingrid? You get your hands on this other money and yippee! Suddenly you can have it both ways. Jenny back and your pay-off for the book intact. You'd have let Bobbie Jean and Frances rot there, wouldn't you, Ingrid? That's why you were so frantic to get your greedy little paws on the bank-draft yesterday afternoon. If it had been Jenny who'd come safely home, how would you have explained how you'd pulled the trick while Paul was still holding the ransom money? Boy, what a nasty little shit you are, Ingrid Pallia.'

'OK—' It was on the word OK that her German accent came through clearest. 'OK, Miss Clever Socks. I've got that bank-draft now and I've got news for you. I'm not signing your lousy copy. You got all that out of me by trickery. Just try to get me to sign it.'

Kate groaned quietly and the sound made Ingrid look around triumphantly, so pleased with the point she had scored that the rest of the problems receded.

'And nobody's getting anything more out of me, either,' she said. 'The rest of you can mind your own business.'

She got up and pushed Charles and Paul out of the way with a hearty shove.

'I'll be in my room if there's any more news,' she said, and sauntered out.

'Insolent bitch!' Kate muttered.

'What if she won't sign your copy?' Paul asked, his voice concerned.

Kate shrugged. 'Print it unsigned and fight about it in the courts afterwards. I've got it all on tape, remember. Locked up. Paul took them back to England for me.' The remark was addressed to Charles. It wasn't the truth, but she felt pretty sure it was a piece of news Monique would impart.

On cue, Monique said: 'I think I'd better go up and see her. I'll try to sort out the situation.'

'You do that,' Kate said, 'and keep us informed.'

But a conviction that Charles had been right in his suspicions and that Monique was playing her own game was growing. What the hell was going on? she wondered. Something a great deal more complex than a simple political kidnapping, that was for sure. And Scimitar was nagging at the back of her mind. She'd have to call the office.

Monique ran lightly up the stairs, still dressed for her early morning jog – the outing that gave her the opportunity to check in and make phone calls in privacy away from the house.

They had called her last night because it had been an emergency. They had broken the rules. But they needed to know that she had no knowledge that the currency Ingrid had handed over was forged. In the end, they'd believed her; she had left them convinced it was Ingrid who had tried to double-cross them.

It had all gone pretty well so far. But the next stage was likely to be tricky and dangerous.

She knocked on the door of Ingrid's room and went in quietly. Ingrid was lying on the bed, her hand over her forehead. She had not drawn back the shutters and the room was deep and shadowy.

'Are you all right?'

'I've got a headache.'

'I'm not surprised.'

Monique went and sat on the bed, gently removed her employer's hand and softly stroked the smooth forehead.

'Any better?'

'No. But it's nice.'

'What went wrong? Was the money forged?'

'Christ knows. I can't believe he'd do that to me. I just can't believe it.'

'I don't understand what's happening. Want to talk about it? Can I help?'

Ingrid was very still, staring at the ceiling, thinking, contemplating what she could or couldn't say, Monique realized. She needed to say a lot if it was going to be over quickly.

'It's difficult,' she said. 'It's not my secret. What the hell am I going to tell the police?'

'As near to the truth as possible?' Monique suggested.

'I can't. Monique, it was my father who swung that funny money on me. Can you imagine? My own father. If he'd even warned me what he was doing it would have been better. The shock, this morning! I couldn't believe it. He might have sentenced his own grandchild to death. Maybe me too, his daughter.'

'Your father!' Monique's voice and face showed amazement. 'But I thought he disappeared in the war.'

'He did. He went back to France – I never lost touch with him – I knew where he was from all the family papers that I had when I got bombed. I knew how to find him. He was working for the Germans in Paris. He was a spy.'

'But he was French.'

'Yes, but he'd been in Germany so long, he felt German. And he admired Hitler. The French never caught him, but he went and settled in Algeria at the end of the war. He was there until de Gaulle gave it back to the Algerians. Funny, you coming from there too.'

'Well, I hardly know the place. I was very little when I left. Where is he now? Marseilles, I suppose?'

Ingrid's face closed again and the set, stubborn look returned.

'He's not in Marseilles. Not now. That was only for that night.'

'But Ingrid, what made you think he could posibly have had all that money?'

'I don't really know—' She was evasive again. 'He had a terribly successful hotel in Algiers. Everyone stayed there.'

Everyone indeed, Monique thought.

'Well, there's no reason why you can't tell the police that your father gave you the money.'

'There is. He's not supposed to be alive as my father, and anyway, I think the French police or somebody want him.'

'What for?'

'I don't know. I don't understand politics. Something to do with the OAS.'

'You mean the French terrorists who tried to keep Algeria for the French?'

'Yes. He wasn't a terrorist, of course. But the French seemed to think he was harbouring people in his hotel.'

'What people?'

'Don't keep asking me questions. I don't know. Just tell me what I'm going to do about this situation.'

It was time to stop probing. And the maddening thing was she hadn't learned a thing she didn't know already. Except that Scimitar wasn't in Marseilles any more.

Claudio had stayed in the room with her through the night because she had discovered that she was frightened and lonely now the other girls had gone.

He had gone out to get her supper, taken away the dirty plates and then returned to stay chastely with her.

'What's going to happen, Claudio?' she had asked him.

'I don't know,' he said miserably, 'but he says I've got to go away.'

'Who *is* he?'

Claudio did not reply and then he said reluctantly: 'Franz? I don't know, I'm not sure. My mother sometimes lived with him, but wasn't married to him. I can't ask him somehow. He frightens me.'

'Can't you ask your mother?'

'No. She's dead. She died for the Cause.'

She clutched at his hand as he sat beside her on the mattress.

'Claudio, that's terrible. What happened?'

'Well, it was an accident really. Some explosives they were working with blew up. And she was killed.'

'Poor you. Poor her.' Jenny said.

'I know. But I'm carrying on in her place.'

There was silence and then Jenny said tentatively: 'Claudio, what is the Cause?'

'To bring down the government and to change life as we know it, to create anarchy and revolution so that all men can be equal and free.'

She snorted. 'And your Cause locks up young girls so all men can be free?'

'I know. I don't like that bit much either.'

She thought again.

'Claudio, could you kill anybody?'

He shifted uneasily.

'Of course, if it were necessary.'

'I don't believe you,' she said flatly. 'You're telling me a lie.'

He fidgeted again.

'Well, I've never had to do it yet.'

'But could you? Could you kill me for the Cause if they told you to?'

'No.' It was anguished. 'Of course not. You know that.'

'All right, could you have killed Bobbie Jean and Frances?'

'No.'

'Or even that man, Bellino?'

He sighed.

'No, I suppose not.'

'Then you ought not to be in the Cause,' Jenny said firmly. 'It's silly. And things aren't that bad; wanting to change everything, indeed!'

He was silent.

'Anyway, what about the man? Is he the head of the Cause?'

'Not our Cause. He just came to help. He's trying to find something. Money, I think. He keeps saying: "Find the man, find the money." He's come all the way from France. Apparently, he's very important in the worldwide Cause.'

'The worldwide Cause!' Jenny said crossly. 'Just lots of nasty people, killing and blowing things up, and for what . . .?'

'You're too young. You don't know anything about it.'

'And neither do you,' she said. 'If you saw the horrible things they do . . .'

'They're necessary,' he said stubbornly. 'The revolution won't come unless we make it.'

'Revolution!' she said. 'I don't want to talk about it. I don't want to think of you being in it at all. I thought I loved you,' she said impulsively, 'but now I've changed my mind and I'm going to sleep.'

She pulled the blanket over her and curled on to her side so that her back was turned to him.

He settled down on his mattress, turning his back to her. They were both silent, and then he said: 'If I didn't belong to the Cause, would you love me again?'

'I might,' she said. 'I'd have to think about it.'

By the morning he had made up his mind. Until very late he had listened to her slow, even breathing and he felt very manly and protective. While he was with her, nothing would happen. She could sleep in safety. He was thinking about the things she had said, and he wished she'd asked if he could kill anyone who tried to hurt her. The answer to that would have been yes, but he wouldn't have been killing for the Cause in that case. He would have been killing for her, and that was different.

But she was right. He wasn't cut out for violence. When his mother had died he had thought he would never stop crying, and it was Franz, the man he sometimes thought might be his father though he couldn't quite believe it, who had told him that he must take her place. Then it had seemed the right thing to do.

The thing that troubled him the most was that he was not sure what they intended to do about Jenny. He could not let anything happen to her. So he had to rescue her or let her go. But if he let her go he would never see her again, so it seemed to him that was not the solution.

He was sitting looking at her sleeping face when she woke the next morning. She looked up, rubbed her eyes, yawned, stretched and said sleepily: 'Good morning, Claudio.'

'You are like a little brown kitten,' he said and he very tentatively reached to stroke her hair.

She wriggled slightly under his touch and then said: 'Did you sleep well?'

'Not very, I was thinking.'

'What were you thinking—?' She was tasting her mouth experimentally, checking on being awake.

'That we must go away from here. Together. With me to look after you.'

She sat up in the voluminous nightgown that he had stolen for her.

'Why do you say that, Claudio?' She was very grave.

'Because I'm a little afraid. I don't know what they plan to do with you.'

'You said they wouldn't kill me?' Her eyes were very round and fearful.

'That was before . . .'

'Before what?'

'Your mother gave them the counterfeit money.'

'My mother gave them counterfeit money?'

He nodded. 'It was your ransom that was paid. Half a million pounds' worth of Swiss francs. But then they changed their minds and Franz rang to say that your friends were to be released and you kept. I don't know why. And then last evening when they found the money wasn't real, they were very angry. If only you had gone yesterday—' he said, his voice despairing.

'Are you leaving the Cause?'

He just nodded.

'In that case,' she said, 'why don't you just let me go? Let me escape.'

'Because they might kill me, and because—'

'Because?' she prompted.

'Because I do love you and I want to be with you.'

'Oh, Claudio.' She leaned forward very slowly, her eyes closed, and to his delight kissed him full on the mouth. 'It's the same for me. What shall we do?'

She had taken his hand and he was squeezing hers.

'We must go from here.'

'But we've no money.'

'My aunt will help us. She lives right in the country, in Penna. It's in Umbria. If we can get a lift on the autostrada and get to her, we'll be all right. It's a long walk to the autostrada, but we can do it.' He looked at her shyly. 'Will you wear the dress I brought for you?'

'Yes, I will,' she told him.

It was after eleven o'clock before they got the chance to go. The other man, whom Claudio said was called Mario, had gone to the café around the corner for his coffee and cigarettes. A pair of conspirators, they hurried through the house together, hand in hand, Jenny trying to see as much as possible of the rest of this place which had held her prisoner for how long? She had lost count of the days.

It was a dirty, gloomy house, obviously inhabited only by men. Washing-up was piled in the sink, and empty beer and wine bottles cluttered the bare wooden kitchen table. Outside there was a courtyard concealing a white BMW and a big wooden gate with a small postern in it.

'This is where we must be quick and careful,' Claudio whispered, 'in case he's coming back.' He peered cautiously into the street and beckoned. Luck was on their side. They plunged without incident into a narrow alley, bordered with similar broken-down houses, and down to a big main street.

'They'll never catch us now,' Claudio said, full of confidence. 'We're free.'

As he spoke she saw a waiting yellow taxi and she thought that all she had to do was to call it and direct it to the house in Parioli and the nightmare would be over. But there was Claudio to think about. She didn't want to leave him, lose him, never see him again. And that would be what must happen if she just went home.

If he came with her they would know he had been part of the plot, and though Jenny had no idea of what the penalty for kidnapping was, she had a shrewd idea that Claudio might have to spend a good slice of his life in gaol if he were caught. If not worse.

She was quite certain how she felt about him. She loved him, and she felt closer to him than she had ever with anyone else in the world. It was as if he had come along to fill an area in her life that had always been barren. She thought perhaps it was because she knew he really loved her, and therefore she was secure in that.

So she let the yellow wasps of taxis buzz by and tramped on.

They had been gone ten minutes when the phone began to ring. There was no one to answer it. Mario heard it as he came in through the gate, but he was too late. Whoever it was had hung up. Still everything seemed in order. The room the girl was in was locked with Claudio inside too busy to answer phone calls, he thought with a leer. He settled down with a glass of *vino* and the morning paper, a small qualm striking him as he read how it was believed that the remaining kidnapped girl was in the Trastevere area. He wasn't surprised when five minutes later the phone rang again and the French girl told him to get out and away, taking the girl and Claudio with him.

'Where were you before?' she asked.

'Only getting breakfast,' the man said defensively.

'Well, your breakfast may cost you your freedom,' she snapped. 'You've got no more than ten minutes. So move.'

Mario moved. He rushed to the kidnap room and banged, bellowing for Claudio and the girl to come out: nothing. He rattled the handle. The door was locked. He banged and shouted again, and it began to dawn that maybe they weren't there. Maybe they had gone. It was time to save his own skin.

He ran back down the stairs and into the kitchen to get into the courtyard. But as he opened the kitchen door he found himself face to face with a very large, slightly overweight, gun-carrying member of the *carabinieri*.

'You're under arrest,' he said, as he stuck a pistol in Mario's ribs.

'We're going home tomorrow morning. I've just come back for my things,' Eileen Elliot was standing in front of Charles, shy again, but the softness from their lovemaking had lingered. She was not the same woman who had come to Rome two weeks ago.

She had returned to his bedroom. It was just before lunch and he had been getting ready to go to see the examining magistrate. On impulse, he put his arms around her full, rounded body and held her tight to him. He knew he didn't love her, but he was grateful to her, and he thought perhaps that she was grateful to him.

'You're going with Alex?'

'For the time being. I'll decide what to do once Frances is settled again. But I don't think she'll be surprised if I leave him.'

'Does he know?'

'I told him.'

He felt that surge of panic that a man feels when caught out in a sexual indiscretion with another man's woman.

'What did he say?'

'That you were welcome to all of me.'

There was an awkward silence, and she laughed lightly.

'It's all right,' she said. 'I don't expect you to take up his offer. What happened was a thing of the moment – something we both needed, Me particularly. You're the strong one, but you gave me some strength and some pride in myself. I keep telling myself that if a man like you can want someone like me even for just a little while, and be so kind, so loving, so reassuring then there must be more to me than Alex ever saw. And I think maybe he is telling himself the same thing. Since Frances has been found, and since I told him, he's looked at me differently. It'll never work between us again, but maybe he'll be able to see now that it wasn't all my fault.' She paused and said gently: 'You are very special, you know.'

'Eileen, don't—' he said.

'I'd ask you to see me in London, but it wouldn't be the same. Our mutual need has gone. Maybe when I've got myself together and I'm free of all those hang-ups that you've started to pull down, I'll ring you. You can buy me a drink for old times' sake. Maybe we'll even go to bed together again.'

There was no desire now in either of them, but he felt a genuine surge of what could have been a kind of love.

'I'll never forget you either,' he said. 'Whatever happens. You were very important. You came when I needed you.'

'And I you.' she paused. 'I'm going now: back to Alex. But not for long. I'm sure of that. Goodbye, darling. And thank you.'

He bent and kissed her forehead, and she smiled once at him, and was gone. Afterwards he realized he could not remember what she was wearing, but he knew he would never forget what she had said.

He went downstairs about ten minutes later. He wanted to give her time to go. Another meeting would have been embarrassing. Bobbie Jean was waiting for him, hopping up and down with excitement in the hall. She seemed more of a child and yet somehow more mature than before. The precociousness had gone, and looking at her he felt a deep sense of relief that she was safely home again.

'Have you heard?' she was asking.

'What?'

'The police found our place. It *was* in Trastevere. But Jenny and Claudio had gone. I bet they've run away together. The man who was guarding us swears he didn't know they weren't in the room.'

'How do you know all this?'

'The inspector's here. He wanted to talk to me and you. I suppose he wants you to break the news to Jenny's mother that she's gone off. And I don't blame her, having to come home to that awful woman. Quick, he's in here.'

Garoni was waiting in the drawing room, courteous and corect as ever. And indeed, he did want Charles to tell Ingrid what had happened.

'But I don't think it will be hard to find the girl,' he said with a small smile. 'It seems certain that she is wearing the confirmation dress that the boy must have stolen for her. She will be conspicuous all in white, I somehow think. And as the signora who owns the dress points out indignantly, it is not even ironed. A crumpled little girl in white with a tall thin boy should not be impossible to find.'

'I get your point,' Charles said. 'But do you think she's safe?'

'I am certain of it. Hungry maybe, and perhaps she will be footsore unless the boy has money, which is doubtful. But safe. They perhaps think they are eloping, eh? Your daughter is convinced that they were in love.'

242

'Well, it sounds like a happier ending than we'd expected,' Charles said.

'True. And not a lira changed hands. But I must speak to Signora Pallia regarding these forged notes that NAP speak of on the tape. Have you an idea of the truth of that?'

'None,' Charles said. 'And I don't think you'll find she's all that forthcoming.'

'Perhaps under the circumstances it would be expedient to forget I have heard that tape,' Garoni said thoughtfully. 'There has been enough international publicity and trouble already. What do you think, signor? As a diplomat what would you do?'

'Forget it,' Charles said promptly, thinking that Pallia, damn her blue eyes, had won again.

'Yes, I think perhaps that is what I shall do,' the inspector said. 'Just between you and I, of course, Signor Dennison.'

'Yeah, just between you and I,' Charles reassured him.

Kate had taken herself off to the Stampa Estera, the foreign journalists' club by the main post office. She wanted to make a phone call to London, and she didn't want it overheard in the villa. She certainly didn't want to make it from a phone box. What she was checking out would take far too long.

She reverse-charged the newspaper who were buying the Pallia story, got through to the library and put in her request.

'George – got anything on something or someone called Scimitar?' she asked. She was glad she had got George. An old newspaper library man, he didn't miss a trick.

'Rings a bell,' he said. 'Is it important?'

'Very.'

'OK, leave it with me. Where are you?'

'Don't worry, I'll ring you back. How long?'

'Twenty minutes,' he suggested.

She amused herself going through the day's periodicals, having a drink at the bar and a chat with some of the other foreign press. They all wanted news of the kidnappings. She gave them what she did not need herself. You never knew when you might need a bit of information in return.

She gave George twenty-five minutes and then called him back.

'Got it,' he said. 'Ready?'

'Carry on,' she told him, the telephone tucked into her shoulder, notebook and pen ready.

He had a lot of information for her, and writing it down took nearly half an hour. She was sweating and her arm aching when he'd finished.

'Sounds like a film script, doesn't it?' he said chattily.

'It does,' said Kate. 'But then there's nothing you can make up that equals real life. Thanks a bunch, George. I'll buy you a big drink when I get back.'

She took a taxi back to Parioli and went to her room, her head buzzing with questions. Then she sat at her typewriter and transcribed the shorthand she'd taken down from George. It still didn't make sense. Not quite. She needed to talk it through with someone. It was half-past twelve and she wanted a drink and she wanted some lunch. Thoughtfully she went downstairs looking for Charles and found he had just come back from the examining magistrate's office.

'Charles,' she said abruptly. 'Can you come and have some lunch – away from here? It's important. And can you extract Paul from Madeleine and bring him too. I know who Scimitar is. Or I think I do.'

Her face was serious enough to convince him.

'Right,' he said. 'Bobbie Jean can entertain Madeleine.'

'Thanks,' she said. 'I can hardly ask Paul myself, under the circumstances.'

He just grinned, nodded and went into the drawing room where Paul was sitting with Madeleine. They were both flipping through newspapers and not speaking.

'Can I have a word with you, Paul?' she heard him say, and a minute or so later, Paul joined her in the hall.

'What's happened?' he asked.

'I rang the office and now I'm totally confused. I don't know if I'm being a fanciful idiot or not.'

'Well, let's go and talk about it and find out,' Paul said.

They asked Verde, who was doing nothing, to drive them down to the town centre and opted to eat at the Piccolo Mondo where the noise, plus the singing waiters and the crowd, would make their conversation totally private. Once they were

244

settled at one of the squashed tables, Kate took out her notes. Then she giggled, looking at the wall across from her.

'Would you believe,' she said, 'a photograph of Pallia?'

And there was, mixed in with a mass of other celebrities' yellowing photographs.

'Can't get away from her anywhere,' Paul said.

'Never mind Pallia. Who is Scimitar?' Charles said impatiently.

'Right.' Kate was suddenly totally serious. 'Scimitar was a man called Raymond Gorel. He was an ex-French army colonel who joined the OAS and became their treasurer,' she said, her notes in her hand. 'They needed a treasurer. From the early 1960s up until 1969 the OAS were pulling off incredibly daring bank robberies all over France as well as in Oran and Algiers to finance their terrorist operation in both France itself and Algeria.

'Apparently their hoard worked out at something between five and ten million pounds – in sterling, that is. It's all in a Swiss bank. To get it out, a twenty-two-figure and –letter combination is needed, plus three signatures.

'One of those signatures was Gorel's. The other main character was a guy called Susini who seems to have been the ringleader.

'According to the *Daily Mail* at the end of 1972, Gorel, who'd become respectable, left home for work as usual one morning and was never seen again.

'It seems that some of his ex-comrades from the OAS had kidnapped, stripped him naked and tortured him in some freezing cold room on the Second Arrondissement.

'Like the tough guy he was, he wouldn't tell them how to get their hands on the loot, so one of them lost their temper and strangled him . . . Or so the story goes. He's never been seen again. There was no body. No real evidence, except some guy called "Little Jim" speaking from Lisbon, who grassed and started telling stories to journalists, swearing that was what had happened.' She paused and shook her head.

'If it's true, it's pretty stupid. By knocking off Gorel, if his *was* one of the three signatures required, they ruined their chances of ever getting near the loot. Strangling him would have been a dumb thing to do, and I don't think that terrorists are all that dumb.'

'You're saying Scimitar is Gorel and that Gorel is something to do with the kidnapping?' Charles asked.

'I don't know. I can't put it together yet.'

'What about the other two signaures?' Paul asked.

'Well, just after Gorel disappeared, Susini and others of the old gang went back to bank robberies. They got caught. And according to *The Times* of February 1974, Susini was on trial in Aix. He was acquitted of the bank robberies, but was going to have to face charges about the disappearance of Raymond Gorel.

'The third man could be a Colonel Yves Godard, who took a million of OAS money with him and his girl-friend to Madrid. Godard was a bit unlucky. He put the money in the bank in her name and woke up one morning to find both the bird and the bank balance had flown. But even if that million was from the secret fund in Switzerland it still leaves a hell of a lot.

'And now we have Ingrid appearing with a mysterious half-million pounds, albeit in forged notes, someone from NAP calling her Scimitar's daughter and saying that, to get the million they're demanding, she'll have to go back to Scimitar. Her father, she says, is French. She also says he disappeared in the war. Conveniently? Unless I've got the wrong Scimitar . . .'

She paused. The waiter had come balancing three plates and a huge tureen of spaghetti which he doled out in generous dollops. They were quiet, watching him.

Charles was ignoring his spaghetti and sitting with his wine glass cupped in both hands.

'I think you could be right. I've had a nasty feeling for some time now that this is not quite so simple as it looked. Monique worried me . . .'

'Me too now. Do you think she's with NAP?'

'I do. But I don't see why NAP should be after the OAS funds, or how they even know of their existence. How could it happen? NAP is about as left wing as you can get. The OAS were just slightly to the right of Hitler. What's the connection? If it were the Red Brigades and not NAP . . .'

'Garoni said that the Red Brigades weren't doing well right now,' Kate reminded him. 'Maybe NAP are on the up and up.'

'Bunglers . . . Garoni said they were bunglers,' Paul said. 'And they haven't done too well with us. They let Bobbie Jean and Frances go for a load of phoney banknotes and they let Jenny escape, and with one of their own members. Not too bright, I would say.'

'I think Monique is the key,' Charles said.

'So do I. I'm not going to let her out of my sight, if I can manage it,' Kate said. 'But what else do we do? Tell Garoni?'

'It sounds so unlikely,' Paul said doubtfully. 'I don't know that we ought to get involved. Just let's get Jenny home safely and then see.'

'But it's such a marvellous story,' Kate protested.

'Oh, you journalists!' Paul said. 'But still, let's get Jenny home first.'

Chapter Thirteen

'I'd just about given you up for lost.' Madeleine was stretched out on the big old-fashioned bed that he had been sharing with Kate for the past seven days. 'What were you doing?'

She was wrapped in a frilly blue crêpe-de-chine robe, one leg, still slim and pretty, sliding through, her blonde hair in a curly halo around her head on the white pillow.

The atmosphere was close and uncomfortable. She had left the shutters open and the sun was streaming in, flooding the room with searing yellow light.

'Aren't you hot?' he asked, ignoring the question.

'Yes, I am. I've been waiting for you to come and deal with the shutters. And I would love a cup of tea.' Her voice was petulant and wheedling by turns. Without speaking he went to the window and opened it wider to pull the shutters across and then said: 'You only had to ring the bell and the maid would have brought you tea.'

She pouted. 'I wanted to sit and drink it with you.' As she spoke, she lifted her head from the pillow and gave him her bright, brave smile. 'And you haven't told me where you were,' she said reproachfully.

In the room next door the typewriter was spluttering. He could hear it clearly and he had a sudden mental picture of Kate, back straight, fingers supple and moving with extra-ordinary speed, her face intent as her mind guided the busy hands. For him there was even an eroticism in watching her work.

His wife's blue eyes were staring quizzically at him, waiting for a reply.

'I was discussing the situation with Charles and Kate. She thinks this whole problem is much more complicated than it appears,' he said.

'Oh? Pass me that emery board from the dressing table, will you, darling. And don't forget the tea. How much more complicated?'

He handed her the emery board and rang the bell for the maid.

'Difficult to put in a nutshell,' he said, all too aware she wouldn't want the details. 'But roughly it looks as if Ingrid's father is a terrorist from another lot entirely – a group who appear to have £10,000,000 salted away in a Swiss bank. Kate thinks Ingrid's father knows the combination. This terrorist gang who kidnapped the girls are perhaps trying to get at that money. It could be.' He knew his explanation was wooden. He also knew she wasn't really concerned.

She was shaping her nails with great deliberation. 'How fascinating,' she said.

She propped herself up against the pillows and looked at him with her interested look. It meant she wasn't interested. When she was genuinely interested her face took on a faintly rapacious expression. Gossip, talk of money, would turn it on. But she was really only interested in herself, her comfort, her clothes, in that order. The condition was not new. Those had always been her only interests, but it had taken him a long time to realize it.

'Fascinating?' he said. 'More worrying.' There wasn't any point in pursuing the subject with her. 'How are you feeling?'

'Well, hot,' she said, and threw him a reproachful little look. 'And thirsty. But not bad. It's not one of my best days, though.' Again the brave smile, her blue eyes wide, then blinking, staring into his. 'I shouldn't really have come, of course. The doctor said not to, but I wanted to be with you. I'm a terrible enough worry for you as it is when you have to leave me. Poor you, to have such a useless wife.'

'Don't be silly,' he said automatically, and changing the subject: 'How are the kids, do you know? Have you rung your mother?'

'Not yet. I couldn't work that funny telephone. I didn't know what to dial. I thought you might do it and we'd both talk to her.'

The maid was at the door and he gave the order for tea. In the next room the typewriter clattered on while his wife asked him if he'd be kind enough to pass her nail polish from the dressing table, and could he just go into the bathroom and find some cotton wool. She thought it was in her sponge bag. It wasn't? Well, maybe in the vanity case, she suggested. He found it eventually in her overnight case, his head running with words that he would very much like to say to her.

'Oh, what a darling you are,' she trilled, and then her voice took on the wheedling note again. 'Could we go somewhere lovely for dinner tonight?'

'I think we should stay here until there's news of Jenny,' he said firmly.

She made a cross little sound with her tongue and her teeth. 'Really, darling, I didn't come all this way and in all this heat just to sit in what looks like the maid's room and with that dreadful typewriter clacking away all day and all night. I do hope she stops soon.'

'I expect Kate wishes she could stop soon,' he said. 'She has a lot of work to do.'

The calculating look she gave him was totally natural. It wasn't one of what he thought of as 'her looks'. There were so many of them – her special look for looking at herself in mirrors, cheeks pursed in, pouting, pleased with the picture she made. Her open, friendly, aren't-I-nice look when she wanted to charm someone for her own good reasons. Her smile that was not a smile, more a baring of the teeth when she was not pleased. Her brave look. Her coy look. Every now and then an unsolicited look came through, one that generally showed the sharp but banal mind under the pretty face, her greed or her incredible sense of self and survival. She knew about Kate all right, he suddenly realized, but she wasn't saying a word. She wasn't rocking the boat. She didn't care – just as long as the *status quo* – her *status quo* – remained intact.

'But what about dinner? Honestly, darling, Jenny's all right. It's just a question of them finding her. She's not kidnapped any more.'

'We don't really know that.'

'Oh, come on. That policeman said she wasn't. Let's go to dinner. Please, pretty please.'

She was pretty – remarkably pretty; and the illness had done nothing to mar her looks. If anything, she seemed suspended: younger. Maybe because others did the worrying.

'OK,' he said. 'Where do you want to go?'

'Somewhere very special. Somewhere expensive. The sort of place you'd take a client to. Somewhere like you'd take Kate.'

Again the calculating look. It was a touch of blackmail – or just malice?

'Kate's not into fashionable places,' he said flatly.

'Well, I am,' she said gaily. 'When I get the chance.'

There was a gentle tap on the door and the maid brought in tea, leaving him to pour it. He did so in silence, and handed her a cup.

'Darling, how lovely!' she said. Then her face parodied disappointment at the first sip. 'Oh, dear,' she said. 'They don't know how to make a good cup of tea, do they?'

She had a point he did not feel like conceding, so he said: 'Why don't you come downstairs and have a drink?'

'In a minute,' she said, pushing the tea cup from her with a fastidious little gesture. 'Do you think I'm looking better for the trip?'

For a brief moment he felt a terrible contrition at what he had been thinking and feeling. She did not look better. Not when she tried to move. There was no improvement.

'I think you look fabulous,' he said heartily.

'I believe it did me good. I enjoyed it enormously. Of course, Karl being there helped . . .' She stopped as if in confusion. He knew his cues. He took this one up.

'Karl?'

'Oh, just one of the young doctors. He sort of fell for me. Kept bringing me flowers and giving me special little titbits and things and not putting them on the bill.'

'That showed good taste, if a lack of professionalism.' He was aware that his voice was expressionless. He wouldn't have cared if Karl had taken her to bed every night she'd been there. But he knew she wouldn't have permitted that. The attraction was the thing. Her game. She had little interest in conclusions.

'Oh, he didn't do anything or even try anything. But he was sweet and it was rather flattering. I talked about you a lot so there was no misunderstanding.'

For years he had been asking himself what ego or uncertainty it was in Madeleine that made her do this; made her flirt, attract, provoke and then report all the details to him almost with indignation, as if the consequences of her sexual signals were nothing to do with her. Just as if she had not been involved or to blame in any way. As a young man, her behaviour had made him burn with jealousy that showed. One man who had kissed her at a drunken New Year's Eve party – against her will, she had protested – he had flattened, and never regretted it. By middle age he still burned with jealousy but knew how to hide it, thinking perhaps she would stop telling him details he did not want to hear if the telling had no effect. But nothing had stopped her, and the tragedy was that now he would not care if the combined armed forces had made a pass at her, or if she told him that the massed bands of the brigade of Guards played only for her favours.

Perhaps the memory of the honeymoon period with Kate wasn't helping. He could picture her in the bed on which his wife lay. He could also hear her working next door. He knew he loved her and he felt he could not bear Madeleine for a moment longer.

She was saying: 'Put my nail polish away for me, darling,

251

will you. And fetch me my turquoise dress from the cupboard, I think I might have a bath.' She paused. This was the moment when he was supposed to say he would run it for her. Today he did no such thing. He ignored both requests and without speaking turned and walked out of the room.

'Paul—' he could hear her saying plaintively as he shut the door. He half stopped, habit dying hard. Then he shook his head and went towards the stairs. The typewriter sounded louder here. Then there was a silence. She would be thinking, staring into space, her green eyes unfocused, hands resting on the keys, her body totally still, deep in concentration. Or, perhaps, had she heard his step on the stair and waited, hoping he would come to her.

He suddenly knew what he was going to do. It hit him with a blinding flash as being the most simple thing in the world. He was going to stop looking at his wife as a sick woman, but as a whole woman, the sickness an unfortunate, but basically incidental element. And he was going to stop living the hypocritical lie he had been living for the past four years. He was going to leave his wife as he should have done long ago, and he was going to live with Kate.

At that moment it seemed so blindingly simple, such an obvious solution and more important, such an *honest* thing to do – far, far better than waiting for Madeleine's slow exit so that he could then live the way he wanted. The decision was honest in that he knew he had loved Kate since before his wife's illness, and that if she had not become so sick he would have left her three years before. Now to live with Kate would mean that he could look himself in the face, even if the rest of the world averted their eyes.

He had been standing on the stair, chaotic thoughts that suddenly cleared into a simple plan of action cascading through his head. He turned abruptly and ran back up the few stairs he had come down, past his own bedroom and straight to Kate's door. Without knocking, the machine-gun sound of the typewriter still rapping out words, he went in.

She did not hear him at first, and not wanting to make her jump he made his footfall heavier as he walked across the room. She turned then, saw him and smiled. She looked tired.

Some of her hair had slipped in damp, dark strands from the drawn-back knot. Her face was bare of make-up and she was wearing her usual working gear of navy blue towelling trousers and a T-shirt.

'I want to talk to you.' Ridiculous! He was whispering, but he was aware of Madeleine's presence in the next-door room and was not certain how much of the sound would carry. The typewriter noise carried. Would their voices?

Sensing the urgency in his whisper, Kate stood up and moved to where he waited with the narrow bed behind him, the window streaming light on his face. A fly battered against the window seeking release. It sounded very loud.

'What about?' She was whispering too.

'Us.'

She nodded, eyes wide, white teeth biting her lower lip.

'I've made a decision.'

She did not speak, but tipped her head questioningly.

'I'm leaving Madeleine. I want to live with you. If you'll have me.'

He had meant to say it with so much more finesse. He was aware that his words made the need all his and perhaps sounded selfish and cold. But she looked at him, her full mouth slightly open with surprise, and then her eyes suddenly gleaming wet, held wide, trying to prevent the tears from falling as she flung herself into his arms.

He held her tight to him, rocking her, his head bent to bury his mouth in her hair.

'You know I love you. I need you. I think you love me. Will you do it? Can we be together?'

She was clinging to him and she did not answer or pull her face away from where it was hidden below his shoulder. And suddenly he was uneasy. He gently pushed her away from him and looked down into her anxious face.

'Well?' he asked quietly.

She was shaking her head, her lips tight together, folded inwards. The facial contortion made her look older.

'We can't.'

'Why not?'

She drew a deep breath.

'Because in a very short time you'd hate yourself. You might even hate me.'

'Kate!'

Her voice had steadied.

'It's true, Paul, darling Paul. We can't. It wouldn't work. Not under these circumstances.'

Her face was loving, tender, but somehow implacable.

'Kate, you don't understand,' he said. 'I've thought it all out. The way we're living is dishonest. It would be better to live with truth. It would be fairer to all of us – me, you and Madeleine – to end the situation.' And again he was conscious that he had put himself first.

'No.' Her voice was decisive. 'You can't leave her. You can never leave her. Until she leaves you . . .'

The last words were spoken so quietly he hardly heard them, then she was silent. He stood holding her arm and staring down at her. He was bewildered and beginning to be angry, and bizzarely they were still whispering.

'You don't love me?'

'Of course. Of *course*.'

'Then why don't you want to live with me?'

'I do want to live with you.' She pulled away from him and took one pace backwards so she could see into his face more easily. 'I want that more than anything in the world. But I've seen her, Paul. I've got to know her as a human being. Sick or well, she's not much, I admit. I don't care for her. I can even understand why you love me. The independence of me must be a hell of a relief. But she's sick, Paul. She's dying. And somewhere inside there, she's terrified. Once she wasn't on your back you'd realize it. You'd either have to return to her or you'd be sick with yourself – hating yourself, hating me for being the cause of all that guilt. You know what you're like about guilt. For Christ's sake, it sometimes makes you impotent when we're making love, even after all this time. What do you think it would be like if you actually upped and left her to make her exit alone? And what about the kids?' she covered her face with her hands. 'You haven't thought it out, Paul,' she said, her voice muffled. 'You've just decided what you'd like to do without a thought to the practicalities.'

254

He could hear the fly again. A bluebottle, he thought. How did a bluebottle get in here? It was easier to think about the fly for a moment.

Her eyes were still overbright, looking at him unflinchingly, and he did not want to hear the truths she was telling. He had wanted unqualified support of his decision; confirmation that it was the right thing to do. Part of him still argued it was the right thing to do, but he was aware that what she was saying was honest too. Yet he felt she had let him down in some heavy-handed way. She should have been joyous at his decision. He had handed her her dreams and she had rejected them.

'What is it?' he heard himself saying harshly. 'Are you afraid I won't be able to make love to you for all that guilt? Is that what you want – a part-time lover? A man about the bed? Freedom to get on with you own life and career, but no real commitment? Would it be inconvenient if I turned up on your doorstep?'

She shut her eyes and groaned quietly.

'Paul! Don't say things like that.'

'It it true?'

'No!' The word was vehement. Too vehement. And suddenly he was afraid that in words that had been said in an effort to wound her he had hit upon some kind of truth that neither of them had understood before.

The following day, the tenth, just some of the smoke began to clear. The first incident, in a day of incidents, was at 10.30 a.m. when NAP rang the villa to declare that they had re-captured Jenny.

'We've got her back, Ingrid,' the whispery voice said. 'And we want the money quickly this time. You have only twenty-four hours. I shall be in touch with you to tell you what you must do. If you do not produce one million pounds in Swiss francs you will never see you daughter again.'

Without waiting for a reply, the red-headed man put down the telephone in the crowded café he had chosen. He was mopping his forehead and he could feel cold sweat running down the back of his neck and under his arms. At the counter he ordered himself a Grappa. He had five men out looking for the boy and the girl. God knew, they should have been distinctive enough and they'd nowhere to go. So where had they gone? The phone call was a last gamble. Finding Jenny and the boy would add credence. He didn't want Ingrid's million – he wanted her to lead them to Scimitar. It was just about the last chance.

'Where the hell are they?' he said out loud, and decided he needed another Grappa.

Garoni, on the other hand, just laughed when he arrived at the villa and heard the latest tape.

'It's a try-on,' he said confidently. 'I don't believe he can possibly have her and the boy. We've had two reports in, and he's no fool, that *ragazzo*,' he said admiringly of Claudio. 'Do you know what he did? He joined a school party on a day's outing seeing the monuments. They were kids from Orvieto and he kidded their teacher that he and Jenny had missed their own bus. He told her they came from Verona.

'She says she chucked them off when the tour was over. She didn't want to be finding them transport to Verona from Orvieto, but they must have hidden on the bus somewhere – probably under the back seat. The driver saw them get off when the bus stopped on the autostrada. Then they got themselves a lift as far as Orte with a *camionista*. Both the teacher and the lorry driver saw their descriptions in the paper – but too late. But they still called in with the information.'

'Good thinking on that kid's part, eh? Who'd look for them in a school outing?'

He chuckled and then shook his head. 'No, I don't believe NAP have got them.'

'It's possible,' Monique said. 'NAP could have followed the lorry and picked them up again.'

'My instincts say no to that,' Garoni said. 'They're trying to force the *signora*'s hand.'

Ingrid looked more exhausted than she had since the girls had been kidnapped. She was bowstring tight; about to snap into little pieces.

'I don't have a million,' she said through clenched teeth.

'What about where you got the money last time?' the inspector asked, tactfully not mentioning he knew it was forged and hoping for some more information.

256

'What does it matter if they haven't got her?' she snapped. 'And anyway, I can't go back there. I don't even know how.'

The information cast a silence over the room. Kate and Paul exchanged glances. Monique's face was totally disinterested The subject was dropped.

By midday the papers were full of the lorry driver's story and that of the schoolteacher. Both had given detailed interviews and descriptions of the bedraggled tiny girl and the tall thin boy in jeans. But neither informant had any idea where the children were going.

The red-headed man was not as impressed with Claudio's quick thinking as the inspector had been. He burned with rage as he read the story over his pizza and coffee, standing in a small crowded bar on the Corso. He chewed thoughtfully. Orte? Why had they wanted to be dropped off at Orte? Then he suddenly remembered. Luisa's sister had had a cottage out there somewhere. Somewhere near Amelia. Could the boy have been taking the girl there? It was possible. But why he was taking her anywhere beat him. Young love? He snorted. Where was that cottage? Think, man, think, he told himself. And presently a smile of satisfaction crossed his face. He had remembered.

The woman who was called Lina Cassuto stood, dressed in her country black, her hair tied back in a black scarf. The face beneath was strong, an arched aquiline nose set between two fine dark eyes. Her jaw was positive, her mouth large with strong white teeth. She was very brown and very sure of who she was. And she was, Kate thought, the most commanding person in the room.

'My family owe you an apology, *signora*,' she was saying in a quiet but carrying voice to Ingrid, who stood, her arm awkwardly around Jenny's shoulder as if she were not sure when she could legitimately let go. 'They thought they were in love, you see, and they did not wish to be separated. Like the young, they did not think.

'But, *signora*, my nephew has not touched your daughter, that I promise you. When I returned home from market this morning, she was asleep in my bed where my nephew had insisted she sleep. I found him sleeping on the floor by the door of the room. He was guarding her. He has never wished to hurt her or take advantage of her.'

Kate felt an uncomfortable lump rise in her throat. Jenny was motionless at her mother's side, her eyes downcast. Claudio had not taken his eyes off her – anxious eyes, devoted eyes. It was obvious that he was terrified he had done everything wrong.

'I was not in when they arrived. Had I been, I would have contacted you before. They had hoped I would shelter them. They were both exhausted and the little one's feet were very painful. Once they had explained to me what had happened, I had to take the cart out again and go to Amelia to the *carabiniere* there. I have no telephone, so it all took time and for that I am sorry. But it was not difficult to persuade them that they must not keep you waiting any longer. My nephew wants only what is best and right for your daughter.

'But now, *signora* – what will they do to Claudio? Can you perhaps speak for him?'

'Signora Cassuto,' Charles Dennison said gently. 'The *signora* only understands a little Italian. I will have to explain to her. And please, won't you sit down?'

The woman gave a slow, determined shake of the head.

'You are kind, *signor,* but it is better that I stand for what I have to say. To whom can I speak for my nephew, the boy of my only sister?'

'To me, if you wish. I am Inspector Garoni of the *carabinieri.*'

The woman gave him a quick glance, and then looked into his eyes. Something she saw there seemed to satisfy her.

'Very well,' she said. 'I will explain it to you.'

The inspector bowed courteously.

'This boy is a good boy who has been led too soon into men's ways. He has no father who acknowledges him; only one who uses him, and he used his mother, my sister.

'My sister was caught up in the terrorism; this man, he is either French or German, led her into it. She loved him, and what she did she did for love. He is called Franz, this man. I do not know his other name. He says he has no other name.

'My sister, Claudio's mother, is dead. She belonged to the

group who kidnapped your children, but she had nothing to do with that. She was already gone.' The woman crossed herself briefly. 'She killed herself with the explosives with which she was preparing to kill others. It was hard to mourn, even for those who had loved her. It seemed like God's justice.

'By then the boy had not been involved. It was the man Franz who said that he must take up where his mother left off. That he must continue her work and that there was no greater glory than to die for the Cause. Or, if necessary, to kill for the Cause.

'Kill for the Cause!' She lost her level tones for a second for one of scorn. 'My nephew is a gentle boy who could not drown a sick kitten. His heart is good, but this man thought he could be taught. Taught to kill.' She made an exclamation of disgust. 'And this man is his father. His own father wanted to teach him to become an assassin.

'Helping with the kidnapping was the first thing Claudio did for the Cause. It will be the last. He knows now he cannot kill, nor can he hate. Like his mother, he has done something for love. But in his case, it is something good.

'He saved this child he loves when he feared perhaps his own people would kill her. He was appalled to realize they were capable of killing her. He has told me this, and he is not a boy who lies. And he understands he can never be an assassin.

'In God's eyes, Claudio has done no wrong. He is seventeen years old, *signor*—' She was near pleading now. 'Must his life be over for ever because he followed the will of those he believed he should?'

Kate was having considerable trouble with both her throat and her eyes. Charles was clearing his throat self-consciously, and he said: 'What do you think, Garoni?'

The inspector looked at him thoughtfully.

'Are you a fisherman, *signor*?'

'As a matter of fact, yes,' Charles said, puzzled.

'I think we should find Franz, the big fish. And tell me, what do you do with the little fish when you catch them in America?'

'The tiddlers? We throw them back.'

'Tiddlers.' Garoni savoured the word as if it pleased him. 'Should we perhaps throw this tiddler back?'

259

'I think so,' said Charles.

'Throw him back?' The woman's voice was respectful but full of anxiety. 'Where will you throw him, *signor*?'

'To you. To your custody. To your care.'

Her face lightened, she smiled, but then the anxious look returned.

'But his father will know where he is.'

'And we would like to know where his father is.'

'I do not know. He is only here when there is trouble. I think he lives in another country. I have never known where he stays here.'

'He is looking for someone with a lot of money,' Claudio said suddenly. 'He keeps saying: "Find the man, find the money." I don't think that the kidnappings were all that important to him.'

'As,' Paul said drily, 'we seem to have all three back safely and not a penny changed hands, it can't have been that important.'

'I don't doubt they would have liked the money,' Garoni said. 'But NAP are bunglers. Claudio – will you talk to me? Tell me all you know? I think you owe me that.'

The boy was looking at his aunt.

'He really is my father?'

'Yes,' she said gently. 'I'm sorry.'

'Now I don't know who I am,' he cried, his voice anguished.

'It is an accident of fate that he is your father,' the woman said calmly. 'And we must help the inspector if we can.'

'Will you come to my offices, *signora*?'

She looked at him, her dark eyes clear and searching.

'I can believe that you will throw this little one back to me?'

'You have my word.'

'Then we will come to your office,' she said. 'Claudio, take my arm.'

While they had been speaking, Monique had picked up her handbag and put her cigarettes and lighter away and was moving towards the door.

'I'll get your room ready, Jenny,' she said.

She had slipped away before Garoni and Lina Cassuto said their goodbyes. Then Charles called the inspector back.

'Can you do something?' he asked quietly. 'Is it possible not to let the papers know that Jenny's safe with us. It may prove nothing, but NAP's reaction might just tell us something.'

Garoni half smiled. 'I think it will be easier to stop Signora Cassuto from telling her story than perhaps the other witnesses we have had,' he said. 'There will be nothing in the papers.'

When Claudio left with an agonized backward look, Jenny started to cry, quite silently; and amazingly, Ingrid was crooning and clucking and murmering consoling words.

'Darling,' they heard her say as she led Jenny away. 'You just don't know how lucky you are to have someone love you like that,' and there was a wealth of yearning in her own voice.

Kate found she had been clutching at Paul's hand without realizing it. 'I wouldn't want to go through that too often,' she sniffed as the door closed. 'Nor I think would you,' she added, with a rainbow smile at the two men, neither of whom had quite recovered composure.

They had the big room to themselves. Madeleine had not appeared downstairs, having no curiousity about the comings and goings of the day, and suddenly self-conscious they busied themselves with cigarettes, plumping cushions and pouring drinks.

'Now what?' said Kate.

'Now Monique has nipped off to inform NAP that they've lost their last ace,' Charles said.

'Correct,' said Paul. 'And then what?'

'Something will happen and pretty damn quick,' Kate said. 'It's got to. I may help it along. I just think I'll go and assist Monique in getting Jenny's room ready.'

This time Monique managed to avoid Kate. She was quite aware that the English girl was keeping tabs on her – even to the extent of catching up with her on the early morning runs. This had caused a slight hiccup – she'd had to snatch other moments for her phone calls – but nothing too serious. A plan was fermenting in her mind into which Kate would fit very nicely. Kate seemed to want to be embroiled, and if Kate wanted to get embroiled she'd have to take her chances with everyone else. Her involvement could prove very useful.

When she left the drawing room she never went near Jenny's room. Her first thought was to get to a telephone, and quickly. She took the Lancia and drove to the nearest phone, not worrying about how she parked, but no one else in Rome worried either; leaving the car half across the pavement wasn't going to get her the death penalty.

Franz was there waiting at the import export office where, no work was ever done. He answered the phone immediately.

'The girl's back,' she said abruptly. 'The boy's aunt just brought her in.'

'I know.' His voice was savage. 'I got there too late.'

'You knew where they'd gone?'

'I guessed. Is the boy with her? Is he talking?'

'Yes and no.'

He grunted. 'He doesn't know much,' he said grudgingly.

'We'd better put my plan into operation,' she said. 'Tonight. The sooner the better. We should have done it that way from the first.'

'It would have made him suspicious.'

'Maybe. Now it doesn't matter. He shouldn't have given her forged money.'

'All right. We'll do it your way.'

'Make sure you're there by nine at the latest in case my charming employer has one of her famous headaches and wants to go. I'm having trouble with the English journalist who wants to be my best friend this term. If I can't unload her, she'll have to come for the ride. Do just as we said. Side entrance and away.'

'Okay.' He hung up.

She grinned at how she, his little bit of recruited stuff, for a flat fee to be paid when the ransoms were delivered, seemed to be in charge now. He must be congratulating himself on his sagacity in approaching her in London before they had left for Rome. A plant in the villa right from the beginning. He *had* been lucky. She moved from the telephone, her lips pursed, going over the ground, going over the possibilities. Could she do it on her own, or did she need help? She was going to get help, willy-nilly. She chuckled to herself wondering just how well the intrepid English journalist would stand up to what she might be facing later that evening. On balance, she decided, she probably wouldn't do too badly.

The intrepid English journalist was regarding her with a great deal of suspicion as she came back into the villa, leaving the Lancia in the drive. She was hovering in the hall very obviously so as not to miss her return.

'I went upstairs to help you with Jenny's room and you weren't there,' she said reproachfully.

'I know. I was *émue*, moved, you know. I had to get out for a while.'

Kate's face cleared. 'It was pretty emotional, wasn't it? I'm glad Garoni turned up trumps.'

'He never did seem like a monster, that one.'

There was an awkward silence and then Monique said: 'I was thinking of taking Ingrid to supper tonight as a little celebration now that it's all over. At Sabatini's. Would you like to join us? Girl's evening. We can cry as much as we like.'

Three expressions chased across Kate's face; surprise, suspicion and then relief.

'How nice of you to ask me,' she said. 'I'd love to. What time?'

'Oh, early, I think. About 7.30 from here. No one will want to be late tonight. We must all be exhausted.'

'True. Jenny's asleep already. Well, see you at 7.30, then.'

She trotted off cheerfully enough, and Monique was reminded of the lines her adopted English father used to repeat: 'Alas regardless of their doom, the little victims play.'

She hoped that Kate would not, unwittingly, become a victim.

If all of NAP's operations went as well as Plan Two, Monique decided, by now the organization could have ruled the world. But then Plan Two wasn't a great deal to do with NAP. It was her and Franz working as a team – very efficient team. They needed no help from anyone else.

It had been a delightful dinner. Kate had listened attentively to all Ingrid's tried and not-so-true stories. The food was good. They drank champagne to the health of all three girls. Ingrid's cheeks were a little flushed by the time the bill came – which Kate insisted on paying – and Monique suspected that she had *almost* been forgiven for asking the journalist to join them. At first Ingrid had not been pleased; had threatened not to come and had required considerable persuasion.

The taxi was conveniently outside in the small alley at the side. Monique had quickly slipped into the front seat with the driver – a habit not encouraged by Roman cabbies, but this one did not seem to mind. The two other women, cheerful and slightly tipsy, seeming almost to like each other, got into the back.

And it was as simple as that. As simple as it had been with Bellino. It became even more simple when Monique produced from her handbag a very unpleasant looking small gun which she posed on the back of her seat, muzzle facing Ingrid. She then suggested that no one should make any attempt to get out if the taxi should have to stop for lights or anything so inconvenient.

Turning to look at them, frozen where they sat, still dressed up for a smart evening out, she began to laugh softly.

'I do wish you could see your face,' she said. 'Sorry, Kate, it's really all your own fault. You were so determined not to let me out of your sight, weren't you?'

'We realized you were with NAP.' Kate's voice was disdainful, as if she were speaking to a social inferior, a despicable social inferior.

'What are you going to do?' Ingrid didn't sound frightened either. Just furious. But Monique was not surprised. She knew her Ingrid. Under all the nonsense was a fighter. She and Franz wouldn't have two hysterical women on their hands, that was for sure.

'Is this the man who kidnapped the girls?' her ex-employer was demanding autocratically.

'Dead right,' Monique said. 'May I present Franz Pallia?'

The gasp from the back seat was nothing less than theatrical and Monique laughed delightedly again. She spoke in French to Franz. 'I just introduced you. It has caused what you might call a sensation.'

'*Bonjour, petite soeur,*' he said, not taking his eyes off the road.

And after that no one spoke until Franz pulled the taxi up in the Porta Pinciana. The street was surprisingly quiet for Rome, the wall of the Villa Borghese bordering one side, on the other, tall well-kept houses, some converted to offices.

'Now don't try anything,' Monique said cheerfully. 'This petite gun of mine has a splendid silencer. The one Franz is carrying would blow both your heads off with one bullet. So be good.'

She meant the warning for her own sake. She wanted them both alive and kicking and she knew perfectly well that Franz would not hesitate to blow anyone's head off. Certainly not Kate Anderson – to him she was entirely extraneous. But not to Monique. Ingrid he wanted information from. So did Monique. After that it would be a different matter. But he would not be his sister's executioner.

She just hoped that Kate would not attempt anything spectacular. She was uneasy at how quiet the English girl was. Her head was obviously working overtime and that could be dangerous.

At gunpoint the two women were hurried into one of the tall buildings and then straight down a flight of stairs behind a heavy wooden door that led to the basement. The whole area they moved through was dimly lit, as if in anticipation of their arrival. Once down the stairs, they were in the big open cellar which could have been used for storage, and which Franz had used when he wanted to screw her. At the end of the storeroom there was a desk in deep shadow with only a lamp in dark green metal which directed light downwards. There was one other plain, wooden, armless chair near the desk which hung from the shade nearer the ceiling. It made a rough and ready interrogation seat. Another plain chair was placed nearby.

'That's your seat, Monique,' Franz was saying, 'but you'd better let our unexpected guest sit there, next to my little sister under the spotlight. Pull up a packing case and settle yourself where you can keep an eye on them both.'

'OK,' Monique said. She settled the two girls in the chairs and then she herself lounged against the wall behind them. It might be better to be mobile, she decided.

'Long time no see, eh, Ingrid?' Franz was saying affably, speaking in English. 'Did you ever wonder if I was still alive?'

'Sometimes.' Ingrid's voice was a monotone. She was shaken, but definitely not stirred.

'Father never said anything about me?'

'No.'

'Well, he wouldn't. We had a parting of the ways – political ways. I couldn't stand his treacherous, creeping, superficially so-respectable activities. I couldn't stand his politics: kill the Jews, kill the blacks, kill the wogs. All that crap about the master-race, and him a Frenchman, though from Alsace Lorraine, as he was always pointing out. No, little sister, we split when I was seventeen and I went and did something positive.'

'Like killing and kidnapping.'

'Positive. Those things have to be done. I got my chance in May 68. You'd have been proud of how much I had to do with those student riots. I honestly think they changed the world. The Left found its heart and spirit there on the cobbles of Paris and the rest of the world followed. Think about it. Nothing has ever been quite the same since.'

He was bragging to his little sister, Monique thought. His face was in shadow where he was seated at the big desk and the room around him patchily lit. But the bravado showed in the set of his huge shoulders, catching what light there was, the lift of his head, the pride in his voice.

'You may be famous, little sister, but I am *secretly* famous. My name in the four corners of the earth means something very special. It means that I can judge. I am jury and executioner. I have no name, or, like God, many names. I am not known as Franz Pallia.'

'And did you pronounce sentence on poor Bellino?' Kate's voice was full of contempt.

'I did. A decadent pervert: did you not think that the punishment fitted the crime?'

Nobody answered. Monique had taken a few paces to get him used to her moving and now she was facing Ingrid. The woman was upright in the chair. As proud in her own way as her brother. She was certainly not cowed – not yet.

'Why are you telling me this?' she asked.

'Oh, there's no danger, I assure you. You won't tell anyone.

Nor will your friend.' Ingrid's eyelids did flicker then, but Kate, sitting four paces away, had her face set in lines of stubborn bad temper.

It was perhaps time that she began preparing ground, Monique decided. She moved a little so that her face was reasonably well lit and in Kate's direct line of vision. Then she said: 'There's no need to look so bad-tempered, Kate. You wanted us to be best friends, didn't you? And now we are.' The words were said sarcastically, but her eyes and eyebrows mirrored a different message, while one swift downward movement of the hand said: Play it cool.

Kate played it cool. So cool that Monique had no idea if the signal had been intercepted. Shit! she thought. A response would have helped. But it had to be a start.

The signal had been received, all right, but Kate didn't trust it. She had no reason to do so. At the moment she had been listening with half an ear to the conversation between Franz and Ingrid, regretting that it looked as if all the gaps in the story she had always felt were there were being filled – and how would she ever get to write them in?

She had no illusions that the brooding Franz would let her live to tell any tales. She was going to do her darnedest to beat him. But for the life of her – a grim pun – she could see no way out of this one.

Monique toted a gun lightly but professionally. And the great ugly monster lying on the desk in front of Franz looked big enough to blow the room apart. 'There is some corner of a foreign field that is forever England,' she found herself thinking, ridiculously, and wishing, wishing, wishing that she had had time to tell Paul once more just how much she loved him. For she did. And tomorrow they would have all gone home. Tomorrow it would have been over without tears.

'However,' Franz was saying, 'enough of my triumphs. Tell me about our mother.'

'Dead. Killed with Joanna in an air raid after you both had left.'

'Tragic.' A small sigh escaped. 'And now tell me about Father. He too must have had his triumphs.'

'I don't know of any.' Kate was admiring Ingrid more and more. She wasn't letting the bastard get her down either. She was managing to sound as if they were having one of the conversations that families indulge in with each other after years of separation. Would they get to aunties and uncles? Kate wondered.

'No triumph for Father?' Franz sounded sad.

'He left France after the war. He'd done a good job for the German High Command, but it didn't seem the best place to stay. The Resistance didn't like him very much. So he went to Algeria, where he opened the Saraband Hotel. It was very successful, the most famous in Algiers. And then came the troubles, of course, and when they were over, once again it didn't seem like a good place to stay. The natives weren't friendly.'

'Poor Papa.' Franz's voice was soft. 'Never welcome for long.'

'Yes. I think he was sad to leave Algiers. He had so many friends.'

'And where is he now?'

Ingrid shrugged. 'You wouldn't have a cigarette, would you?'

He flung her one, and then after hesitating, got up to light it. Monique moved, as he did, so that she was standing just slightly behind his desk.

'You were about to say where Father is?'

'I wasn't, actually, because I don't know.'

'You saw him in Marseilles just a few days ago.'

Ingrid stiffened. 'But I also told your treacherous, creepy little toady –' She stabbed a contemptuous finger at Monique '– that I don't know where he is now. And that was before I realized she was a treacherous, creeping little toady.'

'But, Ingrid, you tell such awful fibs,' Monique put in. 'You'll say anything if it suits you. You're not truthful, Ingrid. You know you're not.' She moved nearer to the desk, Kate noticed, and her hand was lightly on Franz's shoulders. 'I had to warn your dear brother about your lies. I mean, he could be misled.'

Franz seemed to be enjoying the joke, as Monique perched

herself on the corner of the desk where she was half hidden in shadow. She picked up a biro that lay there and began to doodle with it. She was up to something, Kate realized. The signal perhaps was to be trusted and a spark of hope lit in her.

'Nevertheless,' Ingrid was saying. 'I have no idea where he is now.'

'Is he Scimitar, Ingrid?' The question was cream soft.

'No.'

'Is that one of your lies, Ingrid?'

'No.'

'Where is Scimitar, Ingrid?'

'Dead. Where they killed him. His name was Gorel – not Pallia.'

'Ah but neither is Father's any more, is it? What is his name, now, Ingrid?'

'I don't know.'

'Ingrid, Ingrid – that is one of your lies.'

In spite of the combination of hope, sheer terror and determination to show nothing that was battling in her, Kate could not help quietly congratulating herself that all her hunches had been correct. Even the one that something must happen quickly. It had. Her only miscalculation had been to accept the invitation to dinner – and possible death. But then she would never have known the end of the story, and while there was life there was hope, particularly as Monique had just put down the biro and picked up Franz's gun, looking at the dark metal as if she had never seen such a thing before. Still perched on the corner of his desk, with a foot between them, she turned the big black automatic over in her hand thoughtfully, rubbed her finger along the barrel, and then let it drop into her lap.

'All right it is one of my lies.' Ingrid blew smoke at the ceiling, incongruous in the bare room in her floating white chiffon evening dress, her brown shoulders bare, her blonde hair dazzling under the lighting that beat down on her head.

'I think you're going to have to tell me,' he said, his voice still soft.

'What will you do if I won't? Kill me, like those other idiots killed Gorel? A fat lot of good that did them.'

269

'But it did our father a great deal of good, maybe. Perhaps Scimitar passed on his secrets.'

'Maybe.' Ingrid shrugged.

'You wouldn't just like to tell me?'

'Not a lot.'

'I'm afraid, Ingrid, you're going to have to.' He got up from the desk and walked, his footsteps echoing hollow on the bare floors, to a filing cabinet. And as he went Kate watched Monique slip off the corner of the desk, the automatic still casually in her hand, swinging like a child's toy. Franz had turned from the filing cabinet, facing into the room again.

'Ingrid,' he said. 'I am going to know. I want that Swiss money for the Cause. I want the irony of money stolen for the right in the pockets of the left. I want it, and I believe our father knows how to get it. You'll tell me where he is, Ingrid, or—'

'Why should you think he knows?' she interrupted.

'My organization knows that he was deeply involved with OAS. They know that Saraband was a headquarters in Algiers. They know that Gorel and our father were close friends and confidants. The truth about Gorel has never been told. There is still no body, still no real evidence of death. And why has our father never returned to France? De Gaulle forgave and forgot. He could have come back with the generals; with all the others. Why did he not? What did he do that was not forgivable? And where is he now?'

'I don't know.'

The silence was so long that prickles of fear ran up Kate's back. The man by the filing cabinet exuded menace; seemed to grow.

'I shan't kill you, little sister,' he said. 'One does not kill one's relatives. I would never have killed Jenny. Rather kept her with us. She might have made a good revolutionary. No. No killing. But in this cabinet are some interesting little gadgets, mostly electrical. I think I might start with your eyes. Simple to blind with no more than light, and not too painful, when one knows how, as I do. Tongue then, maybe. Difficult for an actress to work if speech has gone. Just small things after that: burns; I believe the fingernails are painful when removed. People scream a lot, I have noticed. It would be simpler to talk, and then Monique will kill you quietly, quickly, tidily and painlessly. Unlike you, I do not lie. You have to die, I'm afraid.'

Amazingly, Ingrid was laughing – genuinely laughing. There was no hysteria in it. Disconcerted, Franz swung round to the cabinet.

'You don't believe me?' He was shouting at her. 'I'll show you.'

He was spilling shining gadgets from the drawer and on to the top of the cabinet, and while he was doing so, Monique had moved to stand near Kate. Very quickly she dropped her small handbag into Kate's lap. The clasp was undone. Inside was the smaller gun.

'*Doucement*,' was all that Monique whispered. 'Softly.'

Ingrid was still laughing.

'It's too silly really,' she said. 'All of this melodrama, Franz. I've acted in better B movies. Brother, there isn't any money in that Swiss bank. It's all gone. Every last franc of it.'

He was totally still, the menace still there.

'Where?'

'Our father, our surviving, wily old father, has had the lot. We are the children of a millionaire, Franz. Isn't that nice for us?' She was still giggling quietly. 'But your organization won't get their hands on it. As you know, I can't get my hands on it. The bit he gave me wasn't even real. No, Franz, the money is in stocks and share, respectable public companies. The money is legit now. Safe from all of us.'

He was closing the drawer and turned back to face her.

'Where is he?'

'At sea. On a yacht. He lives on a yacht. The biggest, most luxurious yacht in the world. The newspapers call it his floating palace. All that money meant a new face, new papers, a new life. Our father is famous, world renowned. We are the children of one of Europe's most famous men. His hotels straddle cities. He is a collossus. And it has only taken him six years. Still one hundred million francs was a good float to begin with, and Father had some money of his own, from Algiers. He was always clever with money. And wasn't he wise to go into hotels? There's an English expression about cobblers sticking to their last. That's what father did. He stuck with his last. Hotels with nice big public companies behind them. His money and lots of other people's as well. Franz, his stocks and shares won't help your cause. The hotels you can hardly steal. Father is safe and a little too powerful to blackmail. I imagine he knows lots of people with the same kind of equipment you've got right there.'

Kate was listening, stunned at the realization of just who Ingrid's father was, but she was still alert enough that the small gun, now in her hand, hidden by the handbag, was cocked and ready for use. It was a bit different from shooting stag or pheasant, she thought, but if necessary she was going to use it. And if she was forced, for the rest of her life she'd never so much as spray-gun a mosquito.

'Father is—'

'Shush—' Ingrid put her finger to her lips. 'We shouldn't mention his hallowed name in front of others – and one of them a journalist. After all, the world believes his money comes from oil – not from terrorism, cold-blooded murder, and bank robberies. Not that father was ever involved with any of that. He just picked up the proceeds. His hands are clean.' She sighed. 'I might not have told you, torture or not, dear brother, if Father hadn't let me down. When he sent me that counterfeit money, jeopardizing Jenny's life, I was through with him. It was a cruel and wicked thing to do.'

'Ah, but he didn't,' Monique was back near the desk again, the automatic held in her hand as if she meant business. 'That was me. I swopped his perfectly good Swiss francs for those bits of paper. Well, not me exactly. My people. We thought it might get things moving.'

Franz took a menacing pace forward and Monique lightly lifted her arm.

'I've got the gun.'

'You treacherous little bitch . . .'

'Well, we're all in the business of treachery in some way, aren't we?' she said chattily. 'Except perhaps Kate here, and she might get the urge to sell us all up the river to her newspaper.'

272

Kate was silent, but Ingrid said, her voice a plaint: 'I can't believe it. How are you involved?'

'Planted,' Monique said laconically. 'You needed a secretary, I applied. We wanted your father, just like your brother does. And I don't mean NAP or whatever mysterious outfit he heads. I mean the French government. We wanted our money back that they stole from our banks, and like your brother, we thought Pallia Père might know how to get it. But we had the same problem – he'd dropped out of sight. Completely.'

'How did you know he was my father?'

'Oh, come on, Ingrid.' Monique was lolling against the wall, the automatic relaxed in her hand. Kate, however, was watching the tense, angry body of Franz, seated behind the desk. His eyes were on Monique and his hand was slowly moving, creeping towards his right-hand desk drawer. 'We knew he had once been Pallia. We knew your name was your own. We tracked you back. You should have changed your name, *chérie*. Why didn't you?'

'It was my name. Me. I had little enough sense of identity.'

'Well, we thought you might just get us there. I must say when Franz made the approach to see if I would join his little outfit – for money, of course – that was a bonus. One of those lucky . . .' She had turned to look at him as she spoke his name and then his hand moved with viper speed and her expression told she knew it was almost too late as she whipped up the gun in her hand.

Except that something happened. A quiet plop, followed by a neat round hole between Franz's eyes where his eyebrows once had met in a peak. There was a faintly acrid smell, a trace of smoke and suddenly a great deal more blood.

'I hope to Christ he was trying to kill you,' Kate said, her voice dangerously calm. 'Because sure as hell I've killed him.'

Monique, paper white, moved to the body. In its clenched hand was an evil looking round grey object.

'He was trying to kill us all. Himself as well. He was blowing us all up with a grenade. And, God forgive me, I almost let him do it,' She straightened and looked at Kate. 'I had a hunch you'd come in handy. Where did you learn to shoot like that?'

'Grouse moors,' Kate said. It suddenly struck her as funny

273

and she was laughing. 'Would you believe, grouse moors. And pigeons and sometimes rabbits and duck and pheasant. And snipe. But they're difficult – they zigzag all over the place. But not people, never people—' The laughter was turning to tears. 'Honestly, never people,' she cried.

Monique hurried across the floor and took the gun from Kate's nerveless fingers, then slapped her face – hard.

'That's enough,' she said. 'It's over. Really over. You've just done the human race a favour.' She turned and said authoritatively: 'Ingrid, get up.'

Automatically Ingrid stood, her knees visibly shaking. 'Listen to me, both of you. You're leaving here now. You are going to walk down to the Via Sistina and go into the Hassler cocktail bar for a very long, very strong drink while the doorman gets you a cab. You both look fine. No one would guess you'd been embroiled in this lot. Drink your drink, take the cab home and forget about tonight. Completely.'

'Where are you going?' Ingrid's voice was small.

'Away – but first I'll get this –' she jerked her head in the direction of the body, leaning back in its chair, eyes still horribly open '– cleared up, then really away. I was a lousy secretary anyway.'

'But cheap,' Ingrid managed.

Monique laughed, and then her face saddened.

'I'm glad nothing happened to you, baby.' She leaned and gently kissed her employer. 'We had our good times.'

Ingrid looked as if she was trying not to cry, but she said gruffly: 'What about that half-million you stole from me?'

Monique laughed again.

'You'll never change, will you?' She turned to Kate. 'This is one good story you should forget. It would be better.'

Kate was mesmerized by the body. 'I'll try, God knows I'll try,' she said 'But I won't be writing it, if that's what you mean.'

'I meant both. Just hang on to the thought that you've done the world a favour. And now get out of here – both of you.'

'Your things,' Ingrid said.

'Keepsakes. I'll be someone new next time – if you don't blow me. Now go on. *Allez*. Push off. *Ciao*.'

They stumbled up the stairs clinging to each other and though Kate did not look back, she knew that those open, bloodied eyes would haunt her dreams until the day she died.

The room seemed very large and very empty as she stood looking at the body in the chair. The shadows seemed to draw in and the shaded light made a cone of brilliance on the floor, illuminating nothing.

She moved closer and stared at him, her face sombre. Living by the sword meant dying by the sword. She always had the same thought at moments like this, confronted with the evidence of violence. And the same nagging fear that a similar fate must be hers when her time ran out.

He was very dead, she thought, remembering the man who had fucked her so crudely on the desk which he now faced in death. He would never fuck her again, and she felt a pang that they had never talked to each other. They had shared the greatest of intimacies without speech.

But she knew his philosophy. She understood the philosophy of the terrorist. Nothing mattered – kin, kith, lover, friend. All would be sacrificed to the Cause, whatever the cause might be.

Yet she had liked him in some odd fashion, as she had liked his sister. Maybe because she understood them. Now they had both gone from her life.

And it was on to the next one.

His face was covered in blood that was darkening and drying. His ice-blue eyes, so like his sister's stared at her accusingly and she was glad that she had not had to dispatch the bullet that lodged in his head.

Very tenderly, with compassion she leaned over him and with her thumb carefully closed his eyes. There was dried blood on her hand afterwards, and she slowly brushed it off with her fingers.

And then she picked up the phone and called the other number.

And After

Kate was the first to arrive at the American Bar in the Savoy, where she was to meet with Paul and Charles Dennison. Looking around the room, she wrinkled her nose a little. Kate hated change and she had not come to terms with the new blue and white décor with the jangling bits of chain mail which now passed for curtains. It felt more like a bar in some oceangoing liner than the sedate British Savoy. But the staff had not changed and they still served a decent-sized champagne cocktail; one of which she ordered. She needed something to relax her, calm her spinning brain so that she could tell what she had to tell coherently.

Before her drink arrived, Charles was at the table. He kissed her, looking at her appreciatively in her white suit with the very deep blue silk blouse; he quickly ordered a Martini for himself, then said, seriously: 'How are you?'

It wasn't a routine question. His grey eyes were searching her face. 'You're still thinner,' he said.

'Well, every cloud has a silver lining,' she said flippantly.

'Are you over it?'

'Not yet. I don't think I ever will be, Charles. The dreams are the worst. In dreams he's always alive and coming for me.'

'Do you think you need to see a psychiatrist?'

She laughed. 'You Americans and your blooming psychiatrists! No, I don't. I know why I'm having nightmares. I killed a man. And I don't think I fired that gun from any deep-seated urge to knock off one of my fellow creatures, nor was I wiping out sexual guilt, mother guilt, father guilt or Madeleine guilt. I killed him because it was either him or someone else. If you like, I chose him to go. I don't have any guilt. Only horror to live with.' She twisted the stem of her glass. 'You know, I just wish I knew what she had done with his body,' she said almost speaking to herself. 'Or what she did with herself, come to that.'

He sighed, the Martini untouched in front of him.

'And what's with you and Paul?'

She looked up and smiled. 'Oh, that's easier. He's marvellous to me. It's terrible to say, but Madeleine has got it into her head to try every kind of cure in every corner of the globe. She's going to be away a lot. I don't blame her, and Paul and I can afford it between us. Not that she knows that. We got all our rightful share of the Pallia money in the end, but to me somehow it's dirty. I don't want to spend it on myself. I don't care if Madeleine uses every last cent of it.'

'And gets cured in the process?' he asked gently.

'Maybe that's what I want. Maybe I don't want any more deaths. As it is, Paul and I can be together a great deal – almost like normal people. If she were cured, I would ask him to leave her. It's my turn for that.'

'What do you mean?'

She half smiled and shrugged.

'Nothing really. It's a bit complicated to explain. He'll be here very soon. He's dealing with a client at the moment whom he says is more difficult than me.'

'Impossible,' he said, his thin face solemn.

She pulled a child's face at him.

'And you?' She had reached across the table to squeeze his hand.

'Bobbie Jean is going to drama school, and this time she hasn't persuaded me, I've *told* her. If she wants an acting career, she may as well do it right. She's fine. No horrors, no nightmares. I think the three of them being together made all the difference.'

As he spoke he knew Kate had seen Paul by the sudden radiance of her smile as she looked up. He turned to see the other man approaching the table.

'Kate has her own lighting beacon which you seem to ignite,' he said. 'I knew you were behind me. What will you have?'

'Gin and tonic,' Paul said to the hovering waiter and leaned to kiss Kate. 'OK?' Again it was a serious query, then he said to Charles: 'It's good to see you. Is all well?'

'All is well.'

'I'm glad you could make it tonight. I've got some news.' He was carefully settling himself in the blue and white tulip-shaped chair that seemed too fragile for his weight.

'Good news?' Charles asked cautiously.

Paul gave a little bark of a laugh. 'Extraordinary news. News you can't believe. Bellino's starting filming again and he's holding the girls to the contracts.'

'What!' The exclamation was from Kate. 'Can he do that?'

'Yes.'

Charles looked winded, as if someone had punched him in the stomach.

'I can't, Paul,' he said. 'I can't take her back to Rome.'

'It's not Rome.' Paul was grinning. 'It seems Bellino's not too keen on another visit to the Holy City. It's changed to glamorous Somerset. To be filmed totally on location with background exteriors in the French Auvergne. The girls have little more to do in the way of travel than to get themselves to Paddington Station. And he's asked Eileen Elliot to be den-mother again. You can't get safer than any of that.'

'I don't think it's too bad,' Kate said suddenly. 'It's cathartic in a way.'

'I'm inclined to think you're right, Kate,' Charles said, his fingers making a steeple above his Martini glass. 'Particularly for Jenny. How is she, Paul?'

'Not too bad. It was a terrible shock discovering that her new-found love was her first cousin and Catholic to boot, and she did mope and rail like an entire Greek chorus for a while there. But after they'd been home for a fortnight, Ingrid came up trumps. She said it was sad that Jenny had so few relatives and they shouldn't lose the one they'd found. So the boy has been invited to spend the summer with them in California. His aunt agreed, and he flew off a week ago. Of course, they'll have to come back for the film now. Anyway, I spoke to Ingrid this morning and she says the adjustment to big brother adoration from young love is coming along nicely.'

Kate's face was sceptical. 'Maybe.'

'Yes, well let's see what the Greek chorus does with it,' Paul said.

'Has Eileen left Elliot?' Charles asked suddenly. He had taken a long sip, longer than usual, of his Martini.

'I think this film will give her the chance,' Paul said. 'She'll be paid. It's the sort of job with a film company that could just go on through inertia. Chaperons are always needed. I would guess that once she leaves for Somerset she'll never go back to

278

Weybridge or Weymouth or wherever it was.'

'Would you like to see her again, Charles?' Kate asked him outright.

'I think so. I don't know. There was something . . .' His voice trailed away.

'You didn't mind her voice?'

'Her voice?' He sounded genuinely puzzled.

Kate opened her mouth but Paul fixed her with a freezing look and she turned bright scarlet.

'Sorry,' she said uncomfortably. 'I'm a bit funny about voices.'

Not sure what it was all about, but sensing her embarrassment, Charles said: 'As long as you don't start hearing them.'

She laughed. 'I'm not sure that I'm imagining *something*,' she said, then stopped, looked around and said: 'I need another drink.'

Paul signalled the waiter.

'Go on,' he said. 'You've been up to something, haven't you.' I knew it.'

She looked a little shamefaced. 'I didn't tell you because – well, I didn't tell anybody. But I couldn't get that story of Ingrid's about her father out of my head when we got back. It's been jostling for position with Franz's body,' she added ruefully. 'Anyway, a month ago, just after we got back, I decided to check it out. What Ingrid had said. Just find out. So I did.'

Paul made a noise that was between anger and anxiety, and Charles said softly: 'Do you think you should have?'

'Maybe not. I don't know if I ever meant to do anything with it, but I needed to know for myself. It was such a good story . . .'

'Where have I heard that before?' Paul asked the ceiling.

Ignoring him, she went on: 'Anyway, I started with the French Embassy and some French newspaper chums and one contact that I have in the French police. I didn't tell them anything about Ingrid, of course, or what had happened. I just said I wanted to find out what had happened to the OAS money and gave them all the background I had, which, of course, they already had.

'Well, every single one of them swears that as far as anyone knows it's still languishing in Switzerland, waiting, like the Sleeping Beauty, to be claimed.

'I didn't take too much notice of that. As far as we know at least half a million of it got away, assuming the money that Monique confiscated for her lot came from Zurich. How could the French know the money had gone, I reasoned, when they didn't know exactly where it was to begin with?'

'And then?' Charles prompted as she stopped for breath.

'I checked him out – the one she implies is him.' She was uneasy at even mentioning the name in a crowded bar. 'I've read every cutting ever written on him in British papers – he's usually in the gossip columns. I asked chums in Paris, Rome and Berlin to do the same.

'I have an incredible dossier on him from doing that and by talking to people who know him. My excuse? I was writing the definitive piece on one of the world's richest men.

'He claims to be English. Well, I have found his birth certificate. He is English. I have his marriage certificate, his divorce papers and the death certificate of his one and only wife who committed suicide long after they separated, but just before he began to get famous. Everything tallies: company records; he's all down in *Who's Who*; it's his picture in the newspapers. I've even seen his mum and dad's signatures in the book at the parish church where he was christened, believe it or not, in Clerkenwell, London EC1.'

She paused.

'He can't be Ingrid's father. He has to be himself – doesn't he?' She sounded almost pleading and then was silent.

'Did you get any aggro when you were inquiring?' Paul asked.

'No more than usual on this sort of job.'

They stared at each other as the waiter fussily arranged fresh drinks and removed their empty glasses.

'Maybe you picked up the wrong clues. Maybe it's another millionaire,' Charles suggested.

'Lives on a yacht. A floating palace. A chain of hotels. Money meant to come from oil. There can't be two. What I want to know is, can you manufacturer a complete life? He even won a competition in the *Islington Gazette*, aged ten. He came up with the best road safety slogan.' She made an exasperated little noise and drank some of her champagne.

'Well, can you do it? Can you plant a private life in public records like that?'

'No,' said Paul. 'You can't.'

She looked as if she had hoped for a different answer.

'But you can,' she said slowly, 'if you steal someone else's.'

Paul stared at her. Put down his drink and lightly slapped the table with the flat of his hand.

'Of course,' he said. 'That's it.'

'I didn't think of it at first,' Kate said. 'I was believing that it was Ingrid's last, greatest and most brilliant lie. I had decided that maybe the idea of being blinded and other unspeakable things had created in her her finest piece of fiction yet. I was full of admiration at the audacity; the way that every single one of us believed her.' She let out a long, low whistle. 'Did Monique believe her?' She answered her own question. 'She must have done. She wanted that information as much as Franz and she let Ingrid go. Franz will never know what she did. I wonder if Monique has realized.'

'How do you mean "steal someone else's"?' Charles asked, leaning forward in his chair. All three were now totally oblivious of the life in the bar around them.

'It may only be possible in Britain,' Paul said. 'I'm not sure. But it happened last year – a cabinet minister pulled the trick. A man called John Stonehouse. He wanted to disappear and start a new life with his mistress. Unfortunately for him, he got caught. How it's done is that you have to find someone who has died recently and is much your own age. They mustn't have been registered *publicly* as dead. It takes six months for a death certificate to turn up in the public records at St Catherine's House where all British births, deaths and marriages are recorded. Anyone can inspect the registers.

'Anyway, once you've got your dead man you can get a copy of his birth certificate from St Catherine's House. And once you have a birth certificate, that gives you the means to get a passport, and bingo, you're in business as a new person.'

'That's it.' Kate had been nodding as he spoke. 'And it explains Clerkenwell. He had to have a foreign-sounding name to cover his accent. And Clerkenwell has a big Italian population.'

'But wait a minute,' Charles said. 'If your original guy died, then surely his death certificate has come home to roost by now. Shouldn't you be able to locate that at your St Catherine's House?'

'Logically, yes,' Kate said. 'But it isn't there. The only person of that very uncommon name who has died in Britain since 1965 – that's as far back as I went, ten years, – is his wife.

'The fact I couldn't find a death certificate made me think I'd got it wrong but then . . .'

'You realized that the donor of Monsieur Pallia's brand-new name met his own death somewhat unexpectedly?' Paul suggested.

'Exactly. Why spoil the ship for a ha'pence of tar?' Kate asked cheerfully. 'A death certificate turning up eventually could have been dodgy. Better a discreet little disappearance, a private burial with no flowers, thank you. As long as the departed's family didn't start squawking, every little thing was taken care of. Maybe there wasn't any family, I thought at first. But there was.'

'Kate – what the hell have you been doing?' Paul said. 'You must be mad!'

'It was all right,' she said with an airy little wave of her hand. 'In the telephone book there is one family of that name in Clerkenwell. They run a funny little take-away – half Italian food, with a small café where you can be served, and a roaring trade in sandwiches.

'I ate there every day for a week. Officially I was visiting a sick auntie in Bart's Hospital. I became friendly with the waitress, starting with how marvellous Italians were at catering, then were these first-generation? Wasn't it wonderful how the families stuck together and got a business going, all helping each other? Then gradually down to the nitty gritty: how big was this family? I asked so, so casually.

'This family wasn't so big. Just three brothers. Not many for an Italian family, I said. Ah, she told me, there were four, but the big brother, the oldest, went back to Italy about six years ago. And this nice little plump girl tapped the side of her head and whispered: "He wasn't quite right, you know." in other words, expendable.'

She stopped.

'For Christ's sake,' Paul said. His face was white. 'Do you realize what you've been messing about in! Kate, I don't want you to have a private funeral with no flowers, thank you. Are you mad!'

Charles was signalling for another drink.

'And what are you going to do with all this information?' he asked her drily. 'Print it?'

'No, alas,' she said. 'Can't prove it. Not unless that family in Clerkenwell come clean, but they run awfully smart cars for funny little café owners. No, nothing for the moment. Maybe one day. When he dies or Monique gets him. I think Monique will get him. She's not a fool.'

'Kate—' Paul's voice was patient. 'Darling, please will you promise me to forget all about it now. Don't go on digging. Leave it. The whole thing could have been a tragedy. At the worst the kids could have been killed. As it has happened, Bellino is the only casualty, and I don't count Franz because he died the way he lived. Monique was right when she said you'd done the human race a favour. I don't want you to be another casualty. And you will be if you persist. Don't you think Ingrid hasn't told him what she was forced to say?'

'As a matter of fact, I doubt if Ingrid has told him anything of what happened that night,' Kate said. 'He wouldn't be too pleased with her spilling his secrets. And remember, our Ingrid is the original survivor.'

'But are you going to leave it?' he persisted.

She turned her luminous eyes on him. The bar was quiet, the drinkers drifting away.

'Yes, darling, I'm going to drop it, because I'm not a fool. And because now I know. I had to know. All stories must have a beginning a middle and an end – my first editor would scream: "Where's the intro? Where's the pay-off?" I had to find the pay-off for myself. Otherwise it's like a piece of music without the last chord played – left hanging in the air, abandonned.'

She sighed and took his hand.

'It's all over,' she said. 'All over. But it was such a good story, wasn't it?'

Unity Hall
Secrets £1.50

Les Hirondelles — the mansion where three generations of the de Courtenays gather under the Mediterranean sky and languish amidst wealth and luxury. Three generations of secrets : the father's passion for an Algerian masseuse ; the eldest son and his illicit love of his own half-sister ; the daughter's insatiable sexuality schooled by her father ; the granddaughter a hireling of the sensuality of pain ; and Anne, the outsider looking for a man to free her from twisted lust . . . Amongst them walks a stranger of powerful wealth — the man who knows the biggest secret of all . . .

Freda Bright
Options £1.50

When she was twenty Catherine made the big decision about all her tomorrows . . .

Kit said yes to the good-looking young lawyer who loved her and married her, building a home and having kids . . .

Kate said no and set out for New York City, for a life of her own, for a career and lovers and success . . .

When she was forty, Catherine could look back over the years of the good times and the heartbreaks, and most of all, the options.

Jackie Collins
Chances £2.25

From the penthouses of New York and the bedrooms of Beverley Hills to the casinos of Vegas and the villas of the South of France — *Chances* was the name of the game. Gino Santangelo was the slum kid who carved an empire out of bootlegging, gambling, extortion, even murder ; his daughter Lucky was as deadly as her father — she accepted crime as a business and power as an aphrodisiac. And Lucky Santangelo was too much like her father not to challenge him for an empire . . .

'Ferociously entertaining . . . outrageously uninhibited saga of sex and ambition' SUNDAY EXPRESS

Tony Parsons
Winners and Losers £1.50

Thorn was born beautiful and she was going to spend a lifetime
selling it at the top of the fashion world ... Johnny was number
nine on the big money tennis circuit, and he was going to number
one. Some day, somewhere, they were going to find each other —
a sleek and searing love story.

Consuelo Baehr
Girlfriends £1.75

They were best friends back when Eisenhower had just been
re-elected President and *Peyton Place* was high on the best-seller
lists. Natalie — betrayed by her first love and consoling herself
with the richest husband in America ; Sara — buried in her ambitions
until a blazing passion reminds her of all she has given up ;
Miranda — exotically beautiful, driven by her own sexuality ...
It was against all the odds they should meet so many years later.

Liza Cody
Dupe £1.25

The case of Deirdre Jackson was a different beat for Anna Lee,
Private Investigator. Ex-policewoman in the pay of a private-eye
firm, she was more familiar with missing kiddy capers. The police
thought Deirdre's death was just another grisly car crash. Her
parents were more sceptical — they hadn't seen her in years.
Anna's job was a series of checkouts, each unearthed contact
stranger than the last ...

'Fresh and fetching no-nonsense sleuth ... watch her' OBSERVER

Robin Cook
Brain £1.75

From the author of *Coma* comes a journey into nightmare, along the white corridors of the surgeons, along the dangerous streets of the porn trade, into a world of gleaming terror where science has finally crossed the borders of sanity.

'Brilliant but brutal surgeons, necrophilious morgue attendants, vanishing patients, corpses minus their brains ... an authentic shiver, an eye-popping finale' GUARDIAN

Ashley Carter
Scandal of Falconhurst £1.75

She was born to Ham Maxwell's bed wench and sired by a handsome mustee slave. At seventeen the belle of New Orleans white society, she married into the city's wealthiest family. But fate had bitter cards to play. The man she loved was shackled in the hell of the Delta canefields, and New Orleans was held in the bloody fist of Butler's Yankee army. She was a true child of Falconhurst and her name was Scandal ...

Wilbur Smith
Men of Men £1.95

It was the epoch of empire, the age of pride, blood and conquest, the time of Rhodes and Jameson, striking north from the Cape in search of gold and diamonds, land and glory. Such a man was Zouga Ballantyne, whose epic journey from the Kimberley mines to the Zambesi grasslands follows a bloodstained road where the death of a king and the destruction of a warrior nation are claimed as the price of empire.

'Red-blooded prose' THE TIMES

Fiction

☐ **Options**	Freda Bright	£1.50p
☐ **The Thirty-nine Steps**	John Buchan	£1.25p
☐ **Secret of Blackoaks**	Ashley Carter	£1.50p
☐ **A Night of Gaiety**	Barbara Cartland	90p
☐ **The Sittaford Mystery**	Agatha Christie	£1.00p
☐ **Dupe**	Liza Cody	£1.25p
☐ **Lovers and Gamblers**	Jackie Collins	£2.25p
☐ **Sphinx**	Robin Cook	£1.25p
☐ **Ragtime**	E. L. Doctorow	£1.50p
☐ **Rebecca**	Daphne du Maurier	£1.75p
☐ **Flashman**	George Macdonald Fraser	£1.50p
☐ **The Moneychangers**	Arthur Hailey	£1.95p
☐ **Secrets**	Unity Hall	£1.50p
☐ **The Maltese Falcon**	Dashiell Hammett	95p
☐ **Simon the Coldheart**	Georgette Heyer	95p
☐ **The Eagle Has Landed**	Jack Higgins	£1.75p
☐ **The Master Sniper**	Stephen Hunter	£1.50p
☐ **Smiley's People**	John le Carré	£1.75p
☐ **To Kill a Mockingbird**	Harper Lee	£1.50p
☐ **The Empty Hours**	Ed McBain	£1.25p
☐ **Gone with the Wind**	Margaret Mitchell	£2.95p
☐ **The Totem**	Tony Morrell	£1.25p
☐ **Platinum Logic**	Tony Parsons	£1.75p
☐ **Rage of Angels**	Sidney Sheldon	£1.75p
☐ **The Unborn**	David Shobin	£1.50p
☐ **A Town Like Alice**	Nevile Shute	£1.50p
☐ **A Falcon Flies**	Wilbur Smith	£1.95p
☐ **The Deep Well at Noon**	Jessica Stirling	£1.75p
☐ **The Ironmaster**	Jean Stubbs	£1.75p
☐ **The Music Makers**	E. V. Thompson	£1.50p

Non-fiction

☐ **Extraterrestrial Civilizations**	Isaac Asimov	£1.50p
☐ **Pregnancy**	Gordon Bourne	£2.95p
☐ **Out of Practice**	Rob Buckman	95p
☐ **The 35mm Photographer's Handbook**	Julian Calder and John Garrett	£5.95p
☐ **Travellers' Britain** }	Arthur Eperon	£2.95p
☐ **Travellers' Italy** }		£2.95p
☐ **The Complete Calorie Counter**	Eileen Fowler	70p

☐	**The Diary of Anne Frank**	Anne Frank	£1.25p
☐	**Linda Goodman's Sun Signs**	Linda Goodman	£1.95p
☐	**Mountbatten**	Richard Hough	£1.95p
☐	**How to be a Gifted Parent**	David Lewis	£1.95p
☐	**Symptoms**	Sigmund Stephen Miller	£2.50p
☐	**Book of Worries**	Robert Morley	£1.50p
☐	**The Hangover Handbook**	David Outerbridge	£1.25p
☐	**The Alternative Holiday Catalogue**	edited by Harriet Peacock	£1.95p
☐	**The Pan Book of Card Games**	Hubert Phillips	£1.50p
☐	**Food for All the Family**	Magnus Pyke	£1.50p
☐	**Everything Your Doctor Would Tell You If He Had the Time**	Claire Rayner	£4.95p
☐	**Just Off for the Weekend**	John Slater	£2.50p
☐	**An Unfinished History of the World**	Hugh Thomas	£3.95p
☐	**The Third Wave**	Alvin Toffler	£1.95p
☐	**The Flier's Handbook**		£5.95p

All these books are available at your local bookshop or newsagent, or
can be ordered direct from the publisher. Indicate the number of copies
required and fill in the form below   5

....

Name_____
(Block letters please)

Address_____

_____

Send to Pan Books (CS Department), Cavaye Place, London SW10 9PG
Please enclose remittance to the value of the cover price plus:
35p for the first book plus 15p per copy for each additional book ordered
to a maximum charge of £1.25 to cover postage and packing
Applicable only in the UK

While every effort is made to keep prices low, it is sometimes
necessary to increase prices at short notice. Pan Books reserve
the right to show on covers and charge new retail prices which
may differ from those advertised in the text or elsewhere